Advance Praise for *In*

"Seduction, scandal and a sexy scientist hero, all wrapped up in Minerva Spencer's trademark wit! *Infamous* is the quirky Regency romp romance readers have been waiting for. Get ready to swoon!"
—Anna Bradley, author of the Swooning Virgins Society series

"Spencer is an absolute wizard when it comes to creating riveting, sensual, and intelligent romances. *Infamous* features not one, but two smart and spirited heroines who challenge the confining gender roles of the day, forging their own futures and happily ever afters. Romance readers need this splendid book—pronto!" —*USA Today* bestselling author Vanessa Kelly

"Five stars for *Infamous*! Spencer has a gift for creating stories that keep you riveted from the first page to the last with complex characters. A sexy, witty, and thoroughly charming read." —Renee Ann Miller, *USA Today* bestselling author

"Why should bad boys have all the fun? In this sizzling Regency, bad girls deserve love too! Snuggle up with this steamy romance and prepare to laugh, cry, and curse the villain. Relatable characters, sharp wit, and a fast-paced story are Spencer's trademarks, and you'll find them here in spades. You won't want to put ... national bestselling author Shana Galen

"*Infamous* i ... orgettable characters, big ... couples to root for. I a ... Darcy Burke

"An incredibly emotional story of redemption and finding a new path when past sins come back to haunt, *Infamous* is a tale filled with angst, regrets, attraction, possibilities and triumph . . . and love. I highly recommend it to anyone who loves an 'old school,' lush, historical romance. Minerva Spencer never disappoints!" —*USA Today* bestselling author Terri Brisbin

"*Infamous* is Minerva Spencer at her best; she takes an 'unlikeable heroine' and slowly chips away at her many layers as the lushly written story progresses, until the reader can't help but cheer for her. Celia and Richard's journey to an HEA is immensely satisfying because it is so hard-won."
—Liana De la Rosa, author of the Once Upon a Scandal series

"Minerva Spencer has knocked it out of the park again with her latest. Weaving a spellbinding tale of romance and redemption that will hook you from the first page and won't let you go until the end, *Infamous* is one not to be missed! With characters so intriguingly flawed you can't help but be draw ... you fir ... !"

Also by Minerva Spencer

Dangerous

Barbarous

Scandalous

Notorious

Outrageous

And read more Minerva Spencer in

The Arrangement

Infamous

Minerva Spencer

www.kensingtonbooks.com

KENSINGTON BOOKS are published by

Kensington Publishing Corp.
119 West 40th Street
New York, NY 10018

All Kensington titles, imprints, and distributed lines are available at special quantity discounts for bulk purchases for sales promotion, premiums, fund-raising, educational, or institutional use.

This book is a work of fiction. Names, characters, businesses, organizations, places, events, and incidents either are the product of the author's imagination or are used fictitiously. Any resemblance to actual persons, living or dead, events, or locales is entirely coincidental.

To the extent that the image or images on the cover of this book depict a person or persons, such person or persons are merely models, and are not intended to portray any character or characters featured in the book.

Special book excerpts or customized printings can also be created to fit specific needs. For details, write or phone the office of the Kensington Sales Manager: Kensington Publishing Corp., 119 West 40th Street, New York, NY 10018. Attn. Sales Department. Phone: 1-800-221-2647.

ISBN-13: 978-1-4967-3288-0 (ebook)

ISBN-13: 978-1-4967-3287-3

First Kensington Trade Paperback Printing: October 2021

10 9 8 7 6 5 4 3 2 1

Printed in the United States of America

For George

Chapter 1

The Duke of Stanford's Ballroom
London, 1818

"Quit yanking on your cravat, Richard—you look as though you've been mauled by those beetles you're so bloody fond of," Lucien said under his breath.

Richard laughed. "Thank you, Luce, I can always count on you to give me the words with the bark still on them."

Lucien's cheeks darkened. "Sorry."

Richard couldn't help noticing that his twin's eyes were in constant motion as he searched the swelling crowds for something. Or someone.

And Richard could guess who.

"I don't mean to be an arse, Rich," Lucien said. "It's just—"

"I know, I know. It's a burden to have a barnacle like me stuck to your side." Richard patted his brother's shoulder.

Lucien snorted. "Idiot."

"Fool."

They both grinned.

Richard squinted around at the multitude of people packing the receiving area of the Duke of Stanford's town house. "Remind me why I'm here again," he asked his far better dressed, more attractive, and more gregarious identical twin.

So, identical in theory.

In addition to the spectacles Richard wore and his brother did not, Richard was a good stone and a half lighter than Lucien, who'd filled out in the chest and shoulders in a way Richard hadn't quite managed yet.

And then there were the spots that had plagued them both from age fourteen. Lucien's had magically disappeared when he'd turned seventeen but Richard's were only now clearing.

Yes, identical, but different. Richard smirked at the thought.

"You're here for the girls," Lucien reminded him, somehow able to speak while smiling, a new skill and something that must have been on the curriculum at Eton those last two years—the two Richard had skipped, instead going straight to university.

Richard snorted. "Yes, because all the girls were so impressed by the way I trod upon—" He made a frustrated *tsk*ing sound. "The devil! I can't even recall the poor girl's name."

"Nobody remembers that incident except you," Lucien said. "Well, and likely her. I don't recall her name, either. You need to stop thinking that nobody likes you, Rich. If you just put yourself out a bit, you'd see."

Richard could not believe his twin could be so oblivious of the insults, mocking names, and even an ode that had circulated about Richard this Season. He could only think that Lucien was so insensible because he was falling deeper in love by the hour and could see nothing other than one spectacularly beautiful face, whether she was in the room or not.

"And," Lucien added, "if a roomful of pretty women isn't enough reason to be here, remember your promise to Mama."

"Oh, that's hitting below the belt," he muttered.

Lucien merely smirked.

Unfortunately, what his brother said was true. If Richard hadn't—in an extremely weak moment—promised their mother to stick it out for one Season, he could have been tramping the Fenlands and adding to his already considerable beetle collection.

But their mother, Baroness Ramsay, had chosen the perfect time to corner him—just after he and Lucien had returned from a year of unfettered hedonism on the Continent—and he had foolishly capitulated.

So, here he was. Thank God it was getting near the end of the Season because he wasn't sure how much more tomfoolery he could bear. In Richard's opinion, a London Season was remarkably like a term at Eton, but with girls to join in the mockery.

Richard sighed and scanned the crowd. And then immediately wished he hadn't. Because, dead ahead, was Sebastian Fanshawe, the Duke of Dowden and Richard's chief tormentor from Eton.

"Good Lord," he muttered beneath his breath, turning so that the other man mightn't see him.

Dowden hadn't changed a whit in the almost three years since Richard had last seen him. He was still the physical embodiment of male perfection, tall, broad shouldered, golden-haired and blue eyed. And he still had the same punishing wit and barbed tongue.

It didn't matter what Richard did or said, Dowden would abuse him. And only the two of them knew the reason why.

The names, digs, and even a snide ode that some wit had composed about him didn't bother Richard any more now than they had at school.

That said, it *was* a damned shame that Dowden had so much influence over the ladies.

Especially over one girl in particular: Miss Celia Trent.

Just thinking Miss Trent's name gave Richard a heavy feeling in his groin—an unfortunate development with the potential to embarrass him right here in the middle of the Duke of Stanford's ballroom if Richard wasn't careful.

He wasn't the only bloke who suffered such a physical reaction to the woman's sensual, almost overripe beauty, but he *was* the only man in the room whose twin was madly in love with her.

Richard felt like a dirty dog about the way his body reacted to the woman his brother hoped to marry, but he was a human animal in his prime breeding years and he could hardly control his body's reaction to such stimulus.

Could he?

But he *could* control his behavior. And so he behaved respectfully and with reserve toward the object of his lust and his brother's love.

Not that his actions mattered to Miss Trent since she seemed to have taken an aversion to Richard before they'd even met.

Lucien leaned close to him and said, "I'm going to speak to Celia's father tomorrow."

Richard groaned. "Why do you feel that you have to marry her, Luce? Just because you kissed her?"

Lucien hissed. "Would you keep your bloody voice down?" He glanced around, as if anyone else cared about their conversation. "You know I've been thinking about it for weeks now. Long before the kiss."

"Yes, but you only started mentioning *marriage* since that irritating lawn party a few days ago—which was also the same day—"

"Yes, yes, you already announced that, thank you very much. It so happens that that particular . . . issue is what has made the matter, er, pressing."

"Why?"

Lucien rolled his eyes. "You know why."

"I don't, actually. It's not as if you ruined her." Richard snorted at the words. "*Ruined her,*" he repeated. "How stupid and dramatic that sounds. Have you ever given any thought to that phrase and what it means? As if she were some sort of object, like a plate you dropped and *ruined* because it is now broken. It's not as if kissing—or even sexual intercourse—can only happen one time, so how can you ruin a woman by having sex with her? I have sex with delightful regularity. And yet nobody says that *I* am ruined."

Lucien was staring at him in a familiar way. Richard could almost predict his brother's next words: *What is wrong with you?*

"What?" he asked when Luce only stared.

"Mother must have dropped you on your head. That is all I can think of to account for it."

"Besides," Richard continued, ignoring the tired insult, "I saw her after you kissed her. I can tell you, without equivocation, that she most certainly did not appear *ruined.* Perhaps you should think on it a few days."

"I don't want to. There have to be dozens of men soliciting her father for her hand."

Richard wanted to ask why they'd do so if she was so clearly *ruined* but kept that unhelpful question to himself.

Instead, he said, "Maybe some of them have also—"

One dangerous look from Lucien's narrowed eyes froze the rest of the words in his throat.

Instead, he soothed his twin. "Even if there are a hundred men, none of them can be more eligible than you. Indeed, you possess the only thing Trent is looking for in a son-in-law: lots and lots of brass. Even I, as woefully ignorant of *ton* gossip as I am, know the man is below the hatches." He smirked. "In fact, if Miss Trent knocks you back, her father would probably marry you himself."

"Very droll."

Richard could see his brother wasn't listening. "Are you sure about this, Luce? You've hardly had a chance to live life or explore the world. We had a smashing time on our trip, didn't we?"

"Yes."

"Well, don't you think—"

"I love her." Lucien's voice was low and firm.

Love. Richard rolled his eyes and heaved a sigh at the ridiculous word. It was his contention that human beings were not designed for monogamy. He strongly suspected what his brother was feeling was really lust.

Even if he did credit love as actually existing, he doubted that a person could fall in love with somebody when allowed no more than a few minutes a week to chat with the object of his desire.

Richard considered trying to tell his brother that it was his breeding imperative that was driving him to distraction and sending him to Miss Trent's father's house tomorrow, hat in hand.

But that was a subject on which his mother had told him he must be circumspect.

"People don't like being compared to ducks or beetles or horses, Richard. You must reserve your observations on man's biology for those who can appreciate and understand them."

Lucien was not one of those people, so there was no point in arguing.

Besides, Richard could understand his brother's fascination—if not love—for Miss Celia Trent.

Before meeting Miss Trent, Richard had believed that all healthy, attractive, unattached females under the age of forty were largely the same. Which was to say desirable. He'd never felt his brother's brand of madness for one woman in particular.

But one look at Miss Trent's gorgeous face, voluptuous body, and lively blue eyes had turned him into a gaping fool just like every other man—married *or* single.

The male populace's reaction to this one woman was laughable, really. Because, as attractive as Miss Trent was, there were dozens and dozens of other women who went unnoticed while the men of the *ton* clamored like a pack of hounds after a single female.

He had observed the same thing in the animal kingdom. Or at least as much of the animal kingdom as he'd had the opportunity to study in his few years.

To his way of thinking, people were no better than the gaggle of geese that roamed Lessing Hall, his parents' country home, terrorizing the populace, both human and animal.

Every year for as long as Richard could remember the two dominant ganders—Wellington and Soult—had warred over a white tufted goose named Harriet. The two males would de-feather each other and end up battered and bloody in their determination to have Harriet.

Meanwhile, dozens of perfectly fine geese went unbred.

Richard glanced around the ballroom that lay below them: yes, the same thing was true here. Except not geese, of course, but hundreds of perfectly breedable young women, a great many of whom were hiding in corners while only a handful were chosen to dance time and time again.

Slave to his animal impulses that he was, Richard caught himself searching the room for Miss Celia Trent.

He shook his head; really, he was no better than a gander, every bit as driven to de-feather all the other males in his vicinity in his pursuit of Celia Trent.

No, not that; she is to be Luce's wife.

Beside him, Lucien heaved a put-upon sigh. "Try not to wear that expression, Rich."

Richard turned to meet Lucien's light brown eyes—identical in color to Richard's, although only half the size since they weren't magnified by spectacles—and found his brother frowning.

"What expression?"

"The one you're wearing right now."

The receiving line inched forward.

"I'm sorry, but you'll need to be a bit more specific, Luce—I know your vocabulary is limited, but give it a go."

"You get this *look*—as if you're observing mankind's foibles from a lofty height."

Richard snorted.

"It's true, and I've seen the same look when you're categorizing beetles or watching animals copulate."

Richard laughed. "Oh, and what look is that?"

Lucien's features shifted until his expression was smirky and heavy-lidded.

Richard had to admit it was an expression that made him want to plant his brother a facer.

"I don't look like that," he objected.

"Not right now. Right now you look annoyed and your eyebrow is doing that thing." Lucien sounded jealous.

Richard snorted; the one thing that he could do that his perfect brother hadn't yet mastered was lifting his eyebrows independently of each other. You'd think that being well liked, more athletic, *and* the Earl of Davenport would be enough for his slightly older twin. But no: Luce coveted Richard's eyebrow *thing*, too.

"I realize the expression is just a defense when you're nervous," Lucien went on, with the assurance of a person who knew Richard almost as well as he knew himself. "But it makes you look like a right arrogant, suspicious . . ."

"What?" he asked when his brother broke off. When Lucien didn't answer, Richard followed his gaze.

Lady Stephanie Powell and Miss Celia Trent had placed themselves in a position to be better observed by his brother and all the other young bucks, most of whom arrived at these affairs as late as possible.

Richard knew the young women's plumage display was for his brother rather than himself, but he enjoyed it nonetheless.

Miss Trent's hourglass figure, ultramarine blue eyes, and mink-colored curls were an attractive contrast to her friend's slender, blond wholesomeness.

"Smile," Lucien hissed as they reached the front of the line and he bowed over the hand of their hostess.

"Good evening, Your Grace," Lucien said in a suave, sophisticated, grown-up voice that Richard didn't yet possess.

"Good evening, ma'am," Richard echoed, his voice breaking in the middle of his three-word sentence.

"Viscount Redvers," the duchess spoke his name with a look of amusement on her handsome face, her gaze on Richard's cravat.

Does it really look that bad?

With the gauntlet of the receiving line over, they headed toward a scene that looked remarkably like the descriptions he'd read of Roman gladiatorial pits.

"Bloody hell," he muttered as they fought their way through the bodies. "Why don't they open a door?"

"The Regent is expected," Lucien explained.

Even Richard, who as good as lived in a cave—well, it was actually shared lodgings off Sidney Street—knew the Regent had a pathological fear of fresh air.

"Davenport, old man," someone ahead of Lucien called out.

"Beaky," Lucien replied, grinning at his best mate.

"Hallo there, Redvers. Didn't expect to see you here," Viscount Beakman said.

"I needed to use a bloody pitchfork to get him here," Lucien said, looking in the direction where Miss Trent had last been spotted. But it was impossible to see more than a wall of people in either direction and none of them were Celia Trent.

"Could I grab you for just a tick, Davenport? I've got that thing to ask you about."

Lucien frowned. "Thing?"

Beaky gave Richard a significant look. "You know—the *thing*."

"Ah, yes. That thing," Lucien said, comprehension dawning, cutting a last, yearning look toward the ballroom. "But I've not got terribly long."

"No, no, it shan't take but a minute. Let's go over to the cardroom. A man can't hardly hear himself think in here."

Luce grabbed Richard's shoulder. "Don't sneak off the minute I turn my back," he warned him, and then pushed his way into the sea of bodies.

Richard sighed; here was the beginning of yet another long, tedious evening.

Celia watched the two brothers leave the receiving line and then disappear into the crowd.

"It is difficult to credit that they're supposed to be twins," Stephanie said to Celia, not bothering to lower her voice.

Millie Bowles, standing on Steff's other side, tittered and leaned toward them, employing her fan to cover her mouth but actually *rais-*

ing her voice. "It's difficult to believe they're even brothers, not to mention identical twins."

"Oh look, there's Phyllida Singleton," Steff said, her glorious green eyes fixed on a slender dark-haired girl greeting several of the other homely, impoverished, or otherwise unpopular wallflowers who were clustered together in a corner.

"Is that the *same* shabby yellow ball gown she wore to the Kittridge, Oldham, and Acton balls?" Millie asked with an avid smirk.

"I doubt she owns three identical, shabby yellow ball gowns," Celia said sharply, earning a hurt look from Millie and an amused one from Steff.

"What's wrong with you tonight, Ceelie?" Steff asked. "You're in a positively savage mood."

"Nothing." That sounded too curt so she added, "I'm just not interested in chattering about people who aren't even worth a moment of my time—like Phyllida Singleton."

Her words caused more tittering, and she knew the verbal cut would make its way to Phyllida's ears before the evening was over. Well, so be it. The unfortunate female should appreciate getting any attention, even if it was cruel.

Some part of Celia's mind cringed at her appalling thoughts and words, but she shoved her qualms aside with practiced brutality.

Celia let the other two women sharpen their claws on Phyllida as she caught sight of a familiar pair of broad shoulders and a golden head. And just as quickly lost sight of Lord Davenport when he disappeared in the direction of the cardroom, leaving his brother to stand alone.

Something about the sight of Richard Redvers just standing there made her jaws clench. Rather than appear anxious or self-conscious, he surveyed the denizens of the ballroom from his taller-than-average height with the confidence of a general observing a conquered battlefield.

Didn't the man care that he was the butt of so many *ton* jokes?

Lily Kendall drifted up to their group. "Did you see who Lord Davenport brought with him again?"

"We already saw," Millie confirmed.

"*Why* does he bother?" Lily muttered. "I've never seen such a lump in my life."

"He asked Maria Trevallion to dance at Lady Warnocke's ball and the poor thing couldn't think of a way to avoid it. He trod on her skirt and ripped off most of the flounce, taking part of the skirt with it."

"I heard he ripped off so much that she was almost naked."

They all twittered over the well-worn piece of gossip.

Celia studied the man in question. He appeared to be staring blankly at the dance floor, his thick spectacles glinting under the light of several hundred candles, looking as if he'd fallen asleep while standing up.

Speaking objectively, Richard *did* look like his brother, but his appearance was like Lucien Redvers's reflection in a warped mirror, with spots, although she'd noticed those had begun to fade. He was just as tall but gawky—too slender—and his clothing was a disgrace, rumpled and without any style.

His lips appeared thinner than Lord Davenport's full, sensual mouth—a mouth more than one young lady had sighed herself to sleep over—but Celia suspected that was due to the odd smirk he seemed to wear in repose.

He stood alone and appeared unconcerned as humanity washed around him like the incoming tide rushing around rocks on the shore.

Celia envied him that—the ability to be comfortable in his own skin. If she were standing all alone like that she'd have developed hives all over her body by now.

That's why she made every effort to ensure she was never in his position.

Almost as if he'd heard her thoughts, he turned in her direction. His expression was lofty and contemptuous: as if he were examining one of his beetles. No, not that, she corrected. Because if he were doing *that* he'd probably look interested. Instead, he was looking at her as if she were a bluebottle fly or some other common insect that wouldn't merit a second of his time.

Perhaps he is correct in his assessment, Celia. After all, what is interesting about you other than your looks?

Ah, touché, she mentally congratulated the inner voice that critiqued her every thought and action.

"Is he a simpleton, do you think?" Millie asked in her piercing voice.

"If you don't keep your voice down, he might think you are interested, and you will be his next dance partner," Celia said coolly.

Millie flushed, but the others chuckled.

"What? Are you suddenly feeling sorry for him?" Steff demanded, her eyes slyly flickering in the direction of Lucien, who'd emerged from the cardroom.

"I'm not—but that doesn't mean I want to make a spectacle of myself."

Millie's eyes became glassy at the implied criticism, her chin quivering.

Celia wanted to stop talking about Richard Redvers.

In fact, she'd like to forget the man, altogether.

No, what you want to do is forget your horrid behavior toward him these past months.

Fine. I would *like to forget that, too. But it wasn't my intention that mocking Richard Redvers would become everyone's amusement of choice.*

It wasn't your intention, but you did everything in your power to make it happen.

Celia was sick and tired of arguing with her conscience—a battered, bruised, and malnourished thing that refused to die no matter how badly she abused it.

Besides, the accusation wasn't fair. While Celia might have spread the rumors and planted the barbs, it was Sebastian who'd conceived of them.

The Duke of Dowden started it, but you fanned the flames, Celia.

Another truth.

Sebastian had been relentless; his quips and slights and comments were cunning and cruel and spread like wildfire. He was so adept at sowing lies that most people never guessed they came from him. Or her.

At least Celia hoped none of the people around them—with the exception of Steff and Sebastian—ever connected her with any of the cruelty this Season.

Part of the reason that Celia had joined in the baiting was the same as everyone else's: to make sure that *she* didn't become the butt of Sebastian's rapier sharp wit.

But more importantly, she'd done everything that Sebastian told her to do because she knew he could wreck her.

He had told her he would.

"You want to become Countess of Davenport, my girl, and there is no need to deny it. But even with a face that could launch a thousand ships, you won't be able to land the handsome young earl without some help. You'll need invitations to the finest events." Sebastian had given her a smile that could probably launch no small number of ships, itself.

But wasn't that how it was in nature? Often the most beautiful creatures were also the deadliest.

Celia had returned his pleasant, utterly empty, smile. "What makes you think I can't secure such invitations on my own?"

The duke had grinned, exposing his pointed canine teeth. "Oh, my dear, sweet, innocent girl. It would take so very little to ensure that the only ballroom you ever see the inside of is a public assembly room."

Celia had been too stunned to reply.

"Don't ruffle your feathers, my lovely. I will *guarantee* you entrance to every single function of any note. All I want in return is a little assistance."

"I don't understand. What can I do that would possibly help you in any way?"

"You can do whatever I tell you."

And that had been the beginning of it all; Celia had become part of Sebastian's inner circle, an esteemed, but not particularly comfortable position to occupy.

A person needed a long spoon to sup with such a dangerous man. Even his ex-lovers—gossip suggested—suffered when Sebastian was finished with them.

The Duke of Dowden was wealthy, gorgeous, and had evaded matchmaking mamas for almost five years.

And, for reasons of his own—reasons she'd never inquired about—he had a vehement hatred for Richard Redvers.

Once Celia had agreed to Sebastian's demands—not that she'd ever had any choice—he had made good on his promise, somehow managing to get her invitations to parties and balls and routs and half-a-hundred other affairs she never would have attended without his connections.

And all she'd needed to do was spread a bit of mischief.

And create a bit yourself—don't forget that.

Celia winced at the reminder of the vicious "Ode to Odious" she'd written, which made it painfully clear who Odious was meant to be.

Other than Sebastian, only Steff knew who'd written it, and that had been by mistake.

Celia should never have told the sly beauty anything private. She knew that Lady Stephanie had befriended her for two reasons, and neither one was because she actually liked Celia's company. First, she wanted to be seen associating with the only woman who could compete with her physical beauty.

And second, she was Sebastian's cousin and did whatever Sebastian wanted.

So Steff had become Celia's bosom companion and the two of them had served up a constant buffet of cruel gossip with a smile.

Had Celia sacrificed Richard Redvers, Phyllida Singleton, and dozens of others like them on the altar of her own ambition?

You know you have, Celia.

But I'll make it all up to Richard when we're sister and brother.

And how is that?

I'll bring him into fashion—introduce him to women who are not wallflowers. There are dozens of things I can do to help him.

Her conscience enjoyed a robust laugh.

Celia fumed in silence.

"I've heard he's quite brilliant and went to university two years early." Millie's shrill voice cut through her uncomfortable thoughts.

"Studying to be a vicar," Steff said with a dismissive sniff.

"No, he's one of that sort who goes about collecting beetles."

"Ewww!" All four of them shivered with disgust.

"Beetles!" Millie screeched.

Either the word itself or Millie's piercing voice drew a glance from the subject in question.

"Oh no! He's looking at us," Lily Kendall hissed.

He appeared to be, but then his attention was caught by Phyllida Singleton, who approached him with another drab-looking female.

Redvers seemed to come to life, a rare smile transforming his usually inscrutable features and making him almost as handsome as his brother.

"Look, he's going to ask Phyllida Singleton to dance," Millie said with her penchant for pointing out the obvious.

"He always does; they're perfect together. An old maid and her specky swain," Steff said.

The others laughed.

But Celia didn't join in.

Instead, anger flared up inside her as she watched the pair. If Richard Redvers had even an ounce of sensibility he would flee London and never attend another *ton* function.

And if he disappeared, then Celia could stop. She could just *stop*.

But he was stubborn and stupid and arrogant and insisted on remaining.

And so she was driven to ever greater heights of cruelty.

She needed it all to end, and end soon, or she'd go mad.

Please God, please let Lucien give me some sign tonight . . . some hint . . . and let this horrid, horrid Season come to an end.

If I were you, Celia, I wouldn't be so eager to attract the Almighty's attention.

Once again Celia had to admit the truth of such moralizing cautions. Given her behavior, she was far more likely to attract punitive lightning bolts than divine benedictions.

All four of them watched in silence as Richard Redvers led the plainly gowned wallflower out to the dance floor.

That was where Celia should be right now—on the ballroom floor, dancing. But she'd purposely kept most of her card free for Lucien because he usually claimed two dances right away. But not tonight.

No, tonight he'd blithely gone off to the cardroom and left her here.

Left her to watch his brother and Phyllida Singleton enjoying themselves.

They might be unpopular, but even a fool could see that both outcasts felt confident and loved and secure. Neither of them would ever have to worry that they'd return home one evening to find all their possessions tossed onto the street.

Celia tasted the coppery tang of blood and stopped chewing her cheek, forcing herself to breathe and relax.

You don't have the luxury of relaxing, my dear Celia; you need to take care of matters before time runs out.

What am I supposed to do? Club Lord Davenport over the head and drag him to the nearest vicar?

Her lips twitched a little at the mental picture.

But the smile was short-lived. She had already jeopardized her fragile reputation by allowing Lucien to detach her from the crowds at not one, but three events.

The young earl had been a perfect gentleman the first two times, doing no more than holding her hand, his behavior forcing Celia to all but launch herself at him the last time they'd been alone together.

Even then, he'd tried to be the gentleman. "I don't want to harm your reputation," he'd protested—but not very strongly—before capitulating and kissing her.

Kissing was a skill that Celia had carefully honed, and by the time she was finished with him, he'd believed that it had been *his* tongue that had first led the charge and *his* hands that were to blame for marauding over her body like Viking invaders.

Indeed, if there had been a vicar with a special license standing beside them at the Lorings' garden party, Lord Davenport would have married her on the spot.

Unfortunately, the only thing present had been his guilt and heartfelt apologies.

And so Celia had been forced to wait and wait and wait.

All the while her father's finances had taken an alarming turn—*downward*. He'd informed her not long ago that she'd better catch herself a wealthy husband before he was hauled off to debtor's prison.

Matters at home—home being the ramshackle collection of rooms he'd leased for the last six months—had become grimmer than ever. They were down to just Henson and a day-maid to wait on them.

And poor old Molly Henson only stayed because she had nowhere else to go.

Which is exactly the choice you'll have shortly.

Davenport *needed* to offer for her, and he needed to do it quickly. Celia had planted the seed almost six weeks ago, but there had been little enough time to cultivate the delicate sprout in his thick male brain. And it bothered her to no end that Steff was always around when Celia had any time near Lucien.

Steff was beautiful, wealthy, and had all the connections that Celia lacked. She'd seen the admiring looks Lucien occasionally gave her best friend.

The voice inside her laughed at the words *best* and *friend* when applied to Steff, who was as conniving and selfish and petty a person as she ever hoped to meet.

A lot like you, in other words.

Celia could not refute the accusation.

Her head throbbed badly enough to blur her vision, but she forced a bored expression onto her face while she swept the room with eyes sharper than any raptor's.

She tried to convince herself that all of this—the incessant balls with the same people, the thinly veiled insults about everyone, by everyone, even the people you believed were your friends, and the constant, crushing fear that you would start slipping down the social ladder and not be able to stop—was not only necessary, but enjoyable.

But the lies and cruelty and duplicity became more difficult to maintain by the day.

This was her second Season and Celia had seen that it was a short step from where she was standing to where Phyllida Singleton lurked with the other undesirables. The only way to keep from *becoming* Phyllida was to make sure somebody else filled that position. It was cruel and unpleasant, but it was the way of the *ton*.

Three young men came to ask them to dance but Celia begged off, offering a vague excuse.

Soon Steff and Millie and their partners were swirling around the floor along with Richard and Phyllida. The last pair weren't exactly swirling and she saw the awkward man tread on Phyllida's toes. It must have hurt, but Phyllida just smiled up at him and said something that made him laugh.

Celia had to admit Richard Redvers was considerably more handsome—a lot more like his glorious, golden twin—when he smiled like that.

She suspected that the gilt on Lucien Redvers was largely a by-product of his money and position rather than any real difference in the twins' outward appearance. As the younger son of an earl, Richard would have only an allowance while Lucien would get all the delicious money and property and status that went with the Davenport title.

Celia's eyes narrowed as she watched the two carefree wallflowers laughing and dancing while she stood on the sidelines ignored and neglected.

How dare they flaunt themselves while she stewed alone on the fringes? If they enjoyed each other so much, why didn't Richard offer for the woman—whose nickname was The Squab? If they—

"What is the belle of the Season doing all by her lonesome?"

Celia started at the sound of Sebastian's smooth, cool voice.

"Hallo, Sebastian." She offered her hand and he bowed over it.

"Where is your beau?" Sebastian was tall—a good head taller than most of the people around them—and glanced around the room with a superior smirk. "Is he neglecting you?" His gaze stopped at something on the dance floor and Celia knew what it was even before he spoke. "Ah, Odious and The Squab."

Celia winced to hear the names—both of which had originated in her mind—spoken out loud.

His lips twitched and he turned his speculative gaze on Celia. "Don't fret, darling. Your young lordling is not avoiding you; Davenport has been dragooned into helping poor Beaky out of a fix." Sebastian cocked his head. "But what if I bring the young lordling to you and lay him at your feet?"

Celia swallowed down her self-loathing and smiled up at him, her expression—she hoped—world-weary and bored rather than desperate. "Would you? That would be lovely, Sebastian."

He chuckled and turned back to the dance floor. "I'm getting the most amusing notion as I stand here. Something . . . devious. Something that will make for a rather infamous end to the Season."

Celia swallowed. "Infamous?" she asked, aiming for an insouciant tone but almost choking on the terror that shot through her at his words. What, in the name of all that was unholy, had he conceived of *now*? She had to force the next words to leave her mouth, "Do tell, Sebastian."

In the years to come, when Celia looked back on that conversation, she would be horrified by how quickly one's life could change.

She didn't know it then, but that exact moment—only a few seconds in time—represented a critical fork in the road of her life.

While Celia could never know if the other fork—the one where she denied Sebastian what he asked—would have been better, she would soon learn that it could hardly have been any worse.

Chapter 2

Ten Years Later

Richard read the sentence once more: *"Antonia is betrothed to the Duke of Dowden,"* and then looked up from the letter, his brain—usually the most agile of organs—struggling with the simple words.

"What is it, Dickie darling?" Lady Honoria Simms asked, running her fingernails up his naked flank when he didn't immediately answer.

"Hmm?" he said, folding up the letter and tossing it onto the nightstand before turning back to her.

They had both been resting—recuperating really—after their last bout of energetic bedsport when Honey's maid had knocked on the bedroom door to deliver Lucien's letter.

"You have an odd look on your face." She gave an indelicate snort. "Even odder than usual. I hope it's not bad news?"

Richard cupped her full breast, absently thumbing the nipple to hardness before taking it between his lips. What *was* it about women's breasts that made him want to fasten his mouth on every naked nipple he encountered?

Honey groaned under his nipping and suckling, her back arching.

"Oh!" she yelped, jerking away just when he was beginning to forget all about the news he'd just read.

He released her taut bud with a wet *pop* and frowned up at her. "What is it?"

"Your glasses."

"Hmm?"

"Your spectacles are cold, Richard—take them off."

"No." He turned back to her nipple, which his thumb had resumed stroking.

She laughed, her body shaking beneath his hand. "You really are the oddest man."

He'd heard that a time or one hundred. "I like to see your body and what I do to it," he explained, even though he'd said that before, too.

"I *know* you do. Believe me—I recall just how much you like to see me."

Richard's mouth pulled up into a smile. He wasn't good at reading conversational subtext, but he knew she was referring to the time she'd drunk too much wine and allowed him to examine her body with his best magnifying glass. "I'll take off my specs if you allow me to use the glass again," he offered, but not with much hope.

"I'm not one of your *beetles*, Richard."

Indeed, she wasn't.

Honoria Simms was a lush, lovely, wealthy widow who was staring her fortieth birthday in the eye and suffering no end of qualms. Richard shamelessly exploited her age-related anxiety—time and again—to allow him to take unheard of liberties with her magnificent body.

His lack of conscience should make him feel guilty, but it didn't.

"I think you were born without a conscience—especially when it comes to women," Lucien had said more than once.

Richard shrugged off thoughts of his brother and turned his attention to Honey's neglected breast: Lord, she was a beautiful specimen of womanhood.

Richard found it interesting that her advanced age—well beyond a woman's prime childbearing years—didn't matter a whit to his breeding organ, which was mindlessly enthusiastic to do its procreative duty.

Human sexual desire, he had discovered after years of close, careful, and diligent study, did not conform solely to the demands of nature or the drive to continue the species. No, indeed—

"What was in the letter?" Honey's voice interrupted his hypothesizing.

"Hmm?" he muttered, sliding down her body until he reached her hips, shoving apart her thighs, and turning his attention to a part of her anatomy she would allow him to pleasure even with his glasses on.

Richard lowered his mouth and inhaled her feminine scent, both aroused and fascinated by her effect on his body.

"Don't think you can ignore my question by—*ah!* My God, Richard."

He gave her the lightest of strokes with his tongue.

She shivered, but then said, "*Richard*. What was in the letter?"

She was tenacious.

He sighed and then reluctantly looked up, settling for stroking her with his fingers. For now.

"My sister is getting married," he said, noticing, as always, that her pubic hair was several shades darker than the hair on her head. That reminded him of their last argument, which had started after he'd innocently, if not wisely, suggested that she let him shave her. When she'd demanded to know what had given him such an outlandish notion, he'd told her the truth: that he'd engaged a prostitute who'd been shaved and had found the experience most illuminating.

Rather than submit to his suggestion—all in the name of science—she had tossed him out of her snug little town house right then and there, even though it had been in the middle of the night and sleeting outside.

And then she had refused to see him again.

She'd only relented after discovering that Mrs. Andrew Martin—

Honey's archnemesis in Parisian social circles—had invited Richard to dine a deux.

"*Richard.*"

"Hmm?" He recognized that tone—it was the one people used when they'd said his name more than once and he'd not answered.

Richard parted her curls and exposed that most fascinating part of her body to his gaze.

"Yes, what did you say?" he remembered to ask.

"I *asked* if you were going home for the wedding?"

He loved looking at women. Indeed, he had something of a mania for it—at least that was what Lucien had accused the last time he'd come to visit Richard, in Vienna.

"Richard!"

His head whipped up. "What?"

"The wedding. Are you going?"

"Oh, yes," he answered, lowering his mouth in the hope it would stop the flow of questions.

It did.

But as Honey squirmed and groaned under his expert manipulations, her question rattled around his brain.

Was he going home? Of course he was. He couldn't miss his little sister's wedding. Nor could he ignore his mother's last letter.

Richard loved his mother, Baroness Ramsay, more than any other person in the world—even more than his twin. She was, in many ways, a female version of himself. Or he supposed it was more accurate to say that he was a male version of her, since she'd made him.

Neither of them got on well with strangers or enjoyed social entertainments. But even his mother—with her love of political history and philosophy—was better equipped to mingle in company than Richard. When people learned he was a naturalist—and just what he specialized in—they became awkward and embarrassed.

And then there was the way he'd been accused of *looking* at people, as if he were visually dissecting them. Well, that could hardly be helped—there was nothing he could do about his face, was there? Besides, wasn't a visual dissection better than an actual one?

Lady Simms thrust her hips, indicating his mind may have wandered in the wrong direction; it wasn't like him to become distracted while he engaged in his favorite pastime.

Home.

The word wended its way into his mind like a serpent, as much as he tried to shove it away. Could a man really call a place home when he'd only returned a handful of times—all briefly—in the past decade?

Richard shrugged the thought aside; it didn't matter, he would go to England.

With that decision out of the way he applied himself to the task at hand—or at mouth, rather.

Lady Honoria shoved her fingers into his hair, pulling hard enough that he swore he heard individual strands being torn out by their roots.

"*My God,* Richard!"

He smiled, all thoughts of his family, England, weddings, and home now filed in their proper places.

The mad jangling of the bell woke Celia with a start.

You'd think after almost a year at Lady Yancy's she would have become accustomed to the shrill, unpleasant sound of servitude. But it made her heart leap into her throat each and every time.

Her feet were already moving before her eyes had focused completely.

It had been foolish to try to sneak in a nap, but she'd stayed up too late last night reading the book she'd borrowed from the circulating library Lady Yancy belonged to.

Celia wasn't supposed to borrow books for herself on her employer's account, but whenever there was room on the card, she did it anyway. And then she read the novel as fast as she could so she would not be halfway through when she needed to return *her* book to check out some improving tract for her employer.

Lady Yancy's house was a snug little bower on the high street in Harrogate. The current Marquess of Yancy had purchased the house for his mother. Celia knew he'd chosen Harrogate because it was as far away from Yancy House in London—which was currently occupied by the pompous marquess, his grasping wife, and their six odious children—as possible.

Celia suspected he would have liked to move his mother even farther north—preferably to John O'Groats—but the old lady had stood firm.

When Celia opened the sitting room door it was to discover Lady Yancy had company.

"Oh, I beg your pardon, my lady, I didn't know you had a guest," Celia said.

"That's why I summoned you. Come here, Pelham," the dowager ordered. "This is Lady Morton and she has come to invite me to spend the Christmas holiday in Eastbourne."

Celia dropped a low curtsey in front of the noblewoman, who was regarding her through a heavily chased quizzing glass, the deep lines around her frowning mouth telling Celia the expression was a common one.

"It is an honor, my lady," Celia murmured.

"Hmmph," Lady Morton snorted, lowering her glass slowly. "She's every bit as pretty as you said, Lenora."

There was a long pause and Celia realized both old ladies were staring at her. "Er, thank you, my lady."

Lady Morton tapped the handle of her quizzing glass against her rather prominent chin. "Pelham, you say?"

"Yes, my lady."

"You seem familiar. Any relation to the Shropshire Pelhams?"

"No, my lady, I'm afraid not."

"I feel as if I've met you before."

"We've never met," Celia said. "I'm sure I'd remember," she added, unable to resist.

Lady Morton's hard gray eyes narrowed at that last comment, as if she suspected some ulterior meaning in her words. She surveyed Celia's plain brown morning gown. "Yes, quite exceptionally pretty."

"She came to me after leaving Bernadette Ingram's employ," Lady Yancy said.

Lady Morton's eyebrows shot up. "Indeed. I can imagine what happened there."

Mrs. Ingram, one of the members of the local gentry, had six sons ranging in age between fourteen and twenty-five. The Ingram men were notorious for their roving eyes and hands. And working as a companion to their rather witless mother had been one of the worst positions she'd had over the course of the last decade. At any given time of the day at least two of the Ingram men could be found importuning Celia.

Not until nineteen-year-old William had trapped Celia against the sitting room door—with William's mother on the other side—had her employer fully comprehended the situation.

Although the incident was, undeniably, not Celia's fault, she was given a week to find a new position.

"She wasn't there long," Lady Yancy said.

Eleven. Endless. Months.

"I should imagine not, Lenna."

Celia's face grew hot as they discussed her as if she were an inanimate object. Still, it wasn't anything new.

"Hmmph." Lady Morton seemed to dismiss Celia from her thoughts and turned back to her friend. "I should very much like you to come and help me, Lenna. You know how much work these things can be and I'm afraid we shan't get *any* assistance from dear Antonia's side—not with Lady Ramsay for a mother."

Celia's head jerked up at the name.

Lady Yancy chortled. "Lord no, she is one of those odd modern young women who insist on engaging in mannish pursuits." Her lips pursed. "Quite a scandal there, if I recall correctly."

"Indeed, the chit married Davenport when she was seventeen and he in his seventies. Bore him the two boys, and *then* married the nephew a decade later."

Their eyes glinted avidly at the memory of such rich, if ancient, gossip.

"And then there is Lady Amelia. You remember her from our come-out Season?"

They cackled like witches.

Celia wondered when their societal debut might have been. Surely during the second George's reign.

"In any case," Lady Morton said, once she'd collected herself, "I am sure I will need your help making ready for a crowd of demanding young people bent on nothing but their own pleasure."

The two women continued to exchange observations while Celia hovered uncertainly.

"Very well, Moira," Lady Yancy said sometime later. "It sounds delightful. I've not attended a holiday house party—nor a wedding—in ages."

"It's shocking the way you bury yourself," Lady Morton chided. "You deserve to get out and about."

Lady Yancy's eyes slid to Celia. "You will finally be able to earn your crust, Pelham."

Celia hesitated, and then asked before she lost courage, "May I inquire as to the names of the happy couple?"

Lady Morton appeared to double in size. "My nephew is Sebastian Fanshawe, the Duke of Dowden. He is the eldest son of my dear departed sister Fanny. He's marrying Ramsay's girl—Miss Antonia Redvers—at their country estate. The wedding is to be held on Christmas Day."

The words were like small fists that knocked the air from her lungs.

"Christmas Day? That is certainly odd," Lady Yancy said, her voice coming from a long way off.

Redvers. The name echoed in her mind. Surely it must be some other Redvers?

"Pelham? *Pelham?*"

Celia noticed that the two old ladies were looking at her oddly.

"Is something wrong?" Lady Yancy asked.

"Not at all, my lady." Celia forced a smile. "A Christmas house party. And a wedding," she said faintly. "My, how very lovely that sounds."

Chapter 3

Eastbourne, Some Days Later . . .

Richard picked up the *dytiscus marginalis* he'd found buried in the slightly thawing mud near the edge of the pond. It was dead, of course—this was not a good time of year for beetles—but it was a superlative sample. He took a glass tube from his satchel and carefully placed the creature inside before corking it.

Hunting for beetles in Sussex during the winter months wasn't nearly as exciting as the places he'd explored over the last ten years, but there was a sort of comfort in seeing familiar species. Like visiting old friends.

Richard smiled to himself as he jotted down a few observations in his notebook; how Lucien would laugh to hear him describing beetles as if—

"Richard!"

Richard jolted at the sound of his brother's voice—as if his very thought had summoned the man. He looked up and smiled. "Hallo, Luce."

Lucien didn't return his smile. "*Here* you are."

"I left word I'd be out here this morning. Why do you look so angry?"

"Because it is after two o'clock, Rich, and the guests are due to start showing up at any minute." Which was when Richard noticed Luce had changed out of his riding leathers.

He pulled out his watch and saw that his brother was telling the truth. "Well, bollocks. Where did the morning go?"

"Come on, we've not got much time. Phyllida and Antonia were supposed to be here but I received a message saying they would be late. And Mama has gone to Whitton Park to make sure all is prepared for those who will be staying there."

Richard picked up his satchel and slipped his notebook inside. "How many guests again?"

Lucien heaved an exasperated sigh. "I'm not sure how you managed to avoid hearing this over the past ten days," his brother groused, "but there will, eventually, be enough of them to fill the guest rooms in both houses, not counting those who live in the area."

"Good God."

"Indeed," Lucien said, sounding aggrieved. "I don't begrudge Toni a large wedding, but I do wish she'd either had it in town or waited until summer. I don't know what she will do with all these people in this weather."

Richard frowned. "What is wrong with the weather?"

Lucien just shook his head, which was when Richard noticed his brother's greatcoat was studded with melting flakes of snow.

"So when is *His Grace* arriving?" Richard asked.

Lucien stared at him through narrowed eyes for a long moment before saying, "Not for a few days."

Well, that was good, at least.

"Is he coming alone?" Richard asked. The man that Richard remembered always traveled in a pack. Like a hyena.

"John Duncan and Viscount Norland will attend him but they can't come until just before the wedding."

Two more of Richard's least favorite people from his school days.

"You are wearing that expression, Rich." Lucien gave him a *look* of his own. "I hope you aren't carrying a grudge. I know Dowden ragged you rather hard, but we were boys then."

"That's true," Richard said noncommittally.

"In less than ten days he will be a member of our family; let bygones be bygones."

Richard didn't comment. Instead, he watched his brother as they walked back to the house. Lucien looked distracted—he'd been vague and out of sorts since the moment he'd come to fetch Richard in Dover a few weeks earlier. Their carriage journey home had been amusing and filled with catching up, but no personal conversation, which was how it had been for years. Ever since Luce's marriage, to be precise. Richard was always surprised by how much he still missed the closeness he'd once shared with his twin.

They trudged in silence, Lucien obviously occupied with his own thoughts.

Rather than part company in the great hall, Luce escorted him to the door of Richard's chambers, as if he couldn't trust him to find his way on his own.

"You've got less than an hour," Luce reminded him before stalking off.

As his valet, Buckle, flapped around making him presentable for company, Richard considered his brother's earlier words about Dowden.

His opposition to the other man went a lot deeper than the fact that the man had "*ragged*" him when they'd been younger. Richard distinctly recalled the event that had triggered Dowden's enmity toward him, the memory still clear after all these years.

He was tempted to talk to his mother about the man his sister would soon be marrying, but he was also aware that his memory of Dowden was almost seventeen years old. Perhaps Lucien was correct; perhaps the way they had behaved as boys had no bearing on the men they'd become.

Somehow, Richard found that difficult to believe.

* * *

In the ten years since Celia had been cast out of the *ton,* she'd experienced the full spectrum of humiliations.

After word of her behavior at the Duke of Stanford's ball had mysteriously gotten into the newspapers—where some clever wag had quickly dubbed her *Lady Infamous*—her friends had distanced themselves *en masse*, all except Sebastian, who, for reasons she wouldn't learn until later, stuck by her.

At first Celia had believed that she would die of mortification and loneliness. But it seemed those afflictions weren't fatal.

Instead of perishing, she'd begun to accumulate a shell—an accretion of insults and slights that eventually formed a hard carapace. Until finally, a decade after her disgrace, she'd believed that nothing anyone said or did could hurt her.

She had been wrong.

As she lugged Alexander the Great's traveling cage, held Percy's lead around her wrist, and clutched the yowling Mr. Fusskins's carrier with her free hand, a voice from the past arrested her.

"Is that *Celia*? Celia Trent?"

Inside her—*deep* inside—the last, feeble sprout of hope that the coming days would not be the equivalent of an extended visit to hell, curled up and died.

"Pelham!" Lady Yancy rapped on Celia's shoulder with her cane. "You are being hailed."

Celia sighed and set down her awkward burdens—burdens she carried because there'd been no footmen available when their carriage pulled in behind three others, all disgorging guests and baggage at once.

"You're young and strong," her employer had barked when Celia suggested waiting for help.

And so that was why she was acting as porter when she greeted her erstwhile friend, Lady Stephanie, for the first time in a decade.

"I *thought* it was you!" Steff shrieked when Celia turned.

Roused from his slumber by the high, piercing voice, Alexander swiveled his great turquoise head, tilted an eyeball at the noisy newcomer and yelled, *"Dirty girl! Dirty girl!"*

Celia tried to smile but knew it was more of a rictus.

Given Steff's relationship with Sebastian, Celia had suspected the other woman might make an appearance, but she'd hoped against hope that Steff would have somewhere else to spend Christmas.

Hope, once again, had abandoned her.

"Is that *yours*?" Steff stared at the bird, giggling just the way she had at eighteen.

Alexander cocked his head and stared back at the beautiful blond woman, his expression ominous.

Before Celia could open her mouth to say . . . well, she didn't know *what*, Lady Yancy barked in her stentorian voice, "Introduce me to your friend, Pelham."

"Pelham?" Steff repeated, appearing not to have heard the old lady's demand.

"My married name," Celia murmured. "I am a widow." Before Steff could say anything else, Celia turned to her employer. "Lady Yancy, this is the Marchioness of Quincy."

Like the rest of the nation, Celia had read about her erstwhile friend's marital triumph in every newspaper, big and small, when Steff had married the stunningly wealthy eighty-year-old marquess several years back.

Steff gave Celia a look that was both mocking and triumphant. "I am a widow now, as well."

Celia wanted to ask if Steff had eaten her mate, but of course did not.

Lady Yancy, who was something of a tuft hunter, perked up. "Why, you didn't tell me you possessed such august connections, Pelham."

Before Celia could think of an appropriate answer, Alexander saved her.

"Once bitten twice shy!" he yelled, and then fluffed up his feathers until he was twice his normal size.

Lady Yancy frowned down at the bird, her attention mercifully distracted from Celia's past. "I believe Alexander is cold, Pelham. Do let's—"

"Yoo-hoo!" Steff called out, fluttering her fingers and looking at somebody over Celia's shoulder. "How wonderful to see you." Her eyes slid to Celia, her smile sly. "Both of you."

Celia guessed, based on the avid cruelty in Steff's eyes, that she wouldn't like what she would see behind her. But her body was already turning.

Coming toward them, looking like double images you might see if you'd been clubbed on the head—which was how Celia was feeling—were the Earl of Davenport and his brother, Richard Redvers.

Steff flung herself into Lucien's arms in a way that made his eyes widen, but he recovered quickly, and gently patted her shoulder before disengaging.

"Hallo, Steff."

"Lucien, my dear, dear friend. It's been *ages* since I've seen you, not since before poor Louis's death."

"Your husband is greatly missed on the bench."

"Oh, *you* and your politics, Luce." If Steff's gaze hadn't drifted to Richard Redvers, she would have seen the flicker of irritation that drifted over Lucien's face at her easy dismissal of what Celia knew—again, from reading newspapers—to be the young lord's passion.

"And I see your famous brother over there helping Lady Sherwood," Steff said. "Why, I don't believe I've seen the two of you together since—"

"Richard spends a great deal of time out of the country for his research," Lucien said sharply. His gaze was not on Steff, but Celia. She watched as realization dawned in his lovely caramel brown eyes.

His dark blond eyebrows pulled into an ever-deepening V as he stared at her, revulsion building in his burning gaze.

Celia couldn't blame him; this was even more dreadful than she had imagined.

But, once again, you are willing to engage in shameless behavior for money, aren't you, Celia?

She couldn't deny the accusation; she was here for money and she would endure whatever ignominy she had to in order to get it.

Steff looked positively gleeful at the silent tableau before her. She stepped closer to Celia and put an arm around her shoulders. "Can you believe it, Luce? It is our own dear Celia Trent—so lost to us all these years. She is a poor widow like me." She looked from Lucien to Celia and clucked her tongue. "It's time we were all friends—is it not? Let us forget ancient history. After all, you and Phyllida have two lovely children and dear Phil is quite the most accomplished political hostess in England. You are the envy of every man eyeing our highest office—at least that was what Louis always said." Steff looked rather sour at that last bit, but then chuckled. "Yes, you are quite the most envied couple in London."

Celia couldn't help thinking there was a snide, taunting undertone to Steff's words, although her assertion was much the same as what Celia had read in various newspapers for years.

"Indeed, Luce," Steff went on, oblivious to the thunderclouds forming in her host's eyes. "You should probably thank Celia for the childish prank that brought you together with Phil all those years ago."

Celia wanted to sink into the gravel drive.

"Pelham!" a familiar voice barked.

Celia gratefully turned away from Lucien's shocked gaze and looked into her employer's angry eyes.

"Are you expecting me to stand here all day while you reminisce?" she demanded.

"I'm sorry, my lady." Celia reached for the animal carriers she'd abandoned. Before she could pick them up, a shadow loomed over her and two large, leather-clad hands landed on the handles.

Celia looked up into magnified brown eyes that she'd thought about far too often over the years.

Indeed, it had always perplexed Celia that it should be Richard Redvers's face she saw in her dreams rather than the man she'd schemed so hard to marry. But see him, she did, and often.

Sometimes she would dream of Richard three or four nights running. She never had any clear recollection of what he was doing in the dreams, just the heavy sense of him lingering in her mind during her waking hours.

Today his face wore a familiar expression: cool, remote, and superior. But the rest of him?

Goodness.

Lucien, who'd once been the sparkling handsome twin, now appeared older, slightly haggard, and far less robust than his marginally younger brother.

And Richard, who'd always been a pale copy of the earl, was now golden, masculine perfection.

Celia's eyes locked with his, and it was an effort to pull away. Her face heated and damp tendrils of hair stuck to her skin, even though the day was cold.

He lifted the animal carriers.

"Oh, you don't need to—"

"I shall show you to your rooms and send a servant to fetch your bags." He turned on his heel.

"Now *there's* a gentleman," Lady Yancy said with a satisfied nod. "Pelham, you may hold Percy and take my arm."

Steff was gazing after Richard's receding back with a speculative look while Lucien was still staring at Celia. His expression was no longer shocked, but cold and pensive.

Lady Yancy patted Celia's arm in an unprecedented show of maternal affection. "Don't worry, Pelham. You'll see your friends again. You will be invited to meals—I insisted upon it with dear Lady Morton, who thought you might feel more comfortable dining in your room. 'No, Moira,' I said to her, 'Pelham knows her presence is a comfort to me. She will wish to attend me at mealtimes, no matter how nervous she becomes in such superior company.'" She looked at Celia as if expecting gratitude for her largesse.

"Thank you, ma'am," Celia murmured.

Steff had pulled her gaze away from the gorgeous man disappearing into the foyer and was staring at Lady Yancy with morbid fascination.

"Do come along, Pelham. No dawdling," Lady Yancy snapped as Celia bent to pick up Percy.

For once, Celia could not have been happier to be hurried along.

Chapter 4

"I can't believe the woman is *here*," Lucien said for the third time, and then sent the ball careening off his cue so wildly it missed the target ball.

Richard stared at his brother in surprise; Lucien used to be an excellent billiards player. Perhaps he'd not played in several years and that accounted for his dreadful shot. If that was the case, why had Luce been so adamant about meeting in the billiards room for a game a good hour and a half before dinner?

Richard leaned low and lined up his shot.

"Can you believe it, Rich?"

Richard jolted at the sound of his brother's voice and pulled back on his shot just at the last moment.

"Oh, sorry about that," Lucien said when he realized what he'd done.

Richard lined up more quickly this time, before Luce could go off on another squawk.

"Where the devil has she been all these years?" Lucien asked as he watched the ball go into a pocket. "And why has she turned up now? And here?"

Richard chalked his cue. "I believe her employer is from Harrogate. That would likely explain why you've not heard any news about her in London—not that you would have recognized her with a new surname."

Lucien didn't appear to hear him. "It's bloody bad luck, I tell you. Phyllida won't like it one bit. Neither will Mama."

Richard snorted. "Please, some days I wonder if Mama even recognizes her own children. She's unlikely to recognize Mrs. Pelham's face after all these years—even if you remind her that her maiden name was Trent." Their mother had a brilliant brain for political philosophy but no actual interest in the people to whom such philosophy applied.

"Even Mama cannot fail to recognize a woman who looks like Miss Trent, er, Mrs. Pelham." Lucien stared at his cue abstractedly, as if he'd never seen one before.

Well, Luce was probably right about that. Celia Pelham had the sort of face a person didn't forget.

And then there was her body.

Richard gave a slight shake of his head as he recalled his own body's reaction to simply walking beside her.

He'd seen similar reactions in the animal kingdom. Some creatures simply exerted an irresistible sexual appeal; Mrs. Pelham was one of those creatures. He was positive it wasn't merely a product of fine looks but, rather, the clarion call of nature: His body knew she would produce fine offspring and was encouraging his mind—with every weapon in its considerable arsenal—to fight off competitors and secure breeding rights.

Richard prudently kept that observation to himself.

"She looked a bit haggard, didn't you think?" Lucien asked.

"No, I thought she looked exceptionally well considering she just got out of a carriage after several days of travel. Especially seeing how she'd been trapped in there with that loud old crone, a bloody parrot, an ancient, piddling dog, and some sort of panther in a carrier." A paw had darted out through the too-large gaps in the wicker basket and Richard had a nasty scratch to show for his efforts.

Lucien gave him a look of disbelief.

"What? What have I said or done now, Luce?"

"You just had to disagree with me, didn't you? You can't help yourself. You have to argue with everything I say or do."

"No, I don't," Richard said, and then grinned.

Lucien returned a weary smile and an even wearier chuckle, but his smile faded quickly. "This is a bloody mess in the making."

"Phil doesn't know she's here yet?" Richard asked after Lucien took his turn and made another dreadful shot.

"No. She was at the church all day with Toni, doing something about flowers or arrangements or perhaps flower arrangements. I need to go up shortly and make sure that she's been warned." He looked as though he were contemplating a walk to the gallows. "I'll finish this game, first."

Richard sometimes wondered about his brother's marriage. There had been a time—when they were younger—when they had discussed everything.

That had begun to change when Richard left Eton two years earlier than Luce. The distance had continued to grow after his brother married. Richard had always supposed that was how things went when a man married: he transferred his allegiance from his friends to his wife and no longer needed male confidants—or even twin brothers.

Between the emotional distance and geographical distance—Richard rarely came to Britain more than once every few years—he knew very little about Luce and Phil's marriage.

He had always supposed that the fact they had two children indicated at least the physical part of their relationship was normal. Then again, he knew there were plenty of *ton* couples who had children but remained strangers to each other and took lovers.

These past few weeks at Lessing Hall Richard had noticed a tension between his brother and his wife. He rarely saw the two together. In fact, he usually saw Phil with Luce's secretary, William Payson—a handsome man a bit older than Richard and Luce.

While Richard believed nothing untoward was going on between the two, he couldn't help but notice how much easier his sister-in-law was with Payson than her husband. Payson accompanied Phil shopping, on estate visits, and even to church when Luce was away. Payson dined with the family and Richard saw firsthand how easily Phil and the secretary got on with each other. Of course Luce and Phil were always . . . cordial . . . to each other. In fact, it seemed they were *only* cordial.

That struck him as being very odd.

Still, what did Richard know about marriage and/or women? His average liaison lasted no more than a few months and he'd not once contemplated marriage. He was aware that many *ton* women had their cicisbeos—oftentimes with the consent and approval of their husbands. The poet Byron had even written about the sophisticated relationships that often existed between a cicisbeo and husband and a wife and mistress.

Perhaps that was the role Payson served in Phil's life? After all, Luce and Phil were, according to the few snippets his mother had passed along, one of the most sophisticated and influential political couples in London.

Did that mean his brother employed a mistress?

For some reason, Richard found the notion distasteful. He could only assume his feelings on the matter were the result of growing up in a household in which his parents had practiced fidelity—an extremely rare situation among their class.

"Richard?"

"Hmm?"

"I asked you what you think happened to Mrs. Pelham."

"Oh." He shrugged. "It's not so mysterious. Her father was—or perhaps still is if he's alive—a mad gambler. I daresay finding a wealthy husband was not so easy for her when word of her, er, prank, became widely known. She probably married a cit, somebody who would have overlooked her reputation for her connections—isn't her grandfather an earl?" Luce nodded and Richard continued. "After her husband died, I daresay she must have been left in the basket if she had to take up working. Aside from marriage, there are very few options for a woman of her class—at least very few respectable options. She would have had even fewer options after that night."

That Night. Richard thought it sounded as if the words were capitalized whenever he spoke them or heard them.

Indeed, That Night was pretty much all Richard recalled from that long-ago Season.

Well, except for the ball where he tore some poor girl's gown half off during the Roger de Coverley; that had been pretty memorable.

"I think Phyllida has aged far better," Lucien declared loyally, and then struck the cue ball with a shattering *crack* and potted a ball. Finally.

Richard thought it interesting that his brother was the only person not to call his wife by her pet name. Didn't that hint at an unusual level of reserve between a man and his wife?

"Well?" Lucien prodded.

"Oh, yes. Phil has aged very well and I'm—"

"Not that—what did you think of *her*?"

Richard tried to get some sense of what his brother wanted from him. Luce's face was drawn—even more so than usual—and intent.

He knew that Lucien had once loved Celia Trent and had been going to offer for her the day after the ball. But that had been a decade ago—surely his brother was not still in love with the woman? Or was that why he was behaving so strangely? Had the prank that forced Luce and Phil to marry, and also cast Mrs. Pelham beyond the pale, left deeper, more painful wounds than Richard had suspected?

He'd always found it ironic that the intended victim of Celia's ill-conceived letter—Richard, himself—was the only one of the four of them who'd escaped unscathed.

Richard looked up from the tip of his cue and saw his brother was waiting for an answer.

"Perhaps her face is not as round and youthful, but there is an expression in her eyes—life experience, some of it harsh if her current employer is anything to go by—that has made her—"

"Made her what?" Lucien prodded.

"It has made her even lovelier," Richard said.

Lucien seemed to deflate. "Yes. Bloody hell. Yes, you are right."

Richard both understood and didn't understand his brother's reaction to this woman's appearance. What difference did it make if she looked well or ill? Luce was married and had children, security, family, friends, and wealth.

Was his brother admitting that he was tempted to hare off with a childhood lover and leave his current life behind? Or take her as a mistress?

Richard simply could not believe it.

And although it *was* unfortunate that Celia was here, it was hardly tragic.

Or was it?

Richard knew he lacked sensitivity when it came to human emotion. But how harmful could Celia's presence here really be? Everything that had happened between them was a decade old.

"I've put that night behind me, but this will bring it up all over again," Luce said, as if Richard had spoken aloud. "I dread the thought of Phyllida learning of Mrs. Pelham's presence," he added softly.

Richard still recalled Lucien's reaction when they'd discovered just who it was that had forged a note and then locked Lucien and Phil into the Duke of Stanford's gun room, where they'd remained trapped until morning, when a servant had finally found them.

Luce had looked devastated that the woman he'd loved and hoped to marry could have conceived of such a cruel plan. Indeed, his brother's revulsion for Celia had been palpable.

Richard frowned as he recalled Celia's reaction when confronted with the note in her handwriting. She had looked guilty, true, but also confused. No doubt she had wondered how Lucien had somehow received the note instead of Richard.

Although he had no proof, Richard was positive that the Duke of Dowden had had some part in the misguided and mean-spirited trick. Even somebody as clueless as Richard had noticed that Dowden and Celia had been as thick as thieves all Season long.

But, if that were the case, surely Dowden would have come forward and taken his share of the blame? And if he'd been too cowardly, why would she have protected him?

Even after all these years, Richard was still perplexed by the entire scheme. Who thought of such mean-spirited plans and then carried them out?

Celia Pelham, apparently.

As beautiful as she was on the outside, she must be ugly within to have conceived of pulling such an infamous trick on another human being. Especially someone as kind and caring as Phil.

Richard found it interesting that Celia's arresting beauty somehow made it more difficult to believe that she'd engaged in such villainy, as if only ugly creatures could be guilty of deception and cruelty.

Lucien took another terrible shot. "You must recall how Dowden and Celia, er, Mrs. Pelham, were back then?" He paused and then said, "Lord, what if they take up their acquaintance again when he gets here? Dowden has a poisonous wit without anyone encouraging him."

Richard bent low over his cue stick. "I thought you were the one telling me to let bygones be bygones and embrace him as a brother," he noted, and then potted another ball.

Lucien scowled. "Bastard," he hissed.

It was unclear whether he was referring to Richard's taunting words or the lovely, clean shot.

"I'll say this to you in strictest confidence," Lucien said, not bothering to wait until Richard finished lining up his next shot. "I do not understand why—"

The door to the billiard room swung open slowly and both Lucien and Richard turned.

"Oh," said Mrs. Pelham, her ridiculously vivid blue eyes wide, her pale cheeks tinted an exquisite shade of pink.

Richard couldn't help it; he gawked. Even wearing a dreadful, old-ladyish frilly cap, she robbed a man of breath.

"I'm so sorry." She didn't look sorry; she looked appalled. "I'm afraid I'm quite lost. I wandered around, looking for a servant, and then heard voices in here, so . . ."

Lucien, generally the spokesman for the two brothers, stared at her, his face creased in a severe frown.

Mrs. Pelham flinched away from his accusing glare and turned to Richard. "Lady Yancy sent me to fetch something—I was in the Yellow Salon. I can't seem to find the stairs."

"You will have taken the second left, instead of a right after coming out of the Yellow Salon," Richard said, replacing his cue in the rack. "People frequently get lost at Lessing Hall, don't they, Luce?"

Lucien's expression was once again that of the consummate host: polite, concerned, pleasant. "Richard can take you where you need to go, ma'am." He turned to Richard. "I need to take care of something before dinner."

Luce had to pass Mrs. Pelham, who stood in the doorway. She recoiled from him as though he might strike her.

For his part, Luce took extra care not to so much as brush against the hem of her hideous gown, as if she were coated in poison.

Once Lucien had gone, Richard's eyes locked with Mrs. Pelham's.

She had rarely ever looked at Richard a decade ago—at least not without her mask of scorn in place. The look she gave him now was anxious and weary and it reminded him of that long-ago day—right after she'd been confronted with the damning evidence of her handwritten note—when she'd been caught in a trap of her own devising.

"I'm sorry to disrupt your game," she said as Richard strode toward her.

"It was all but over. Come, I will take you back."

She melted against the doorframe, making it easy for him to slide past her without touching her.

But his body—acting without permission from his mind—lightly brushed against her shoulder as he passed.

It was only his upper arm against hers, but the touch seemed to reverberate through him.

Nothing but simple sexual attraction, old boy.

Richard knew that was true. He imagined that such a siren call was a burden to a woman forced to earn her living in the homes of the wealthy. No doubt Mrs. Pelham had become adept at dodging roaming hands.

Richard resolved that his brief touch—a bullying behavior considering her status—was the only one that he would indulge in.

He ignored the mocking laughter that echoed through his mind at such a resolution.

They walked in silence, even though Richard knew it was likely his gentlemanly duty—even with a paid companion—to fill the quiet with meaningless chatter.

"I read about your impending honor."

Richard turned to her. He couldn't help noticing, yet again, how much nature had favored her. Her eyelashes were thick and dark and curly, the tips a piquant auburn that matched some of the darker red lights in her mink-colored hair. Her lower lip was . . . well, decadent. There was no other—decent—word for it.

He saw the trace of a smile on said lips and realized he'd been staring. Again.

"Honor?" he repeated, perplexed.

"Your knighthood," she said, a touch of humor in her voice.

"Ah, yes. That." Richard had forgotten. No doubt he should keep that admission to himself.

"Are you looking forward to meeting the king?"

"Not really."

She choked on a laugh.

"I probably shouldn't say that," he admitted dryly.

"No, probably not."

"It's just that I have met him before, you see. That's what I meant. My father was one of his advisors when he was a very young man, still a prince. The prince had largely distanced himself by the time I was old enough to notice such things, but he visited twice from Brighton and he also came to my father's funeral." Not that Richard could recall him. No, all he remembered of that day was his choking, overwhelming grief.

"We are men, now, Rich," Lucien had told him that morning when they'd waited for one of their male cousins to accompany them to the vault where their father would join his ancestors. Where they, themselves, would one day go. "It is up to us to take care of Mama now that Papa has gone."

Richard smiled at the memory of his nine-year-old brother taking up his responsibilities even at that age; Lucien had truly been born for his position as head of their family.

"I saw your collection at the museum when I was in London."

Richard realized—yet again—that he was doing a less than admirable job holding up his end of the conversation. "Oh, did you? It is not such a popular exhibit with the ladies."

She smiled up at him and his heart felt as if it had leapt into his throat, even though he knew that was a physical impossibility

"I must admit that I was relieved the specimens were behind glass. Even though they were dead. That one beetle in particular was—" She shivered.

"You must be referring to *goliathus regius*. Or, more popularly, the Goliath." Richard recalled the day he'd found that exquisite specimen, when his heart had lurched almost as passionately for a beetle as it was currently doing for the beautiful woman beside him.

"Yes, that is a magnificent example of the breed, just shy of ten inches. I am surprised you enjoy insect exhibits, Mrs. Pelham."

Her nose wrinkled, adding adorable to the list of adjectives one could use to describe her. "Well, to be honest, it would not have been my first choice that day. I accompanied Lady Yancy to London and it was my honor to escort three of her six grandchildren—all boys below the age of ten—to various educational exhibits."

And she'd not been very pleased with the task, by the sound of it.

"And did they enjoy it?" he asked, already knowing the answer.

"They were deafeningly enthusiastic. I daresay the beetle population of West Africa would be terribly depleted if one were to deposit a ship full of English boys in Freetown."

"That sounds like something you've contemplated, Mrs. Pelham."

She gave a startled laugh—which exposed a small dimple on the right side of her mouth—as if not expecting him to possess any humor. "Well, perhaps a few times," she admitted.

"What would have been your exhibit of choice?"

"Oh." She appeared nonplussed, as if unaccustomed to being asked her preferences.

Richard supposed that was the lot of a servant.

"Well, to be honest, I would prefer a visit to the National Gallery. But if forced to make do with the British Museum"—a trace of a smile curved her lips—"I would like to see the recent acquisition of Babylonian antiquities."

"Ah, yes, Mrs. Claudius Rich's donation."

"You've seen it?"

"I had that opportunity before the exhibit was put on display as I am acquainted with the curator. It is quite an impressive collection and well worth seeing." Richard stopped and turned to her. "Here we are."

She blinked up at him, her lips—which were the exact color of the interior of the *lobatus gigas* he'd seen in the British West Indies—parted slightly.

Richard visualized himself leaning down and claiming her mouth. For a fraction of a second, he contemplated the effect of such behavior.

But she was a servant in his family's house, and such behavior would be predatory.

So, instead, he opened the door and said, "Here is the main entrance to your suite of rooms, Mrs. Pelham."

Chapter 5

Celia leaned against the door and exhaled a shaky breath. They say that with age comes wisdom, but for the first time in her life, she knew what that saying really meant.

When she'd opened the billiard room door looking for help, both brothers had turned to face her. It was a jarring experience to be confronted by two individuals who looked so very much alike. But what jarred her more was how she had ever believed that Lucien was the more handsome of the two brothers.

Come, Celia, it wasn't only a handsome face you wanted back then.

No, that was true. She hadn't loved Lucien, although she'd been infatuated with him. Perhaps even more infatuated with what he could give her: wealth, comfort, and security.

While it was true that Richard Redvers's clothing was more stylish now and his haircut more *la mode*—two things her younger self had valued—that wasn't what drew her eye. No, Richard Redvers seemed to smolder, to throw off enough heat to leave her eyeballs hot just from looking at him.

Celia suspected he'd smoldered all along, but she'd been too young and naïve to know about sexual attraction. Now, after far too many years' experience with the opposite sex, she could recognize and appreciate his simmering sensuality.

Oh, his spectacles were every bit as thick—perhaps even thicker—as she remembered, his golden-brown eyes still distorted by the lenses. He sported the same expression she recalled—a sort of confident, superior smirk that used to make her itch to bring him down a peg, but now made her want to—

What? Want to throw yourself at him?

She groaned at the stupid, mortifying, self-destructive thought.

But her imagination—ever willful and fertile, even after years of humiliation and abuse—continued to dwell on Richard's person.

His body had fulfilled the promises of his young, lanky frame and he filled his closely tailored clothing to perfection. Indeed, his coat adhered to his body like ink poured over his powerful shoulders. And his black pantaloons snugly sheathed exceptionally well-formed muscular thighs and calves.

Lord Davenport was as handsome as ever, but he now seemed less substantial beside his brother, and Celia didn't think it was her imagination that he was thinner than he'd been a decade earlier.

Oh, he still emanated sunny charm and golden gorgeousness, but his brother *exuded* a masculine confidence in his own skin that Celia found as alluring as she'd once found Lord Davenport's plump pockets and illustrious title.

Yet, despite his rugged, virile exterior, Richard Redvers was undoubtedly a cerebral man who valued thought as highly, if not more, than action.

Celia could only suppose that he had developed such an intriguing character thanks to years spent in some of the most far-flung, exotic, and dangerous parts of the world.

And he had never married in all that time. Because he'd loved the woman his brother had been forced to marry? It had certainly looked that way during that long-ago Season.

Richard Redvers and Phyllida Singleton had, at one time, appeared almost inseparable. They'd danced together and sat together and laughed and chatted together at every function. If they had been in love, then that was yet another crime to lay at Celia's door.

Was that why Richard had never married? Because he was the sort of man who only gave his heart once in a lifetime?

Celia grimaced at the horrible thought, praying it was not true.

He'd not looked unhappy—nor had he looked happy. Instead, an aura of aloofness clung to him—just as it had all those years ago.

While Lucien had regarded her with all the disgust and scorn she deserved—although he'd done so for only an instant, before his breeding took over—and Steff had looked at her as the most diverting part of what would likely be a younger person's romp of a house party, Richard had looked *through* her, no more interested in her than he'd been in Lady Yancy.

Celia had to admit that his cool, bloodless courtesy had been more painful than open derision would have been.

Oh, but he brushed your shoulder, did he not?

Yes, she had to admit that small action had surprised her. Were it another man—a less *sinuous* man—she might have believed it mere happenstance. But she didn't think Richard Redvers had any problem controlling his body; nor did she believe that he did much that was inadvertent.

So what if he wanted to touch you, Celia? What man below the age of ninety hasn't? All he wanted to do was demonstrate that you are powerless—a member of the servant class who will have to endure whatever he dishes out, and do so with an obedient, pleasant expression on your face.

True, true, and true.

Anger churned in her belly—an anger she'd thought she'd rid herself of years ago, back when Sebastian had brought home to her how powerless she was and just how much she could suffer at the hands of her *betters*.

You have no right to be angry about your current, lowly position or how these people treat you. You should be ashamed of being here; you should be saying a prayer of thanks that Lord Davenport didn't have you tossed out into the cold. Perhaps his wife still might do that when she learns of your presence.

Celia *was* ashamed. It was as if God, or the cosmos, or Loki or some other omnipotent being with a cruel, remorseless sense of humor, could not keep from enjoying a laugh at her expense.

Of all the houses in Britain, why did Lessing Hall have to be the one where she found herself?

Weeks ago, after she'd overcome her initial shock about who was getting married, she had considered feigning illness, but Lady Yancy most certainly would have called a physician to look at her.

And the woman would discharge her before traveling with her dog, cat, and parrot across the country without Celia to manage for her.

And Lord Yancy would not give Celia the end-of-the-year bonus he'd promised, the hazard pay, as he'd laughingly—and disrespectfully—termed it, for staying an entire year in his mother's service.

The end of the year was only weeks away—surely she could last that long?

Celia thought of the Earl of Davenport's expression just moments earlier and was not sure the money was worth it.

It will be worth it to Katie.

As ever, thinking about Katie's sunny, beautiful face—which she loved with all her heart, no matter how much she resembled her father—made Celia smile.

Yes, she could tolerate any amount of humiliation for her daughter.

Chapter 6

Lucien rarely entered his wife's chambers. Indeed, he could count the number of times he'd come into her bedroom: nineteen. Nineteen visits in almost ten years.

Eleven visits for their first child, his heir, and eight visits for his daughter. A daughter whose existence was the reason that he would be allowed into his wife's bed yet again, beginning tomorrow evening.

And if she bore him a second son this time? Well, then the coming days—until Phyllida was breeding—would be the last visits to his wife's bed for the rest of their lives.

Lucien could not look forward to the evenings that lay before him—even though he wanted them so very, very badly.

Instead, he felt sicker with every day that passed.

Sick about his wife's refusal to be his lover, sick about his inability to mend their relationship, and sick at the deep, aching sense of hopelessness that what they had now—this platonic marriage of business partners—was all they would ever have.

And it was all Lucien's fault.

Stop stalling, Lucien.

Lucien knocked on the door and then entered his wife's room.

Phyllida's eyes met his in her dressing table mirror and widened. "Is aught amiss, Davenport?"

Lucien forced a smile he wasn't feeling. "Will you excuse us a moment, Barnes," he said to her maid.

"Of course, your lordship." The older woman dropped a curtsey and hastily left the room.

"What is it? Is it one of the children—"

"No, no—nothing like that. It is just—well, Celia Trent has come with one of the guests. Er, she is here. At Lessing Hall," he added, as if there were any other here, here.

Phyllida stared and he cursed himself for his blundering and blurting.

"She is a companion to some woman who accompanied Dowden's aunt," he explained. "She's—well, she's a servant. And her name is Pelham now. Er, Celia Trent's name is Pelham, not the aunt's name."

You're babbling, Lucien.

He shut his mouth.

Phyllida's expression was so inscrutable that Lucien had often thought she should be the one with political aspirations. Not that her unreadable face was the only thing to recommend her. She was also a good deal smarter and better educated than he.

Although she'd not gone to university—neither had he—she had as good as earned honors just living with her brilliant father and acting as hostess at his famous dinner parties.

Several of those years hosting had been while Rich was Sir Gael's pupil.

Lucien knew that his twin's association with Phyllida had been the start of a deep and abiding friendship—if not actual love.

"That is . . . unfortunate," Phyllida said after a long moment of silence.

That was one word for it.

"Well, there is nothing to be done, I suppose." She dropped her gaze to the diamond and emerald bracelet he'd bought her on their fifth wedding anniversary. "Would you fasten this for me, please." She held out her wrist, her expression remote.

In all the years they'd been married, he'd never helped her put on a piece of jewelry, even though he'd bought her several fine sets. His fingers shook slightly, the feel of her warm skin so close to his fingertips sending a frisson of excitement shooting from his hands directly to his groin.

Good Lord. He was in a bad way when mere proximity to his wife's wrist was enough to get him hard.

What would she do, he wondered, if he dropped to his knees, lifted the heavy turquois velvet of her skirt and various petticoats, thrust her thighs apart, and buried his face in her sex?

She would likely scream and then kick you in the jewels. Or perhaps kick you and then *scream.*

"Davenport?"

He looked up from the bracelet to find Phyllida studying him, her brow wrinkled with concern. "Hmm?" he asked, his mind on his current physical predicament.

"I know this must be hard for you."

For one horrifying moment he thought she was referring to the erection currently pressed against his fall.

But then he saw that she was looking at his face, not his crotch.

He dropped his hands to the front of his hips, placing them in a way that should hide the truth of his condition.

He cleared his throat, scrambling to remember what she'd asked . . . Ah, yes—about Mrs. Pelham—whose face he couldn't recall right now even if his life depended on it.

"Er, no, actually."

Her velvety brown brows pulled down over her sharp little nose. "You don't mind her being here?"

"Oh. Well, I'd rather she was somewhere else—anywhere else—obviously. I just meant that it was no h-harder for me than it is for you, Richard, or—I daresay—Mrs. Pelham, herself."

Based on her deepening frown, he should have omitted the last name.

"I doubt Richard will even notice," she said, her expression once again aloof.

Lucien didn't think it wise to tell her that his brother not only noticed but had evinced a clear—at least to Lucien's way of thinking—interest in the still very beautiful woman.

"I don't suppose there is any way to keep her away from the festivities?" Lucien asked.

Phyllida gifted him with one of her rare smiles. "I don't see how, my lord." She shrugged. "It will be a mild, brief tempest." She hesitated. "I suppose you should tell your mother, Antonia, and Lord Ramsay. You know how—"

Lucien grimaced. "Yes, I know how Hugh enjoys poking the hornet's nest. Although I don't think that even my mischievous stepfather can find anything entertaining in this situation. I think—"

There was a soft knock on the door.

Lucien cast an irritable glance toward it; couldn't the bloody woman stay away until Phyllida rang for her? "Yes?" he snapped, and then recalled it wasn't his bedchamber he was standing in.

But when the door opened, it wasn't Barnes, but William Payson, the secretary he and Phyllida shared.

Payson was the younger son of a squire. At first, he'd worked only for Lucien, but he'd soon made himself indispensable to both of them.

Phyllida got to her feet, her expression not so much embarrassed as . . . distracted. "Oh, Will—you must be here for the letters I was preparing for Lady Lindham. I'm terribly sorry, I forgot to send them down to you. Wait just a moment and I will fetch them from my desk."

She went to the adjoining study, leaving Lucien alone with the other man.

Just how often did Payson visit his wife's chambers, anyway?

Lucien must have been giving William a hard look because the other man's handsome face reddened. "I'm terribly sorry to interrupt, my lord. Normally I would not bother her ladyship, er, here, but these letters needed to go out on tonight's mail coach."

Payson sounded neither guilty nor alarmed, merely apologetic.

Still, Lucien did not like seeing the man in a room he'd visited nineteen—now twenty—times.

"Here you are, Will." Phyllida passed in front of Lucien, the lemony scent she wore teasing his nostrils. "I'm so relieved that you remembered."

"My pleasure, madam. Er, shall I accept Lord Bexhill's invitation?"

Phyllida absently turned her bracelet on her wrist as she considered the question. "I think that is wise. He was rather on the fence about whether to double his donation. Please add it to my calendar."

"Yes, my lady." He dropped another bow. "My lord." And then took his leave.

"What thing with Bexhill?" Lucien asked before he could stop himself.

She appeared surprised at his interest. "Oh. Bexhill is giving an afternoon concert featuring a pianist he's brought over from Rome. William and I will go sit through the performance and then approach him about his donation to the Trapston School. He usually funds one scholarship but we were hoping to talk him into doubling it this year. Bexhill is a close friend of Will's father and the squire promised to work on him for us."

Lucien wondered when his wife had begun calling Payson *Will*. Even he called the man *William*.

"Davenport?" she asked.

Lucien scowled. And that was another thing; why the hell did she never use *his* pet name? In fact, had she *ever* called him by his Christian name at all? If she had, he couldn't recall it.

"Yes?" he said, rather sharply.

"Was that all you needed to tell me? About Mrs. Pelham?"

"Oh. Yes."

"Very well, then I will summon Barnes back to finish getting me ready."

So, there was his dismissal.

He strode toward the connecting door, passing through it for the fortieth time in his life.

"Oh, my lord?"

Lucien stopped, hope surging in his chest as he turned. "Yes, Phyllida?"

"Will you explain what happened to Antonia?"

Lucien blinked at her question—not what he'd been expecting.

What were *you expecting?*

He didn't know, but something . . . more. Something foolish.

"I daresay she knows nothing about it," Phyllida said, no doubt interpreting his perplexed expression as having some other meaning. "She was only eight at the time. I would rather not have her know of it, but it seems unfair to keep such information from her at her own wedding."

"Yes, I'll tell her," Lucien said.

"Oh, Antonia received word that there has been a setback at the London house and Dowden is staying even later to set things to rights."

Lucien was relieved to hear it. Dowden could be . . . awkward and Lucien would rather not deal with his presence just yet.

He would never admit as much to Richard, whom he knew despised the duke, but he had never quite trusted Dowden, not even years ago when they'd briefly run together during Lucien's first and only Season.

Lucien also knew that his future brother-in-law kept a mistress in London.

Although the knowledge irked him—it was his sister the man was marrying, after all—it was not his affair—no pun intended. Their mother would have told Antonia the realities of married life, even though Hugh didn't keep a mistress.

But Hugh's behavior was far from the norm when it came to *ton* marriages.

Almost every man Lucien knew—married or otherwise—kept a woman or frequented brothels.

So, it was not his place to point a finger at Dowden. Especially not since he'd kept a similar secret for years.

"Davenport?"

Lucien saw that his wife was staring at him. "Hmm?"

"I said perhaps you might go to Antonia now, my lord. You should have enough time to explain matters to her before she needs to go down for dinner." Phyllida turned back toward the mirror and commenced screwing in her earrings.

Their meeting was apparently over.

Chapter 7

Phyllida waited until the door shut behind her husband before closing her eyes, tossing the earring onto her dressing table, and slumping into a shaky sigh.

Celia Trent.

Phil hadn't told her husband that Stephanie had already made it a point to convey the delicious news the moment she'd arrived from the church with Antonia and Lady Morton, Dowden's obnoxious, overbearing aunt.

While Phil did not like Stephanie, she'd been forced to put up with her for years, especially when the marquess was still alive, as he'd been a great friend of Lucien's.

"You'll never guess who is companion to Lady Yancy," Stephanie had blurted before the butler was out of earshot.

"You're probably right," Phyllida agreed. "Who?"

"Celia Trent. Well, except she's Celia Pelham, now."

Only because Phil had been practicing obfuscation for a decade was she able to cheat the other woman out of a satisfying response.

"What a remarkable coincidence," she'd said mildly, stripping off her gloves as she'd begun the long trek from the massive front entry hall to the family wing of the ancient building. "How are you finding your rooms, my lady?" she'd asked.

Stephanie had looked so crestfallen that Phyllida would have laughed if her stomach hadn't felt as if she'd just swallowed broken glass.

"Oh. It is lovely, thank you, Phil."

The other woman's use of a name reserved for family and friends irked her, but her smile didn't waver. "I'm pleased you like it. It is quite my favorite of the guest suites. Do tell me if there is anything you need," Phyllida said. "I'm afraid my rooms are this way," she added when she reached the landing. "I shall see you at dinner, my lady."

As much as Phil had enjoyed leaving Steff stewing in her disappointment, she'd barely made it to her room before cracking.

"My lady?" Barnes, her maid, had gasped when Phyllida had entered the room, closed her eyes and sagged against the door. "Is anything—"

"I need a quarter of an hour alone, Barnes," Phil said in a shaky, hoarse voice.

"But it is almost six thirty and—"

"A quarter of an hour, Barnes."

Once her maid had gone, Phyllida dropped into a chair and stared without seeing at the opposite wall. But instead of the beautiful fifteenth-century French tapestry, she saw Celia Trent as she'd been not only that fateful Season, but all the years before, when they'd attended the same school in Cambridge.

Year after year of taunts, slights, and digs rose up like specters.

She could still recall the day she met Celia. She'd been seventeen and Celia, twelve. Even then there had been something about the other girl that had drawn every eye—male or female—in her vicinity.

Phyllida had thought that day, and countless times in the years that followed, that it wasn't right for one woman to have so much beauty.

Their school—Mrs. Bennington's Academy—had been operated by a friend of Phil's mother. Although most of the students lived in the grand old mansion that housed the school, Margery Bennington had allowed Phyllida to attend as one of her few day students. The schoolmistress had known of Phil's responsibilities at home and understood that often she could only manage half days.

During Phil's first two years at the school, her mother had still lived at home and Phil had spent as much time with her as possible. By her last year, when she'd been nineteen—a bit older than her classmates because of her irregular schedule—her mother had been moved to a sanatorium in Bath, where she'd died before the school year was finished.

Her mother's dying wish was that Phil have a London Season.

"It was the best time of my life, darling. Just two years—promise you will give it two years."

And so Phil had promised.

But not long after her mother's death, her father became dangerously ill and Phil's Season was put off twice.

Mrs. Bennington knew that Phil was alone for those two long years and had begged Phil to offer a painting class at the school.

"You can't be nursing your father day and night, Phyllida. You need a few hours for yourself. Besides, I desperately need a painting instructor after Miss Quimby left so suddenly."

What began as a favor to her old schoolmistress gradually became one of the joys of her life. Phil discovered that she had a gift for teaching and loved her students.

Well, with the exception of Celia Trent, Margaret Croy, and Jennifer Trethaway—or the Unholy Trio, as Mrs. Bennington termed the three beautiful girls.

It was likely that Phyllida—drab and plain and reserved—would never have attracted Celia's attention if she'd not stopped the willful beauty from teasing one of the younger girls, who'd been homesick and crying.

"Just because you teach *painting* here," Celia had spat the word like it was poison, "doesn't mean you are in charge."

"I couldn't agree more, Ceelie," Lady Margaret Croy agreed with an evil smile on her lovely face.

"Perhaps I should tell my father that Mrs. Bennington is allowing the daughter of a school teacher to instruct our behavior?" Lady Jennifer Trethaway chimed in. "Papa has already been saying a journey to the Continent is the only way to achieve *true* polish."

Mrs. Bennington barely made enough to survive as it was. And there Phil was, jeopardizing her friend's precious crust with her interference.

And so that had been the last time she'd corrected any of the girls' behavior.

She'd hoped to avoid them entirely, but then all three had signed up for her painting classes.

And so Phyllida had gritted her teeth and tolerated their snide comments, disruptive behavior, and negative effect on the other students.

Until the day her satchel went missing.

Phil had left it in the cloakroom, as she always did. But that day it wasn't there after her class. She'd retraced all of her steps and then torn apart the cloakroom before notifying Mrs. Bennington.

Still they'd not found it.

The following day, after a sleepless night, she received a message: the satchel had been discovered.

Phil had rushed to the school to collect her precious bag, pathetically grateful it had been found—until she learned that one item was missing: her diary.

Against her better judgment, she'd been entirely candid in her journal. That was something she never, ever made the mistake of doing again. In fact, she'd stopped keeping a journal after that.

The first of her poems appeared a week after the journal's disappearance.

Phyllida had walked into her class that day and was immediately aware of the strained atmosphere. Girls kept giggling, eyeing each other, and were slow to get out their watercolors.

"What is wrong with everyone today?" she'd asked, more amused than angry.

"Oh, nothing," Celia Trent said with a die-away sigh. "It is simply a day to allow one's heart to soar . . ."

All the girls except Mary Winthrop had collapsed into giggles. Mary, a stolid, old-before-her-time American girl, had frowned at the others and said to Phyllida, "I believe one of your poems is pinned on the message board in the sitting room, Miss Singleton."

After that, it had occurred every few days.

"Oh, dear," Mrs. Bennington had fretted, but Phyllida could see the older woman was more annoyed than angered by the theft and subsequent posting of poems. "Some of the girls are such trouble. Why is it always the ones whose fathers pay their tuition on time?"

So, in other words, Phyllida could expect no help from that quarter. She had two choices, either quit, or endure.

One look at Celia Trent's smug face had made her choice clear; she would not let the vicious little witch drive her away.

So she'd stood her ground, only truly relaxing after Celia was taken out of school eight months before the year was over.

But her relief was short lived.

Phil's debut had been pushed back so often due to one catastrophe or another that she'd begun to hope it would never happen at all. Just when she'd begun to think she'd not be able to keep the promise to her mother, her aunt had decided to take matters in hand and launch her niece into society, no matter how ancient Phil was.

When Phyllida finally made her debut at the grand old age of twenty-two, one of the few faces she'd recognized at her first London ball was Miss Celia Trent's.

The Season had been dreadful.

Phyllida immediately fell into a group of wallflowers and spent every event she'd been invited to—not many—on the fringes.

The second Season, while much the same as the first, had settled into a predictable, if humiliating, pattern. No matter how much effort her aunt expended to find her dance partners, the only person who ever asked her willingly was Richard Redvers, one of her father's past students.

Although Richard was several years her junior, he'd gallantly sought her out at every function, dancing with her wallflower sisters, as well. He was charming, handsome, and a terrible disaster at *ton* functions, where his thick spectacles, disheveled appearance, and direct manner drew more censure from *the beautiful crowd* than even Phil and the wallflowers.

Phil had always enjoyed Richard's company when he'd come to dinner at her father's house, but she'd viewed him as a sibling rather than a suitor. She knew that he wasn't interested in her romantically, either.

Richard Redvers was not the kind of man who wanted to marry. Phil was familiar with his sort—earnest young men who lived for science rather than human interaction—and she felt comfortable with him. Indeed, he reminded her of her father, who'd not married until his forties.

The only reason Richard was in London was because he'd promised his mother that he would attend at least one London Season.

Phil had always known he had a twin brother, but she could hardly credit that scruffy, awkward, beetle-obsessed Richard was related to the glorious, golden, godlike Earl of Davenport.

Like every other woman that Season, Phil fell in love—or at least infatuation—with the young earl.

Not that Lucien Redvers had even registered Phyllida's existence, of course.

Well, at least not until the night of the Stanford ball.

Phil woke slowly from her dream of the past to find that she was staring blankly at her looking glass and late for her hostess duties in the Yellow Salon.

She attached her earring and then examined her person: tidy, matronly, and handsome. That was the best that could ever be said of her short, far-too-slender body. As for her face? A series of nondescript features united to create nondescript looks. Only her wavy, glossy, chestnut hair was anything out of the ordinary. Unbound, the heavy curtain fell past her hips.

But not even on those few nights when her husband came to her had her hair ever been loose.

She smoothed a hand over the sleek chignon she favored, which all but eradicated any curl or wave.

This is not a time for pensive daydreaming, said the militaristic voice that kept her moving whenever she faltered.

Indeed, it was not.

As Phil made her way through the grand corridors of her home, she tried to console herself that she now had all the things that Celia Trent had once schemed and yearned for. She had Lucien, his money, his status, and even his children. Rather than resent Celia's presence in her house as a servant, she should enjoy the opportunity to lord her material and emotional wealth over the other woman.

But the cloak of love, respectability, and family that Phil usually wrapped around herself suddenly felt ragged and worn rather than comforting and warm.

Chapter 8

Celia got the impression that if she could have been seated in the cellar—or dungeon, as Lessing Hall looked as if it might have one—her hostess would have done it.

To tell the truth, Celia would have liked eating alone in a dungeon better than enduring the waves of hostility emanating from the Redvers clan.

Not that any of them were so ill-bred as to openly display their dislike.

Richard had never been one to show his emotions and was even more aloof than he'd been a decade earlier.

Antonia, or Toni as her intimates called her, was a breathtakingly beautiful young woman with vivacious blue-green eyes, masses of golden-red curls, and a loving smile for her family and friends.

Interestingly, Sebastian's bride-to-be was a difficult woman to read for all that she looked so very, very young.

Although Celia saw enough awareness in Antonia's clear, forthright gaze to know that somebody had informed her of what had happened a decade earlier, the girl's expression was enviably inscrutable.

Lord and Lady Davenport had, of course, been the consummate host and hostess.

Both had smiled politely—if frigidly—while Lady Davenport introduced Celia to her mother and father-in-law, Baron and Baroness Ramsay.

"This is Lady Yancy's companion, Mrs. Celia Pelham. Perhaps you might recall her—her maiden name was Trent."

It had been a masterful, subtle set-down.

Lady Yancy, who'd been right beside her, had said in her strident, carrying voice, "My goodness, Pelham, you seem to have a goodly number of friends here. I'm afraid my companion has been hiding her light under a bushel," she'd explained to the startled baron and baroness with an amused chuckle. "If you can believe it, she has been in my employ almost a year and has, thus far, kept her august connections quite a secret from me."

Celia had been surprised that flames hadn't begun leaping from her head.

Well, she could only hope that she kept the horrid truth from Lady Yancy long enough to collect her bonus from Lord Yancy. Because—stickler for propriety that the dowager was—she would sack Celia in a heartbeat if she learned that Lady Infamous was living under her roof.

Phyllida—Lucien's wife and the current Lady Davenport—was a woman Celia had tormented and taunted almost from the first moment they'd met.

But a person would never guess at their shared past from Phyllida's cool gray eyes, which showed absolutely no awareness or interest in her.

Exhibiting such an utter lack of interest was far more effective than a sneer. Phyllida's expression said, and rightly so, that Celia was so far beneath the countess's status that it was difficult to see her at all.

And Celia, more than anyone in the dining room, knew that was the truth: she was a servant and this woman was a well-respected and wealthy peeress.

Celia also acknowledged, with some pain, that both she and Lady Davenport had gotten exactly what they deserved in life.

Celia was seated between Mr. Philbin, an aged curate, and a lad named Jonathan, yet another of the numerous Redvers offspring.

Jonathan Redvers was a tall, handsome boy who bore a striking resemblance to his piratical father—but without the eyepatch. He couldn't be more than sixteen, but he was already heart-poundingly handsome.

Celia spent most of the first course listening to the curate maunder on about the unseasonably warm spate of weather, the difficulty of fitting so many wedding guests into the small church, and Lord Ramsay's generous endowment of the bell repair project.

By the time the curate's companion on the other side, a school friend of Miss Antonia Redvers, distracted him, Celia felt as if her attentive expression had calcified on her face.

She turned to Jonathan, who gave her a knowing smirk that was remarkably like his half brother Richard's. "Old Philbin jabber your head off?"

"My head is still attached but there's a ringing in my right ear."

An inelegant guffaw slipped from his mouth and she saw a new glint in his eyes; a glint that said perhaps the old bird he'd been stuck sitting beside wasn't as senile as he'd first suspected.

Celia knew she shouldn't encourage the young sprig in such disrespectful behavior, but her better angel had been clubbed over the head by its more vicious partner about five minutes after she'd stepped out of Lady Yancy's carriage.

"So, what did you do that's put everyone in such a pucker?" Jonathan asked, his fork and knife skillfully dissecting his gamebird with no attention from his eyes or brain. "Or shouldn't I be asking?"

"You may ask anything you want. But I'm not sure you're old enough to deserve an answer," she taunted, enjoying his narrowed eyes and flushed cheekbones. There, that was much better. Now he looked like the boy he was rather than the heart-slaying sophisticate he'd be in the next few years.

"I say, that's rather harsh," he said.

Celia smiled. "Where do you go to school?" she asked, moving the conversation, not too subtly, away from herself.

"One more term at Eton."

"What will you do then? Go to university?"

His horrified expression was comical. "Lord no. I'll be going into the navy."

It was easy to keep him talking, just as it was with most people.

Celia had learned, during her decade of subservience, that it was best to ask questions and allow others to do the talking. After all, what did she have to talk about that wouldn't get her ejected from a room, discharged by an employer, or shunned by even more of the populace?

By the time the last course was carried away, Jonathan had lost all pretention to being a jaded young buck and was, instead, a charming boy who chatted happily about the small sailboat his father had given him a few years earlier.

"You should come and give her a look," he offered as he stood to pull back her chair when Celia rose with all the other women. "I could take you up and down the coast. She's at anchor just outside town, the *Unsinkable II.* And before you ask," he said with a wry grin, "yes, there *was* an *Unsinkable I.*"

Celia chuckled. "That sounds like a story worth hearing." She dropped a curtsey and went to offer her arm to Lady Yancy.

The old lady leaned more heavily on her than she had a mere year earlier and Celia knew she was becoming frailer by the day. At least her body was. In spirit, she was as vigorous as ever.

Yet as rough and demeaning as Lady Yancy could sometimes be toward her, Celia did not dislike her. She was old, lonely, and knew that her son—her only surviving child—did not like her. Her daughter-in-law was disrespectful and dismissive and her grandchildren were unruly and rude. And yet she woke up every day, got dressed in the formal and complicated garb of a long-gone age, and kept going through the motions.

Celia could respect that; she knew how difficult it was to even crawl out of bed some days.

"Would you like to go up to your room, my lady?"

To her surprise, Lady Yancy nodded. "I *would* like to do that, Pelham. But it seems impossibly ill-mannered to retire so early."

"Oh, I'm sure the countess will understand." Celia hesitated and then added, "I believe Lord Ramsay's aunt lives here but rarely attends dinner. I'm sure it will not look amiss if you turn in early."

Lady Yancy perked up. "I knew Lady Amelia, even though she was older than I. She was tall—almost as tall as Miss Antonia—but not much to look at. She was in love with Lord Synton"—the old woman chuckled—"but then we all were. Such a shame, it was. He went off to fight the French in the colonies and died unmarried." Her voice hushed to her idea of a whisper. "Lady Amelia was heartbroken—half mad, some said—with anguish. And then there was a scandal with a *man*—some say a servant—and poor Amelia was plucked from London in the middle of the Season and sent home. I believe she's been hidden away here ever since."

Celia felt an instant kinship with the exiled, scandalous old woman.

"Dear me, she must be getting on," said Pot about Kettle.

Celia had to bite back a smile at that. "Shall I take you over to say good night to the countess before we go up?"

"Yes, yes, I'd better."

Lady Davenport was surrounded by her mother-in-law, the vague but beautiful Baroness Ramsay, her sister-in-law, Antonia, three of her school mates who'd doubtless come to take part in the wedding celebrations, and Lady Morton, whose ringing voice was audible from the far side of the room.

Lady Yancy waited until her friend finished declaiming before speaking. "I beg you will forgive me, Lady Davenport, Baroness, Lady Antonia, but I'm afraid I must turn in early this evening."

"Of course, of course, Lenna. It was a very long journey for you," Lady Morton said, forgetting that she wasn't the mistress of this particular house. She looked at Celia and sniffed. "I daresay *you* will come back to join us, Mrs. Pelham?"

"Oh no, Pelham needs to take care of poor Percy, Mr. Fusskins, and Alexander," Lady Yancy said, patting Celia's arm like a dog.

Celia swore she heard a collective sigh of relief and, for once, she was glad of the old lady's order.

They said good night and made their slow way back to their wing of the house.

"I'm not sure why Moira thought her assistance would be needed with the wedding," Lady Yancy said. "Miss Antonia is quite an efficient and organized young woman. I have seen the schedule of events she has planned for everyone's pleasure and there is nothing left to organize. Moira must have misunderstood her nephew."

Celia thought it was far more likely that Lady Morton hadn't consulted Sebastian, at all.

Sebastian. Ugh. Thank God his arrival had been delayed.

"You shivered, Pelham. I told you to put on your heavier shawl for dinner."

Her heavier shawl bore a striking resemblance to a yak pelt she'd seen on her last visit to the British Museum. "I expect I should have, my lady."

"That younger boy—Lord Davenport's twin—he is rather . . . odd, isn't he?"

Celia smiled; she'd seen that Lady Yancy had been seated beside Richard and wondered what shocking pronouncements the naturalist had made over dinner.

Because Celia was poor, bored, and desperate for some news of her old life, she'd read a copy of the last paper Richard had submitted to the Royal Geographical Society.

The treatise was so popular that it had been published as a small bound copy that had been available at Lady Yancy's lending library.

When Celia had seen his name on the cover, she'd been unable to resist.

Everything in the brief book was shocking, from his views on man's origins to something he termed *the breeding imperative*. Even the term itself was shocking.

"He has an entire room devoted to discoveries made during his travels—insects, I believe—at the big museum in London. Beetles and such." Lady Yancy's expression told Celia what she thought about *that* hobby. "He's a very strange young man. Nothing at all like his brother—not nearly so elegant or stylish."

No, he wasn't.

Unfortunately for Celia, somewhere along the way, she'd come to find Richard Redvers's dangerous sensuality far more attractive than modish garments, plump pockets, or pleasing manners.

Chapter 9

Richard loathed port and found most after-dinner conversation insipid. The only time he'd ever enjoyed after-dinner drinks and cigars had been at Sir Gael's house, back in Cambridge.

Not only had Lady Singleton, and Phil after her, set an excellent table, but neither woman had squawked about Sir Gael filling the house with young men, who would often stay smoking or conversing until morning.

Richard had received a letter from Gael just this morning. It seemed there were a pair of very promising cousins, William Fox—whom Richard had met briefly—and a younger man whose name was either Charles or Thomas Darwin, he couldn't recall. In any event, Gael told him that he *must* come down for at least a few weeks before setting out on his next journey in March.

Richard would take the now-retired don up on the invitation. A fortnight with Gael would be an excellent chance to—

"*Richard?*"

He looked up to find his stepfather smirking at him. "You are looking remarkably like your mother right now, which tells me you are bored and have retreated to some mental cave full of more interesting, but probably long-dead, people and books."

Richard grinned at Hugh. "I was actually thinking about a letter I received from Sir Gael this morning."

"Ah, and how is Phil's father?"

"He is very excited about some new students that he met through a fellow professor. I'm thinking of spending some time with him in the New Year before I head off."

"See if you can convince Sir Gael to come up for a visit—maybe over Easter. I don't like to sound like a meddling old woman," Hugh said, "but I do wish he'd come see Phil more often—and his grandchildren, of course."

There was something about the older man's expression that told Richard more about Phil and Luce's relationship than either his brother or dear friend was willing to do.

Richard cleared his throat. "How has Luce been? He looks a bit, er—"

"Weary?"

It was more than that, but Richard nodded.

"Your brother is a very private person, Rich. As is his wife. Although we might all live under the same roof, we are not in each other's pockets. You know how it is."

Indeed, Lessing Hall was so sprawling it was like a small village. A person could wander the hallways for days without encountering another person.

Hugh gave Richard a rare look of indecision. "Perhaps you might . . ."

Richard could guess what his stepfather was suggesting. "I'm afraid that Luce no longer speaks to me as he used to, Hugh."

"I still think you have the best chance of getting him to confide in you." Hugh glanced around, as if to ascertain whether anyone was listening; no one was. "I've been meaning to ask, but there never seems to be a good time. What do you think about Dowden? Lucien tells me you two were at loggerheads when you were lads. You are like your mother—slow to rile; I trust your judgment."

Richard thought back to that long-ago day in the stables at Eton, when Dowden was sixteen and Richard eleven. "It is true that I do—*did* not like him. To be honest, it all stemmed from one event.

There was a boy—a friend of sorts—he was a year older than I, but small and weak. He was one of the lads who waited on Dowden that year and the man rode him ruthlessly." He looked at Hugh. "You know how some boys can be when they get that first taste of power." Although Dowden, as the heir to a dukedom, would have had considerable power from the time he took his first steps.

"What are you saying, Rich?"

"I walked into the stables one afternoon and found the two of them alone. It was clear they'd been involved in some sort of altercation. Tim—my friend—was crying, his clothing torn and one of his eyes swelling. Dowden told me to be on my way but I refused."

Lord, Richard could still recall the terror he'd felt facing up to such a grand, popular, and powerful boy.

"What happened next?"

"I accused him of being unnecessarily harsh on Tim, and then I took Tim with me. But when I asked him what had happened, he refused to tell me."

Hugh's expression turned chilling. "So, in other words, he's a bully at best and a rapist at worst?"

"I don't feel right in accusing him of the latter as I have no proof."

"No, that would be spreading a rumor." He sighed, looking distracted. "It's a damned shame you don't know exactly what happened. A cuffing is one thing, but if it was worse—" He grimaced. "That is a disturbing piece of information."

Richard wondered if he'd made a mistake telling Hugh the story. In his day, Hugh had been more fearsome than the pirates, slavers, and killers he'd hunted. The expression on his face made the hairs on Richard's neck stand up.

"To be fair, sir, it was a long time ago. Perhaps he has grown out of his bullying ways. A man does a lot of changing in seventeen years."

"Hmph. That's true, but I need more assurance. I need to know if he is a brute, Rich. And I want to know *before* he has Toni within his power. Perhaps your friend Tim might tell you the truth now—if he knew your reason for asking?"

"I'm afraid he couldn't."

"I know a gentleman doesn't tell tales, but surely—"

"He is dead, Hugh. He hanged himself not long after leaving school."

"That is . . . unfortunate." Hugh paused and then asked, "Did he leave any indication why?"

"Not that I heard. His parents were devastated—he was their only child."

"I don't even want to imagine such a thing." Hugh shook his head as if to dislodge the upsetting thought. "So I have no proof of anything when it comes to Dowden—only my gut instinct for danger."

Richard suspected that there were few men in England with a more honed instinct for danger than his stepfather.

"Have you said anything to Toni?"

Hugh scowled. "You know how your sister is."

Richard smiled at that; Toni was as stubborn and willful as the man who'd sired her.

"She is so very determined about all of this." Hugh's expression was one of profound perplexity. "She fixed on Dowden only a few weeks into the Season. And after she made her decision, she sat me and your mother down and told us the way it would be—that she would marry him when he asked and that she would tolerate no meddling in her betrothal, wedding, or marriage."

Richard knew the older man was not speaking in jest; his sister was a force to be reckoned with.

"You are concerned about her age?" Richard guessed.

"She is only *just* eighteen. Because of how her birthday falls, we allowed her to come out at seventeen—although I don't think we could have stopped her. The only reason their marriage wasn't announced back in the spring is because we told her she could, if she still felt the same, announce it after she turned eighteen. Dowden is almost twice her age. Both your mother and I agree that is a worrying age gap."

Richard frowned. "My mother and father had a much larger age difference than that and they were very well suited and happy." Richard didn't realize until after he'd spoken how sharp he sounded.

Something flickered in Hugh's eyes and he laid his massive, four-fingered hand on Richard's shoulder. "You make an excellent point; your mother and father had a very happy marriage."

Richard had always been sensitive about any criticism—real or imagined—of his father.

Although Thomas Redvers had died when Richard and Lucien were not quite ten, Richard had missed his sire every day of his adult life. His father had always loved Richard best, even though he wasn't the heir. And even though he was so much clumsier and duller than his magnificent twin.

"Anyone can master horses or boxing or fencing, Richard," his father had told him one day, after Richard had once again demonstrated his ham-fisted equestrian skills by allowing his pony to scrape him off on a tree. "But you have the sort of intellect that comes along only a few times in a generation." The earl's stern face had flexed into one of his rare smiles. "I'd like to claim my part in your cleverness, but you get your big brain from your mother."

Though the earl had already been seventy when his sons were born, he'd still taken the time to teach them to ride, shoot, and how to be gentlemen. His love for them had been palpable.

And yet now, not quite twenty years after his death, nobody spoke of him or seemed to remember him.

Not even Lucien mentioned him anymore.

His brother had lived in a house with Hugh longer than they'd lived with their real sire, and Richard knew that Lucien had come to think of Hugh as his father.

As much as Richard loved Hugh, he was not his father.

Thinking of his beloved papa caused a familiar itchy feeling behind his eyes. He blinked rapidly and looked away from his stepfather. Good God, he was twenty-nine, not twelve. Was he about to blubber in the middle of port and cigars?

"Richard?"

He cleared his throat and forced himself to face Hugh's too knowing gaze. "Tell me more about your gut instinct," he said, mainly to move the conversation along.

"I had Dowden looked into and found out that he is no worse than any other young buck. Moderate drinking, gambling, doesn't go to his country estate often but has been wise enough to leave it in the care of an excellent steward, attends to his duties in town and on the bench." His frown deepened. "He's always kept mistresses but—" He glanced at Lucien. "Well, he's hardly the only man who does."

It took Richard a moment to absorb Hugh's words and significant look.

"What? Is that true?" he asked rather stupidly. "About Luce?"

Hugh nodded.

Richard stared at his brother, hoping to see something that would contradict Hugh's claim.

But all he saw was Lucien's familiar, amiable face as he chatted with one of Lessing Hall's neighbors.

Lucien kept a mistress?

That was . . . disappointing.

Did Phil know? If she knew, did she care? Richard didn't like to think of her knowing and suffering. It made him feel quite grim toward his twin.

"Rich?" Hugh prodded.

He turned to his stepfather. "Do you think someone—perhaps Mama—should tell Toni about Dowden's mistress?"

"She already *knows*."

"What?"

Hugh looked exhausted as he leaned back in his chair, his six-foot-five body causing even that substantial piece of furniture to creak. "I don't understand her interest in him, but your mother says Dowden is accounted an extremely handsome man and he demonstrates magnetism whenever I've heard him speak. And then there is his rank."

Richard scoffed. "Surely she doesn't give a toss for that?"

"Who knows? All I could get out of her was that she finds men her age callow, undeveloped, and uninteresting."

Richard winced. "That's rather harsh, isn't it?"

"Well, Jonathan certainly took issue with it."

"Can't say I blame him. Still feel a bit callow myself on occasion."

Hugh gave one of his bellows of laughter. "Me as well, Rich."

Around them, the men began to extinguish cigars, finish their port, and move toward the door.

"I have to go and give Newton his nightly constitutional," Richard said. "But tell Phil I'll return."

Hugh walked out with him. "Lord, that dog must be what—thirteen?"

"He is twelve," Richard said rather abruptly, and then took his leave.

He didn't like to talk about Newton's age, or even think about it. He knew that it was foolish for a naturalist to pretend his dog would never die. But he didn't mind being accused of foolishness on occasion.

Buckle was waiting so close to the door that Richard almost hit him with it when he entered the room.

"He is impatient, Sir Richard."

"I heard his *impatience* all the way down the corridor." Richard frowned at his servant. "And you shouldn't be calling me that, I've not been knighted yet."

"I'm just practicing, sir."

Richard gave a bark of laughter and turned to his still-howling dog. "Come, old fellow," Richard said, scruffing the spot just behind Newton's big ears that turned him into a slobbering beggar.

Richard had decided to stay in the Rose Suite, which was the only ground-floor bedroom in the house. It was used as a convalescent room, which both his father and stepfather had occupied at different times, because it was closer to the kitchens and had no stairs. He knew Newton would appreciate the lack of stairs—and also the proximity to the kitchen.

He opened the French door that led to the terrace and Newton trotted out before him, looking interested and vigorous as he sniffed the crisp night air. Richard allowed Newton to pick their destination as there were few obstacles or dangers for the old dog near the house.

They'd only walked a couple steps before Newton caught the scent of an animal and began trotting for the first time in recent memory, quickly disappearing into the nearby shrubbery.

Richard smiled. There, see? He wasn't quite so old—

Newton gave one of his spinetingling bellows, and Richard heard two dogs snarling, punctuated by a feminine yelp, and then, "Percy! Percy, come back!"

Richard jogged toward the sound of the ructions. There was a half moon and the cloud cover was sparse, so he saw her immediately. She'd taken off the horrid mobcap she'd worn earlier and was wearing a bonnet of some sort. She'd also covered up her high-necked, dowdy frock with a plain dark wool cloak that was a perfect foil for her fair-skinned beauty.

Well, listen to you. A poet now? Or an aspiring lady's milliner?

"What happened?" Richard asked as he jogged up to her.

"Lady Yancy's dog ran away," Mrs. Pelham said before charging off into the darkness.

"Mrs. Pelham, please do be careful. There is a—"

"Aaargh!" The scream was followed by a soft *oof*ing sound.

"—sharp drop-off," he finished.

Richard followed the sound of groaning and found three lumps: one large, one smaller, and one very small.

"Did you hurt yourself?" he asked, dropping to his haunches beside her.

Part of his brain pointed out that she smelled nice: a slightly soapy scent blended with female sweat. Feminine sweat was, in his opinion, an aphrodisiac. Or at least that was the effect it had on his body.

"I think I might have twisted—ah!" she whimpered when she tried to turn her very lovely ankle.

"Here, let me see," he said.

Because you are such an expert?

Richard frowned at the snide thought and took her ankle, exposing it to the moonlight. But all he could see of her slim and trim leg was her stocking.

He'd never realized that plain white stockings could be as appealing as silk or lace or the sort that he was used to seeing on the older, more sophisticated ladies he preferred.

"Mr. Redvers?"

Oh yes, the ankle. "Well, it's difficult to say—I see no swelling, but the light is poor. I believe it would be wise not to put any weight on it. At least not immediately," he said, lowering her foot and then bending over to scoop her up before she could protest.

She started squawking before he'd even stood all the way up.

"Oh, you needn't, really, Mr. Redvers. This is quite unnecessary. I can walk. You—"

"Oh, but I *need*, Mrs. Pelham. Besides, the ground is damp. There is a bench just up here. I will set you down and give you a moment to rest, and then we will take stock of the damage."

"But the dog—"

"I daresay the dogs are already fast friends and are doubtless right behind us."

"No, Percy is blind."

"He doesn't need his vision as he has a superior sense of smell, which is far more important to canines, who have inferior night vision."

Richard could feel her eyes on him even though he was facing straight ahead, focusing on getting to their destination.

Bollocks. You're focusing on how soft she feels and that tantalizing soapy-sweat smell.

Very well, so it was bollocks.

"How do you know that?" she asked, interrupting the scornful laughter of his scoffing conscience.

"I'm sorry, but how do I know what?"

"About dogs having bad vision."

"I participated in a study in which we had dogs read off numbers and letters on a chart. Only poodles could read the smallest line."

She paused so long he didn't know what to think.

He stole a glance down at her. "What?" he asked, although he could already guess.

"Nothing."

"No, it was definitely something," he said, lowering her to the bench as he'd promised.

"I just didn't know you possessed a sense of whimsy."

"Ah, and that's because you know me so well?"

It was too dark to see whether she blushed, but her expression was wry.

"Touché."

The two old dogs ambled up, Newton breathing heavily. Percy bumped his head against the stone base of the bench.

"Oh, poor Percy," Mrs. Pelham crooned, leaning forward to scoop up the white-muzzled little creature. She looked up at Richard. "Please, have a seat. It looks as if your basset will not be moving soon."

As if he'd heard her, Newton bent his stubby legs and lowered himself to the ground with a low *wuffing* sound.

So, Richard sat and stared up at the night sky.

The clouds were sparse and he was getting his bearings with the familiar constellations of his boyhood when she spoke.

"It is quite cold. Do you think it will snow for Christmas?"

Richard smiled; ah, the weather—a staple of English conversation everywhere. "There is a very old woman in Eastbourne whose name is Nancy Grinstead, and every year she gives a forecast. She claims to be over one hundred, but nobody knows for certain as there is nobody who remembers. Her forecasts have been remarkably accurate and she says this year will not be as cold as the Year Without a Summer, but that we will get a great deal of snow. So, there you have it from a self-appointed expert. Do you like snow, Mrs. Pelham?" he asked, deciding it was time to do his conversational share.

"I like it when it is fresh and white. Do you?"

"I would like it this year because Toni is hoping to have a chance to put our old sleighs to work. However, she is also planning a *winter picnic*, which I doubt would be so enjoyable in the snow and slush."

In Richard's opinion his sister was approaching her wedding with an almost manic energy. He believed it covered other feelings, perhaps even misgivings.

"You spend a great deal of your time away from England, traveling," she said.

"I do," he agreed.

"Where will your next journey take you—somewhere far away and exotic?" She sounded wistful.

"I don't know; it depends whether you consider the Italian states exotic?"

"Oh, yes. How lovely. All that art and architecture."

Richard grunted.

She laughed and the sound was pleasingly earthy and an interesting contrast with her fine-boned, almost ethereal beauty. "You don't appreciate art?"

"It's not a matter of appreciation. I'm afraid I don't take much notice of it."

"How is that even possible?"

"Because it does not interest me." He turned to her. "Do you take notice of things that do not interest you?"

"Well, when you put it that way, I suppose I don't."

He paused and then said, "But what you said is more or less correct; painting and sculptures and such are not my idea of beauty."

"Really? What is, then?"

You, he could have said, but prudently did not.

Richard couldn't help noticing that she sounded livelier than she had before, as if his answer really interested her. He also couldn't help contrasting this Celia with the one he'd observed ten years ago.

Not just her clothing, but her demeanor.

As far as what she was actually like, he didn't have much to compare because a decade ago the only thing about Richard that Celia Trent had found interesting was his brother.

And perhaps making mock of him on one of those occasions when he'd embarrassed himself, something he'd done frequently in the unfamiliar milieu of *ton* parties.

As little as she had spoken to him, he had felt her gaze on him more than a few times, usually when he'd just done something clumsy or buffoonish. He recalled a certain scornful lift of her upper lip and disdain in her dismissive glance.

Fortunately, Richard hadn't cared about her perception of him back then, nor had her scrutiny embarrassed him. Why would he care if he were a *ton* failure when he held the opinions of its members in such low regard?

As he allowed himself a slow perusal of her classically beautiful features—not disdainful, but genuinely interested—Richard told himself that her opinion of him mattered even less now.

Oh, Richard.

Instead of bickering with his inner critic, Richard decided that he would examine his thoughts on the subject more closely later, when he was alone and at his leisure.

But for now, he thought about her question and the things he considered beautiful.

He met her curious gaze and said, "The convex image in a bead of moisture. Crystalline structure in sulfide minerals—have you ever seen iron pyrite?"

She shook her head.

He would have to show her some. "The elytra of some *buprestidae*," he said. "The iridescent carapace of jewel beetles," he explained at her confused look. "They are as highly prized as real jewels in countries like Japan. I could continue, but I'm sure you have discerned my gist."

"You find beauty in the natural world."

It was too dark to see the color of her eyes, but he knew they were the shockingly pure azure of the Blue Morpho butterfly, a creature he'd had the privilege of seeing in the wild.

"Yes," he said, holding her gaze before she lowered her eyes to her clenched hands.

They sat quietly for a time, hearing nothing but the sound of Newton's snores and the occasional rattle of a few dry leaves still clinging tenaciously to their branches.

"I never apologized to you."

Richard did not need to ask what she meant. "Do you believe I hold a grudge?"

She considered him for a long moment and then shook her head. "I doubt you've given me two minutes' thought since then."

Richard smiled at that. *Oh, Mrs. Pelham—if you only knew the truth.* But he said nothing.

Her beautiful face was taut and intent, as if she were driven to speak. "I should have, at the very least, sent a letter of apology to Lord and Lady Davenport."

"Probably. But it is too late, now."

"Yes. Far too late." She sighed.

"Something went wrong. It was meant for me, wasn't it?"

She didn't need to ask him what he meant, either. "Yes."

Richard thought about asking her why she would have done such a thing, but he decided he did not care about her motivations. After all, they would hardly have been good or noble impulses, would they?

"Are they happy?"

Richard found the question surprising. "Does that matter to you?"

"It would . . . make me feel better. Maybe not better," she amended, "but certainly less guilty."

"You'll have to ask Luce or Phil that question, Mrs. Pelham."

"You don't know? Or you won't tell me?"

Richard smiled. "How is your ankle?" he asked, his prosaic question putting an end to a topic he did not wish to discuss with her.

She lifted her foot and slowly rotated it. "A bit of a twinge, but nothing too painful, I think."

Richard stood. "Take my arm and keep the weight off while you walk."

Her hand was like a small white star on his dark sleeve, her cotton gloves insubstantial protection against the chill. In his mind, her presence was larger, but, really, she was a diminutive female, nothing like his mother or Toni, both of whom were closer to six than five feet.

He waited as she tested the foot by gradually putting more weight on it. "It is fine," she said, taking a few steps to demonstrate.

Richard released her arm and bent to pick up the fragile old dog.

"Thank you," she said when he laid the shockingly weightless beast in her arms.

Newton had already struggled to his feet and was trudging in the direction of his warm bed and food dish.

They walked toward the house in silence, Richard taking her around to the main entrance rather than any of the side doors.

The huge foyer was lighted by several red-glassed sconces and they cast a warm, almost barbaric glow that gave the illusion of flames dancing across her pale skin.

He stopped at the foot of the grand staircase. "Shall I guide you to your chambers?"

"No thank you, I can find my way." She paused as if to say something, but then closed her mouth and smiled.

"Then I bid you good night, Mrs. Pelham."

Richard was not the sort of man who believed in anything other than what he could see, hear, or touch, but he swore he felt the weight of her eyes on his back as he walked Newton back toward his chambers.

Chapter 10

Breakfast at Lessing Hall had always begun at an exceptionally early hour, even by country standards.

Usually it was only Richard or Hugh who ate at such an ungodly time so Richard didn't expect to find Lucien already dressed and at breakfast before him.

"I didn't think you cared for early mornings, Luce?" he said as he went to load a plate at the sideboard.

"I don't, but I remembered you said something about going shooting and thought I'd join you. I've got a new fowling piece and haven't taken it out yet. Besides," he added with a smirk, "Phyllida said we need ample grouse for the group arriving in a few days and we both agreed you were more likely to come back with a game basket full of aquatic beetles if you went alone."

Richard laughed. "I'm so pleased to discover you have listened to my many hours of discourse on the beetle life of Sussex."

Lucien grunted and put aside the paper he'd been browsing.

He sat across from his brother and nodded his thanks to the footman who poured him a cup of the black, inviscid liquid their stepfather considered proper coffee.

"You'd better eat more than that," Richard said with a glance at Luce's half-eaten toast and nearly empty plate.

Lucien grimaced. "I dislike eating so early."

"You've lost weight," Richard pointed out.

"Yes, thank you for your unsolicited observation." Luce watched with a look of distaste as Richard swabbed up egg yolk with a chunk of ham. "You were outside with Mrs. Pelham last night—I saw you come in together."

"Yes." Richard finished the last of his ham and deliberated on having another piece.

"You had better watch yourself with her, Rich."

Richard looked up from his food, chewing thoughtfully as he stared at his brother.

Lucien's face was flushed, the skin around his eyes tight. "What?" he demanded when Richard didn't speak.

Richard shrugged.

Lucien gave an irritable sigh. "Your savage habits and lack of civility might stand when you are out in the wilds with nobody but insects for companionship, but I would ask that you answer me when I make the effort to speak to you."

"Good God, Luce—you do sound very lord of the manor."

"I *am* lord of the manor."

Richard grinned. "Well, to answer your question—or observation, more like—I suppose that being trapped into marriage with Mrs. Pelham isn't the worst future I can imagine."

Lucien's expression was priceless.

"What?" Richard demanded, his word a mocking echo of his brother's of only a few seconds earlier.

But apparently it was Lucien's right as lord of the manor to ignore *his* questions.

His brother pushed to his feet. "I'm going to change. I'll meet you down by the gun room in thirty minutes. I need to get out early if I'm to return in time to go on the tramp Toni and Phyllida have planned for the younger people. I take it you are coming?"

"No."

"Why not?"

"Because I don't fancy a tramp with giggling, barely out of the schoolroom chits and green young men trying to impress them."

Lucien scowled. "You might consider putting your duty above personal preference, for once."

"No, old man, I think I'll leave duty to the lord of the manor."

Richard wasn't surprised when his brother stormed from the room, muttering under his breath. Lucien was certainly out of sorts this morning. Still, it was better to see him exhibiting some emotion rather than walking about like a man in a trance.

Richard finished off his sizeable portion and debated whether he should have another. Why not? He might as well eat while he waited.

He was piling more food onto his plate when he heard the door open behind him. "Back to apologize?" he said, replacing the cover on the chafing dish before turning.

Mrs. Pelham stood in the doorway, her gaze flickering around the empty room before settling on him. "Should I be apologizing?"

"Good morning, Mrs. Pelham. I thought you were my brother."

She headed for the sideboard. "And should *he* be apologizing?"

"It would certainly be unusual," Richard said, dipping the corner of a triangle of toast into his coddled eggs and munching.

"Siblings do not normally apologize? Or Lord Davenport in particular?"

"Luce is actually quite good about apologizing when he thinks he's been wrong. The problem is, he rarely thinks he's wrong."

She chuckled and turned back to the food, leaving him free to study her body.

Just like yesterday, she wore a hideous cap covering her masses of mahogany hair. Today's dress was a dirty tobacco color. Richard wondered if she thought such drab shades camouflaged her beauty. He supposed that was an issue for a companion; one wouldn't want to attract the attention of one's employer's male relatives.

But if she thought to hide her beauty with mobcaps and ugly clothing, she was terribly off course. What she ended up doing was making her exceptional loveliness even more conspicuous. Like a masterpiece painting with a cheap frame.

"You have no brothers or sisters, Mrs. Pelham?"

She turned from the sideboard with a heaping plate. "No, I am an only child." She saw him looking at her breakfast and smiled, her peaches-and-cream skin darkening slightly over her high cheekbones. "Lady Yancy believes in the health benefits of having only porridge for breakfast, so I'm taking advantage of this delicious spread while I can," she explained.

"Hmm." Richard approved of a healthy appetite in men or women; it was also wise to eat when food was plentiful, as he'd learned more than once on his travels. "You are an early riser," he said rather stupidly as she was sitting across from him.

"Percy needs to be walked twice in the night and again before first light. He, er, well, he cannot wait long."

"And it is you rather than a servant who takes the dog out in the middle of the night?"

"I *am* a servant, Mr. Redvers. Besides, I like it. I am a light sleeper and wake often."

"Ah, the sign of a guilty conscience—or so I'm told," Richard said.

Richard marveled at how easily she blushed; he decided he liked it.

"There is to be a tramp this afternoon. Will your employer allow you to take time off from your duties?" he asked.

"She probably would."

"But you will not go?"

She cocked her head at him, her expression wry. "I think the fewer activities I engage in, the better for everyone."

"You believe my family will take vengeance on you if you participate in the festivities?"

"Of course not. But I cannot think my presence brings anyone happiness."

Richard could have told her she was wrong about that.

Instead, he said, "Perhaps you place too much importance on the role you played in my family's lives?"

This time her flush wasn't delicate, but mottled and splotchy. Ah, she was . . . angry? Insulted?

"*Perhaps* I made little difference in your life, sir, but I was rather—well, there is no other word for it—dreadful to Lady Davenport."

"I don't recall ever seeing the two of you together."

"We rarely spoke during our time in London. But one does not need to be proximate to another person to be awful to them."

"True."

"I went to a girls' school in Cambridge where her ladyship was a day student."

"You went to Mrs. Bennington's?"

"You know of it?"

"I was a student of Sir Gael's and had dinner at his house many times. Phil was his hostess, as her mother wasn't well enough."

"Well enough?" she asked, arrested.

"Lady Singleton was not in good health the last five years of her life. A degenerative disease of the spine. She was in constant pain for the better part of two years and died in a sanatorium in Bath."

Mrs. Pelham's gaze was intense. "How old was her ladyship when all this was happening?"

"Oh, all through school. The reason she had such a late come out was because of her mother's death, and then Sir Gael was ill, and not long after that her grandmother died. It was not a happy time for her."

Mrs. Pelham turned toward her plate. Her hands, he noticed, had stilled.

The door opened and Lucien poked his head in. He looked from Richard to Mrs. Pelham and then did a double take, his lips compressing into a frown.

"Good morning, Mrs. Pelham," he said abruptly, looking away before she could answer. "I am ready, Richard—we need to be off if we're to do this." He turned and left, not bothering to close the door behind him.

Richard wiped his mouth with the napkin, tossed it down on the table and stood, his eyes on Mrs. Pelham's bowed head. "Have a good morning," he said.

"Thank you, Mr. Redvers." She did not look up when he left the room.

Her mother had been dying all that time.

Celia pushed away her half-eaten plate, sickened by what she'd just learned. All the time she'd believed Phyllida Singleton was nauseatingly happy, loved, and secure, her mother had been dying a slow, painful death, hidden away in a sanitorium.

As she sat there, staring at her rapidly cooling coffee, she tried to recall who'd told her about Phyllida's happy homelife. Or had she simply inferred it from the other woman's pleasant, helpful, and kind demeanor?

Celia still became bilious when she thought back on those years in Cambridge.

Just like every other period in her life, school had been yet another time when she could never let down her guard. Even though Mrs. Bennington's was one of the least expensive finishing schools in Britain—notorious for allowing shamelessly late tuition payments, thanks to the widow Bennington's generous nature—her father still managed to push the schoolmistress's generosity beyond the point of civility.

Four times a year Celia had needed to be vigilant, sending frantic messages to Molly Henson, the only servant she could trust in her father's London lodgings, begging her to make sure he didn't forget to dispense the quarterly payment for the school. The money had not even come from Cedric Trent's own pocket, but his wife's. Celia's mother had, on her deathbed, foolishly put the money into her husband's keeping. She'd extracted a promise from him to disburse it only on behalf of their daughter.

Celia's mother had been an actress—not a particularly good one, but one of the great beauties of the stage. She'd married Celia's father believing that he would take her away to a life of wealth and ease. Instead, her father's family had disowned him and it had been Ophelia Trent who'd supported herself, her husband, and eventually her child, before she'd succumbed to an influenza when Celia was ten.

While Celia had been fretting herself to stomach pains, losing sleep, and expecting—every moment of the day—to be pulled out of school, Phyllida Singleton had smiled and painted and blithely come and gone every day from her loving home to Mrs. Bennington, a woman who adored Phyllida like a daughter.

Phyllida's seeming good fortune had infuriated Celia. Why should *Phil* have loving, caring, financially solvent parents, *and* the adoration of the school's owner, other teachers, and most of the students? Why should she be so happy when Celia's every waking moment was spent walking the razor's edge?

And so Celia had behaved like an odious beast toward her. Not only had *she* been beastly, but she'd led a small cadre of other girls—wealthy, beautiful, and spiteful—in her campaign to harass and torment Phyllida Singleton.

In retrospect, her own behavior horrified, mortified, and sickened her—even before Richard's disclosure about what the other woman had been going through. Why had she been so ugly? So lacking in sympathy?

You've no shortage of sympathy now, have you?

No, she thought as she stared out the breakfast room window at the crepuscular light; she had no lack of sympathy now.

Chapter 11

Richard could see that his brother was in a vile mood, so he decided to keep his mouth shut and not risk saying anything that might annoy him.

"God, please tell me you're going to speak more than ten words to me this morning," Lucien said after they'd walked in silence for a bit.

"I know it seems fitting, Luce, but you probably shouldn't call me God."

"Ha, ha. That never gets old."

Richard tried again.

"Perhaps you'd like to hear about the titan beetle I captured while I was—"

"No. Beetles. Absolutely none," Lucien said, turning to stare at him. "That doesn't just go for me and right now, that goes for everyone else and this entire house party."

"Hmmm," Richard said, amused rather than insulted by his brother's queasy feeling about insects of any kind.

"Well, if you don't want to talk about beetles, may I talk about the funnel spider I—"

"I said *no* bugs."

"But spiders aren't bugs, Luce, they're—"

"Nothing with more than four legs. Unless—" He squinted at Richard. "Are there bugs with four legs?"

Richard grinned. "If there are, I certainly hope I'm the first to discover them."

Lucien grunted, unamused.

"What is it, Luce? You're as tense as an *Arotes amoenus*."

"I don't like the sound of that."

Richard suspected he wouldn't much like the look of one, either.

He turned the subject away from his life's passion to something that had been nagging at him for quite some time. "I'm pleased to see Mother isn't pregnant. Do you know if Hugh has plans to breed her again?"

Lucien stopped and turned, his eyes and mouth round. *"Good God, Richard!"*

"What? She is at an age where childbearing is more dangerous. I would think you'd care about such matters. You know how Mama is—such considerations would never cross her mind. Therefore it needs to be Hugh who puts a stop to more children."

Lucien snorted and resumed his trudging. "The last thing I want to think about is Mother and Hugh doing . . . *that*."

"You can't even say it—how the devil do you ever manage to do it?" He barked a laugh. "Well, at least twice."

Lucien wheeled on him. "*What* did you say?"

"Hold a moment, Luce," he said as Lucien advanced on him, murder in his eyes. "I was only jesting."

"What were you doing with Mrs. Pelham in the breakfast room?"

Richard blinked. "Is that a trick question?"

The beaters and loaders had stopped and were trying to pretend that they weren't listening to their master and his brother fratch.

"Go along," Luce ordered, not looking away from Richard. "We'll be right behind you."

He waited until the men were out of earshot and then said, "You think this is amusing—having that woman here?"

"I think it hardly matters if she is here." Richard's eyes narrowed at his brother's furious visage. "Why the devil are you so angry, Luce?"

"Why do you think?"

"I genuinely do not understand."

Luce's familiar face distorted with a most unfamiliar rage. "You don't understand?" he repeated, his voice louder. "You don't understand why it bothers me to see that—that vile *bitch* in my house? A woman who purposely, and without any sane reason, wrecked my life—" He seemed to realize what he'd said.

"Luce, you can't believe that?" Richard asked. "You have two wonderful children, a wife who loves and adores—"

"Of course, I don't believe that," he snapped, his eyes wild. "I misspoke because of your—because—ah, bloody hell."

"Is something wrong, Luce?"

"Wrong with what?"

"Between you and Phil?"

"No."

"You seem—"

"I seem *what*?"

"Unhappy."

"I am *not* unhappy. I'm just—" He yanked off his hat and shoved a hand through his hair. "God, I don't know what I am. I daresay you'll think me a terrible gudgeon if I tell you what is bothering me."

"You'll have to try me to find out, Luce."

"Phyllida and I *do* have a very successful marriage. It's just . . . well, it's just that we are so far from each other."

Richard didn't understand what his brother meant.

Fortunately, Lucien didn't need questions to keep talking. "The truth is, I know no more about her than I did when we married." There was a faint tinge of hysteria to his voice and two bright red spots stained his cheeks. "I sound like a bloody fool," he said, more to himself. "I've never said this to you—" He stopped, biting his lip hard enough to make Richard wince.

Richard set a hand on his brother's shoulder and gave him a gentle squeeze. "We used to be so close it was like being one person. Now all I know is that you seem deeply unhappy."

Lucien shook off his hand, spun on his heel, and strode away. "I don't know what you're talking about. I came out to shoot, not gossip like old women."

And that was the last thing his brother said for the next four hours.

It alternately misted, rained, and then snowed all morning, so by the time they returned to Lessing Hall they had to shuck off muddy boots, soggy leathers, and heavy, sodden wool coats.

"Where are you going now?" Lucien demanded, finally breaking his silence.

"I promised Jonathan that I'd go for a ride on his boat this week and I've yet to go."

Lucien scowled out the sidelight window that ran beside the big metal-strapped door. "On a day like today?"

"It's just a bit of water, Luce, not locusts or plague."

His brother didn't laugh or even smile. It was as if some strange entity had taken over Lucien's body and replaced his normally witty, clever, and happy personality with one that was suspicious and humorless.

Lucien grunted. "I doubt the tramp will happen in this weather. No doubt poor Toni is tearing her hair out; you know how she hates it when her plans fall through."

Richard thought their sister would do better to let the guests entertain themselves, but he kept those words behind his teeth.

"Well, don't dawdle all day and force me to come find you." Lucien rammed his feet into the slippers his valet had brought for him and then stalked off.

Richard knew he should go after him and get him to talk, but he had no experience with his brother when he was in such a dark mood. Besides, he'd spent scarcely a moment with Jonathan since coming home.

Half an hour later, dry, warm, and dressed in yet another pair of buckskins, with an oilskin over a dry wool coat, he went to the stables.

Daniels, one of the older grooms, was leading a big gray gelding into the courtyard when he arrived. He gave Richard an odd little smirk. "I know you took Knight out the last few times, sir, but the baron has him today. So, this is, er, Magic."

Richard looked at the stolid horse; a less magical beast he could hardly imagine.

"Let me guess," Richard said as he mounted. "Lord Ramsay is still allowing my little brothers to name the cattle?"

Daniels chuckled "Aye. I thought steam would come out the earl's ears when he learned his new hunter's name was Fluffy."

Richard threw his head back and laughed. "It will be good for my brother." He nodded at the older man and headed out.

As he rode, his mind kept returning to Lucien's face this morning—upon seeing Mrs. Pelham and then later, when he'd told Richard that the long-ago prank had ruined his life. Could he really feel that way?

Lord. Richard wished he were more attuned to human interaction. He'd never been the sort of person who easily hid his likes and dislikes and lying was simply too much effort. But he knew those around him—even the people he loved—wore layers and layers of masks. Some they wore to protect themselves, but some they wore for others.

He wanted to ask Phil, Luce, or both what was wrong, but the defenses they'd both constructed told him that such inquiries would not be welcome.

He should keep his nose out of their affairs.

As it had done earlier, the weather alternated between rain and tiny flakes of snow as he rode into the small town of Eastbourne. The dark gray sky promised heavy snow soon, but he thought that wouldn't start until later today, or tonight.

Jonathan's boat was at anchor and Jonathan himself was rowing a dinghy toward the pier.

Not until he had dismounted and was almost at the bottom of the stone steps did Richard realize there was somebody waiting.

"Why, Mrs. Pelham, what a surprise."

She jerked around. "Oh. Mr. Redvers." Her eyes slid from Richard to the rapidly approaching skiff. "Jonathan invited me to see his boat," she said, more than a little defensive.

Richard experienced an unexpected pang of jealousy at the sound of his brother's Christian name on her tongue.

How interesting; jealousy was a new emotion to him. He would have to consider its sudden appearance more closely when he was alone.

"I see," he said.

She shifted from foot to foot. "Lady Yancy was going to spend the afternoon with your Aunt Amelia, so I thought—"

"That you'd spend the day with my younger brother."

Her cheeks, already attractively pinkened by the chill weather, darkened further at the slight emphasis he put on the word *younger*.

"If you think it improper, *sir*, I will gladly—"

"Why should I think that?" he asked, although they both knew it was exactly what he'd meant. Jonathan, not quite seventeen, was an earnest, sheltered youngster who had probably been drawn to the beautiful, mysterious female. Although Mrs. Pelham looked every bit of her seven- or eight-and-twenty years, she was still exceedingly lovely. Richard could not like the thought of her ensorcelling his brother.

As she has you?

"I should probably just go back." She strode toward the steps Richard had just descended.

He caught her arm and drew her close. "You should probably stay, as my brother is almost here. Otherwise he will think I said something to drive you away."

"And we wouldn't want him to know the truth, would we?"

Richard smiled and she recoiled. "Yes, we wouldn't want to turn you into a romantic rescue fantasy that would appeal to his chivalric male tendencies. Come, I will go out to the boat with you."

She yanked her arm away. "Worried I'll overpower your brother's good sense and convince him to run away to Gretna Green with me?"

"It's not his *good sense* I'm worried about."

She gasped at his insulting innuendo.

Before she could think of a retort, Richard turned to help Jonathan bring the boat up onto the shingle.

Chapter 12

Insufferable, arrogant, conceited—

Jonathan grinned up at Celia as he reached the landing. "Hallo, Mrs. Pelham—Rich. Did you two come together?"

"No. I had the great fortune to meet your brother here."

Jonathan's smooth brow creased at her acerbic tone and he looked from Celia to Richard. The sweet young man could sense tension but had no clue what it was. And she was behaving like a shrew with the wrong person.

"I'm very much looking forward to seeing your boat," she said in a much more pleasant tone. She actually had been looking forward to it. Until Richard's arrival.

Liar. You love being around him; he makes you feel more alive than you've felt in years.

Celia scowled at the unwanted, but accurate, thought.

"Help her in, Rich," Jonathan said. "You can shove us out."

Richard Redvers complied without speaking, his big hands warm and solid beneath her worn mittens.

Once she was settled on the narrow bench seat, Richard pushed and nimbly hopped into the small boat. There was only the one seat, other than Jonathan's, and Richard sat down beside her, his body pressing against hers from hip to shoulder. When she tried to scoot away, she discovered there was nowhere to scoot.

He looked down at her and gave his customary smirk. This close, she could see the lines around his eyes and mouth. His skin still bore the effects of a dark tan, the sort that could not be achieved under the pallid English sun. His hair was lighter than his brother's now, the roots a dark blond but the rest lightening until the tips were all but bleached of color. The fairness of his hair made his eyes all the more startling. She couldn't recall seeing blond hair and brown eyes before. All the other Redvers children had blue or green eyes. Only Lucien and Richard had the golden brown.

His thin lips curved into a superior smile that made her realize she'd been staring at him.

She whipped her head around and looked at his younger brother, instead.

Jonathan was breathing hard as he pulled, the oars moving in time with his motions. The boyish excitement on his face was obviously reserved for his boat and had nothing to do with her presence. And yet his brother—and likely the rest of his family—feared she would try to snare a sixteen-year-old boy in her web.

Celia shoved down her anger; these people had every right to believe the worst of her.

"You do not get seasick, Mrs. Pelham?" Richard Redvers's deep voice vibrated through her body.

"Apparently not."

One blond eyebrow arched high. "This is your first time on the water?"

"My first time on the ocean. I've been on a barge on the Thames." On her way to Vauxhall Gardens, hardly more than a brief ferry ride.

"And you trusted me enough to come out today." Jonathan sounded shyly proud.

"You said you knew what you were doing," Celia reminded him tartly, not nearly as sanguine to be floating around the ocean in a twelve-foot dinghy, no matter how close to shore they were.

Jonathan laughed. "You're safe as houses in my hands."

* * *

The snow had begun to fall heavily by the time Jonathan brought the boat back to his anchor spot. He'd taken them—with impressive skill—up and down the coast, staying close enough to shore that she never became nervous.

Celia had sat beside him and they'd chatted. Richard, to her relief, settled into a low-slung wood-and-rope chair at the front—or the bow, as Jonathan gently corrected—and appeared to doze the two hours away, seemingly uncaring of the weather. Only when they came back in sight of town did he rouse himself, crewing for his brother without being asked.

Celia couldn't help but watch as he competently carried out chores usually managed by a sailor—or so she imagined.

"Your brother appears comfortable on a boat," she said to Jonathan.

"Oh, Rich has his own boat—a *real* one. It used to belong to my Uncle Martin, back when he still patrolled with the West African squadron."

As Jonathan and Richard took care of the anchor, battening down the various covers and hatches, and putting the little dinghy into the water, it occurred to her that Richard Redvers was, in every way—except money and title—more impressive than his brother. He was more educated, he engaged in a more interesting occupation, and he was certainly more masculine and physically impressive than Lucien, who appeared pale and bland next to his strapping twin.

A strapping twin, indeed, Celia.

She gritted her teeth against that part of her brain which seemed devoted to taunting and prodding and tormenting.

I find him attractive—what of it? she demanded.

But the voice had already gone, like a vandal that left bloodless, yet lasting, damage in its wake.

Richard's piercing, knowing gaze made him an invigorating, but uncomfortable, person to be around—well, at least to Celia.

The cynically amused look in his eyes whenever he glanced at her—not often, as if just about anything else in his vicinity was of more interest—goaded her, bringing out behavior she had long ago believed—and hoped—to be behind her.

Like their bickering on the pier, for example. As a servant, Celia could not afford to brangle with people who were now her superiors, especially about matters like pursuing young, unwed male relations.

Besides, Richard was right to find her association with his sixteen-year-old brother concerning; young boys were notorious when it came to forming attachments to inappropriate women.

"Let's stop in at the Pig and Whistle," Richard said, gesturing to the weather-beaten public house that stood just beyond the pier.

As they walked, his hand was barely a whisper beneath her elbow, but she was sharply aware of his nearness.

"You're buying?" Jonathan asked, looking even younger than his sixteen years as he gamboled like an excited puppy beside his brother.

"It's the least I can do after such a relaxing tour." Richard stepped ahead of Celia to open the door to the small public house.

A man who was obviously the innkeeper rushed out to greet them. "Ah, Mr. Richard, Mr. Jonathan," the publican said, smiling from ear to ear to see the township's wealthiest residents.

"Good afternoon, Mr. Eames. We'd like the private parlor if you have it."

"Of course, sir, right this way."

"The Pig has the best hot chocolate anywhere, Mrs. Pelham," Richard said as he pulled out her chair, his words earning him a proud grin from Mr. Eames. "A pot of chocolate for the lady and the young captain," he said, not bothering to ask Celia. "And I'll take a porter, and we'll have an assortment of Mrs. Eames's delectable pastries."

Celia bristled at his high-handed treatment, tempted to tell him she didn't want chocolate, but of course she did.

The room was cozy and an oversized hearth did a wonderful job of keeping the cold and damp at bay. Heavy drops of precipitation splattered against the room's one window.

Celia squinted. "It's no longer misting. Is that sleet? Or rain?"

Jonathan chuckled. "Neither—Richard created a special word for it: sneet, a combination of snow and sleet."

Celia snorted.

"I don't think this has approached sneet level quite yet," Richard corrected.

"Looks more like snizzle to me," Celia said, giving Jonathan a conspiratorial smirk.

The younger man gave a boisterous hoot of laughter. "Well done, Mrs. Pelham."

"Snow and drizzle; I am impressed," Richard said, visibly amused. "Well, whatever we call it, it seems to be settling in." He turned to Jonathan. "Once you've had your chocolate and some pastries, you can take Magic back home and send the carriage for us."

This time Celia could not allow his high-handed order to stand unchallenged. "That's not necessary. I can walk."

"I'm sure you can," Richard said. "But you don't have to."

She opened her mouth to argue.

Jonathan laughed. "Oh, Mrs. Pelham—you need to recognize that expression on Rich's face. When he looks like that, he always gets his way."

Richard's unsmiling gaze was fixed on her, the intensity of his stare causing an annoying quiver in her belly.

"Maybe it's time for that to change," she suggested.

For some reason, Jonathan found her pronouncement hilarious.

"You live in Harrogate?" Richard asked, examining her from beneath heavy lids.

"Yes."

"How long have you lived there?"

Celia wondered if he was asking because he was interested, or because he wanted to poke and pry. Somehow she suspected the latter.

"I moved there almost four years ago." After she'd voluntarily left her last employer in Bath.

Celia's lips twitched at the thought of telling the sly, superior man across from her about the sort of work she used to do.

Jonathan pointed at something outside the window. "Oh, I say, Rich—there's Denby. Will you excuse me? I need to talk to him about fixing the crack in the gunwale."

"I'm not the one whose pardon you should beg, Brother," Richard retorted sternly.

Twin red flags flew on the younger man's cheeks. "Er, begging your pardon, Mrs. Pelham, but—"

She smiled. "Go, now, before your chocolate comes. If you don't return quickly enough, I'll drink it for you."

He grinned and darted from the room.

Leaving her alone with his saturnine sibling.

She fixed Richard with the most aloof look in her arsenal. "Your message has been received, sir. I shall not spend more time with your brother—or any other male in the vicinity. You needn't stay to make sure that I behave."

"Thank you for your permission to leave. But I believe I shall stay all the same." He cocked his head at her. "Are you looking forward to seeing your old friend Dowden?"

Her gut clenched at the sound of the hated name. Ever since learning whose wedding this was, she'd repeated the name in her mind over and over, hoping to rob it of its power to incite fear and revulsion. The repetition didn't appear to have worked.

"We were acquaintances, at most. And I've not seen him since that summer." And that had been enough to last a lifetime.

"I recall the two of you being as thick as thieves."

"Perhaps it only looked that way from your vantage point."

"You mean from outside the golden, inner circle?"

She shrugged. "If that was the way it appeared to you."

"I always thought it odd that he didn't have a hand in that last evening's . . . *entertainment* as he'd always been so engaged in your games before then." He raised his eyebrows. "Was it you or Dowden who composed that charming poem about me? Let's see—what was it called?"

Celia's face flamed, yet again. "It was 'Ode to Odious.' I'm afraid that was all me."

He grinned, the expression so rare—and gorgeous—that Celia stared.

"What?" he said when he saw her surprise. "You don't think I enjoy a good roast? I'm afraid all that embarrassment you hoped to cause was wasted effort on an insensitive, oblivious bloke like me."

"You did appear indifferent to gossip," she agreed. If he'd only allowed all the rumors and taunts to drive him out of London, then Celia would have been free of Sebastian far earlier and never would have drafted that missive.

Oh, Celia. Blaming it all on Richard's thick skin?

"If I recall correctly," Richard went on, his expression thoughtful, "it was quite a clever poem. Especially that part about my accidentally tearing that poor girl's skirt off, where you managed to rhyme *spilling orgeat all over thee* with *Roger de Coverley*."

Celia's lips curved into a slight smile. "Yes, I was rather proud of those two lines."

He laughed, a low, honey-smooth sound. "So, which of you conceived of the note that was meant for me?"

"I've already told you it was only me, but you will have a chance to ask His Grace yourself when he arrives. When is that, by the way?"

His gaze was knowing, almost as if he could feel the beating of her heart, the pounding of her pulse, her sweaty palms. "I believe he was delayed for a few days."

She wanted to weep with relief, although it didn't really matter how much he was delayed; she would have to see him eventually.

"Tell me what happened to put you in your current position, Miss Trent."

"Why? So you can gloat?"

"What have I done to you that would make you believe me capable of taking pleasure in another person's misfortunes?" He didn't sound angry or insulted, just curious.

He was right; it had not been Richard Redvers who'd spread rumors and taunted those less fortunate.

"I'm sorry," she said, meaning it. "That wasn't just rude, it was unfair. You are correct, I don't know you well enough to make such an assumption. But I also don't know you well enough to confide the painful details of my past to you."

"Fair enough."

The door opened and the innkeeper came in, accompanied by a serving woman. Once they'd put out an attractive array of pastries, two small steaming pots—one with a knitted sock to keep it warm—and a tall, dark glass of beer, the man asked, "Anything else, sir?"

"No, thank you, Eames, this looks marvelous."

"My," she said, looking at the abundance before her. "I hope you are planning to help with all of this."

He sipped his beer. "Porter and tarts don't really mix. Don't worry, Jonathan is perfectly capable of eating not only all those pastries, but the tray itself."

Celia laughed.

"I'm not jesting. You'd better secure what you want while he is out of the room."

She put two pastries on one of the three plates, poured out a thick stream of chocolate, and then took a sip. Her eyes closed in silent, profound, ecstasy. She opened them at the sound of his soft chuckle.

"Thank you for the recommendation," she said, her cheeks hot at her carnal display.

"My pleasure entirely." His eyes had darkened and his disconcerting gaze made her skin prickle.

Watching her eat was an erotic experience.

Richard knew he should be ashamed for treating her so stiffly and rudely—he didn't really believe she was angling for his young sprout of a brother—but there was something . . . irrepressible about her that brought out the brute in him.

Most women in her situation would be beaten down and broken, but not Mrs. Pelham.

Even poor, garbed in either a castoff or a much-altered gown, wearing a hideous bonnet, and occupying a servile position, the woman appeared proud and unbowed.

It was not like him to want to see a subordinate bend—to *make* one bend. But then, she had occupied a singular position in his life, so he was going to allow himself a bit of latitude when it came to bad behavior.

Jonathan burst into the room, rubbing his hands eagerly. "Oh, I say—I'm just in time for my chocolate."

The charged atmosphere dissipated, and Jonathan kept up a steady stream of chatter that allowed Richard an opportunity to study the woman. He knew she felt his gaze—how could she not—but he made no effort to hide his scrutiny. Being the exceptionally beautiful creature she was, being looked at was probably something she'd long become accustomed to.

Already he could see his brother falling under her unconsciously broadcast spell. Not only was she surpassingly lovely, but she was genuinely interested in his boyish prattle. If she had been as personable and enchanting ten years ago, it was no wonder that Lucien had fallen in love with her.

But Richard suspected—although he had no proof—that her younger self had been far more guarded because there had been so much more to lose.

Unlike a decade earlier, she no longer seemed to be looking for a man—young, wealthy, handsome, or otherwise—to rescue her from her situation.

Rather than repel him, her self-sufficiency and independence only served to make her more attractive.

He did not believe Celia wanted male attention. Quite the opposite; he believed she did everything in her power to avoid it.

Richard swallowed the last of his porter and stood, his abrupt action stopping his brother's chatter.

"You stay and finish your food," he said, when Jonathan made as if to stand. "I'll go to Lessing and send the carriage back for you." He ignored their surprised looks and left them to their chocolate, paying the innkeeper on his way out of the Pig and Whistle.

After he'd mounted Magic and turned the horse's head toward Lessing, the sneet began in earnest. That was fine with Richard.

A bit of rotten weather was a lot safer for him than a ride alone in a carriage with Mrs. Celia Pelham.

Chapter 13

Richard opened the breakfast room door and paused.

Part of him had expected Mrs. Pelham again. Part of him had hoped to see her. Part of him had hoped to dine in peace.

But no part of him had expected to see the Duke of Dowden sitting in Lucien's breakfast room reading one of the daily newspapers his brother had delivered from London.

As a scientist, Richard found his reaction to the other man interesting. He had fully expected his strongest emotions: loathing and repulsion. But he was surprised by some of the other feelings that assaulted him: anxiety, worry, and even fear.

All these emotions, he suspected, were on behalf of his sister.

Toni could not marry this man.

Richard only wished he knew how to stop it.

Whatever Dowden saw on his face made the other man grin—that same cocky, arrogant, smug smirk as ten years ago.

"Good morning, Richard, it's been a long time."

Not long enough.

"Good morning, Dowden. Coffee, please," he said to the hovering footman.

Dowden looked just the same as ever: golden, handsome, and utterly at home in his own skin.

"I thought you weren't due for another couple days," Richard said, taking a plate and going to the sideboard, even though he'd lost his appetite the moment he saw the other man's face.

"I probably shouldn't have left, as the men working on the roof of the London house disappear if you turn away for even a moment. I want everything perfect for Toni, but I also hated missing even a moment of the festivities."

Richard was glad his back was to the other man so Dowden couldn't see his glower at the duke's use of his sister's pet name. Unfortunately, he couldn't stand there loading his plate at the sideboard all day.

He took the farthest possible seat away from the other man.

The slight, wry smile that curved Dowden's lips told Richard the other man was amused, rather than insulted, by his action.

Dowden pushed aside his half-eaten plate, placed his elbows on the table, and steepled his fingers. "I'm glad to get you alone for a few moments, Redvers."

Richard raised his eyebrows and sliced a piece of thick-cut Taunton ham.

"I know we were often at odds when we were younger men. But now that we are to be family, I hope that bygones can be bygones. For my part, I'd like to apologize for my—admittedly—obnoxious behavior toward you. Especially during that last Season. Pax?" he said, his confident expression telling Richard he wasn't in any doubt of his response.

Richard opened his mouth to tell him—what? Get stuffed? Piss off? Over your dead body?

Instead, he smiled and said, "Of course."

"Excellent. I knew we could put that behind us."

After that, Dowden filled the room with vapid nattering that required very little in the way of contribution from Richard. The way the man yammered one would have thought he was nervous, but Richard suspected that he simply enjoyed the sound of his own voice.

Richard had been bolting down his meal more quickly than was healthy and was finishing his breakfast when he heard the door open. He just happened to be looking at Dowden, which was why he saw fear, fury, and disbelief flicker across his face in rapid succession. Richard knew without turning that it would be Mrs. Pelham.

So, that was interesting.

Richard wouldn't have spared the duke a second thought if it weren't for the fact that he was engaged to marry his sister. But, if he were to stop that from happening, he needed to employ those same skills that made him a good scientist—patience, logic, and detached assessment—to study and discover the real Dowden, and then expose him. Much the same way he would set about debunking a competitor's hypothesis.

In short, Richard needed to become a Dowden expert, and he had barely a week to prove what he'd always suspected about the man—that he was brutal, rotten to the core, and dangerous.

It had been almost ten years since Celia had last seen the angelic, handsome, and hateful face that rose to meet her.

"Celia, darling! It's been forever and a day." Sebastian came toward her, his familiar smirk twisting his full, expressive lips.

He engulfed her hand in both of his.

Celia always forgot what a big man Sebastian was—perhaps an inch taller than Richard Redvers—and thought that was probably due to his foppish appearance. He was always a bit too extravagant, his clothes the bright colors of a bygone age when men wore buckles on their shoes and lace at their wrists.

Today, for instance, he wore a dark cherry cutaway coat over not one, but two, waistcoats—one of which was a rather glaring yellow-gold—and his cravat was the sort of white frothy masterpiece he must have woken his valet before dawn to create.

Although he wore buckskins, they were far paler than usual. They fit his powerful thighs so tightly it was a wonder he could even sit, not to mention ride.

"You look marvelous—no older than a schoolgirl," he murmured, not caring or noticing that Celia was trying to tug her hand away.

She knew he wasn't supposed to be here for a few more days; it was her guess that Steff had dashed off a letter to him minutes after she'd seen Celia.

"Thank you, Your Grace," she murmured.

"Oh, please, Celia—no *your grace*-ing me when we used to be such dear friends. I have wondered about you many, many times over the years." The gleam in his eyes was the unholy one that had always made her feel ill, because it meant he was scheming something unpleasant. The look was even more potent now and she felt like voiding the contents of her mostly empty stomach.

Indeed, she was considering excusing herself and leaving, on some pretext or other, when Sebastian resumed speaking, this time to Richard.

"Don't you think it's a shame that Celia should have hidden herself away just because of that little incident?"

Celia was tempted to tell him that it was actually Sebastian who'd caused her to hide herself away—and not just because he'd purposely delivered that fateful note to the wrong brother—but she was no more interested in drawing the duke's ire than she'd ever been.

"Would you like to sit, Mrs. Pelham?" Richard asked, his calm gaze on Sebastian's hands, which still held her fixed in place.

"Oh, how terribly rude of me," Sebastian said with a chuckle, finally setting her free. "I was so excited to see you that I forgot my good manners."

Celia went to the sideboard, relieved to have a moment to gather her wits.

Behind her, Sebastian said, "Toni tells me that your family has some very entertaining Christmas traditions." He spoke in the same jovial, false tone that had always grated on Celia's nerves. "There is nothing so charming and quaint as Christmas in the country, don't you think, Rich?"

There was a long pause, and then, "You shall be in seventh heaven, here, Your Grace."

Celia bit back a laugh at Richard's frosty, repressive tone.

She heard the scrape of a chair on wood and turned to find that Richard was standing.

"If you will excuse me, Dowden, Mrs. Pelham."

She nodded, her eyes darting from Richard's empty plate to his half-full cup of coffee.

He gave her a perfunctory bow and then left her alone with the person she disliked most in the world.

Once the door had closed Sebastian chuckled. "He's quite as . . . unusual as he ever was. It seems fame and fortune have not changed him a whit."

Sebastian smirked as Celia forced herself to take the seat directly across from him.

"Thomas," Sebastian said to a footman she knew was named Daniel. "Fetch a fresh pot of coffee. This one is cold."

The handsome young footman's eyes narrowed slightly—he'd only just entered with the coffee—but he turned and left without a word.

As soon as they were alone, Sebastian's smile fell away, like flesh rotting off bones, exposing what was beneath: cold fury. "What in the name of God are you doing here—*Mrs. Pelham*?"

Celia poured herself some of the *cold* coffee, which was still producing steam from the spout, topped her cup with cream, and then took a sip and sighed with genuine pleasure. "I'm sure Steff will have told you that I'm a companion to a friend of your aunt's."

"And you didn't think it wise to find an excuse *not* to attend this particular house party?"

"I would love nothing more than *not* to be here because I don't enjoy situations in which my reduced circumstances are fodder for humiliation and degradation. However—and this might not have occurred to you, Your Grace—but people who work for their living must do so at their employer's direction. They can't pick and choose."

Sebastian snorted. "Well, look who has learned to stand up on her hind legs." His mouth tightened, the expression making him look a good ten years older than his thirty-four years. She suspected the deep lines around his eyes and mouth were the results of a dissipated lifestyle.

Celia could not understand why the baron and his wife—who seemed to be genuinely kind people uninterested in dynastic unions—wouldn't have looked into Sebastian's murky background and come up with a reason to dissuade their daughter from marrying him. Antonia Redvers was intelligent, vivacious, and gorgeous—she didn't need to settle for an aging rattle like Sebastian.

"You are sorely mistaken if you believe I will tolerate impertinence from you, Celia. I think you know I do not take kindly to upstarts who do not know their place."

"Oh? And what will you do to me *this time*, Sebastian?" she asked, pleased that she spoke with bravada rather than terror. "Get me discharged from my current dogsbody position? How fortunate for me that such demeaning positions are thick on the ground." She snorted rudely. "You would be doing me a favor." That was not actually true, but she had to use the very limited weapons at her disposal; demonstrating how little she cared was pretty much all she had in her arsenal these days.

Rather than look angry, he smiled—and it was not a pleasant expression. "You think there isn't anything more I can do to you? You think that by calling yourself Mrs. Pelham, you are safe from me?" His quietly menacing tone was chilling. Before she could answer, he asked, "Tell me, Celia, how is our daughter these days?"

Chapter 14

"If I have to go, then you have to go," Lady Ramsay muttered under her breath.

Richard smiled at such a juvenile response coming from such a serious, mature, and intellectual woman.

"I take it Hugh rousted you from the library, Mama?"

The baroness scowled at him, which meant *yes*.

"All right, ladies and gentlemen." Hugh's voice—honed by decades of yelling at sailors—probably carried all the way to Eastbourne. "This is not simply a day for unfettered pleasure and hedonism. My daughter, Miss Antonia Redvers, although not for much longer"—he cut Dowden a smile that only those closest to Hugh would see as thin—"has decreed that collecting Christmas greenery is today's activity. That means it will be a day of hard labor for all of us." There were a few chuckles. "Although this is a picnic, there will be no food or beverage served until—"

"Papa!" Toni said with a huff of annoyance.

She broke away from her group of friends and glared up at her towering, smirking father, shaking her head at him before turning to her guests. "My father is jesting. You do *not* have to gather greenery in order to be fed. However, there are going to be prizes for the most ambitious gleaners among you."

Some of the younger people—there were perhaps thirty of them—demanded to know what was on offer, but Toni handled their impertinent questions and comments like a seasoned matron.

Richard hadn't realized just how tall she'd gotten—taller even than their mother, and certainly not much less than Richard's six foot one. Her hair, which she wore unbound and loose to her waist, in contravention of the style that women her age generally adopted, flowed around her like a rippling golden-red cape as she fielded questions from the restless group of young people.

"A pavilion has been erected, complete with food, drink, and comfortable chairs. Our winter picnic will take place next to a delightful little wood where fir and pine are plentiful. If you are so *inclined*"—she cast a chiding look at her father—"you may help in the gathering of garland and mistletoe—" The small crowd erupted with whoops and cheers at this last piece of information. "There will be several braziers to keep you warm as well as extra mufflers, gloves, and cloaks for those collecting greenery, so that you do not spoil your clothing." She stopped and smiled at her betrothed. "Do you have anything to add, Your Grace?"

Dowden stepped up beside her and took her gloved hand in his.

Richard hated to admit it, but the two tall, blue-eyed, blond gods made a strikingly handsome couple.

He glanced at his mother to gauge her reaction, but she was looking down at something—a book!—she'd pulled from the pocket of her heavy blue cloak.

Richard reached out and gently—but firmly—closed the small book and took it from her hands.

Naughty, he mouthed at her, amused by her scowl.

"I'd like to thank you all so much for coming to spend this very special Christmas with us." He looked down at Toni in a way that caused her to blush, making her even lovelier. "I have waited a long time to find the perfect lady, and am thrilled that you all could join us for this rather unconventional—but delightful—house party and wedding."

Richard had thought it a bit odd to have a wedding at Christmas, himself.

"I am eager to become acquainted with all Toni's friends and family."

Richard could only hope that he imagined Dowden's pointed look in his direction.

"Let the festivities begin." The duke kissed Toni on the forehead, the affectionate gesture earning dubious frowns from the baron and baroness, vigorous clapping from the younger set, and tittering from a few of the older ladies in attendance.

The group broke up and Richard turned to his mother. "Shame on you," he said, glancing at the book he'd taken, which was written in German. He recognized enough words to know it was another political tract of some sort.

"When did you become such a bully?" Lady Ramsay groused.

Hugh came toward them as the majority of the guests broke into groups and set out on foot. There was a little snow on the ground, but not enough to make walking unpleasant.

"Do you want to walk with us?" his mother asked her husband in a plaintive voice.

Hugh grinned. "Ah, my poor, put-upon, cruelly mistreated wife. It's good for you to get out from behind a book once every ten years or so, darling. Don't fret—you shan't have to do it again until Jonathan marries. So, I'm guessing you'll be safe for at least another decade."

Richard found it interesting that Hugh had not mentioned his name as the next marriage candidate.

"You are a pest," the baroness said, glaring at her teasing spouse. "And you didn't answer my question."

"No, my dear, I can't go with you. I am to transport Lady Yancy, Lady Morton, and Lady Yancy's dog to the picnic." Hugh smirked at Richard. "I convinced Lady Yancy to allow me to put Alexander in the library with the Great Sou'wester for the day.

When I left, the two of them were having quite an interesting conversation."

"Oh, Hugh! You didn't," his mother said, shaking her head. Still, Richard could tell she was fighting a smile.

The Great Sou'wester was an ancient parrot who'd learned his vocabulary from privateers. His language was, to say the least, colorful.

"Well, shall we get on with it?" his mother said after Hugh left.

"Where is Luce?" Richard asked as they headed for a shortcut that Toni hadn't shared with her guests.

"He had a meeting with his steward this morning but will come when that is finished. Phil is spending the morning organizing the boxes but shall join us later."

By boxes, she meant the gifts the Earl and Countess of Davenport gave their employees and tenants every year on Boxing Day.

"She makes all the boxes herself?" he asked as he lifted a leafless branch to allow his mother to pass.

"She has help making them all up, but she's adding special gifts for the children and women."

"What, nothing for us menfolk?" he teased.

"You menfolk get womenfolk—which is more than many of you deserve."

Richard snorted. "Speaking of menfolk—just what is wrong with Luce these days? He looks so . . . grim."

His mother's face, which had been relaxed a moment earlier, tightened. "Oh, I sometimes despair over your brother. And Phil."

"Why?"

She cut him a wary look. "It is not like me to notice things such as other people's marriages."

He laughed; Baroness Ramsay's obliviousness to anything except political philosophy was legendary.

"It is Hugh who drew my attention to it. You know how he is."

Indeed. His stepfather was an avid people-watcher—not to mention a people manipulator.

"What did Hugh say?" he asked, although he already knew something of what Hugh thought.

"He believes Lucien and Phil were wrong-footed from the beginning and have never managed to sort matters out."

"Mother, if there is a person less in tune with other people's emotions or motivations than you, it would be me. I'm afraid you shall have to be blunt. What do you mean by wrong-footed?"

"It all goes back to that dreadful night," she said. "Hugh believes that Phil thinks Lucien was—and still is—in love with Mrs. Pelham." She frowned, as if saying the name pained her. "I'm sure you knew that Lucien was going to offer for her?"

"He told you?"

"Why do you sound so surprised? He spoke to us just before the two of you left for the Stanford ball. He said he felt it was respectful to inform us of his intentions."

Yes, Richard could imagine his brother saying such a thing. "So, what did you say to him?"

"What *can* a person say when their child comes to them with a perfectly respectable choice? Everyone knew that her father was in the basket, but the family has a noble lineage. Trent had apparently married somebody unacceptable and his family cut him off without a cent—" She waved a hand irritably. "I don't know the full story, but it didn't matter that Miss Trent was penniless. Our only concern was that Lucien was too young to know his own mind. But it was pointless to bring up such notions to a boy of nineteen. So, we gave him our blessing. We couldn't have done otherwise. You must have seen that he was in love. Or perhaps in love with love—far more likely in my opinion—and he could think of little else except for Miss Trent."

"Yes, that was true," Richard agreed.

"Phil is a smart woman, and I'm sure she knew which way the wind blew. Indeed, I doubt Lucien did anything to hide his affection for Miss Trent that Season."

Richard recalled his brother's enthusiastic pursuit of the woman the *ton* had called the English Aphrodite—before she earned a far less flattering sobriquet.

"But, Mama, this is a *decade* ago. Luce and Phil have always seemed so . . . I don't know the words for it, but I've heard them compared to Robert and Emily Stewart."

"And we all know how well matters ended for poor Castlereagh."

His mother was referring to the downward spiral and tragic suicide of Robert Stewart, the Marquess of Londonderry, several years earlier.

"That's true," Richard conceded. "But before Stewart's illness, he and Emily were one of the *ton*'s most successful couples," Richard reminded her. "Even I know that an invitation to dinner at Davenport House is among the most sought after in Britain."

Even such an infamous ascetic as the current prime minister—the Duke of Wellington—had publicly stated that a meal and conversation at Davenport House were not to be missed.

"It's true that Lucien's marriage to Phil has been advantageous to his political career," she admitted.

"And then there is the fact that they have two children."

The moment the words left his mouth, Richard felt a bit foolish. After all, breeding offspring did not indicate deeper feelings. There were *ton* couples who couldn't stand to be in the same room with each other who had numerous children. Even the king had gotten a child off his wife and their enmity was legendary.

But his mother did not bring him up short on that point. Instead, she said, "Hugh has said more than once—"

He turned to her when she stopped and saw that her pale cheeks were stained red.

Well, this was interesting.

"Hugh said what?"

"Oh, I shouldn't tell you. It's not proper."

"He'll tell me if I ask, Mother."

She pulled a face. "Fine. Hugh has often said that he doesn't know how Lucien and Phil ever had children as they actively avoid touching each other—even in the most harmless or innocent of ways. Not out of dislike or loathing, but more out of . . . fear. After he mentioned it, I watched when I was around them. It is true."

"Well, not everyone is as, erm . . ."

"I know what you are trying to say. Not everyone is as demonstrative as Hugh. And I, on occasion," she admitted when Richard laughed. "But there is a palpable reserve between them."

Richard thought he knew what she meant, but he wasn't sure he agreed with her assessment. "Are you saying that Lucien is still in love with Mrs. Pelham?"

"I don't know. But I do agree with Hugh—that Phil believes her husband loves another."

"But . . . ten years?" Richard was not an overly emotional man, but even he found the notion of such a marriage agonizing.

"Ten years," she repeated softly.

They walked in silence after that.

Chapter 15

Celia put on her hat and cloak and took them off three times before she finally succumbed to her more willful impulses.

Why shouldn't she go gather greenery? Everyone else was going—even Percy with Lady Yancy.

Alexander and Mr. Fusskins aren't going.

Celia chuckled at the foolish thought. No, the parrot was off paying an avian morning call to a vulgar bird and Mr. Fusskins was sprawled out in the middle of Lady Yancy's bed snoozing soundly, the housekeeping staff having been sternly warned to avoid the bedroom.

Indeed, Celia took care of her mistress's room herself—along with the help of Lady Yancy's maid. Though cleaning was not a part of her job, seeing to the old woman's rooms herself avoided complications with the animals.

Can you imagine cleaning an old lady's room with a smile on your face ten years ago, Celia?

No, she couldn't. She'd been a spoiled, willful brat growing up, even though her father had scarcely had two pennies to rub together. They'd rarely had more than a handful of servants, and those had usually been either young and green or the sort who'd been discharged one too many times from wealthier and more discerning employers.

All except loyal, competent, caring Molly Henson, whom selfish Celia had always run ragged with her demands.

Poor Henson had needed to play lady's maid and dress her for balls, maintain her clothing, and somehow remake Celia's pitiful number of gowns over and over so that they would appear new and different, all in addition to a hundred other domestic duties the older woman performed in her father's dreadfully understaffed household.

Henson.

Thinking her old servant's name made Celia's heart clench. As hard as her life was, it would have been a thousand—no, a million—times harder without Molly Henson's loving help.

"—her ladyship wanted to know which of the champagnes we should bring over with the wheel of Wensleydale, my lord?" The voice drifted up from the foyer as Celia made her way down the main staircase.

Celia froze when she realized to whom the servant must be talking.

"Take the 1809 case, which will probably be shy a few bottles, so add a few from 1808," Lucien Redvers said.

She was just about to retreat to the upper landing when Lord Davenport appeared around the huge newel post at the bottom of the stairs. He glanced up absently, pulling on his gloves, gave her a vague look, turned away, and then his head whipped back, the muscles in his handsome face tightening. "Oh, Mrs. Pelham."

Celia forced a smile and resumed making her way down the stairs on wobbly legs. "Good afternoon, my lord."

Lucien Redvers looked from Celia to the hovering servant, whose eyes were wide enough to tell Celia that the servants knew exactly who she was and what she'd once done. "Anything else, Watson?" Lord Davenport asked rather sharply.

"Er, no sir. Thank you, sir." The butler scuttled out of the room in a dignified, butleresque fashion.

Lucien pulled on his second glove, his honey-gold eyes frigid as they swept over her not very appealing outerwear, his gaze lingering on her woolen mittens, the warmest hand coverings she possessed. "You are going to the, er, picnic?" Before she could answer, he grimaced. "Seems stupid to call it a picnic, but I suppose that is what it is." He snorted. "A picnic in December."

"At least it is a lovely day for it."

"Except for that." He pointed to the black cloud that hovered to the south of them.

"I understand your family gathers greenery every year?"

"Yes, but we don't usually invite half the *ton* and all the local gentry. A light snow might be pretty today, but I'm not sure my sister understands the muddle she'll have on her hands if that cloud brings real weather with it." His mouth tightened and he seemed to shrug away whatever was bothering him. "If you like, I can fetch one of the carriages to take you over."

"I was looking forward to a walk." She had no wish to be shut up in a carriage either with him or by herself.

He nodded, his body tense, as if his legs wanted to be off, but his torso refused to listen. After a moment, he gave an abrupt nod. "Very well, I'll join you. I am going that way, myself."

What else could she say except, "Thank you, I would be honored."

He opened the huge door and held it while she exited. Although the sky was clear, there was a brisk, cold breeze that stole away her breath. Celia pulled her cloak tightly around her person.

"Is that the warmest cloak you possess?" he asked as they walked down the drive, gravel crunching beneath their feet.

"Yes." That was a lie; she had another but it was gray, ugly, heavy, and so worn it would likely be rejected as a poorhouse donation.

"Would you like to go back? I know Toni rounded up a great many garments for guests to wear."

"I'm warm enough," she said, ruining the claim by shivering

He snorted. "Let's take this shortcut." He struck off across the manicured lawn that bordered the pebble drive and Celia followed him, having to take two steps to keep up with every long stride.

He'd only pulled ahead a short way before he stopped suddenly.

"Ooof." Celia slammed into him and staggered back, treading on her cloak hem so that a tearing sound filled the air.

He reached out and grabbed her upper arms to steady her. "I'm sorry. That was clumsy of me," he said, not taking his hands from her even when she was stable.

Celia stared up at him. For a moment she was transported back ten years. His hands on her body as he led her during one of the dozens of waltzes they'd shared that Season. At a hair under five feet four inches, Celia was not a small woman, but the top of her head only reached his broad shoulders. Back then there had been something comforting about being in his gentle, proper embrace that she'd never felt with other young men.

Now, she felt nothing.

"I just wanted to say that I have forgotten—or *had* forgotten—what happened all those years ago." His fingers squeezed into the soft flesh of her arms as his eyes flickered over her face, as if searching for something. "I admit I would rather you hadn't come here, but I do not wish to provide an amusing show for either my guests or employees."

"I agree."

"It was a long time ago."

"Yes."

Celia had no clue how long they simply stared into each other's eyes searching for . . . something. All she saw was a stranger; Celia hadn't known him a decade ago and she knew even less about him now.

He looked away first, breaking the strange spell, his gaze drifting to where he still clutched her arms. He jerked his hands away. "Lord, I'm sorry. Did I hurt you?"

She would have bruises. "No, I'm fine." She hesitated and then said, "I'm sorry."

He blinked, clearly perplexed.

"About what I did. I should have apologized a long time ago," she said, her face remarkably hot considering how cold it was outside. "I wrote letters to both of you—you and Lady Davenport—but they never seemed—" She shrugged. "Letters just seemed inadequate, and I couldn't face either of you. It was cowardly." She wanted to look away from his eyes, which had gone from vague to coldly penetrating.

"Why did you do it?"

She should have known he would ask that. "I'm not sure I can explain. I—I was jealous."

"Of Richard and Phyllida? Because that was who the note was meant for, wasn't it? You were hoping to humiliate them publicly and trap them into marriage."

It wasn't a question, but she nodded anyhow. "I was jealous of them." She tilted her head back and stared at the sky, blinking back the tears that threatened to fall as she dredged up that horrible time. "I was—"

He cleared his throat. "Come, Mrs. Pelham, you don't need to explain it to me," he said gruffly, offering his forearm, his smile strained, but genuine. "It is a long time ago and your reasons no longer matter. I forgive you. Now, you'd better let me help you as this first part of the path is quite rocky and might be slick with ice."

Celia took both his forgiveness and his arm, although she doubted she deserved either.

Chapter 16

Phil couldn't pull her gaze away from the window.

She'd just left the schoolroom, where she'd promised Marcus he could come to the picnic after the curate had released him from his daily lessons. Her daughter Lizzy would have to stay in the nursery as she'd developed a bit of a cold and should not be out in the weather.

Fortunately, Lizzy had the company of her favorite uncle, Lord and Lady Ramsay's youngest son, David, who was almost the same age as his own niece.

Phil had just taken leave of her son and his tutor and was turning away from the schoolroom door when something caught her eye out the beveled glass window that cast such lovely light on the dark paneled corridor.

She would recognize Lucien's golden hair, broad shoulders, and confident stride anywhere.

And the figure beside him . . . Well, she wouldn't have known it was Celia Pelham if she hadn't seen the woman in her homely bonnet and threadbare cloak several times already, out walking her employer's ancient dog at all times of the day and night.

Her dowdy, drab clothing should have made her look like a pitiful ragamuffin, and yet somehow her attire managed to enhance her already extraordinary beauty—giving her the haunted, tragic aura of a gothic romance heroine.

If Phil were to wear those exact same garments, she'd resemble a governess. Or somebody's spinster aunt. Or a spinster governess.

As she watched, the couple stopped and Lucien grabbed Celia's upper arms, the two standing less than a foot apart. It was too far away to see their faces, but their postures broadcast tension even at a distance.

Phil was unable to get enough air into her lungs, as if somebody were standing on her chest.

Only after her husband released the other woman was Phil able to suck in a ragged breath.

Instead of moving on, they stood talking.

What were they talking about?

I doubt you want to know the answer to that, Phyllida.

No, she probably didn't.

A moment later Lucien held out his arm, Celia took it, and they headed toward the shortcut path.

Phil couldn't look away. What sort of person couldn't stop staring when doing so caused real physical anguish?

She didn't know why her behavior should surprise her after all this time. Right from the moment Lucien had asked her to marry him—not that he'd had any choice—she had done things that caused her pain, and then kept doing them year after year.

Things like telling her husband to engage a mistress.

Not only had she told him to go find a lover, but she'd then proceeded to ensure he did by denying him the pleasure of the marriage bed. Year after year she'd lain in her room, right next to his, and imagined where he was on those nights he didn't come home, tormenting herself with visions of her beautiful husband in some other woman's arms.

And when they were in the country for those blessed few months of the year—when she *knew* that he occupied his own bed—she'd stood by their connecting doors times beyond counting with her hand raised to knock.

Only to drop her clenched fist to her side and go back to her bed.

While Phil had never seen one of her husband's mistresses—

Lucien was not so insensitive as to escort his women places that his wife might frequent—she'd heard about one of them.

It had been an accident—something she'd overheard while in the retiring room at Lady Bruxton's annual masquerade ball, only the second year they were married.

The overheard words were forever burned into her mind.

"Louisa really does not deserve her good fortune," the first woman, dressed as Marie Antoinette, said as she adjusted her eighteen-inch-high wig, which had tilted to one side.

"No, she doesn't," her friend—one of the many Cleopatras in evidence—had agreed. "It didn't take her long to sink her hooks into him, did it? He went scarcely a week after discarding poor Mary."

"Can you blame the man? His wife might be a superlative hostess, but poor Luce never wanted to marry the dowdy little squab."

Cleopatra had giggled. "The woman looks like she was carved from a piece of ice."

"Louisa told me his lordship brings a prodigious appetite to her bed as often as six evenings a sennight."

Her friend groaned. "I've already heard her boasts about how deliciously vigorous he is, wanting her two or even three times a night."

The women's laughter had been as ribald and earthy as their words.

"It is not fair that Louisa has access to such riches. My poor Andrew is so stout he is barely able to *rise* to the occasion once in a fortnight."

The women had cackled as they'd wandered from the room, utterly unaware that she'd been only feet away, mending her costume behind a screen.

The last bit of foolish hope that Lucien might one day come to love her as much as he clearly appreciated and relied on her—had died that night.

And the knowledge that it was entirely her fault made the realization all the more devastating.

And now there was this . . . *woman* back in their lives.

Why was Lucien with her? Where were they really going—to the picnic or to one of the small hunting cottages that were scattered about the property?

You are being foolish, the cool, calm part of her mind chided.

Phil had no interest in listening to that voice just now. Right now she wanted to *hurt* something.

Or someone?

She was seized by a powerful sense of urgency; she needed to do something, but what, she didn't know. The entire situation defied comprehension. How could this horrid, meddling female be in her life again? It was like a recurring nightmare.

How could Celia hold her head up among the very people whose reputations she had overtly attempted to destroy—or at least besmirch? Had the woman no shame after what she'd done—putting all three of their names, not to mention their families, not only in the gossip sheets but even on the front of the *Times* for one dreadful day?

Phil snorted. She knew the answer to that; Celia Trent had always been the most selfish, vindictive, cruel person of her acquaintance. Whenever the woman had wanted something, she took it, no matter who she hurt.

Like your husband?

"No," she whispered fiercely, her breath fogging the glass and bringing her back to herself.

Lucien was *hers* under the law. Celia could not take him away.

Maybe not legally, but you are the one who has spent the last decade pushing him into the arms of other women. What if he takes this opportunity to reestablish himself with the woman he once loved, and likely still does?

As for Celia—why wouldn't she leap at the offer to become Lucien's mistress? It isn't as if she could ever show her face in society after what happened. As Lucien's mistress her life would be far easier than it is laboring for Lady Yancy.

Indeed, if she became Lucien's mistress, her duties would not be onerous at all. Her duties would be—

"Shut up," Phil hissed, squeezing her eyes shut at the horrid pictures that leapt into her head.

You could change all that if you swallowed your pride and went to him, Phyllida.

Phil snorted. If only that were true. But it was far more likely that she would only fall more in love with him—although she didn't see how that was possible.

And Lucien? Well, he would take her to his bed, for a while, until she was no longer a novelty, and then he would return to his other women. That's what the men of their class did.

Lord Ramsay does not keep a mistress.

That was true, but he was a singular man. Besides, Lord and Lady Ramsay's marriage had been a love match.

While her marriage had been the furthest thing from love.

He has never once made you aware of what he lost. It's you who have pushed him away from the beginning.

That was true; Lucien Redvers was a gentleman. From the night they'd spent trapped in that room to the day he knelt and proposed, he had always behaved with exquisite breeding. Nobody watching him would have seen anything other than a young man kneeling before his betrothed.

Not then, or after they married, had he pouted, taken to drink, reproached her, or behaved like the brokenhearted lover she'd known him to be.

Phil might have believed she had imagined that Lucien Redvers ever loved Celia if she'd not come upon him once when he had believed himself to be alone and unobserved.

It was the day before their wedding and she'd been at Davenport House with her Aunt Vickie and several of Lord Ramsay's female cousins, preparing for the wedding.

Lady Ramsay had been there, as well, although the bookish woman had spent most of her time reading, only speaking when consulted by one of the other ladies.

Although Phil had grown up with a professor and had been surrounded by brilliant young men, she'd never met a woman who devoted herself to her studies.

Lady Ramsay had been kind to Phil in her own absentminded way. "If you need something to read," she'd said, just before Phil and her aunt were leaving that day, "you should feel free to borrow from the library. Ramsay has a great love for fiction and always orders the latest novels."

Phil had taken her up on the offer. She'd been about to leave, after having found a copy of *Frankenstein; or The Modern Prometheus*—a story that seemed guaranteed to drive her comparatively mundane problems from her mind—when something caught her eye outside the window that overlooked the large garden.

Lucien had been sitting on a stone bench that was tucked near a veritable hedge of roses. He would have been hidden from any vantage point other than that single bank of library windows.

Shrouded as he was by hundreds of tiny pink flowers, he'd looked like a storybook prince held in some sort of enchanted prison. His magnificent shoulders were slumped and he was staring blankly at nothing, his expression that of a man who'd lost all hope. As she watched, his face seemed to crumple and he lowered his head into his hands.

Phil never knew whether his shoulders shook from grief or merely the effort to breathe, but it was painfully obvious that the sunny, pleasant façade he'd been showing her was just that: a façade.

Somehow, his kindness and forbearance in the face of all he'd lost had made matters far, far worse. If she hadn't witnessed that one unguarded moment, she might never have known what his beautiful face hid.

But she *had* seen and she *did* know.

And so, when he'd come to her on their wedding night—valiantly prepared to pretend their wedding was a real one—Phil had already devised a plan.

That night, she put her plan in motion.

That night—and every night after—she systematically destroyed any chance for a normal marriage.

It was a process she'd continued to implement over the course of ten long years.

All so you can cling to the dream that keeps you going: that he has never yet rejected you. That maybe one day he will come to you and tell you he has come to love you.

She could not deny it. "You are a fool, Phyllida. A fool," she told herself.

Long after Lucien and Mrs. Pelham had disappeared into the woods, Phil stood gazing out the window, unable to look away.

Chapter 17

If one had to have a winter picnic, Richard's sister had certainly selected the perfect location for it.

At some point in the distant past one of his ancestors had contoured the land, diverting a stream to create a surprisingly large lake at the foot of a slight hill.

The pavilion was an enormous woven tent in exotic shades of pink, red, and gold that appeared magical against the slate gray of the Sussex sky.

Richard handed Toni a glass of hot mulled cider. "Who the devil are all these people?"

She glared at him. "My friends. Why?"

Everyone Richard knew—at least to call friend—would fit into a traveling coach with room left over.

"Don't rip up at me, you little shrew. I know Lessing Hall is big, but where will you put them all?"

"At least two-thirds of the group are from nearby—they won't be staying at either Lessing Hall or Whitton." She hesitated, and then added, "I know it seems excessive—"

"Hush," he soothed, smiling at her concerned expression. "I'm just doing my job as your curmudgeonly brother and teasing you. If I didn't do it, who else would?"

"Ha! Let's see . . . there would be Lucien, Jonathan, Matthew, and David—although he's a bit young yet. Oh, and don't forget my father—you know that he always likes to get in his fair share of teasing."

That was true; Hugh was the very devil when it came to teasing his wife and children.

"We only tease you because you are our favorite sister and we all love you so," Richard assured her.

Toni rolled her eyes at the old jest—she was their *only* sister. "Yes, well, I could sometimes do with a bit *less* love from the bunch of—" Her gaze flickered to something over his shoulder and her eyes widened. "What's going on there, Rich?" Toni asked softly.

He turned; Lucien and Celia were standing together under the pavilion, chatting away as if they were old friends.

Richard and Toni watched in silence as Lucien took her hand, raised it to his lips, and said something that made Celia laugh.

"I don't know," Richard admitted as an unpleasant sensation unfurled in his stomach.

"I don't like it," Toni said, echoing his thoughts. "Surely she must have known it was our house that her employer was coming to visit?"

"One would have thought so."

"What sort of woman could come here after what she did?"

A desperate one? Richard didn't say that.

Or merely an employed one. He didn't say that, either.

"Sebastian said that he knew her—back then," Toni clarified, as if Richard might get the wrong idea: that her betrothed would know such a woman *now*.

"Oh?" he said.

"He said he did not want to speak ill of a lady, but—"

But he did, anyhow, didn't he?

"But what?" he asked his sister, turning to find her pink-cheeked, and not, he believed, solely because of the weather.

They watched as Dowden broke away from Stephanie to approach Lucien and Celia. He greeted the pair and then set about filling several cups from the enormous silver bowl that contained their cook's prized mulled cider.

Although the duke behaved as though the punch had been his object, Richard thought it was really speaking to Lucien and Mrs. Pelham. Or, more likely, overhearing what *they* were saying.

Beside him, Toni shook her head. "It isn't right that I'm telling tales, no matter what the woman did," she said, her gaze fixed on her betrothed, whose arrival had stopped the comfortable tête-à-tête the other two had been having.

"Why don't you like Bastian?" she asked Richard. "And don't lie and tell me you do." Her brows drew down in a way that made her look remarkably like Hugh. "I'm young, Rich, but I'm not foolish. And I shall soon be a married woman; I deserve the truth."

Richard thought she did, too.

He didn't believe the truth was something only to be parceled out to those who were deemed old enough or only given to men. Richard knew his opinion was not a common one among his sex, most of whom believed that women, as the weaker gender, needed to be protected.

But he wasn't withholding the truth from her, was he? Because he had no proof that Dowden had buggered an underclassman against his will. Telling her about his suspicions would only be spreading a rumor.

"Richard?" she prodded.

"Hmm?"

"Nothing you will say can shock me. I know that Sebastian keeps a mistress," she said in a low voice, her eyes once again back on her betrothed, who was standing with Celia now that Luce had been accosted and carried off by Stephanie—or *Steff*, as she kept insisting that Richard call her.

"Richard? Did you hear me?"

"I heard you." He couldn't think of too many eighteen-year-old girls who would calmly discuss their husband-to-be's mistress. "And doesn't that bother you?" he asked, genuinely curious.

Rather than quickly deny it, Toni considered the question, a characteristic she'd likely inherited from their thoughtful mother, rather than her mercurial father.

"I don't like it," she finally admitted. "But it will be my duty to make sure he does not require a mistress."

Ah, now *there* was an eighteen-year-old's response.

Richard considered telling his young sister that a husband's propensity to wander had almost nothing to do with his wife's behavior.

It was his experience that certain men—or women, for that matter—took lovers regardless of what happened at home. If he had to attribute infidelity to any single cause, it would be that most people in the *ton* took lovers because they were bored.

Of course, many people of their class were forced to marry for expediency, rather than love. It was understandable that the men and women in those marriages of convenience often fulfilled their duties and then took their pleasure elsewhere.

But his sister and Dowden—as far as Richard knew—were both free to marry whomever they wanted. Shouldn't Toni want a man who intended to be faithful?

"You don't think I should marry him, do you?" she asked when he didn't respond.

"It is *you* who will have to live with him. Besides, as a confirmed bachelor I am a poor source of information. You should ask somebody who has a successful marriage—what does Mama say?"

"She says I shouldn't marry a man I don't love."

"You don't love him?" Richard had believed that all young ladies dreamed of marrying for love.

Well, that would teach him about the inaccuracy of stereotypes.

Toni's forehead furrowed, and he didn't know whether it was because she was thinking, or because she was watching Dowden walk arm in arm toward the lake with Mrs. Pelham.

"I don't think it is a very comfortable feeling to be in love," Toni said, her eyes flickering briefly to Lucien, who was staring at Mrs. Pelham as she walked away and clearly not listening to whatever it was that Stephanie was saying to him.

Richard considered asking her what she meant by such a look, but decided he'd already said enough to his young sibling on the matter. At least for now.

"Do you?" she asked him, her gaze switching back to Dowden and Mrs. Pelham, her eyebrows knitting as the pair strolled out of sight.

"Do I what?" he asked.

"Do you think being in love would be comfortable?"

"I've never given it any thought."

Toni laughed, her expression brightening as she turned away from the departing couple and back to Richard. "Oh, Rich—you are such an odd bird. Who does *not* think about love?"

"Me, I guess. I'm not sure I believe in love."

She pulled a face. "I've heard your theories: it is nothing but s-sexual attraction between men and women." Her voice broke on the scandalous word, her expression one of mortification—either at the word itself or her inability to toss it off like a sophisticate.

Richard smiled. "And the breeding imperative."

Her color deepened and her lips pursed in a disapproving way he found adorable—and also very youthful.

"Yes, yes, yes," she said with a dismissive jerk of her chin. "You needn't go into it all. I've read your papers—at least some of them."

"Have you?"

"You must know that Mama gets copies of everything you publish."

"I did not know that. But just because Mama gets my papers doesn't mean you have to read them."

"Ha! You clearly don't know Mama as well as you think you do. She gave them to me and Jonathan and told us they were required reading."

Richard laughed. Only *his* mother would believe that a paper on the breeding habits of beetles was suitable reading for a young woman.

"But don't try to distract me," Toni said, her expression once again becoming serious. "Why don't you like Sebastian?"

Richard considered his sister, who was about to marry a man he despised, not just disliked. Didn't she deserve to know? No matter how *ungentlemanly* such behavior—tattling, in essence—would be?

Are you more worried about your reputation as a gentleman or your sister's future?

That clinched the matter.

He didn't need to be explicit, but he could certainly mention Dowden's brutal behavior, which he'd witnessed on more than one occasion.

"He mistreated his fag."

She stared, momentarily perplexed. "You mean one of the younger boys who act as servants to older boys at school?"

"Yes."

She shook her head, her brow once again furrowed. "But I thought all boys were beastly to each other."

"We were," Richard agreed.

"So then what do you mean by *mistreated*?"

"I won't go into details. No," he said when she opened her mouth to argue. "I shan't, Toni, no matter what you say. I've already said more on the topic than I should. You were right about there being plenty of barbaric behavior at Eton. But you also know *me*, which means you should know what I consider unacceptable behavior. And that is what I am trying to communicate—not carrying tales, not gossiping, as you pointed out only moments earlier."

"Fine, so Sebastian behaved cruelly back when he was what—sixteen or seventeen?"

"Something like that."

"So over fifteen years ago."

"Yes."

Toni stared at him. "What would Sebastian say if I asked him about this behavior? Would he even remember?"

Oh, yes, I believe he would remember it quite clearly.

"You'd have to ask him, Toni. I hardly know the man." *And what I do know, I heartily dislike.*

His sister didn't say anything. Instead, she stared pensively in the direction that her betrothed and Mrs. Pelham had last been seen.

"I was surprised to see you waltz up to our little picnic with the master of the house, Celia—especially after our conversation earlier today."

Sebastian sounded amused, but she heard the fury beneath his words.

"I told you that I would mind what I said about you to anyone, Sebastian. I don't recall agreeing to lock myself in my room for the duration of my stay."

"I hardly expect you to lock yourself in your room, and I'm perfectly aware you are here in a servant capacity. But I hardly expected to see you arm in arm with a man whose life you destroyed."

"Destroyed? He hardly looks destroyed to me."

"*Tsk, tsk*, my dear, you need to take a peek under that handsome exterior. He is as tightly strung as a bow. His marriage, while successful, is not a happy one. Anyone with a particle of discernment can see that."

"I'm not sure I believe your assessment," Celia said. Not after the conversation she'd had with Lucien just a few moments earlier.

"You shouldn't be apologizing for what happened, Mrs. Pelham," Lord Davenport had said as they'd walked. "Indeed, I should be thanking you."

That had surprised her. "Oh, how is that, my lord?"

"What happened a decade ago was the best thing that could have happened to me." He'd given a wry chuckle. "I would have preferred to marry my wife without the accompanying scandal, but I know that would never have happened as I would not have noticed her otherwise." His eyes had softened as he spoke about Lady Davenport. "And that would have been a tragedy."

"It hardly matters, Celia." Sebastian's sharp tone brought Celia back to where she was right now: alone with a man she distrusted, feared, and loathed.

"So what *does* matter, Sebastian? I already promised you that I would not say anything about you or attempt to besmirch your character. You can trust my word on that."

"I certainly hope so, darling. I'd hate to take my lovely daughter—what is her name, again?"

"Katherine," she said between clenched jaws.

"Yes, I'd hate to have to take Katherine away from you. You might think I cannot do it, but I wield the power of a dukedom, my dear, and there is very little that is beyond my purview."

"I know all that, *Your Grace*—you needn't threaten me again."

His full lips curved into a hateful smile. "I'm pleased to hear it."

"Where are we going?" she asked, lifting her hand from his arm as he headed for the small wooden dock that extended out onto the lake, a charming boathouse on the end.

He took her hand in his, his grip unbreakable. "Come."

Like a dog, she went.

"Can you swim, Celia?" he asked as he led her down the narrow dock.

"No."

"Does it frighten you to be surrounded by water?"

"This does not look very deep." Indeed, she could see the bottom, for which she was pitifully grateful.

He reached for the door to the boathouse and pulled it open. "Ah, unlocked. No doubt for our pleasure." He glanced around and then gave her arm a brutal jerk.

Once they were inside the dimness of the small structure, he slammed her up against the wall hard enough to knock down oars, buoys, and miscellaneous boating items that hung from hooks.

Celia gasped, her back rammed up against something sharp and painful. "What are you—"

"Shut up." He crushed her mouth with his, mashing her lips between their teeth and stabbing into her with his tongue.

Celia tried to turn her head but he grabbed her jaw in a brutal grip. She struggled to wrench herself away, but he just held her tighter. He kissed her—although it was less like a kiss and more like an assault—until she went limp.

The moment he pulled away she said, "You're hurting me."

"Keep your voice down," he ordered, his eyes displaying all the savagery that he usually concealed behind his attractive, civilized mask.

"Let me go, Sebastian." Celia was mortified by her pleading tone.

"You will listen to me first." He raked a hand down her throat, over her chest, and then grabbed her breast in a viselike grip.

Celia bit her lip against the sharp stab of pain as he squeezed. "Please," she gasped.

"Or would you rather I subdue you a bit more?"

"No. I'm listening, I'm listening."

"When I tell you to *stay away* from these gatherings, I mean *stay away*. These next few days are far too important to me. I refuse to allow a slut like you"—his upper lip lifted in disgust—"to ruin my plans."

"What am I supposed to say if my employer tells me to do something—or go somewhere?"

"I don't care what you say or do. Besides, even if you were told to be here, you didn't need to mingle with the master of the house. If you want to thrust yourself on somebody, do it with your own kind." He snorted. "A stable lad or gardener." His nostrils flared, as did his pupils, and she knew what he'd say before he said it. "Perhaps I might even allow you to come to my room." His lips curved into a smile that made her flesh crawl. "I recall that you were an eager, shameless little jade and learned all the tricks I taught you quite speedily, didn't you?" He ran a gloved finger back and forth over her lower lip. "When Monty gets here the three of us might have a reunion. Just like old times."

Celia pursed her lips and tried to jerk away from his loathsome touch, but he just sneered and squeezed her jaw harder.

"Why don't you keep that in mind, darling? The next time you disobey me, I shall pay you a midnight visit." His eyes narrowed. "And while I teach you some new tricks, I shall send one of my servants—a great brute of a man who carries out my every order most vigorously—to Chesterfield to fetch *Katherine*."

"No, I promise—"

He raised his voice and spoke over her. "And when I have her, I will lock her away somewhere you will never, ever find her." He cocked his head. "Perhaps I shall do the same to you—"

The door swung open and Sebastian dropped her arms as if she were on fire.

Celia sagged without his support and staggered to one side before she caught herself on the exposed rib of the wall.

Sebastian took a step back, his face already rearranged in its normal, handsome mask as he turned toward the open doorway.

"Well, hallo there, Redvers. Were you looking for us?"

Chapter 18

Richard was not the sort of man to notice nuances such as atmosphere. But even he could not miss the emotionally charged environment in the boathouse.

"Well, hallo there, Redvers," Dowden said. "Were you looking for us?"

Richard glanced from the duke to Celia's sweat-sheened, red face, then back to Dowden. "My sister needs you. She wants to start the garland hunt."

"Ah, yes. Of course, of course. We'd thought to put out one of these skiffs and paddle about, but then Celia told me she simply didn't have the time—she needs to get back to—" He turned and gave the flustered-looking woman a questioning look. "What was it? The parrot?"

"Yes, that's right, Alexander. I need to get back. I forgot to put him in his cage and left him out with Lady Yancy's cat." She managed a sickly smile. "Mr. Fusskins and Alexander despise each other; it is a disaster in the making, so I really must go. "

"You only just arrived," Richard pointed out. "You could send one of the footmen back."

"Oh, I couldn't. Alexander is—well, he's a handful and Lady Yancy would be terribly upset if I tried to delegate my job to somebody else. If you will excuse me, Your Grace, Mr. Redvers." She pushed past Richard and was gone in a flurry of skirts.

Richard and Dowden watched her go.

"Poor thing," Dowden said. "I can't imagine life is very enjoyable with that demanding old crone."

Richard ignored his observation, more interested in why she'd lied about the bird—which Hugh had told him was in the library.

"Did you want me to help you put out a boat before I go back up?" Dowden offered.

Richard stared at Dowden's handsome, jovial face; why did he always feel that something lurked behind his attractive features? Something calculating, cold, and reptilian.

"No, I only came down to fetch you for Toni. She's split the younger people up and wants you to lead one group."

Dowden chuckled. "Poor Toni, I'm afraid she doesn't have much tolerance for the sorts of antics young men and women generally get up to."

"No," Richard agreed as he shut the boathouse door and started back up toward the pavilion. "She is old beyond her years."

"I prefer to think of it as maturity. She will make an exquisite duchess." Dowden's eyes glittered in an avid way that Richard could not like.

"My sister is exquisite—and impressive—no matter what her title."

Again Dowden gave that annoying, jolly chuckle, patting Richard on the shoulder harder than necessary. "Ah, spoken like a loyal brother."

Richard ignored his violent urges, instead plodding up the slight hill.

"I understand you are up for honors in the New Year, Redvers. Congratulations."

"Thank you."

"I read your paper on, er, the breeding imperative in—damme, I can't quite recall—"

"Coleoptera."

"Yes, that's right—beetles, isn't it?"

"Yes."

"In any event, I thought your theory was damned interesting."

"It's a hypothesis."

"What?"

"What I proposed was a hypothesis. A theory has undergone extensive testing and is supported by evidence. The same is not true for a hypothesis."

"Is that so?" Dowden said, giving Richard a look of exaggerated fascination. "A person learns something new every day."

"I hope a person learns more than that."

"I beg your pardon?"

"You are thirty-four, are you not?"

Dowden's face was a study in confusion. "Er, more or less."

"Well, thirty-four years multiplied by three hundred and sixty-five is 12,410 *things*. Not a great deal of knowledge when it comes down to it. I should think the subject of what constitutes a decent hunter would absorb at least a year's worth of days—perhaps even two if you are as obsessed with horseflesh as my brother."

Dowden stared, his mouth open.

"Of course, I didn't account for leap years," Richard admitted. "Nor the *more-or-less* you mentioned."

Fury spasmed across the duke's face before his characteristic smile slid over his features. "You just did that multiplication in your head?"

Richard frowned. "Where else would I do it?"

Dowden gave a bark of laughter. "I am recalling you more and more."

Whatever that meant; Richard did not ask.

"Well," Dowden continued, "what I really wanted to ask you is whether this breeding imperative you speak of applies to anything other than beetles?"

"It is likely, although I can't speak with authority about the existence of the phenomenon in other species."

"But it's possible that humans, too, might be controlled by a breeding imperative?"

"It's possible." Richard looked at the other man. "Why do you ask?"

He shrugged. "Just curious."

"Curious or concerned?"

"I beg your pardon?"

"Well, you are about to enter the married state. While it might be true that biologically the male of any species is compelled to disseminate sperm as widely as possible to get offspring on as many females as possible, I *do* know that socially, at least, that behavior is frowned upon among humans. Particularly when one is married."

Dowden burst out laughing. "Oh, I say! I didn't know you were so very, very droll."

Richard didn't bother to tell him that he wasn't jesting.

They crested the rise just then and Toni came rushing toward them. "*There* you are, Sebastian."

Richard thought his sister looked . . . irked.

"You are the last two group leaders; the others have already gone."

"I'm sorry, my dear. Mrs. Pelham wanted to take out a boat but then recalled she was needed back at Lessing Hall."

"Yes, I spoke to her," Toni said, rather abruptly. "Everyone is ready to get started."

Indeed, Richard was impressed to see that the remaining young people were standing about in small, orderly groups rather than wandering off.

"Papa thought it might motivate everyone if we offer prizes for both quantity and quality of garland."

"Very clever," Dowden agreed, earning a smile.

"As the leader of your group, you will keep count of how much each pair—one lady and one gentleman—bring back to the wagons. Sebastian, your group is there." She gestured to three fidgeting young men and three giggling young women. "Richard, your group is there. Stephanie has kindly offered to help you keep count." She gestured toward another clutch of people that included the attractive widow, who was smiling at Richard in a raptorlike fashion.

"Actually, Toni," Richard said, feigning a regretful smile and proceeding to lie blatantly, "I told Mama I would ride herd on Jonathan and his mates."

"Oh," Toni said, discomposed for only a moment before making the necessary adjustments. "That's no bother. I'm sure Stephanie can manage her group without any assistance."

Dowden chuckled. "Trust me, Steff doesn't need any help keeping a few youngsters in hand. Especially the young men." He smirked at Richard. "As much as she might want some help."

Toni looked uncertainly from Richard to her betrothed.

Dowden chuckled at her innocent confusion and slid a gloved hand under Toni's chin, tilting her face slightly to meet his eyes. "And what about you, sweet?" he asked in an amused, caressing tone. "Whose group will you join?"

Richard would have expected his sister to find the other man's condescending manner offensive, but, to his surprise, she blushed prettily and became flustered.

Well, that was interesting. And a bit disappointing. Apparently Dowden had an appeal that overwhelmed even women of sense.

"I'll be staying to entertain your aunt and the other ladies, *my dear.*" She motioned toward the braziers, where Lady Yancy, Lady Morton, and three other matronly looking women were clustered around a table, draped in thick furs and lap rugs.

"You deserve a reward for such selfless behavior," Dowden murmured, but still loudly enough for Richard to hear him. "I shall have to conceive of something . . . suitable."

Richard grimaced at his sister's entranced expression. It revolted him that an intelligent woman like Toni could find such moony-eyed bobbery appealing. He cleared his throat. "If you'll excuse me."

She nodded absently, her attention riveted on her betrothed.

His mother was seated beside Hugh near one of the copper braziers.

Richard rubbed his gloved hands—which were still cold—and held them over the bowl of fire. "Lord, these things throw a shocking amount of heat."

Heaping plates of food sat in front of both the baron and baroness.

Richard frowned. "How can you possibly be eating again? I saw you coming out of the breakfast room not an hour before we left."

"I am a growing boy," Hugh said. "Besides, if we say we are eating, we don't have to go bumbling through the underbrush leading an assortment of infants to defoliate trees."

His mother's eyes tracked the noisy groups as they melted into the woods. "Your sister should be a general in the army," she said, heaving a sigh of relief when the boisterous crowd disappeared. She pushed her full—and untouched—plate away.

"Don't let us stop you from competing for fabulous prizes," Hugh said to Richard, pulling his wife's plate toward him and taking a lobster patty.

"Oh, and what would those be?" Richard asked, snagging a patty for himself and earning a territorial frown from his stepfather.

"A scimitar for the winning gentlemen and a bracelet and earrings for the lucky ladies."

"Hmm, princely," Richard said, eyeing Hugh's remaining lobster patty and deciding it wasn't worth risking his hand. "Where are Jonathan and his mates?"

"They didn't wait around after they heard there were prizes," Hugh said, tapping his temple with one big finger. "I know how to motivate young men."

"If Toni asks after me, tell her I forgot something at the house but will be back," he said.

"What did you forget?" his mother asked, giving Richard a skeptical look.

"My knife for cutting boughs."

"Your sister brought spare knives."

"Yes, but I want *my* knife."

She gave a slight shake of her head. "Be careful, Son."

"Oh, I know how to handle a knife."

"I wasn't talking about the knife."

Celia sagged against the trunk of a huge chestnut when she thought she was far enough away from the festivities.

She rested her head against the rough bark and closed her eyes as Sebastian's words echoed in her head. She'd been foolish to doubt him this morning; today would be the last time she'd try to thwart his will. Sebastian not only had the power to do the vindictive things he'd threatened, he also had the inclination.

You should know as you were once his handmaiden. What is the saying? As you sow, so shall ye reap.

And reap and reap and reap.

Sometimes Celia felt as if she would pay for the cruelty of her youth for the rest of her life. Oh, she didn't believe it was anyone else's fault but her own, but she couldn't help wondering if she would still be paying when she was old and gray.

"Mrs. Pelham?"

She jolted and turned.

"I'm sorry to scare you," Richard said. "I'm afraid I didn't see you until I was almost upon you."

"What are you doing here?" she asked, realizing as the words left her mouth how rude she sounded.

"I was looking for you."

It wasn't the answer she was expecting; it was an answer that made her heart leap into her throat. What now?

"You were?"

"Let me escort you back to the house." He glanced at the tree. "Unless you'd like to stay here?"

"No, I was just . . . resting."

They began to walk. Unlike his brother, Richard Redvers did not offer his arm.

"Why were you looking for me?" she asked a moment later, after she realized that the man could quite happily walk in silence all the way back to the house.

"I wanted to know why you lied back there."

Celia stopped. "I beg your pardon?"

"You lied to me and His Grace."

Fear, rather than anger, stabbed at her and Celia hoped the man across from her couldn't tell the difference. "Do you think you can insult me because I am a servant in your house?"

"It's not my house."

She scowled. "You know what I mean."

"I don't believe in insulting anyone, anywhere—scullery maid or sovereign. But you lied and I want to know why."

"About what?" Oh, God. Had he heard their conversation?

A V formed between his golden-brown brows. "What do you *think* I mean?"

She turned away and marched on. "I will not be toyed with."

He followed her in silence. All the way back to his family's sprawling ancestral home.

When she headed up the stairs and toward the corridor where the guest rooms were, he followed.

"What are you doing?"

"I had an urge to see your parrot—Alexander his name is? I'd also like to meet the cat. Mr. Fussykins?"

"Mr. Fusskins," she said, biting back a smile at hearing him say such a ridiculous name.

He nodded but didn't speak, his disconcerting gaze fixed on her.

Celia flung up her hands. "Fine. I lied about the bird."

"Why?"

"Because . . ." For one mad moment she contemplated telling him the truth of her relationship to Sebastian.

There were at least a dozen reasons why that would be foolish, not the least of which was that acknowledging who Katie's father was would only give Sebastian more power over her daughter.

So, instead she said, "I lied because I decided that attending the party was foolish. I felt like a specter at the feast." That, at least, was the truth.

"Did Dowden tell you that?"

"No. In fact, he told me that I should not feel guilty—that I was welcome." Even to her own ears the lie clanged. "He said it was time to let bygones be bygones."

Redvers's eyebrows arched up above the glinting glass of his spectacles. His lips curved into a wry smile that suddenly made him very . . . kissable.

Good God, Celia! What is wrong with you?

The voice shocked her to her senses and she dropped her eyes before she did something stupid.

"That was very magnanimous as well as solicitous, two characteristics I have never associated with Dowden."

His words startled a laugh out of her. "You don't care for His Grace?"

"I think you already know the answer to that." He stared at her in a way that made her very aware of her uneven breathing. She wanted to demand that he leave her alone.

But she also wanted to reach out and take off his spectacles and see if his gaze stripped her quite so effectively without them.

Wisely, she did neither.

"Since you don't have to rescue Mr. Fusskins from Alexander," he said, smirking, "would you care to look at the portrait gallery?"

What *was* it about this man? Every third statement from his mouth was unexpected. It was impossible to get the rhythm of the conversation. He was not a comfortable man to talk to.

Especially if you're a liar.

Well, that was true enough.

Celia was just about to manufacture some new duty when he offered his arm.

"Come," he said when she hesitated. "You will be quite safe with me. And there are some magnificent paintings."

She swallowed.

He reached out, took her wrist, and gently set her hand on his arm. "Let us look at some art, Mrs. Pelham."

She nodded and they headed back toward the main staircase. Celia tried to keep track of the turns, but she was too aware of his big, solid body beside hers. Her skin felt many times more sensitive than usual, her belly a mad collection of flutters. His silence didn't help matters.

"I understand the house has Saxon origins?" she said, before she ran yelling down the corridor from sheer overstimulation.

"There is nothing that remains of the original structure, of course, but the family dining room—the smaller of the two dining rooms—was the location of the great hall for the village. By great hall I mean it was the home of the local chief. Apparently, the Saxons favored one-room dwellings so the only thing to distinguish the chief's house from the others in the village would have been the size."

He took her down a wing of the house she'd not entered before. "The main part of the house is Elizabethan, but there were considerable additions during the Stuart Era."

He pushed on one door of a double set, exposing a long, wide corridor with an intricate *parquet de menuiserie* in a complex geometric pattern.

Along one side there were giant rectangular windows with double fan arches at the top, the glass set in lead cames as thick as a finger.

On the opposite side was a dazzling array of paintings—not only portraits, but landscapes—that had been hung cheek by jowl so that there was scarcely any wall visible. The paintings went up at least fifteen feet.

"My goodness," she murmured, needing to stand on the opposite side of the corridor to see the uppermost paintings.

"I'm afraid I don't know much about art," he said, standing beside her and gazing up. "But since you mentioned liking it the other night, I thought you might enjoy this."

"It's . . . spectacular. Also rather overwhelming."

"Do you paint, Mrs. Pelham?"

"I used to dabble in watercolors, like every young lady. Now I prefer to sketch." She strolled down the corridor, trying to take in everything at once. "Do you know who some of the subjects are?"

"Yes, that I can help with. The one you are in front of right now was painted by William Dobson and his subject is John Redvers, Baron Seacliff. John performed no impressive deeds, engaged in no influential politics, but fathered an unprecedented—for a Redvers—seventeen children. All with one wife."

Celia shuddered, recalling her single—painful and terrifying—experience. "Poor woman. Where is her portrait?"

"Hmm, I'm ashamed to say I don't believe there *is* one. That is because his son Richard was an ardent Royalist and played a dangerous game that had some rather dire results. A large section of the house was put to the torch and it is likely my prodigious ancestress's portrait was lost in that blaze." Almost without pause, he asked, "Your father is the youngest son of the Earl of Trent, is he not?"

Celia experienced the same hopeless desolation that she always felt whenever she thought about her father. "Was. He died on the Continent almost seven years ago."

Richard nodded without offering the normal platitudes. "Do you have any connection with his family?"

"Do you think I would be employed as a companion if I did?"

"I suppose not." To her surprise, he chuckled, the skin at the corners of his eyes crinkling in a charming fashion. His teeth, she noticed, were white, but the center teeth on the top overlapped slightly; so, another way that he differed from his brother, who had one of the most perfect sets of teeth Celia had ever seen.

"Why have you brought me here, Mr. Redvers? What is it you want to know about me? Is it something specific?"

"I'm merely curious about you, Mrs. Pelham."

She felt a chill at his words and turned away, walking down the corridor, and staring at the paintings but not really seeing them. "Why? My life—I assure you—has been most mundane over this past decade. Indeed—it was before then, too, unless one considers a girls' school and two London Seasons the height of excitement. Certainly my life has been uninteresting when compared to yours."

"How is it that you know so much about me, Mrs. Pelham?"

She gave him a sidelong look. "It is nothing nefarious, I assure you, sir."

He smiled—a sort of smile she'd not yet seen. Or at least an expression he'd not directed her way: an open, boyish, genuine grin that turned his already handsome features into something that made her already staggering heart lurch even more wildly.

"What?" she asked, wondering if she had a smut on her nose. "Why are you smiling like that?"

"I like the word nefarious."

Celia laughed at his unexpected comment.

"I also like the sound of your laugh." He took several long strides, closing the distance between them.

She swallowed, making a mortifying gulping sound, and wrenched her now-wide-eyed gaze from his too-distracting person, resuming her stroll—away from him—and ignoring what sounded like an invitation to flirt. Celia would not have believed Richard Redvers even knew how to flirt.

She prudently steered the topic away from her laugh. "You asked how I knew so much about your life. I only know what I've read in the newspapers. It is not surprising that your journeys always excite a certain amount of interest."

"Yes, but not usually among laymen. Or laywomen, I suppose."

"Well, there is heightened interest when one knows the author of such articles."

"And do you know me . . . *Celia*?"

She spun on her heel, giving a laugh of frustration to mask her shock at the sound of her name on his tongue. "You are a persistently . . . *literal* person, aren't you?" She paused for a moment and then said, "And I did not give you leave to use my name."

His lips curled into a slow, dangerous smile. "My family would agree with you on your first point. As to the second, I thought we might use Christian names as you claim to have such intimate knowledge of me."

"I didn't say my knowledge was intimate." Why did she have to sound like such a breathless chit?

"Did you go to the Continent with your father?" he asked, jerking the conversation abruptly into a zig or a zag.

"No." She turned away. "I was not interested in the sort of life he lived." She hesitated and then added, she knew not why, "Besides, he did not ask me along."

"He left you here? In whose care?"

"My own care."

There was a long pause. Even without looking at him she could feel his astonishment. "He left you alone." It was not a question. "That's rather harsh for a girl who was what—eighteen? Nineteen?"

"I was eighteen by the time he left." *And two months pregnant.* "I suppose it appears harsh, but the truth is that my father never had much to do with me. My mother—somehow—managed to put aside enough money to ensure I went to a good school. I owe her foresight everything because my father was never afflicted with any paternal ideals."

"But even so—to leave you alone after what happened?"

Celia reached the end of the long gallery and turned, not surprised to find that he was right behind her. His proximity made him appear even bigger. She was torn between fear of her reaction to his masculine physicality and an almost delirious elation that her body could still *feel* such intense attraction. When was the last time she'd reacted so strongly to a man?

I believe that would be ten years ago and the man was his brother.

Celia flinched away from the thought. Besides, she didn't believe that was true. What she'd felt for Lucien hadn't been lust or attraction, but desperation.

She wrenched her attention back to the unpleasant conversation. "My father believed, quite rightly, that I had made my bed and should get comfortable in it. Abandoning me was harsh, but—ultimately—he could have done nothing for me. He'd been dodging dunning agents for years—all the years I can remember. So, leaving me to get on with the life I had made for myself was probably the best thing he did as a father. You see, he was killed after being caught cheating at a card game. The only thing worse than being abandoned in London would have been being abandoned in some foreign country where I did not know the language." When he didn't answer, she looked at him. "What is it?"

"I was just thinking you had a difficult time that Season, but it never showed."

"You know what showing any sign of weakness does for a person among our crowd."

"Yes. Weakness to the *ton* is like fresh blood for sharks."

Celia shivered slightly at that all too accurate analogy.

"So, you needed to marry rather desperately."

She gave a bitter laugh. "That sums it up succinctly."

"Lucien was going to speak to your father the day after that ill-fated ball. I believe he expressed something of his feelings to you earlier that week at one of the interminable functions."

"Ah, you must mean Mrs. Emily Lowell's Venetian breakfast." Celia cut him an amused look. "I don't recall your being there?"

"No." He did not appear to notice her humorous expression. Instead of returning her smile or flirting—as a normal male would do—Richard Redvers shook his head, visibly confounded. "If you knew that salvation was within reach, then . . . why? Why would you do such a thing?" For the first time since she'd met him, he turned the full force of his attention on her, his intelligent eyes intense and all-too-piercing.

For a moment, Celia had the wild thought that he could look *into* her.

She wanted to shove him aside, run out of the house, and all the way back to Chesterfield—and Katie.

Instead she inhaled deeply and let her breath out slowly. "What do you want from me, Mr. Redvers? I've already apologized. I don't—"

He closed the small bit of distance between them, coming close enough that she could smell him: faint cologne, fresh winter weather, and wool. "I don't want another apology—I didn't need the first one. What I want is to understand." He gave her a wry look. "I'm afraid that is yet another of my many flaws: a compulsion to understand that which perplexes me. And you, Mrs. Pelham, have long perplexed me. You had your future in the palm of your hand and yet you wanted to bring harm to two others—Phil and me—you did not even know."

He was looking at her earnestly, with no judgment, just curiosity. She wanted to tell him the truth—tell him that she'd made a dreadful mistake, a fatal miscalculation, and could find no other way out. That, even now, ten years later, she *still* could find no way out from under Sebastian's thumb.

Instead, she schooled her features into a sultry, taunting expression that had long ago been her mask of choice. "You want to know why I did it? You won't like the answer," she assured him before he could speak. "I did it because I wanted to. Because I was a vindictive, mean-spirited little cat. I don't try to make excuses for myself because there are none. I was horrid and my behavior—which destroyed my life—actually liberated your brother from a marriage to the woman I was."

"The woman you were," he repeated. His brows drew together in an expression of frustration—the look of a man close to unraveling a mystery, only to have the answer snatched from him.

As she stared up at him his pupils swallowed the amber-brown irises as his eyes roamed her face. His gaze spoke of confusion but his tightened jaw and flaring nostrils spoke of another emotion, an emotion that Celia had read in almost every man's eyes who'd ever looked at her: lust.

That was her power—her only power: the power to incite raw yearning.

And so she tilted her chin, swayed ever so slightly toward him, and exercised her power.

Chapter 19

As Richard leaned toward her and slid a hand beneath her jaw and around her neck, he was reminded of the time he drove Hugh's curricle into a ditch and flipped it onto its side.

The event had happened in a few blinks of an eye—he knew that—and yet time had slowed to a crawl, as if to allow him the opportunity to savor in full the disastrous event.

That's how time was behaving right now.

He was aware of his hand, out of the corner of his vision, but he could not pull his attention from her face—from those heavy-lidded madder blue eyes and those plump, pouting, slightly parted lips. Were they the pink of a peony? Coral? Rose?

Richard covered her mouth with his, holding tightly to the reins of his desire. A gentle kiss—a flimsy veil for the lust that she evoked merely by existing.

But Mrs. Pelham—*Celia*—had other ideas.

Her hands snaked around his waist and there was strength in her fingers, which grabbed and squeezed. And then she slanted her mouth over his and stabbed into him with a groan that vibrated down his neck, through his chest, straight to his overstimulated cock.

Richard backed her into the corner—the only spot of wall not taken with windows or paintings—pressing his body against hers, thigh to thigh, hips to belly, and breasts to chest. She was all soft, yielding feminine curves, a profligate voluptuousness that begged—no, demanded—to be penetrated, explored, and dominated.

She shuddered beneath his hand, which, he discovered in some surprise, was cupped over her breast; a hardened nipple peaked against the cheap brown muslin of her gown. Richard watched as his second hand moved to caress her other breast, both his thumbs stimulating her nipples while he cradled the soft weight of her in his palms.

Her fingers dug painfully into his waist and she yanked him toward her, trapping his hands in a blissful prison between them.

Her mouth claimed his, teeth nipping and biting, lips sucking, the suggestive thrusting of her tongue causing his already aching prick to pulse with need. The desperate little grunts and breathy sounds she made were like the prod of a whip, and he crushed her against the wall, grinding his erection into her belly like an animal in full rut.

And then she slid both hands down his lower back, grabbed his buttocks, and ground against him.

"Bloody hell," he murmured against her lips, pulling away from her questing tongue—not the clumsy, earnest kisses of a maiden, but the carnal, skilled exploration of a widow—so that he could see her face.

"Mrs. Pelham?"

"Hmm?" Her eyes were lust-drunk blue slits that probably mirrored his own dazed, wanting stare.

"I am half a tick away from raising your skirts, spreading your legs, and mounting you right against this wall."

Both their bodies tightened at the image his crude words created.

She swallowed, her heavy lids lifting as if they weighed a hundred pounds.

Richard knew the feeling; he had to keep blinking to focus, his own eyes hot and pulsing, his vision dazed and blurred, images of plunging into her body vying with the cold, hard reality of the gallery around them.

"Oh," she said.

It was barely a puff of air and part of his brain—the less civilized portion—urged him to capture her mouth and resume their tussle.

But she swam more quickly toward awareness than he and her hands dropped from his buttocks as if she'd been scorched.

Now there's a wasted opportunity, old boy.

Richard couldn't argue. Instead, he stepped back, watching raptly as she changed before his eyes: from erotic enchantress to tousled temptress to mortified matron.

"I'm sorry," he said. The words were a reflex that came unbidden.

Richard absently stroked his lower lip—which she'd bitten quite thoroughly—and stared at her flushed and forlorn expression.

He dropped his hand and shook his head. "No, actually, I'm not sorry."

The skin around her beautiful eyes tightened until her expression became one of near agony. "*I'm* sorry enough for both of us." She pushed past him, taking several long strides before breaking into something that was part-trot, part-run.

When she reached the doors, she flung her body at the one on the right, shoving open the heavy slab of wood and iron only a crack before flickering through the gap, like a swallow darting out from under an eave.

Richard released the lungful of air he hadn't realized he was holding and made a few critical adjustments to his person, still staring at the now closed door—as if she might change her mind and come barreling back through it.

The tiny hairs on his arms and the back of his neck stood upright, as if he'd just passed through an electrical storm—or been struck by lightning.

He hoped that wasn't true, because lightning, as the old proverb went, rarely struck the same person twice.

Chapter 20

Lucien had dismissed his valet and was pacing his room, glancing at the clock with each pass by the mantel.

The party had broken up early tonight—likely due to the exhaustion of a day spent outside—and there had been no calls for a second round of charades—thank God.

This evening was the first night of what he'd mentally termed the *mating schedule* and here Lucien was, waiting to go into Phyllida's bed as nervous—no, *more* nervous—as his first time with a woman at the age of sixteen.

Of course, back then he'd been in a group of schoolmates and there was strength—or bravado, at least—in numbers.

Lucien smiled as he recalled the momentous occasion. It had been late one night when they'd sneaked away during term.

When Lucien had invited Richard along—certain that his brother would be eager to join them—Richard had refused to go. After Lucien had pressed him, Rich had shared the fascinating, and shocking, information that he had no need to pay a woman to rid him of his virginity as he'd already lost it at the tender age of fifteen.

Lucien could still recall his utter stupefaction that his awkward, reclusive, and scrawny brother had been with a woman before he had. Inconceivable!

"Who?" Lucien had demanded, over and over, only to be confronted with Richard's amused, dismissive smirk, as if Lucien were a mere Johnny raw.

"A gentleman does not kiss and tell, Luce."

Lucien snorted as he recalled his brother's smug face.

But the one characteristic that he shared with his twin was persistence. Lucien had badgered and badgered until he'd gotten the information out of his brother—but not until that summer, after he'd caught Richard sneaking out of the house one night to go visit his lover: a thirty-three-year-old widow who owned the small millinery shop in Eastbourne.

"How the devil did you even meet the woman?" Lucien had asked, incensed that he'd been such a sexual slow top while his brother had been secretly trysting with older, *willing* women he didn't have to pay.

"I was gathering specimens near the stream that runs behind her cottage," Richard said in a calm, practical tone—as if collecting specimens was an activity that naturally led to bedsport.

Hell, obviously it did.

Lucien had been impressed and awed by his brother's carnal confidence.

A few years later, after they'd turned eighteen and spent a year touring the Continent together, he'd learned that even though Richard had the social sophistication of a twelve-year-old boy, he attracted women—experienced, older, amorous women—the way Lucien attracted giggling, blushing debutantes.

Even back then Lucien had known which group he would have preferred to appeal to.

Well, that had been how he'd once felt. For years now, he'd only wanted to appeal to one female, for all the good that wanting did him.

As always on these nerve-racking evenings, Lucien inevitably recalled their wedding night.

He had arrived in Phil's bedchamber freshly shaved and optimistic about his marriage because he'd spent the days before their wedding coming to terms with his new life. It was true that Phyllida was not the woman he would have chosen, but there was no point in repining.

When he'd entered his new wife's chambers she had been lying in bed, wearing a sleeping cap and heavy flannel nightgown. Lucien still recalled the book she'd been reading: Louisa Gurney Hoare's recent tract on the subject of education, *Hints for the Improvement of Early Education and Nursery Discipline*.

She had looked surprised, and not especially pleased, to see him.

Lucien had watched with increasing apprehension as she'd calmly put the marker in her book, laid it on her nightstand, and then turned her full attention on him.

"I think it is time we discussed a few things."

Foolishly, his initial reaction to Phyllida's statement had been a combination of fear and hope. Fear that his soon-to-be wife—almost four years older than himself—could exhibit such sangfroid in a situation that had tied his stomach in knots.

And hope that she wished to clear the air of any residual doubt between them.

"Yes, excellent notion. We must make a clean breast of things," he'd offered, believing himself to be magnanimous and sophisticated to make such an offer.

She'd nodded calmly and then proceeded to stupefy him.

"It is about children," she'd said, coolly. "Our children."

Lucien had reached up to loosen his cravat, and then recalled he wasn't wearing one. "Er, yes?"

"I know you want an heir."

He'd nodded.

"I also want children."

He'd nodded.

"I also know you are quite serious about your position in the current government."

At the time, he had just accepted a junior position in Lord Liverpool's government and had immediately taken to the world of high politics.

"Yes," he'd said again, even more cautiously—and even more confused as to the direction she was heading.

For the first time, he'd seen signs of nervousness on her rather plain face. "I believe we can safely schedule births every three years, until matters are settled in that department."

Lucien hadn't been sure that he'd heard her correctly. *"That department?"*

She'd ignored his interruption. "I should hate to have you disturbed in the midst of a Session by childbirth," she'd continued, apparently unaware of his hanging jaw. "Therefore, I believe we should limit conception to December and January."

His ears had admitted her words to his brain, but his understanding had lagged far behind.

"Er, you don't wish to conceive tonight?" he'd asked, blushing furiously at having such a conversation with a maiden.

"Correct."

"Ah. Well, there are ways to avoid it, although of course they—"

"You misunderstand me. I do not wish to commence—" She'd faltered, her own color finally deepening.

"Yes? You do not wish to commence?" he'd asked, no doubt looking stupid as he'd stood clutching a bottle of wine and two glasses.

She frowned. "I thought we just determined that December or January was the best time to begin such activities?"

"Activities?"

"Yes, to embark on creating a child?"

The meaning of her prior words hit him like the cold, crushing snow of an avalanche. Yet again he'd been a slow top. His wife did not want him in her bed—at least not for anything but conception.

At that point, Lucien wouldn't have been physically capable of completing the act even if she had begged him to.

"I understand that men have needs," she'd continued.

Dumb from shock, Lucien had merely nodded.

"My only request is that you employ a mistress rather than utilize brothels."

Lucien's jaw, already sagging, had hit the floor.

When he'd been unable to comment, she'd gone on to say—with a tolerant smile, "I am not so ignorant of men to know that this is an inevitability."

To be honest, keeping a mistress or visiting brothels had never entered his mind; he was a *married* man.

Although he'd never articulated his thoughts on the subject of marriage and love, he had hoped to have a marriage such as Hugh and his mother's: a marriage that was not only a union of mutual respect, but love.

At the time of his marriage, Lucien had never done much whoring, nor had he kept a mistress. He'd only been with a small handful of women, most of those on his Grand Tour with Richard, whom he'd discovered—to his shock—had a rapacious sexual appetite. Not only did his brother have a constant parade of lovers, but he was adventurous and did not shy from amorous experimentation.

Oh, Lucien greatly enjoyed the act—like any young man—but he found frequent, casual amours unappealing. While his brother took lovers in almost every town—no matter how small or remote—they passed through, Lucien found that taking a succession of women to bed left him empty and dissatisfied.

Then his new wife had told him, on his wedding night, that taking lovers would henceforth be his only choice if he wanted physical intimacy.

If Lucien hadn't believed that Phyllida meant the words she'd spoken on their wedding night, he'd certainly believed her in the weeks and months to come.

Rather than warming to him, she had sedulously reinforced the distance between them.

When he'd offered to accompany her to balls, parties, or the many talks she enjoyed attending, she'd told him his presence was not necessary. She was never rude or cruel, just relentlessly pleasant and cool, making sure he received her message: She would assist him in every way possible when it came to supporting his interests, but she had no desire to become anything other than his helpmeet.

By the time December came around, Lucien knew that his new wife was deadly serious. There would be no carnal relations between them, except what was necessary to bear him two sons.

Even so, Lucien hadn't been able to face the thought of taking a lover. At first.

Instead, he'd continued to hope that when he finally came to her bed in December, they might both at least enjoy the process. Perhaps relations between them might thaw and she would change her opinion on the matter of allowing him to be her lover as well as her husband.

Once again, he discovered he was wrong.

Even after all these years his face heated to recall that first night in December—their first scheduled mating, as he'd come to think of it.

She'd been in bed with an improving book, dressed in almost exactly the same fashion as before, a cap on her head, strings tied under her chin.

The sight of her had set off a sinking feeling in his stomach. But, optimist that he'd been, he'd persevered.

Before he could remove his robe, she had asked, "Will you extinguish the candles, please?"

Well, virgins were known to be shy, so he'd cast the room into darkness before undressing.

When he went to the bed, he discovered that she'd pulled her nightgown up to her waist. When he made as if to remove it completely, she asked, "Is that necessary?"

Lucien had laughed, believing she was jesting. "Necessary to procreation? No. Necessary to giving us both pleasure, perhaps."

"Oh." The one syllable conveyed volumes.

By that point, his cock—which had been stiff and waving about in anticipation—began to flag.

"What is it, Phyllida?"

"It's just that I wish to get on with it. Unless this is something you find necessary," she added hastily.

Her words released a veritable hurricane of emotion inside him. Anger and despair chief among them. She wanted *nothing* from him aside from a child—nothing. No tenderness, intimacy, or love—physical or emotional.

It was, Lucien knew, his legal right to bed his wife as often as he pleased, but the notion of forcing her—of forcing any woman—was repulsive to him.

And so he'd done his duty over the coming weeks, until she'd become pregnant, but there had been no joy in the act.

When it was over, he'd decided that if she didn't want his touches or affection, surely some other woman would.

And so, less than a year after their wedding night, he'd engaged his first mistress.

For those first few years, he'd been furious at Phyllida for what she'd done to their marriage. He'd told himself that if he engaged in enough debauchery he could wipe her entirely from his mind.

Instead, he just wanted her more with each year that passed.

It drove him half mad that he found his wife so appealing—even though she managed to make him feel like an inexperienced boy.

Phyllida was only four years older than he, but Lucien often felt as if the age difference were a decade or more.

Even that fateful night, when they'd been locked in the Duke of Stanford's weapons room for hour upon hour, it had been Phyllida who'd maintained an almost eerie stillness while he'd fidgeted like a sullen, restless child.

All Lucien had been able to think about was Celia and how important it was that she never find out he'd spent hours alone with another woman.

But as one hour followed another, he knew that marriage to the woman he loved was less and less likely.

He recalled Phyllida's words even now: "I know this is very unfortunate for you, my lord. And I am sorry."

He'd been humbled, awed, and terrified by her composure. *She is more and more likely my wife-to-be,* he'd thought at the time. *And she's behaving like more of a man than I am.*

Lucien laughed bitterly at his younger, foolish, and naïve self. Not much had changed, apparently, because he was still pacing and fidgeting ten bloody years later.

He stared at his reflection in the mirror, feeling as though a stranger looked back at him. He wasn't sure if he could do this anymore.

He also wasn't sure why he was feeling such despair now.

Could it be the sudden reappearance of *that* woman?

Aren't you even man enough to say her name in your own mind?

Lucien groaned. *Fine: Celia. There, I've said it.*

Could that be true? Was it Celia's presence in their lives again—after so many years—that was making him see the truth of his empty existence? Making him remember the dreams he'd once had for his life? For his marriage?

Oh, he adored his children, and his anger toward Phyllida had long ago burned out.

He'd stopped taking lovers after that third, bitter, endless year. He'd simply become too guilt-stricken and miserable to find any joy with other women. Instead, he'd learned to appreciate the bounty he had, rather than yearn for what he didn't. He respected and admired and relied on his wife—how many of his peers could claim such a relationship with their spouses?

It was Phyllida whom he went to when he wanted to test the soundness of some improvement or plan. Lucien always solicited her opinion of a particular piece of legislation before he committed to a course of action. Oh, he didn't always take her advice, but he certainly relied on her help—more than his secretary's—to polish his ideas into something compelling and cohesive.

But he'd become increasingly weary of living with a woman who treated him like an employer rather than a lover.

Indeed, she treated William Payson far more like a lover—or at least far more like a husband.

It wasn't seeing Celia herself that made him feel restless; it was more that she'd made him recall how he'd felt back then, his hopes for his marriage and wife.

Hope? I think what you mean is lust or infatuation.

Lucien believed that he had once loved Celia, though not the way he now loved Phyllida.

How could the emotions be the same? He and Celia had spent mere minutes together over the course of weeks and weeks, and during none of that time did a person show their true self to anyone. The *ton* was all about appearance—substance was never a consideration.

Lucien had learned that being married, even as stiff and distant as his marriage might be, meant you truly had the opportunity to know another person.

When he'd broken his leg while hunting—the fourth year of their marriage—it had been Phyllida who'd stayed by his bed day and night for weeks, nursing him back to health.

When Phyllida had almost died giving birth to their daughter and had spent an unprecedented six weeks in bed afterward, Lucien had stayed with her at Lessing Hall rather than doing as she had constantly bade him and gone hunting with the Melton Pack, as he had every year since they'd married.

"How can you think I would enjoy going hunting when you are ill?" he'd asked her, earning yet another of her opaque, unreadable looks.

So, yes, they knew each other—or at least they knew each other's mettle.

Seeing Celia had been a bizarrely eye-opening event. It had

made him realize that for a decade he'd held on to some vague belief that his love had been torn from him. Even though he'd never dwelt on the thought or allowed it at the forefront of his mind, it had lurked all the same.

He stared blankly at the door that stood between him and his wife; he had no idea what he would do when he went in to her. But whatever it was, he could not continue on the way he had been doing.

Chapter 21

Phil sat exactly where her maid had left her: on her chair in front of her dressing table.

Her hair had been brushed to a shine and then plaited into a heavy rope that hung down her back. Barnes had then tied her sleeping cap over it, just as she did every night.

For one mad moment Phil had considered taking it out and letting it hang like a curtain of silk about her shoulders.

Foolishness.

She sighed and her eyes wandered to the clock; he was late. He usually would have come, done his business, and gone, by now.

Perhaps he was finding this as trying as she was this year. Or more trying, now that Celia Pelham was under their roof. Was he thinking about her—the woman who'd managed to steal all the light in the dining room yesterday evening?

Phil could see by looking at the faces of her family that everyone else had felt the pull that far end of the table seemed to exert on their conversation.

Even though she had seated Celia as far away as possible, it wasn't far enough to dull the woman's light—her beauty.

Phil had been almost weak with relief when the woman had sent her regrets and eaten in her room tonight.

Hate, she knew, was always more corrosive to the bearer than the target.

But she could not help it. Looking at Celia's beautiful—albeit drawn—face had reminded her of a time when those preternaturally blue eyes had stared at Phil with dislike and disdain.

Would it be painful for her husband to come to her tonight while the woman he'd once loved—perhaps still did—was only a short distance away?

Phil had foolishly hoped that Celia's absence tonight would allow everyone to relax and enjoy the evening. Instead, the gathering had seemed flat, dull, and lifeless without her.

She felt flat, dull, and lifeless. An interloper among the beautiful, talented, charismatic family she'd stumbled into by accident. Celia would have fit in well with Lucien's family—like the most spectacular gem in a beautiful crown.

Instead, her husband and his family were stuck with Phyllida Singleton. Plain, stiff, and practical with not even a slight claim to being decorative.

Phyllida Singleton, married to the man every other woman had dreamed about and wished for that year. Golden, gloriously handsome, kind, funny, intelligent—was there any desirable attribute her husband did not possess in abundance?

And yet you have driven him away at every turn.

Phil didn't deny the accusation. It was either drive him away or lose herself. But keeping him at a distance had become its own kind of suffering. Could allowing him to see the truth of what she felt for him really be any worse than the suffering she'd been experiencing for years?

There was a soft knock, and then the connecting door opened.

Phil stood and turned. As it did every single time she looked at her husband, her heart swelled with pride and love. And something else: agony. Because he wasn't hers, not truly.

He was wearing a banyan that his mother and stepfather had

brought back from their journey to China several years before. It was gold and umber and ivory and flattered his dark blond hair and golden-brown eyes.

He gave her the pleasant, polite smile that killed any ill-conceived hopes or dreams she might have allowed to flourish in her breast.

"You must be exhausted after today," he said.

And then he did something he never did: he came to stand before her and took her hands.

"Cold," he murmured, lifting her fingers to his mouth and kissing them.

Phil swallowed, careering between the urge to pull her hands away and the desire to fling herself at him.

She was still staring in shock when he lowered his mouth over hers. His lips were warm and unspeakably soft.

"Mmm," he hummed against her, the slight vibration traveling between them. He sucked lightly on her upper lip before his tongue teased into her mouth.

Phil started at the invasion, her breathing rough and shallow, her body shaking.

"Shhh," he whispered.

Somehow, without her realizing it, his hands had released hers and one rested on her hip, burning through the layers of her clothing. The other hand cradled her head gently, holding her steady for his wit-scrambling kisses.

He'd kissed her before, of course—hundreds of dry pecks on her cheek or forehead—but never when he came to breed her; not since that very first time, when she'd rebuffed him so coldly.

This kiss was like none of the others. This was . . . the kiss of a lover.

He tasted so warm and real and the low, encouraging sound he made deep in his chest caused a clenching in her belly that set off an unspooling sensation, as if her inhibitions had been severed from their moorings and were floating away.

Phyllida's mind fogged and her body heated, her skin becoming tight and hot beneath his hands, which stroked and caressed and incited.

She blinked to clear her vision, but the haze of arousal was inside her head—not inside the room—and only becoming thicker.

What was happening?

He's kissing you, as a lover would.

Her heart quickened and it was all she could do not to melt into his touch.

His expert touch—

An expertise gained from his mistresses . . .

The thought snapped her back from the edge of madness.

What was he doing? Hadn't she told him that she didn't want such things? She was not his lover; she was his wife. This—this whatever he was doing would be the ruin of her; already her body was shaking, wanting—

He pulled away with a low moan. "Mmm, Phyllida," he whispered against her temple, and then looked down at her, his eyes heavy-lidded in a way she'd only imagined. He stroked her jaw and chin with his thumb, his gaze flickering to her mouth. "I want things to change between us." He looked almost as surprised as she felt, hearing his words. "I no longer want our nights together to be scheduled like meetings." His chest rose and fell against her unbound breasts, the feel of his hard, hot, and intensely male body making her usually sharp mind woozy and sluggish. "I want this marriage to be real, Phyllida."

Her thoughts were like rats that had long been accustomed to darkness and were now exposed to the light—fleeing blindly.

"My dear?" he said when she could only stare.

"I thought we had an arrangement that was effective and efficient."

His beautiful mouth curled up on one side, the smile sad. "Yes, effective and efficient."

"Why do you say it like that?"

"Because I want more."

"But—but why now? Why tonight?"

She could see from the tightening of his handsome features that he knew what she was asking.

"Does it matter why? It is almost ten years that we have been married. I no longer want this coldness—this distance. I want us to live like man and wife, Phyllida," he said, his tone gentle but firm.

She swallowed convulsively, her head throbbing. "Do you—should I get on the bed?"

His smile, this time, was resigned. "I want to make love to you, not merely cover you as a stallion mounts a mare."

She flinched at his words, even though he'd not raised his voice.

"I want you to come to my bed, Phyllida. I want you to be my lover."

Phil gaped. "You want me to go to your room?" Even she could hear the hysteria in her shrill voice.

His face took on the fixed look of a person forced to hold a smile too long, and he dropped his hands from her face and body and took her hands, which she'd fisted between them. "I can see the idea is a shock—I have surprised you with the suddenness. You need time, I suppose. Take all the time you need, my dear. I will not importune you or visit you again. If you want to be my lover as well as my wife, then come to my bed when you want me—as your husband. Not only as the father of our next child."

"You want me to come to you," she repeated blankly.

"Yes, but only if you wish it. I have never forced myself on you, but this . . ." He gestured to her bed. "What happens in this room at carefully planned intervals, like a stud breeding a mare . . ." He inhaled deeply and then released his breath with a noisy sigh. "I should have said something long ago, on our wedding night, when you sent me away and told me to take my pleasure elsewhere."

Phil opened her mouth, but then realized she had nothing to say. He was right; she'd sent him away.

"It is my fault that it has gone on so long," he said. "But now—well, now I want us to be honest with each other. It is far, far past time we were honest. I no longer want these dispassionate, impersonal encounters. I want—no, I *desire* you as a man desires a woman."

His words set off a cacophony inside her skull, the din so oppressive she could barely hear herself think. "But *why*?" She was yelling, she realized. When was the last time she'd raised her voice? Decades ago—not since she was a child.

It felt . . . *good.*

Phil glared up at him, pleased when he flinched at whatever he saw on her face. "Isn't our life good as it is? The children? Working together for our various causes?" she demanded tightly.

Inside her head, she didn't curb her words or her fury: *Or do you have to take that little bit of me that I keep for myself? Must you take all of me, and then cast me aside and destroy me when you find I am not enough for you?*

"Our life is good. But could it not be better?" He hesitated, his gorgeous cheekbones flushed. "Don't you want a lover as well as a husband?"

She stared.

"Phyllida—" He frowned. "Why is it that I call you by your full name? Why do you not call me by my Christian name as the rest of my family does?" He scowled, but more at himself than her, and shook his head. "That doesn't matter. What matters is that I no longer want this reserve—this stiffness—that has been between us since the day we married. Perhaps at the beginning, given how we were thrown together, such distance was understandable, but we've been married almost a decade. We have two children together. And yet we have never once enjoyed the pleasure of each other's bodies like lovers."

His words were like hornet stings, sharp, painful, and startling. Phil shook her head, as if to shake away actual buzzing. "Why now? Why *this*? Isn't it enough for you that I don't care if you have m-mistresses? Aren't *they* enough to keep you happy?"

You are such a liar, Phyllida. Your jealousy rips you to shreds and then sets fire to all the pieces.

He dropped her hands as if scalded. "No, Phyllida, that is not enough. I've been a fool to allow this to go on for so long. I suppose I felt guilty—that you'd been forced into this union when it was so obvious that it was not me you wanted."

Phyllida's jaw sagged. *Her* not wanting *him*? Was he deranged?

"I've been a coward, but now it must stop. I do not wish to go on like this until the end of my life."

His weary, hopeless gaze was the last straw.

"This is all because of *her*, isn't it?"

He recoiled from her fury.

"Isn't it, my lord?" she demanded when he didn't answer.

"Why won't you call me Lucien? Or Luce?" he retorted, just as heatedly. "At first I thought you were merely reserved—shy. But I was wrong. You use my title to keep me at a distance. And yet you call Richard Rich, Antonia, Toni, and even William Payson you call Will."

She opened her mouth, but nothing came out.

"Why must you always enforce this distance between us?" He took a step toward her, not menacingly, but Phil backed away, shaking her head.

"Don't touch me," she hissed.

His eyes widened.

"What?" she asked. "You are surprised that I am angry after you've told me that everything I've given to this marriage—to you—is not enough? You want more? To have me as a lover? Why? Because it will be a novelty? At least for a little while." She gave a rude snort, not waiting for his answer because she didn't want one. "When have you ever indicated such a thing in ten years? When—"

"I came to you on our wedding night and—"

"That was not the act of a lover." She knew she was sneering but could not stop it. "You came to me for sexual gratification. You knew *nothing* about me and had hardly spoken to me before. From the moment you proposed until the day we were married, you scarcely exchanged a word with me. You made no effort to know me, no effort to charm me or set me at ease, no flirtatious words—*nothing* of what I saw all Season long between you and the various beauties of the *ton*. With you and *Miss Trent*. No, with me you were all bleak, noble sacrifice—doing your *duty* by me, your family, your reputation. Marrying *me*, a woman you'd never once looked at. I daresay you couldn't have picked me out of a crowd of wallflowers before that night."

Phyllida could see from his flushed cheeks and pursed lips that her words had hit their mark.

"Am I to be eternally punished because I did not know you?" he demanded. "Because I never sought you out to dance?"

"I am not punishing you by withholding what you want—my sexual submission in your bedchamber—I am merely pointing out the truth of our relationship. I wasn't what you wanted back then and I am not now, either."

"That is not true. I have come to care for you a great deal."

She wanted to scratch his beautiful face and hurt him for such a lie. Never—*never* had he looked at her with the same worshipful gaze that he'd constantly given Celia Trent all those years ago.

"I am the mother of your children. Of course you care for me—"

"No, it is more than that, Phyllida. That is what—"

"I am not a fool—or one of your fancy women—to be won by pretty, hollow words, my lord."

He winced, as if she'd clawed him the way that she'd wanted to do.

His expression had gone aloof—and distant, but Phil could not stop herself now. "I was a chore for you and we both knew it then and I still know it now, for all that you appear to have told yourself some other story. A chore. And yet you ask why I didn't want you to touch me on that first night or any other? A woman four years your senior and never blessed with beauty even in my prime. A woman you were forced to marry as the result of a vicious practical joke that went awry. No thank you, my lord. I value myself too highly to capitulate to your momentary whim for dalliance."

This time it was Phyllida who took a step toward him. Unlike her, however, he held his ground.

"And now, after seeing the woman you'd always hoped to marry, you suddenly wish to grasp at some childish fantasy of marriage? And you wish me to submit to you like the obedient wife I have always been?" He recoiled at her bitter laughter. "I will not indulge your wish, *my lord*. If you want to bed me according to our agreement, then extinguish the candles and exercise your legal right here. If not, I bid you good night."

Phyllida turned away from him, horrified by the bile coming out of her mouth. But as horrible as her words were, the thought of giving her soul to him, along with her body, was not to be borne. It was already awful enough to surrender to him every three years and experience unspeakable joy at his careful, gentle, and all too brief lovemaking. She suffered enough after those encounters, crying herself ill in her bed after he thanked her politely and left.

That small, precious bit of distance between them had been all that kept her sane these ten years. And now he wished to strip her of those meager defenses?

No. At least not with her assistance.

When Phil heard the soft rustle of silk and gentle click of the door, she realized that she was alone.

Lucien had, once again, given her exactly what she'd asked for.

Chapter 22

Richard couldn't help noticing the extra tension between Phil and Luce when he entered the breakfast room the next morning.

But Luce and Phil weren't the only ones behaving strangely lately.

Mrs. Pelham had not attended dinner last night.

"Mrs. Pelham is of a retiring nature," Lady Yancy said when pressed by Lady Morton, Dowden's abrasive aunt.

"Oh, stuff! She is here to attend you, and so she should."

Richard had shamelessly eavesdropped later, in the drawing room, while the two old ladies had talked themselves into a state of dudgeon about the ingratitude of servants these days.

After discovering that she would not be coming down, Richard had excused himself to walk Newton, hoping he'd see her out with the little dog. He had no idea what he'd say to her—

Liar. Speaking was not what you had on your mind.

Oh, very well. That was the truth. He felt a bit like a gin addict or opium eater. Except it wasn't another drink that he needed, but more time in Mrs. Pelham's company.

Rather than be alarmed at such a singular emotional response—for indeed he'd never experienced such intense yearning for a female's company before—he was eager to explore these unprecedented feelings and their motivations.

But she did not walk the dog. Or if she did, she found someplace else to go.

He'd come down early for breakfast, hoping to catch her, but the only people who'd come down at such an uncivilized hour were first Lucien, and then Phil. Both of whom had looked at each other as if they were complete strangers, and then proceeded to dine without hardly exchanging a word before going their separate ways.

If Mrs. Pelham was invisible, then Dowden, by contrast, seemed to be everywhere.

In fact, Richard sometimes felt there might be two, or even three, of the man.

He found it slightly alarming that the duke seemed determined to systematically charm Richard's entire family.

And it was *extremely* alarming that he seemed to be succeeding.

The duke had inspected the home farm and Luce's new drainage project—a subject close to his brother's heart—and he'd even managed, if not to win over Richard's mother, to at least intrigue her.

"He attended several of Friedrich Schelling's lectures in Munich," the baroness said when Richard asked her why she was looking at the man with such a benevolent expression.

Richard sighed and shook his head. "Oh, Mother."

"What?" she demanded, her guilty expression telling him that she was well aware of her self-interested defection. "Oh, don't worry," she added. "Hugh still mistrusts the man—even without any evidence—enough for all of us."

Even Phil—who'd been the target of Dowden's barbed tongue on more than one occasion during that wretched Season—appeared to have forgiven the duke.

Richard was so stunned by his sister-in-law's change of heart that he decided he needed to speak to her, one-on-one.

So he sought her out before going for his daily ride.

This was not as easy as it sounded.

Although Lessing Hall was a huge house, it was stuffed to exploding with what seemed to be hundreds of young men and women, veritable mountains of greenery, two enormous trees, and more ribbons, decorations, and Christmas gewgaws than Richard had seen in his entire life.

"Have you seen Phil?" he asked Toni, who was looking a bit frazzled as she attempted to direct her youthful army, who were far more interested in kissing beneath the dozens of pieces of mistletoe than doing any actual decorating.

Toni pulled a face. "Marcus and Jason were decorating one of Aunt Amelia's pugs, so Phil took the boys and left."

His Aunt Amelia was close to one hundred and her pugs—only three of them now—were the same age, in dog years.

Toni turned to stare at Jonathan and his two mates, who were wrapping Lucien's daughter, Lizzy, in yards of ribbon. "Jonathan, I meant for you to decorate the *house,* not our niece."

"What?" their younger brother asked, his expression the very definition of innocence. "She said she wanted to be a Christmas tree." His friends collapsed in laughter.

"You would think they were six, rather than sixteen," Toni muttered.

Richard glanced around at the stately hall and staircase, which was full to overflowing with greenery. "It looks like a forest vomited in here."

Jonathan and his mates howled but Toni hit him in the arm. *Hard*.

"Dammit, Toni." Richard rubbed his shoulder.

"We could use your help," she said.

Richard laughed at that. "Maybe if you were decking the hall with beetles." He smiled at her look of disgust. "It's looking lovely," he lied, and then headed to the stables before somebody started decorating him.

He entered the courtyard just as Phil was mounting her dappled mare, which one of the children had humorously dubbed Thunder.

"Uncle Richard!"

"Richard!"

His nephew and second-youngest brother both shouted at the

same time, and then launched themselves at him, almost knocking him off his feet in their enthusiasm.

"You are coming with us, Rich," his sister-in-law said before Richard could offer.

He chuckled as the stable lad led out the mount he'd called down for. "Need some help, do you, Phil?"

She gave him a frazzled, withering look.

In a few minutes they were all mounted and headed out, the boys tearing ahead on their ponies, trying to shove each other off.

"To what do I owe this honor?" Phil asked once they were headed across the park.

"Why does there have to be a reason?" he asked, trying to mimic his brother Jonathan's innocent look.

Based on Phil's reaction—scoffing disbelief—he failed, terribly. "Being coy does not become you, Rich."

"Very well. I want to know why you've relented toward Dowden—especially when he was always such a beast to you."

She groaned. "It was all so long ago. You must resign yourself to his becoming your brother, Richard."

"I am already resigned, Phil. What I'd like to feel is something better than resignation. I'd like to feel sure that Toni knows enough about him to make her choice."

"I think that Toni has already made her choice," she reminded him gently.

So did Richard, and the thought left him profoundly unhappy.

They rode in silence as he tried to come up with some other way to phrase what he meant.

Nothing came to him.

"You've spoken to her?" Phil asked.

Richard frowned. "Spoken to Toni? Of course I—"

"Not Toni, Richard—Mrs. Pelham."

Richard swiveled his body toward his sister-in-law, giving her his full attention. How the devil had they gotten to Mrs. Pelham?

But Phil was now staring straight ahead, studiously avoiding his gaze. "Marcus, stop baiting your uncle and trying to make him perform circus tricks on his pony."

"Sorry, Mama," Marcus said, and then proceeded to lure his young uncle into yet another race.

Richard and Phil rode for a moment in silence, watching the children.

"Well?" Phil prodded.

"Yes, I've spoken to Mrs. Pelham."

I've kissed her, too. We also indulged in a bit of mutually satisfactory groping. I'd like to pursue both activities further, however only a dog would hound a woman who was the next thing to a powerless servant, and without a friend in the world and nobody to protect her. I might as well pester that pretty little housemaid who was tidying my bedchamber.

The last thought revolted him—as it should. Entertaining amorous thoughts about one's subordinates was the act of a predator.

So why aren't you revolted by your lustful desire for Mrs. Pelham?

"Rich?"

"Hmm?"

"Mrs. Pelham," she said with exaggerated patience.

"Oh. Well, Mrs. Pelham is not the same person she once was, I think."

"What do you mean?"

"I think she regrets what happened."

Phil barked a laugh. "I should think she does."

"Not only because of what happened to *her*," Richard clarified. "I think she regrets being so spiteful. Especially to you."

"She said she was sorry for that?"

"Er, no, but she admitted she'd been horrid to you."

"She was certainly that."

Richard felt torn. He abhorred prying into people's personal business, yet on this trip he seemed to be doing nothing *but* prying. He couldn't seem to stop himself.

His brother and Phil were in pain over something that simply did not matter any longer. Perhaps Lucien and Mrs. Pelham had once loved each other, but Richard was sure that was not the case any longer.

Based on what evidence?

Richard shivered at that question. He *never* made important decisions without ample study, consideration, and evidence and yet here he was, doing exactly that.

This is different, he told himself.

His inner voice laughed.

"I do not think Luce is still in love with her."

There, he'd said it.

Rather than look pleased, Phil glared at him. "I resent your impertinence, Richard."

"I didn't mean to be impertinent. I'm merely no good when it comes to talking about such matters."

"I couldn't agree more."

His face heated at her well-deserved scolding. His first reaction was to stop talking about something that he'd already discussed too freely.

But then an image of his brother's gaunt, lined face flickered into his mind's eye.

He'd already made an arse of himself—why not complete the job thoroughly?

"Even an unobservant lump like myself can see that you and Luce are not happy. He is my twin and I feel his unhappiness keenly. If that unhappiness is in any way due to a misconception, then I feel compelled to do all I can to help correct it."

The muscles and tendons in her jaw flexed beneath her smooth, pale skin, and Richard—as inept as he was at reading emotions—could read his sister-in-law's face clearly: she was experiencing an agony of indecision. It was an unusual look for Phil as she was usually such a self-assured woman.

"How do you know?" she asked in a choked voice.

Richard didn't have to ask her what she meant. "I know he doesn't love her because we spoke of her—of her presence here—and his reaction made his feelings clear."

"What reaction—what feelings?"

"He is far more concerned about how her presence is affecting *you*. He exhibited no desire to see or talk to her, Phil. Her presence here pains him. All he wants is to make sure you are not hurt."

"I *saw* them together."

Richard shrugged. "Yes, I saw them, too—so did a dozen other people. They looked like two strangers who'd accompanied each other to an afternoon function. Whatever they talked about—the weather, the upcoming wedding, or what happened ten years ago—neither of them looked euphoric, despondent, or anything other than polite."

"You said Lucien looks haggard and unhappy."

"Yes."

Her mouth worked, as if she were struggling with a particularly unappetizing mouthful of food. "How do you know the pain he is feeling is not that he can see and speak to his *love*"—her lips twisted as she spat out the word—"but she is still out of reach?" She turned away, but not before he saw the glassy look to her eyes.

"I know that is not the case because he's looked this way since I returned home—before she arrived."

"He was ill not two months ago, with an influenza that laid many people low. Perhaps *that* is what you've noticed."

Richard sighed and considered her original question. How did he know that Luce no longer loved Mrs. Pelham? Or was he just telling himself that because *he* had an interest in her?

Is that what you call that thing in your buckskins? An interest?

Richard scowled and dragged his attention back to Phil's question.

"It pains me to say it, but the reason I believe what I do is based on my intuition as his twin."

Phil's head swiveled back toward him and she gaped. *"Intuition?"*

Richard's face flamed. "Yes, yes, I know. Please don't *ever* tell your father I said that," he pled, only partly in jest. "He'd have my qualifications revoked or repudiated or some such thing. But that is the truth, Phil—I know my brother. Whatever he feels about Celia Pelham is not love. It is closer to annoyance. Almost as if she arrived just in time to frustrate something he'd planned."

Phil started at his last words, her eyes wide.

"You are his wife—why don't you ask him?"

She snorted. "Oh, how delightful to get advice from a confirmed bachelor on the subject of marriage."

Richard felt as though she'd struck him across the face with her crop.

Just then, Marcus and Jason came trotting toward them. "Please, Uncle Richard," Marcus said, "you promised us a race."

He smiled at his nephew and half brother and nodded. "A race it is."

Chapter 23

Lucien stared unseeingly at the pile of correspondence that his secretary had left stacked on his desk as Richard's words of a half hour earlier still rang in his ears.

He thought there might be something wrong with his twin; Richard had actually been *lying* in wait for Lucien—like some sort of big-game hunter—and had leapt out of the billiards room and grabbed him by the arm.

"Ah, just the man I'm looking for." He'd smirked in an almost maniacal fashion and then yanked Lucien into the billiards room, but not to play billiards.

"I'm busy, Rich—what do you want?"

"I've been thinking."

"Oh? Does it hurt?" Lucien took pleasure in using one of his brother's favorite lines against him.

Instead of looking annoyed, Richard just grinned. "It warms the cockles of my heart to know that you've learned from me, Brother." He'd frowned. "What exactly *are* heart cockles, do you think?"

Lucien sighed. "What do you want?"

"I was out riding with Phil and the children yesterday morning—"

"How nice for you." Lucien ignored the stab of jealousy he felt at his brother's words.

"—and something struck me," Richard continued, apparently not hearing him.

"I'm all agog, Brother."

"You need to court Phil."

"What?"

"You need to court her."

"Court her?" Lucien repeated, sounding remarkably like one of the huge parrots currently shouting expletives at each other in his library.

Richard nodded authoritatively, as if he were putting one of his bizarre naturalist arguments before a committee. "Remember you said to me, the morning we went hunting, that—"

"Yes, yes, yes," Lucien said. "You don't need to repeat what I said." He foolishly glanced around, as if somebody might be lurking in the billiards room listening to their conversation. "I wish I'd never said it, because it wasn't true." And he'd felt like a bloody fool ever since.

Once again, Richard didn't seem to hear him. "It occurred to me that the, er, distance between you might be because you never had an opportunity to court her properly." Richard flushed at whatever he saw on Lucien's face and raised his hands. "Before you bite off my head, just listen. In the normal course of events a young woman and man spend time together before they become betrothed. But the two of you hadn't even met until the Stanford ball. And then you were married, and then there was Phil's presentation—a horrifying event for anyone. My point is, you were both pitchforked into marriage without knowing each other. Have you ever stopped to get to know each other, er, romantically?" His face had been flaming by the end of his tirade.

Lucien had been so stunned that his coldly scientific brother—a man who steadfastly refused to admit that love even existed—was talking about courtship, that he'd almost swallowed his own tongue.

Richard had chuckled nervously. "I know I'm no expert. All I'm saying is this: I notice that your wife spends more time with your secretary than—"

Lucien's body was in motion before he knew what he was doing, and he'd slammed Richard up against the wall. "Have a care what you say, *Brother*," he'd snarled, his face less than an inch from his twin. Lucien could hardly see Richard's startled face through the red haze clouding his vision.

Richard being Richard—which was to say the most bizarre man in Britain—had laughed. Not a chuckle, but a big belly laugh.

Lucien had dropped his hands and stepped back to stare at this person who looked exactly like him but who could hardly be more different. "What the devil is wrong with you?"

"Oh, Luce." Richard had clutched his stomach as if he were in pain. "You poor bastard."

Lucien briefly considered hitting his brother over the head with one of the pool cues that was conveniently close to hand. "What is so bloody funny, *Richard*?"

"Don't you see?" Richard had asked, wiping the tears from his cheeks. "You're in *love*, old man."

Lucien had stormed from the room in disgust after that.

And then he'd come to his study to stare at his desk like a man in a stupor.

"My lord?" William Payson was standing in front of his desk looking down at him, a notch of concern between his eyes.

"What is it?" Luce asked.

"Er, you sent for me, sir."

"I did?" Lucien racked his brain to recall what it was he'd been going to say. He noticed the pile of letters. Yes, that was it—letters.

He gestured to the correspondence. "Do any of these need my immediate attention, Mr. Payson?" He bloody well hoped not, because he had the attention span of his eight-year-old son this morning. Actually, that was probably maligning poor Marcus, who could be quite persistent when it came to matters like pestering Luce for a new hunt pony. Which reminded him . . .

"Just the letter from Sir Robert Peel on top, my lord."

"Ah, good. I'll give that a look right away. Before I forget, do you know when Marcus and Lizzy's new mounts are due to arrive?" His daughter was already an avid equestrienne and Lucien had been teaching her on Marcus's pony, but she'd been demanding a horse of her own.

"That letter is in the stack as well, sir. The duchess promises to have them here by Christmas Eve."

"Eva wrote to me herself?" Lucien asked, not waiting for an answer before flicking through the letters until he saw the ducal seal of the Duchess of Tyne.

He grinned when he saw Eva's messy scrawl across the elegant stationery; the woman hated writing letters and usually had her secretary draft them.

When Lucien had been younger, he'd been madly in love with Eva de Courtney, as she'd been called before her marriage. But the willful beauty had had no time for either Luce or Rich, both of whom had followed her around like puppies the summer they'd been sixteen.

Lucien read through the brief letter, his eyes dropping to the postscript.

P.S. Please stop your stepfather from naming hunters from my stable things like Buttercup, Cherry Tart, or Snugglekins—it is mortifying to put such names in the breeding book.

Lucien laughed out loud. He'd have to give this to Hugh to read—the other man would get a—

The library door opened and Lucien looked up.

He stood when he saw it was his wife. "Ah, good afternoon, my lady."

Phyllida gave Lucien her characteristic distant smile; it was significantly frostier than usual after his truncated visit to her bedchamber the other night. "Good afternoon, Davenport."

When she turned to Payson, her entire expression changed to one that she never used with Lucien: friendly and open. "Ah, Will. I was hoping to find you here."

William Payson's pale cheeks flushed at her warm greeting—so pronounced after the chilly way she'd spoken to Lucien.

Whatever he saw on Lucien's face made his color deepen. "How may I serve you, my lady?"

"We've wrapped all the toys and I'm ready to bring them to the orphanage."

William turned to Lucien. "Did you need me for anything just now, my lord?"

Lucien sat back in his chair and looked from his employee's red face to his wife's coolly distant one.

He heard Richard's voice: *Court her.*

Phyllida was absently smoothing the fingers of her gloves, which were a shade of emerald kid that was particularly flattering to her sea-colored eyes. She was avoiding Lucien's gaze and it occurred to him that she could just as well have sent a servant to fetch Mr. Payson. Indeed, that would be far more like her. She almost never interrupted him in his study.

So why was she here today?

Court her. You've never courted your own wife.

The words were like a mallet to his forehead, and he stared at the two people in front of him.

For years he'd known that William spent more time with Phyllida than he did. He told himself it was the way of the *ton.* Some women had cicisbeos, but his wife was too practical for such foolishness.

William, the son of a gentleman, was the perfect companion for all those charitable events, educational talks, and other functions that Lucien didn't have either the time or inclination to attend.

In essence, his secretary had managed Lucien's wife as much as the man managed all his correspondence.

Hell, the man had even purchased parting gifts for several of his mistresses, back when he'd kept them.

But never for my wife. Only I *have chosen Phyllida's gifts.*

Somehow that wasn't very reassuring.

"Is aught amiss, Davenport?" his wife said, her look of concern telling him that he was behaving strangely.

"Your mother and father must be here by now?" he asked William, who was the youngest son of Squire Leonard Payson, one of Lessing Hall's nearest neighbors.

"Er, yes, my lord. They arrived last week."

Lucien smiled, not taking his gaze from Phyllida's narrowing eyes. "Actually, William, why don't you take today off. In fact," he said, his smile growing in direct proportion to his wife's glower, "I shan't need you until after Boxing Day."

William's eyes darted back and forth between his master and mistress. "Er, but Lady Davenport—"

"I shall escort Lady Davenport to any of her obligations."

William hesitated, and then said to Phyllida, "Was there anything—"

"I don't need you," her ladyship said shortly, her gaze burning a hole through Lucien's head. "You deserve a holiday."

"Excellent," Lucien said before the younger man could dither any longer. "Give your family our felicitations and enjoy yourself."

"Thank you, sir." William gave him a puzzled smile, cut Lady Davenport a nervous look, and then scooped up his satchel, which sat ready and waiting beside his smaller desk.

Phyllida spun on her heel and marched toward the door, apparently intending to accompany him out.

"Might I have a word with you, my lady?"

She stopped, squared her shoulders, and turned. "Yes, my lord?"

They stared at each other—Phil silently seething—until the door closed softly behind Payson.

"How may I help you, sir?" she prodded when Lucien paused for a moment to enjoy the sight of his wife's small, stylishly dressed body.

He wasn't sure when the mere sight of her had become enough to make him harden, but he wanted her with a painful ache, and had done for longer than he could recall.

Perhaps it is only a matter of wanting what you cannot have?

No, he didn't think that was it. Not at all.

Luce knew she was furious and impatient to get on with a duty that would now take twice as long since he'd deprived her of her helper, but he was tired of constantly bowing to the exigencies of their busy life. He wanted to look at her. While he would have preferred to look at her naked, she was delightful garbed in her smart riding kit.

Her wool habit was trimmed with black leather and was the same jewel green as her kid gloves. She wore her tiny beaver shako at a jaunty angle and it bore three peacock feathers—yet more colors that suited her unusual eyes and flawless, pearly complexion.

He had watched her ride off in years past, sometimes with his parents, sometimes with his sister, and sometimes with Payson, always mounted on her favorite cover-hack. Following her was at least one wagon—sometimes two—heaped with thoughtfully chosen gifts for their tenants.

She was beloved by the people who lived on his land and made sure to have gifts delivered at Lucien's other three estates, even on those years when they could not find time to visit personally.

And, right now, she was very, very annoyed with him.

"My lord?" She shifted from one foot to the other, the fidget uncharacteristic.

Lucien looked from her slender body to her frowning face and smiled. "I will go to the orphanage with you today, Phyllida—it occurs to me that I've never been." Lucien saw that his offer surprised her.

Whether she was pleasantly surprised, Lucien could not tell.

Chapter 24

Richard was lurking. There was no other word for it but lurking.

Toni, Dowden, and most of their guests, including old Lady Yancy and Lady Morton, had left shockingly early—to hear the younger crowd tell it—to go junketing off to the sprawling Christmas fair that was held just outside Bexhill every year.

His mother was in the library, somehow able to work on her latest paper even with the two parrots going at it hammer and tongs.

Hugh, along with Richard's younger brothers, was out on Jonathan's yawl.

And Luce and Phil, he'd been *very* interested to notice, had gone off *together* to deliver a wagonload of toys to an orphanage.

That left a house that was largely occupied by servants.

And Mrs. Pelham.

He knew she was somewhere in the house because he'd watched as the carriages had loaded up to leave: no Mrs. Pelham.

He'd not seen her for over twenty-four hours, and he didn't like it. Today he was going to see her, no matter how slyly he needed to go about it.

It was, he supposed, possible that she'd sneaked out while he was in the breakfast room. But, otherwise, he'd positioned himself in the sunroom, with the door open, which gave him an excellent view of the stairs she would use if she left the suite of rooms she shared with her mistress.

Richard took out his watch; it was approaching noon. He'd been sitting and not-working on his paper for almost two hours.

He sighed, stacked up his notes, and stood.

And then he heard footsteps on the marble stairs and looked up just as Mrs. Pelham walked past the sunroom.

He left his papers and strode after her; he'd only gone a few steps when she glanced over her shoulder and then stopped.

She stared straight ahead for a long moment before sighing heavily and then turning. "Mr. Redvers." She dropped a stiff curtsey.

Ah, they were going to pretend what happened in the portrait gallery never happened?

Richard gave her a courtly bow fit for a king, pleased to see she was wearing an amused smirk when he met her gaze.

"You are dressed to go out," he observed.

"Yes."

"Where are you going?"

She pursed her lips. "Don't worry, I'm not going back to your brother's boat. Although . . ." She frowned and then opened the battered brown leather satchel she had with her, almost identical to the one he used, and pulled out a small velvet box.

"Here." She held out the box; she was wearing the same mittens she'd worn at the picnic and also that first night, when she'd walked the dog. Did she not own a proper pair of gloves?

The notion that she didn't was oddly bothersome.

"Well?" she asked when he continued to stare at her hand, which was now clutching her satchel, as if she were trying to hide her ragged mitten.

"Well what?"

"Open the box."

He did so; it contained a rather pretty necklace and earbobs. He looked up. "Very nice. Garnets?" he asked, somehow doubting she'd possess rubies.

She made a sound that was half laugh and half snort. "Jonathan gave them to me—at least I believe it was he. I didn't know the other boys in his garland-hunting group. It was one of their prizes," she added when Richard continued to look puzzled.

"Ah, that's right. It was his group that won." He frowned. "This was what he won?"

"Apparently there weren't enough swords or whatever to go around, so he got that."

Richard handed the box back to her. But she shook her head. "No, I don't want it."

"What do you want me to do with it?"

"I don't care."

"What were you going to do with it if you hadn't seen me today?"

"Give it back to your brother." She hesitated, grimaced, and then said, "Along with the letter he sent."

"You said you didn't know who it was from."

She gave him a look that indicated he was being an idiot.

"What does the letter say?"

"It's a private correspondence," she said, her tone chiding.

He continued to hold out the box. "Well, you can give it back to him if you think that is necessary."

"You don't think it is—necessary to return it, I mean?"

"It's a trifle that he had no use for. Why shouldn't he give it to a pretty girl?"

"I'm not a *girl*, Mr. Redvers."

Richard was amused by her chilling tone.

"I'd rather you returned it to him," she insisted.

"So, you're asking me for a favor?"

"I'm asking for your help because I know you don't wish me anywhere near your young, clearly impressionable brother."

Richard was bored with the subject of Jonathan. "You never told me where you were going."

She glared, gave an irritated huff, but snatched the box from his hand, dumping it back into her bag. "Why do you care?"

"Because I've been waiting for you." He smiled at her nonplussed expression. "I'm sorry, I daresay that was too direct. But I am dismal at flirtation. The truth is that I need your help with something," Richard lied. He'd spent a good deal of time coming up with an excuse that would convince her.

"So, you're asking me for a favor?" she asked, her words a mocking echo of his own.

"Yes. I have yet to buy several Christmas gifts."

"Why didn't you go with the others to the fair?"

"There are far too many tents and booths at the fair. I wish to shop somewhere more limited."

She laughed. "You have to be the only person in Britain who wishes for *less* choice."

"I doubt it. I'm sure there are plenty of men—and probably some women, too—who find excessive variety overwhelming. Besides, I didn't wish to be crowded into a carriage for hours on end just to do a bit of shopping." When she only stared, he said, "Where were you going?"

He thought she might tell him to go to the devil. But then she said, "As it happens, I was reading this." She rooted around in her bag, extracted a book, and handed it to him.

"Ah," he said. "A guidebook. Going to look at St. Mary's?"

"Yes, and also the Lushington monument."

"Mmmm-hmmm." He opened the book to the page she'd marked, his eyes skimming over the story. "You have an interest in the Black Hole of Calcutta atrocity?"

"I'd heard of it, of course, but not read extensively about it."

"Well, I'm not sure this account is honest—this is double the number of prisoners I've read about." He looked up and handed her the book. "But it is true that a good many men died horrifically in a short amount of time." He cocked his head. "If you help me choose my gifts, I'll take you to the Pig for more of that hot chocolate you consumed with such unladylike haste."

"You have quite the silver tongue, Mr. Redvers."

Richard grinned in what he hoped was a winning manner.

She heaved an exaggerated sigh. "Well, you drive a hard bargain. I suppose I could help." She tucked her book back into her satchel. "Who usually manages such purchases for you?"

"Luce is dashed clever at buying for ladies, but he's busy today." He glanced down at her shoes, pleased to see she was wearing sturdy-looking half boots. "I'm afraid the only conveyance left on the property is the gig—it's not exactly luxurious."

She laughed but made no comment.

"Who cares for Percy while you're gone out?" he asked as they made their way toward the north exit.

"One of the footmen offered to walk him this afternoon."

Richard just bet the male servants were lining up to offer pet-care.

He couldn't really blame them.

What are you doing, Celia? What are you doing?

The question was going around and around in her head, but she had no answer—other than the foolish truth: she was going to spend the day with a member of the Redvers family, explicitly against Sebastian's instructions.

But Sebastian won't know because he is gone to the fair with his betrothed and all the others.

The voice in her head ignored her.

Celia couldn't blame her inner companion; she *was* foolish.

Sebastian wasn't the only danger; there was Richard, himself—and the effect he had on her.

She tried to keep from touching Richard's body but the gig seat was so narrow that was impossible.

Celia glanced at his profile; was he *smiling*?

"What?" he asked rudely, his smirk growing.

"This is rather cozy, isn't it?"

"You could always ride in the back." He gestured to the straw-filled wagon bed.

"Very droll."

He just smiled.

"All right," she said, opening her satchel, taking out her sketchpad and graphite stick, and turning to a new page. "Whom do you need to buy gifts for?"

He raised an eyebrow in that maddening way.

"What?" she demanded, just as rudely as he just had.

"I'm impressed that you carry a notebook and writing implement in your bag."

Celia refused to be pleased by praise for such an inconsequential matter.

"Why do you keep such a large notebook?" he asked.

She shrugged, the action inadvertently rubbing her arm up and down his. She inched away, or at least tried to. "It is for sketching—not notes."

"Let me see some of your sketches," he said.

Celia snorted. "No."

Rather than be offended, he grinned. "Why not? I sketch a bit, myself."

Celia clucked her tongue at his understatement. "You forget that I've *seen* your drawings, sir." And they were jaw-dropping in detail, so lifelike they looked as if they might crawl right off the page. Perhaps not the best thing for a nine-inch beetle, but the butterflies had been gorgeous. "Did you take drawing instruction?" she asked.

"No. I'm not really very good—I'm not," he insisted when she scoffed. "You should see Phil's father's drawings. Sir Gael could have been an artist if he'd not been a naturalist." He slanted her a look. "Is that why you don't want to show me? You're intimidated? Or is there another reason?" A slow, sinfully handsome smile stretched across his face. "Are there drawings of me in there, Mrs. Pelham? Is that what you don't wish me to see?"

"Let's see—that's no, no, no, no, and no, again," she lied. Actually, she had several pages of sketches of him.

He chuckled and the low, masculine sound suffused her body with warmth—almost enough to drive the chill from her fingers.

"Are those the best gloves you have?" he demanded, staring at her hands, which she was unconsciously flexing.

"You are very nosy. Has anyone ever told you that?"

"All the time," he said mildly.

"Gifts," she repeated, tapping the sketchbook.

"Everyone."

"What? You've not bought anyone anything?"

He shrugged at her disbelief. "There's loads of time yet."

"Six days. Well, five and a half, if you want to be precise."

He turned to her. "I adore precision, Miss Trent." His eyes, usually so golden brown, darkened beneath his lowered lids.

Celia swallowed and stared at the blank page as if it were a lifeline rather than mere paper. "So, that is the baron, your mother, your sister—and *how* many brothers do you have?"

"Five."

"Goodness. I've only seen the two."

"The others are still in short pants. In fact, two of them are younger than Luce's two."

"So, toys, then?"

He wrinkled his nose, the boyish expression adorable on his strong, chiseled features. "I usually give books."

"What, improving tomes?"

He chuckled. "No, books about insects, plants, animals, that sort of thing."

"Can you find those in Eastbourne?" she asked doubtfully.

"There is a fine bookshop in town."

"So that leaves the adults. Your mother?"

"A book."

Celia laughed.

"What?" he asked, genuinely confused.

"You asked me along to help you pick out books?"

Celia swore that the skin over his lovely cheekbones darkened.

"I'll get her a pair of gloves," he said after a long moment.

"You think she'll like that?"

"She's always losing one glove of a pair; she'll appreciate it," he said, sounding certain.

"All right, gloves. And Lady Davenport?"

He grimaced. "Ugh. This is giving me a headache." He scowled at her when she laughed. "That's unkind. I despise shopping."

"Well, you're in luck today, Mr. Redvers, because I adore it."

Four hours later, Richard realized that she hadn't been speaking in jest.

The bookshop had been a joy. Not so much the dress shop—shawls for Toni and Phil—the milliner's for a hideous bejeweled and feathered turban decoration for his Aunt Amelia—and now, the glover's.

"This one, or this one?" She held up two different gloves. They were *surrounded* by gloves.

Richard groaned. "I'm tired. And hungry," he whined.

She just chuckled, as he'd hoped she would. Her laughter was proving remarkably addictive.

"Pick one pair and then we can have some hot chocolate."

He perked up. "Put one of each on, so I can compare them."

"But my hands are not the same size as your mother's—she is four inches taller."

"Model them," he insisted "It will give me an idea." He already had ideas; none of them involved his mother.

Richard glanced around, his gaze immediately snagged by a pair of oxblood gloves lined with black fur. He gestured for the shopkeeper, who'd been circling like a buzzard. "Do you have these in the lady's size?"

"Oh, of course, Mr. Redvers." The clerk glanced at Mrs. Pelham's hands, opened a drawer beneath the counter and came up with a box with several other pairs. "Hmm, size six, I think."

They looked tiny. But then the hands that emerged from the horrid mittens were small and delicate. Just looking at her slender white fingers made his body heat. He was a very visual man and the visions her hands elicited were extremely arousing; thank God he was wearing his overcoat.

Richard watched her ethereally lovely face, rather than her hands, as she pulled on the gloves. Her soft smile and glowing eyes told him that she was enjoying trying on the expensive handwear. But there was a reserve beneath her pleasure, and he recognized it: it was the knowledge that she could not have them, and that it was better—safer and less painful—not to want them.

She glanced up and caught his gaze, her cheeks flaming at whatever she saw in his face—likely the raw desire he was feeling—then quickly looked away.

"What do you think?" she asked, looking everywhere except at Richard.

"I think my mother would prefer the blue," he said. To the clerk, he said, "The navy ones in size eight. Wrap them up and have them sent to the Hall, please."

"Of course, Mr. Redvers." The saleswoman hustled away, visibly pleased by the expensive purchase.

Richard turned back to Miss Trent; she was chewing her lower lip, her gaze on the red gloves that were now back in the box.

"Ready for hot chocolate?" he asked.

She looked up; her smile a little too bright. "And some pastries?"

"Wait a minute—did I promise pastries, too?" he teased, opening the door for her. "I don't recall being so reckless."

"Yes—unlimited pastries were your words."

Out on the street he waited as she pulled on her pitiful mittens.

"Drat," he said.

"What is it?"

Richard held up one glove. "Would you believe I left my other glove in the glover's?"

She laughed. "You are quite the scatterbrain today. You left your hat in the modiste's, your cane in the milliner's, and now a glove in the glover's. It's a good thing your head is attached."

Oh, if she only knew . . .

"Shall we pop back in?" she asked.

"I'll do it—the Pig is just there." He pointed to the black and white public house, which was looking festive with pine garlands and holly berries festooning the little building. "I'll join you in a tick."

Richard watched her walk for a moment before turning back to the shop.

Are you sure you know what you're doing?

"It's only a bloody pair of gloves," he muttered under his breath as he pushed open the shop door.

And a gown, shoes, and some head frippery.

Richard ignored the mocking voice and smiled at the surprised clerk. "I decided I want those oxblood gloves after all—but in a size six, please."

Chapter 25

The South Sussex Home for Foundlings was an hour's ride from Lessing Hall.

They'd take Lucien's curricle and the fourgon, loaded with all the gifts, would follow them.

As he handed his wife into the smart rig he used all too rarely, Luce shook his head at John-Jacob, his favorite groom, who generally rode behind him. "You get to ride with the toys, John-Jacob."

The older man laughed. "Aye, my lord."

Lucien climbed in beside Phyllida, who was tucking the heavy fur rug over the jade green traveling costume she'd changed into. "Will you be warm enough?" he asked, settling beside her. "We could put the top up and send for another lap-rug?"

She glanced at the sky, which was the color of slate. "I'd rather leave the top down for the time being. And I am plenty warm. Here," she said when he lowered himself beside her, their hips and thighs touching on the narrow seat. She tucked the rug over his lap, needing to lean over him to do so.

Lucien's body—already primed just from this little bit of proximity—throbbed.

Phyllida looked up when she realized he'd gone still. "That should keep you warm," she said, pink-cheeked.

"Thank you."

She nodded and looked away.

"Let 'em go," he told John-Jacob, who held the horses' heads.

Phobos and Deimos sprang forward and Phyllida laughed as Lucien let them have their heads on Lessing Hall's long driveway.

"Goodness! They're so frisky," she said, clutching her hat.

"It's probably wiser to allow them to kick up their heels for a bit," he said, glancing down at her. Her eyes sparkled and she looked like a young girl enjoying a treat. How was it he'd taken so long to realize that he would enjoy such a simple activity?

Why had he been a fool for so damned long?

Phil was afraid that she was too happy.

I wonder if you know how ridiculous that sounds?

She grimaced; it *did* sound ridiculous. But it was better than becoming accustomed to something only to have it yanked away.

Perhaps he was only paying attention to her because there was nobody else? After all, his mistress—whoever she was—would be in London and his needs would be going unmet.

Good, that's good—think about his mistress. That should take care of any excessively happy feelings.

It had. Immediately.

Whoever Lucien's lover had been these past six or seven years, he'd been extremely discreet.

After that horrid time overhearing women gossip about him, she'd never heard another peep.

"The new horses will be here by Christmas Eve."

Phil turned at the sound of his voice, needing a minute to comprehend what he'd said; ah, yes—the gifts for the children.

"That will be perfect," she said. "I'm afraid Marcus has taken to visiting the stables once an hour to check and see. The last time I caught him, he had Lizzy with him. Now they are *both* pestering poor Mr. Standish."

Lucien chuckled. "Well, I have to admit it feels good to know that we are getting them such perfect gifts. Marc has outgrown Prince and Lizzy is ready for a mount with a bit more spunk than poor old Dobbin." He cut her a sideways look. "Do you think you will be all right with Lizzy joining the hunt next year?" he asked.

"Well, five is rather young, but Marcus loved it so—although I think he was most excited to be with you." Phil had been touched by how close Lucien had stayed to his young child, deferring his own pleasure in hunting to make sure his son was not frightened or hurt.

"It's rubbish hunting around these parts but it is a good place to start for the children." He cut her a glance. "It's a pity you don't care to go."

Phil blinked. "You mean you would not mind if I went with you?"

He gave her an odd look. "Of course I wouldn't mind—not if you cared for it."

"I thought—" Phil bit her lip.

"You thought what?"

"I just thought you didn't want to be burdened with an inferior rider."

"Phyllida—" And then he muttered something beneath his breath and shook his head.

"I'm sorry?"

"I said it feels damned ridiculous to keep calling you that when everyone else calls you Phil."

It was a day for surprises. "Why *do* you call me Phyllida? Not even my mother called me that," she added. When he didn't answer, she gave a breathy laugh. "I always thought that you didn't like my pet name—it is so mannish."

He slowed the pair and turned to her, his brown eyes darkening. "I like it very much. It's as if you are two persons—Phyllida is the sophisticated London hostess, and Phil is the girl who is game for anything."

"Hardly a girl," she demurred, mainly to hide her pleasure in his words.

They sat in silence for a long, charged moment. To Phil, it felt like those few times when a young man had asked her to dance and shown genuine interest in her. They were, she realized, engaging in mild flirtation.

Lucien said, "When you came to Lessing you weren't comfortable in the saddle."

"No," she agreed. "I'm afraid I did very little riding in Cambridge."

"And yet you took to it so quickly," he said, smiling at her. "You've an excellent seat—I saw you out riding with Rich and the boys and meant to comment on it."

He'd been watching her? He'd been impressed?

"I should have asked you to join me years ago." He held her gaze for a long moment. "I should have asked you many things years ago . . . Phil."

He seemed to struggle with himself, as if to say something, but then looked away. They were approaching the junction with the road up ahead and he needed to pay attention to the horses.

That was just as well, because Phil could barely hear, her heart was thudding so loudly in her ears.

Her husband thought she was a good rider; he wanted her with him.

He wanted to call her Phil.

Those might be small things to other women but Phil felt as if she would explode if she didn't let some of the happiness out.

"I would like to go with you and the children . . . Lucien."

His lips curved into a smile, but he stared straight ahead, slowing the pair slightly before turning onto the narrow, rutted road.

Once they were on the main road, he turned to her, looking almost as joyful as Phil felt.

"I should like that too, Phil—a great deal. I'll talk to Eva about a hunter for you. Next year we can all ride together—as a family."

Chapter 26

Richard realized he'd been gritting his teeth and forced himself to relax.

Yet again, Mrs. Pelham hadn't been at dinner last night.

Nor had he seen her on his walks with Newton.

Nor was she in the breakfast room when he'd entered bright and early this morning.

Indeed, he'd seen nothing of her since their ride home in the gig yesterday. And, oh, what a ride it had been.

He'd felt as if he were in a snow globe. It had been . . . magical—there was no other word for it—the snow blanketing them as they trundled along in the sturdy little cart, packed nice and tight together on the narrow seat. She'd smelled of woman and chocolate and the ineffable scent of freshly fallen snow.

It had been . . . romantic.

Richard bit back a groan at his idiocy and turned his mind back to Mrs. Pelham and her annoying disappearing act.

Even a fool could figure out that she'd been coming to meals before Dowden's arrival, and now she was hiding in her room—or her employer's room.

If the duke was threatening her in some way, Richard wanted to know about it.

Still, there was nothing he could do if the woman wouldn't talk to him. He'd given her plenty of opportunities during their shopping expedition yesterday, bringing Dowden up several times, usually in conjunction with Toni's name. He knew he was the farthest thing from subtle—she must have guessed what he was asking.

But she'd confided nothing. Indeed, she'd almost seemed . . . frightened when the man's name came up.

Richard frowned down at the article he was meant to be reading and enjoying but had not understood a word of.

Put her out of your mind, old chap. This cannot end—

Toni burst into the room, a whirlwind in woolen skirts. "Ah! There you are."

Richard looked up at his sister, a sinking feeling in his gut. "Was I supposed to be somewhere else?"

"One hour until the snowman building contest."

Richard squinted. "Come again?"

She made a low, almost feral, growling sound. "Snowman. Building. Contest. What about that is vague?"

"Er . . ."

"I want Mama to judge, but—well, Mama has refused to cooperate, point blank."

Richard bit his lip to hide his smile.

"I'm so pleased to amuse you," she said, making him realize he'd not hidden his amusement well enough

"I'll talk to Mama," he said.

"Oh. Good—I'm sure you can convince her." She paused and gave him a narrow-eyed look. "Since you're her favorite."

Richard grinned; this was a common complaint among his siblings. Everyone was convinced that somebody else was Mama's favorite.

He turned to leave but her next words stopped him.

"Luce and Phil went off again today—some do or other at Lord Bexhill's." She paused and chewed her lip, seemed about to say something, but then shook her head. "So I need you to make up the tenth team."

"You want *ten* teams?"

"Mmm-hmm," she said, jotting something down—probably Richard's name—on the infernal lists she carried about with her.

"I'm terribly uncreative—you know that. Why don't you ask Hugh—"

"He and Jonathan are partners."

Richard perked up at that information. Beating Hugh at anything was always enjoyable. The man was the most competitive person he'd ever met and he had no qualms about cheating shamelessly. And Jonathan was almost as dismal as Richard when it came to artistic endeavors.

Hmmm, this might be entertaining . . .

"Who are you partnering me with?" he asked.

"If you can't get Mama to judge, maybe you can talk her into competing. You know how she loves to clobber Papa."

"That's true."

"Or you could ask Sebastian or John or Montgomery," she said, her look hopeful as she named her fiancé and his two best friends, whom Richard had seen arriving late last night. Back in the day, the two men had joined in tormenting Richard almost as enthusiastically as their ringleader.

Richard didn't tell his sister that he'd sooner gargle nails than do anything with any of the three, but she must have recognized his expression.

Toni heaved a sigh of annoyance. "Go try the music room—I saw five or six people in there a half hour ago. Surely one of them will meet your exacting standards."

Or you could find Celia . . .

"Well?" she demanded, her boot *tap-tap-tap*ping on the wooden floor. "Can you manage this yourself, or do you need my assistance?"

"Don't worry about me," he said, smirking. "I'll be ready and raring to go when the time comes."

* * *

"Mrs. Pelham."

Celia leapt a good foot in the air, dropped the little metal bucket of food, and screamed before spinning around.

"Are you *mad* to be sneaking up on someone like that?" she demanded, clutching her chest, as if that would somehow stop the pounding of her heart.

Richard bent and picked up the bucket that had fortunately landed on its bottom rather than its side. He examined the contents of the small pail. "Hmmm, dried cobs of corn and shriveled apples." He looked up at her. "You told me that Lady Yancy had a strange diet."

She couldn't help laughing. "I *was* going to feed Alexander, before you frightened me half to death."

"I'll go with you."

"I don't need—"

"I'm sure you don't," he said, striding toward the library so that all she could do was follow. "Where have you been hiding, Mrs. Pelham?"

"I haven't been hiding."

"*Tsk, tsk.* No fibbing, now," he said, opening one of the massive library doors and waiting for her to enter.

Celia flounced—yes, she did—into the massive, toasty room.

You're only flouncing to hide your happiness at seeing him, Celia. You can't fool me.

No, but maybe I can fool Richard.

Alexander—who was standing on an open perch across from Lord Ramsay's foul parrot, the Great Sou'western—started bobbing wildly when he saw her. And then he crowed, sounding so much like a real cock that it was eerie.

Richard laughed, a rich, uncontrolled belly laugh, grinning at Celia as if *she'd* been the one to crow. "That's fantastic." He turned back to the bird. "Do it again," he ordered.

Celia snorted and took the bucket from his hand. "Don't waste your time. Alexander does only what he wants, when he wants. Doesn't he?" she asked the bird, scratching beneath his monstrous beak.

"Is he *purring*?" Richard asked.

The bird cocked its head, giving Richard a knowing look, and Celia could guess what Alexander was going to say.

"What does a kitty say?" Alexander squawked in a voice that sounded far too much like Lady Yancy for Celia's comfort.

Richard gave Celia a questioning look.

"Well?" she said, smirking. "What does a kitty say?"

"Um, *mreowwwww*?"

"There's a good pussy," Alexander praised.

"He's dicked in the nob!" the Great Sou'wester shouted, clearly unhappy at being left out.

"What does a froggy say?" Alexander shrieked back.

"Bird-witted fool!" the other parrot squawked.

And then it was parrot pandemonium.

"Now you've done it," Celia said, having to yell to be heard over the screeching of the birds.

"Good God," Richard shouted. "It's bloody deafening!"

Celia reached into the bucket and handed each bird a dried corncob.

Alexander snatched it from her hand like a gin addict grabbing at a fresh bottle. The other bird was less aggressive, but that was probably because he got the treats all the time. Alexander had never had dried corncobs before.

The silence—except for the sound of two giant beaks gnawing—was loud.

"Well, thank the lord for corn," Richard muttered, watching Celia as she filled each parrot's bowl with pieces of fruit, some chestnuts, and a mixture of grain.

When the bucket was empty, she could no longer ignore him. "What did you need?" she asked in an unfriendly voice.

"What is wrong?" he asked, coming toward her, his brow wrinkled with concern.

Celia could hardly tell him that Sebastian had paid her a midnight visit. He'd been furious when somebody let word slip that she'd spent the whole day with Richard. She had the bruises on her arms to prove his anger.

"Nothing," she said shortly, turning toward the door.

"Celia."

His voice was soft, yet she could not ignore him.

She spun around. "What do you want from me, sir?"

"What has happened since yesterday afternoon? I thought we enjoyed ourselves in Eastbourne. Did I do something wrong? I know I can be obtuse. If I did anything that—"

"You didn't do anything." She felt like an ogre for making him feel bad when all he'd done was give her the most wonderful day she'd had since she'd last seen Katie.

And that scared her even more than Sebastian's threats.

He closed the gap between them, until he was standing close enough that she caught a faint whiff of whatever intoxicating cologne he wore. Close enough that she could see the fine details of his face: a comma-shaped scar over his right cheekbone, the faint grooves bracketing his mobile, sensual lips, and the unspeakable beauty of his honey-brown eyes.

"What do you want, Richard?"

He jolted slightly and she knew he was surprised that she'd used his name. He'd asked her yesterday to call him Richard, but she'd resisted.

"I thought we had a good day."

She swallowed, looking down at the worn toes of her ankle boots. "It was a lovely day," she said, hoarsely.

His warm, slightly calloused fingers slid beneath her chin and tilted it up and up until she couldn't avoid his dilated gaze. His chest was rising and falling as fast as hers.

"Celia."

She swallowed at the sound of her name on his tongue—a loud, gulping, mortifying sound. "Yes," she whispered, her voice a husk.

"I want you to be my partner in the snowman building contest."

It was so utterly absurd and unexpected—and so Richard—that she gave a snorting laugh.

He grinned, his expression one of pure joy. "There, that's better." His right eyebrow rose. "Will you? There are prizes, hot chocolate, and apple buns, and the opportunity to thrash an infamously competitive ex-privateer and perhaps even make him cry." He released her chin, and it was a struggle not to follow his hand, to press her face into the comforting strength of his palm.

"So, what say you?" he asked, his face eager and hopeful because this man did not dissemble.

Celia, the warning voice in her head said. *You need to go back to your room. Or go hide in that tiny parlor you found under the stairs. Or—*

"You really think we could make Lord Ramsay cry?" she asked.

He laughed. "I'm sure of it."

"Just let me go and get my cloak, hat, and mittens," she said, her grin as big as his.

Chapter 27

"This isn't *fair,*" Hugh complained—for the third time—to Toni and all the others who'd gathered around Richard and Celia's masterpiece.

"Nothing quite like hearing a grown man blubber, is there, Mrs. Pelham?" Richard asked in an exaggerated whisper.

The small crowd laughed but Hugh cut Richard a menacing, narrow-eyed piratical look.

"It's supposed to be a snow*man,*" Jonathan said, his voice just as whiney as his father's. "Not a snow*beetle.*"

"Specifically, it's a snow *oryctes nasicornis,*" Celia corrected, her smug smile so adorable that it was all Richard could do not to scoop her up in his arms and spirit her away to a secret lair—if only he had such a thing.

"Well . . ." Toni said, unable to suppress her amusement as she looked at her father's grumpy face. "I suppose we could—"

"My goodness."

Everyone turned at the sound of the new voice.

It was Richard's mother, and she was staring fixedly at Richard and Celia's creation.

"Why, it's a snow beetle. How charming." She gave one of her rare laughs. The low, slightly snorting chuckle made Richard grin just to hear it. "It's magnificent. However did you get the legs to stick out like that?"

"They *cheated*," Hugh said, glaring at his wife.

"No," Toni said, "they used branches—just like everyone else, only they used them more, er . . ."

"Cleverly," Richard supplied. He smirked down at his partner. It had been Celia's idea to pack the snow around each branch, wet it a bit, and then pack more snow and shape the appendages. As a result, they had six remarkably beetle-ish looking legs and even a little rhinoceros horn.

Hugh scowled at his wife, who was still admiring the snow beetle. "What are you doing here?"

"I'm one of the judges," she said.

Hugh flung up his hands. "Well, *this* isn't fair."

"Have you ever seen such terrible sportsmanship?" Richard asked Celia.

"It's shocking." Celia frowned at Hugh and Jonathan's snowman. "And I've never seen such a terrible snow—well, I'm not sure what it is."

Jonathan crossed his arms. "What's wrong with it?"

"What's wrong with its head?" Richard asked.

"It's more of a snow*creature*," Celia said.

Jonathan made a strangled noise and turned to Hugh.

Hugh's expression promised retribution.

Celia and Richard sniggered.

Fragments of sentences drifted toward them over the din:

"—should have built a snowturtle," somebody complained.

"Never heard of such a thing," Stephanie said to her partner, a strapping young lad with a lovely profile and a vapid expression, as they hovered possessively around the voluptuous snowwoman they'd created, complete with a generous bosom.

"Disqualified."

"Not fair."

"My nose is freezing."

These were some of the other comments.

"Everyone," Toni called out over the babble of voices. "All three judges are here." She gestured to Richard's mother, Will Standish—Hugh's childhood friend and also the master of his stables—and Watson, their butler. "Let's give them an opportunity to consider the entries without coercion and *in peace*," she added when Hugh moved toward Standish and Watson.

The various teams drifted away, forming two-person cabals who stared suspiciously at one another.

Beside him, Celia smacked her mittens together. They were knitted from thick wool and the snow tended to stick to them in clumps. Richard wished he'd sneaked the new red gloves into her room somehow.

"Cold?" he asked.

She looked up at him, her delicate nose rose-tinted on the tip. "A little."

"Let me see."

Her forehead furrowed. "What do—"

He slipped off one of her mittens and scowled. Her slender white fingers were red and chapped. Richard pulled off his gloves and handed them to her. "Put these on."

"I don't—"

He raised his eyebrow and gave her the look his family feared, pleased when it seemed to work on Celia, too.

"Fine." She snatched the gloves from him and shoved her hands inside. "Ooh," she said, her eyes going wide as she buried her fingers in the warm fur.

"There, you see?"

She made a purring sound that went straight to his groin. "Thank you." She tucked her hands into her pockets, her cheeks turning pinker, and not from the cold, he suspected.

"Would you like—"

"You see who is here, Monty?" Dowden boomed out behind them, loud enough to make Richard jump.

Because Richard was looking right at Celia, the transformation that occurred on her face at the sound of the duke's voice was all the more striking.

It put him in mind of a house that had been lively and warm and welcoming—and then instantly became a burnt-out, empty shell.

She turned slowly as Dowden and his two mates approached them.

All three men wore the sort of smarmy smile that brought to mind back-alley pimps or hole-in-corner perverts.

And they were all looking at Celia.

"Well, it has been a long time, Celia," Monty said, his use of her Christian name making Richard's fists clench.

"It has, my lord. Hallo, Mr. Duncan," she added, dropping a brief curtsey to both men. Whatever she was feeling, her voice and demeanor were as cool and collected as ever.

Dowden looked from Celia to Richard, his expression avid and unseemly—as if he were watching a cockfight.

Richard took a step forward, rudely pushing between Celia and the leering men, forcing all three to take a step backward.

"The baron was looking for you, Dowden," Richard lied.

"Was he?" The duke cut him a mocking look. "Well, I wanted to introduce Monty and John to him." He glanced at his friends, who were glaring at Richard for his boorish behavior. "Have you ever met Baron Ramsay?"

The men pulled their gazes away from Richard with obvious reluctance and looked at their friend.

"I've not had the pleasure," Monty said.

"Nor I," Duncan said, still scowling at Richard.

"Well, then you're in for a treat." Dowden smirked at Richard and led the two men over to Hugh, whom Richard hoped would eat them alive.

Richard turned and laid a hand on her shoulder. "Celia—"

"I just recalled something I was supposed to do." She spoke quickly and wouldn't look at him. She took several long strides, stopped, turned back, and shoved her hands at him.

Richard glanced down; oh, his gloves.

He took them. "Tell me what is wrong," he asked, already knowing what she'd say.

"Nothing is wrong." She spun on her heel and all but ran back to the house.

Richard looked away from her departing figure and stared across the distance to where Dowden and his friends were talking with Hugh. The duke's eyes were on him and Richard knew the other man had seen Celia's departure.

Fury leapt in his chest at Dowden's amused, knowing look.

Just what in the devil was going on between his sister's betrothed and Celia?

Chapter 28

Celia didn't stop running until she was safely in her room. She squeezed her eyes shut hard enough to cause white stars to explode behind her eyelids, relieved that she could drive away—even temporarily—the memory of Monty's and Sebastian's smug, evil smiles.

She never should have come here. She'd known Sebastian and Stephanie would be here, but she'd not even considered Monty, which was unutterably stupid of her.

Of course he would be here; how could her humiliation be complete, otherwise?

Celia slid down her door, landing on her tailbone with a painful thump as that summer came flooding back.

The weeks after that wretched ball had been a blur. Her friends hadn't been able to abandon her quickly enough.

The day after the ball, her father had returned—after an almost two-month absence.

By then, the bill collectors had taken to standing on the stoop of their small lodgings, and Celia rarely even left her room. After all, where did she have to go?

Her father had bruises and a broken arm, but at least he'd been able to pay off some of the dunners.

He had then dismissed their one footman—a fourteen-year-old

boy they'd paid only with food and housing—their cook, and the scullery maid, leaving only Henson.

And then he'd called Celia into his bedchamber-cum-study-cum-sitting room. It hadn't even been noon, but her father already had a bottle of wine open and three-quarters empty.

The Honorable Cedric Trent was as handsome as his daughter, or at least he had been before years of drink and dissipation took their toll. But that morning her father had looked all his thirty-nine years and then some.

"Well, darling," he said with a sad, wry smile, "you'll be proud to know that news of your *little mess* is circulating even in London's seamiest hells."

She waited in vain for him to offer help.

Instead, he said, "I'm afraid I shall be leaving you soon."

"Leaving?" she repeated stupidly. Even after all those years of casual neglect, she wasn't able to believe that her father would abandon her at such a dire time. "Where are you going?"

"I've managed to secure an invitation to the Duchess of Winchester's villa in Tuscany. I'd take you with me, but Her Grace doesn't care to have young lovelies around her."

"When will you be back?"

"I'm afraid I couldn't say, darling. But I've paid for this"—he waived a dismissive hand at the sooty, grimy walls around them—"until the end of next month."

"But . . . that's barely six weeks away, Papa."

He shrugged, something like shame flickering across his features more quickly than a comet. "It is already more than I can afford to pay."

"Where will Henson go?"

This time she recognized the expression on her sire's face as amused surprise—as if it was piquant or eccentric of her to be concerned about the welfare of one's oldest and most loyal servant.

"I've not paid her for months, Celia—perhaps even as long as a year. I have no idea what she will do."

Henson had stayed without payment? She'd tolerated Celia's

snappish temper and excessive demands and lack of gratitude without getting money for it?

The shame Celia experienced at that moment had been life altering.

For the first time in her life Celia had seen herself as she really was: self-centered, thoughtless, and shallow. Nothing but an empty, hollow shell of a person who took and took and took, giving nothing in return.

And yet Henson had stayed.

Her father had been oblivious to the shift that was occurring within her. His bored, peevish expression and the dismissive flick of his hand told her that he'd already wasted more time on a servant than such a lowborn individual deserved.

Instead, he asked the question she feared. "What about Dowden? I know you were his particular pet this Season. Or has he fled, too? Because he is your best option at this point."

"He would never offer for me, Papa," she said, even though her secret hope was that Sebastian might, out of guilt, swallow his expectations of a grand marriage and help her out of this mess—a mess that he had instigated.

"Oh, darling. I wasn't talking about marriage." He had chuckled at her shocked expression.

"You . . . you would have me become his—" Back then she'd been unable to push the word past her lips.

"Whore—you're old enough to say it, my dear. A whore. Although there are much more pleasant names for it: mistress, demimondaine, to name a couple. Latch on to a wealthy protector, darling. I'm afraid it is the best you can hope for after that stunt you pulled."

He'd given her overripe, voluptuous body—always a burden to her—an amused look. "Some women quite enjoy that life. I daresay you will find you are one of them. As for Dowden? Well, he is plump in the pocket, not hard to look at, and seems interested enough. You'd be well advised to latch on to him with both hands while you have the opportunity."

He'd given her a look of true disgust then. Celia knew it wasn't because he was appalled by her immoral, vindictive behavior, but disappointed by her stupidity. "It is time you faced the life you have, Celia, not the one you dreamed about."

That had been the last time she'd ever spoken to him. He'd left the next day, not bothering to take his leave.

Celia saw nobody except Henson for a week after the ball.

And then Sebastian had arrived at her door.

Had that surprised her?

It shouldn't have, if she'd been thinking straight. But she'd been so pitifully grateful for his presence that she'd welcomed him into the dreadful lodgings she called home.

"Why darling," he'd said that first time, his chest rumbling with laughter as he held her in his arms, "I think you're glad to see me."

She should have been ashamed—she'd flung herself at him—but instead she'd laughed with him, although her laughter had verged on hysterical.

"Shh, shh, now. Everything will come around. You'll see."

"It will?" she asked through her tears. "But how?"

"Well, first we must wait until the Season is over and Davenport marries the Singleton chit," he'd said. "Once another scandal seizes the *ton*'s attention, we will quietly bring you back into fashion. It will not be easy, but with my considerable influence I will be able to secure an invitation to a house party for you, and we shall work slowly from there."

"How ever did the note go to Lucien instead of Richard?" Celia had told herself not to ask the question, but it burst out of her.

His expression had tightened slightly at her accusatory tone. "They are twins—the footman I gave the message to obviously got muddled. Not that it matters now. What is done is done."

Celia had understood the threat implicit in his words: If she wanted to place blame, he would not linger.

And so she had stifled her suspicion and rage.

Besides, she deserved what she'd gotten—it didn't matter that the message had gone astray.

After that day, he'd come to her every day for a week, staying only thirty minutes. She had looked forward to his visits with pathetic desperation, frantic when he left her.

And so, when he'd come the second week, she had been easy prey for a predator like Sebastian.

"I think of you all the time, Celia," he'd said, sitting beside her on the settee, his big, powerful body warm and comforting. And then he'd kissed her.

"Mmm, such a lovely mouth you have, my dear," he'd murmured against her throat. "You're so very beautiful. You must know that I've always wanted you, Celia." The next kiss had involved touching, fondling, and—eventually—the lifting of her skirt.

She could still recall lying on the worn settee in the room they used as parlor, study, and sitting room, looking up at his angelic face. Never before had he worn such an expression while looking at her: one of dire need and adoration.

"It will only hurt a little, Celia, and I will make it so good for you."

He'd been half right.

Afterward, he'd held her until his body had softened inside hers. She hadn't realized that he'd fallen asleep until she heard his heavy, regular breathing.

I have him, she'd thought. *He is mine, now.*

Celia could only think of that younger woman now with amazement.

And Sebastian? Well, he'd returned daily—for a while. And then every few days.

And then London emptied of everyone who was anyone and the heavy, motionless heat of summer settled over the city.

Yet Sebastian lingered in town, his presence the only thing feeding her rapidly diminishing hope.

By the time six weeks passed, Sebastian no longer mentioned

possible invitations to country house parties or reviving her ruined reputation. And more and more time passed between each visit.

The visits themselves had become so brief that only an idiot could fool herself any longer.

And then, one week, he didn't come to her at all.

The worst part hadn't been her shredded pride or her cheaply discarded maidenhood.

No, the worst part had been that she would have taken him back even then—after he'd been using her for weeks and weeks. Celia would have submitted to Sebastian's—by then—loathsome attention simply because she'd been so desperate for the touch of another human being.

Celia still recalled his last visit. He'd taken his pleasure with the haste that had become usual by then—not bothering to do more than unbutton his fall, lift her skirts, and mount her against the sitting room door.

A few minutes later, when he'd been adjusting his cravat while examining his reflection in the room's one glass, he'd said, "I'm sorry, darling, but my last hope—Mrs. Leggett's rather pitiful gathering—fell through. But do not despair," he'd assured her with a cavalier grin. "I have not given up my efforts on your behalf. Unfortunately, *I* must attend several of these bothersome functions—no matter how much I'd love to cancel and stay here with you."

Celia had remained silent. After all, what could she say?

He'd shrugged one elegant shoulder and then turned to smile down on her. "Don't pout, my lovely. You know how it is—one cannot accept invitations and then change one's mind without getting a certain reputation." He'd smiled sadly at her. "Even somebody like myself must be careful. Don't despair, my sweet. I'll be at the Earl of Thornton's, which is just a few miles south, so I shall be able to pay you a visit—albeit brief—once or twice over the coming weeks. But then I am all the way up by the border at the Duke of Carlisle's."

When she still didn't speak, he chuckled and rubbed her upper arms, as if to warm her up. "I *do* have some rather good news."

She'd been afraid to ask.

"You've said your lease here is almost up?"

"In five days," she'd said through numb lips.

"It just so happens that my dear friend Monty has to remain in the City for the next two months. He's just returned from Paris, where he was with the diplomatic corps, and needs a governess for his two children before he moves to his parents' place in Yorkshire in September. I know it's far beneath you, but . . ."

Rather than be offended, she'd been overjoyed: a job. A way to avoid ending up homeless and penniless? "Thank you, Sebastian—that would be wonderful."

He'd smiled, clearly pleased and amused by her gratitude for a governess job. Oh, how the mighty had fallen.

"There, you see, kitten? I am always thinking of you. You are fortunate in that Monty knows you don't have any experience as a governess, but the children are young, so the duties will not be arduous. By the time September comes, everything will have turned around for you."

He'd been right about that last part, but not in the way Celia had hoped.

Chapter 29

Richard was just finishing up his meal when the handle turned on the breakfast room door.

His head whipped up, only to find his twin standing in the doorway. And Lucien was . . . Richard squinted . . . *smiling*.

"Rich, I'm so glad I caught you." Luce's eyes were bright, his grin so big it exposed his impressive mouthful of teeth.

He grabbed Richard's shoulder and gave it an almost painful squeeze before all but skipping over to the buffet. "Oh, good—I see cook made plenty of ham."

The door opened and a footman popped in, visibly flustered at having missed his master's earlier-than-usual entry. "Coffee, my lord?" he asked.

"Yes, indeed, Thomas. Also tell Cook I'd like a beefsteak this morning—bloody."

The footman blinked; it was common knowledge that Lord Davenport usually had to be tempted to his meals. "Very good, sir."

"More coffee, Mister Richard?"

Even though he needed to piss like a racehorse, Richard couldn't leave just yet. "I'll take more coffee."

The door closed and Richard turned to his brother, who was still engaged in loading his plate.

Richard cocked his head. "Are you humming, Luce?"

The humming stopped immediately. "No." He turned on his heel, still smiling, his plate heaped with ham, eggs, a devilled kidney—which he'd believed his brother *hated*—and one of every other item on the sideboard.

Luce dropped into a seat across from Richard and spread his napkin on his lap, staring at the pile of food with obvious relish.

He sawed off a chunk of kidney and was about to pop it into his mouth when he noticed Richard staring—likely with his jaw hanging.

And then something truly strange happened: his brother *blushed*.

Richard opened his mouth just as the door swung open.

Both he and Luce turned like eager spaniels hoping to see their master.

"Phil." Richard stood, his brother mirroring his action.

And then something else interesting happened: Phil blushed.

"Good morning, Richard, er, my, er, Lucien."

Luce grinned like a man whose horse had just won the purse at Ascot. "Good morning, Phil."

They stared at each other as if Richard wasn't even in the room.

All this blushing and stammering put Richard in mind of Toni's young friends, who'd spent the evening last night playing multiple games of *I Dare You*, kissing beneath anything green and giggling and blushing the color of the holly berries that seemed to be everywhere one looked.

Richard peered at his brother and sister-in-law. They were both blushing. Although he'd seen no kissing, both were smiling rather . . . strangely.

Hmmmm. Could it be that Lucien had taken his advice and was courting his wife?

Richard opened his mouth—to say what, he wasn't sure—but the door opened behind Phil.

Just when Richard had stopped expecting Celia to show up at breakfast, there she was.

Lucien's eyebrows pulled down into a V, Phil lost her pretty flush, and Celia looked as if she wanted to turn and run out of the room.

"Oh. I thought I'd be the first one down," she said, and then *she* colored up, as if realizing how odd that might sound to the master and mistress of the house.

"I beat all of you by an hour," Richard said when the awkward silence continued to stretch and stretch.

Celia headed for the buffet while Phil sat beside Richard, nodding to the footman who entered with her customary pot of tea.

"Why are you still here if you started eating an hour ago?" Luce demanded, dropping into his chair, his eyes never leaving his wife.

Richard shrugged, his own gaze drawn to the woman currently at the sideboard, who'd hunched her shoulders, trying to make herself small. "Why not?" he asked.

Luce snorted.

Richard suddenly remembered something and turned to Phil. "Isn't today the day you wanted help distributing all the boxes? Or is Payson attending to that?" They were usually given out on Boxing Day, but this year, with the wedding, Phil was getting them out early.

Phil smiled. "Yes—thank you, Rich, that would be lovely."

"I'll go, too," Luce said, cutting Richard a hard look and then commencing to glare at him. As if he wanted . . . something?

"Oh," Phil said, coloring up for the second time in as many minutes. "That would be nice . . . Lucien. But are you sure you—"

"I'm very sure."

The heated look that Luce gave his wife made even Richard blush.

Phil ducked her chin and messed about with her tea and Lucien turned to Richard, his sultry expression turning to annoyance.

Richard mouthed, *What?*

Lucien's eyes swiveled to Phil and then back to Richard. And then he gave a slight shake of his head.

Richard tried to cover his bark of laughter with a cough; judging by his brother's furious glare, he wasn't very successful.

He cleared his throat, getting his amusement under control, and then said, "Dash it, Phil, I *just* recalled that I have something else I have to do this afternoon. I'm afraid I shall have to shab off."

Phil looked ready to break into a jig before she recalled she shouldn't appear so elated at not having his company.

"Oh. That's a shame, but don't worry about it, Rich," Phil said, cutting a look at her husband. "If, er, L-Lucien will help me, then I shall be fine."

Richard couldn't help noticing his brother's fatuous smile had returned as he gazed at his wife's pink cheeks.

This was promising. Very promising, indeed. And Richard felt that he deserved no small amount of credit.

"So, what are your plans for today, Rich?" Phil asked, sipping her tea.

"What plans?" he asked, and then recalled what he'd said not thirty seconds ago.

Lord, he was as bad as Luce and Phil.

A soft snort came from the direction of the buffet.

"You just said that you had plans this afternoon," Phil reminded him.

"Ah, yes. Well, yesterday I was telling Mrs. Pelham that I'd recently seen a *vanessa atalanta* out by the old weaver's cottage."

Phil frowned. "At this time of year? That *is* unusual."

Blast and damn. How could he have failed to recall that Phil had forgotten more about insects than most people would ever know? Not only would it be unusual to find a red admiral butterfly moving about in this weather, it would be a bloody miracle.

Still, in for a penny . . .

"It's hibernating, of course."

"I didn't think they *did* hibernate?"

Richard gritted his teeth. "No, that's true; in general, they don't. That is why this situation is so, er, interesting."

"Ah." Phil was staring at Richard the same way he often stared at beetles.

"Anyhow," he said, charging ahead. "We talked about going today, didn't we, Mrs. Pelham—before the weather changes?"

Celia turned slowly from the buffet, Lucien looked up from his plate, his mouth full of food, and his sister-in-law stopped with her teacup lifted halfway to her mouth.

Damn. Richard really was a dreadful liar.

Celia was looking at him as if he'd grown a second head.

"You are interested in insects, Mrs. Pelham?" Phil asked. Skepticism—with a slight tinge of amusement—colored her tone.

Celia's eyes moved from Richard to Phil to Richard.

Richard gave her an encouraging smile.

"I, er, well, who doesn't like butterflies?" she asked rather lamely. And then went on, "I became quite interested in all sorts of insects after seeing Mr. Redvers's display at the museum in London."

"It is a magnificent display," Phil agreed.

"You saw it?" Richard blurted.

"We took Marcus, Jason, and David when we were last in London."

Richard was delighted that she'd taken the time. Her father was the foremost authority on beetles in all of Britain, so she probably knew more on the subject than Richard.

Lucien frowned and asked his wife, "Who is *we*?"

"Will accompanied me and the boys."

Lucien's frown deepened, his gaze riveted to Phil. His normally mild-mannered brother looked positively barbaric.

This was more than interesting; this was *fascinating*.

Phil gulped down a mouthful of steaming tea and coughed under her husband's primitive, possessive stare.

Lucien finally wrenched his eyes away and turned to Celia. "You're braver than I am, Mrs. Pelham. That huge beetle—" He shivered and looked at Richard. "The whoosy-whatsit?"

Richard opened his mouth.

"The *goliathus regius*," Celia said. "More commonly known as the Goliath beetle."

Richard could only gaze at her in silent adoration; never in his life had he become so hard, so quickly. Could there be a more sensual sound in the world than the words *goliathus regius* coming from between her perfect, pillowy lips?

Lucien's stunned expression grew into a smirk. His twin might loathe insects of any kind, but he would know the effect of Celia's words on Richard.

Richard didn't care. Just like yesterday, he was seized by a desire to scoop Celia up in his arms, run from the room, and take her somewhere intimate and force her to speak Latin to him. All day and night. Preferably wearing no clothing.

"Indeed, that is the correct Latin name," Phil said.

"When did you say you wanted to go, Mr. Redvers?" Celia asked. "I'm afraid I can't recall." Her blue eyes glinted with amusement.

"Whenever you finish breakfast. I shall wait for you in the library."

"I've already eaten. This is for, er, Lady Yancy."

He clearly recalled her comment about the old lady only eating porridge. "Quite the meat-eater, isn't she?" Richard teased.

"Voracious," Celia agreed with a slight smile on her delicious mouth. "I shall be ready to go in half an hour." She turned back to the buffet.

Richard smiled at his gaping brother and winked at Phil. "If you'll excuse me, then, I'd better go get ready."

Chapter 30

Richard was waiting where he'd told her he would be, leaning against the doorway and reading a book.

Celia took a moment to admire him—because he was certainly worth admiration. His leathers were dyed a dark brown that was almost black.

"It is better for hiding all the muck and dirt I tend to get all over myself," he'd said yesterday when she'd asked him.

His boots were black and glossy, but hardly shiny enough to see one's reflection. They were the footwear of a man who spent a great deal of time being active. His head was bent over the book in his hands and a lock of burnished golden hair had fallen over his forehead. He kept his hair shorter than his brother—unfashionably short—just as he'd done all those years ago.

He looked dauntingly large and masculine in his black wool overcoat, his shoulders seeming twice as broad.

Beside him was a big wicker basket that she assumed carried whatever a beetle scientist, an entomologist—she'd looked up the word—would need.

As he'd done all those years ago, he looked serenely confident by himself, the aura of stillness around him almost soothing. He was a man who gave no thought to appearances, and Celia—a woman who'd spent a good deal of time disguising *her* appearance—respected and envied that quality.

He turned a page, glanced up, and then did a double take when he saw her hovering by the doorway. His surprise was fleeting, the smile that replaced it genuine and stunning.

And—she realized with a pang that started in her chest and ended somewhere south of her belly—it was the sort of look that was catnip to a woman who'd been treated like a half person for longer than she cared to remember.

Oh, Celia. You are *in trouble, aren't you?*

Richard put a marker in his book and closed it. "You are as quiet as a cat," he said with a charming smile. "Ah—I have this for you." He dropped his book into his bag and pulled out a small red leather box.

She did not reach out to take it. "What is it?"

"You look so suspicious," he chided. "Are you worried it might be a Goliath beetle?"

"Not at all—I know you'd never part with one of those."

He chuckled. "I cannot deny your accusation. It is the prize from yesterday's contest—we were the winners. I looked for you all yesterday afternoon and evening. And then you didn't come to dinner . . ."

He trailed off, obviously waiting for her to explain. But the last thing she wanted to do was confess how she'd spent yet another evening cowering in her room.

Celia realized his hand was still outstretched and took the box. Inside was a beautiful hand-blown bottle. She looked up to find him gazing at her, his smile gone, his expression . . . hungry.

Celia swallowed. "It is lovely."

"Open it—there is perfume inside. Toni chose it and said it is all the rage."

Her hands shook as she took out the delicate stopper. The scent that assailed her was heavenly.

"Thank you," she said, her face hot under his stare.

He nodded. "All ready?"

"You don't have to do this," she blurted. In fact, it would be better for her—probably for both of them—if he didn't.

His smooth brow furrowed. "Do what?"

"Take me out to see this hibernating butterfly. I know what you were doing in the breakfast room this morning; you were just coming up with an excuse to step out of the way so your brother and Lady Davenport could spend some time together. But you don't have to really take me with you."

It took her a moment to recognize the expression on his face because it was one she'd never seen before—at least not on him. He was hurt. All those hundreds of barbs and digs that Season and never once had he looked hurt.

He did now.

"Of course." His smile this time was one she was familiar with. Not until now did she understand it. While he appeared remote, smug, and even disdainful, she realized it was his protection—his defense against rejection. He bent to pick up his basket.

"Wait," she blurted when he turned on his heel and grabbed the door handle.

He stopped but did not turn. "Yes?"

"I want to go." More than anything she could remember in a long, long time. "I just . . . well, I didn't want to be a burden for you."

He turned slowly, his expression still stiff. "I would not have offered if I did not wish to take you with me."

She swallowed, chastened by the coolness in his tone. "I *do* want to go." She smiled, giving him the same genuine look of pleasure that he'd just given her—before she'd snuffed it like a candle. "How often does a person get to see a *vanessa atalanta* in the middle of winter?"

The corner of his mouth twitched and he raised his eyes to hers; they were as big and brown and beautiful as they always were, but this time she saw the reserve in them for what it was: a shield. This seemingly impervious man could be hurt. Even by somebody as insignificant as Celia—an impoverished servant, a woman far past her bloom, a spinster staring thirty in the face.

A woman with a child born out of wedlock.

A woman who'd been a whore.

"I should probably confess that I spotted it a while ago—not long after arriving at Lessing Hall—but I *did* see it before the snows came."

"It is a beautiful day for a walk," she said, wanting him to know she simply wanted to be with him—viewing hibernating insects, or not.

His expression grew a little less guarded. "I'm impressed that you recalled the name at breakfast—*Goliathus regius*."

"I cheated." She reached into her own satchel and pulled out a book, handing it to him. "I had to look it up."

He read the spine, his eyebrows creeping up his forehead. He had the same hopeful look he'd worn at breakfast, when she'd shocked him with the Latin name.

"This is an excellent beginner's field guide to beetles."

Celia reached out and turned the page to the front flap of the book.

"Property of Richard Thomas Redvers," he read, and then smiled. "I recall the day I bought this. It was on one of the few trips Luce and I ever took with my mother and father."

He must have seen her surprise because he said, "Lord Ramsay is not my real father—although he is much beloved by both Luce and me."

"So, your real father and Lord Ramsay both share the same surname—they were related? I'm sorry, I don't mean to pry."

"It's no secret. Hugh was my father's nephew." He gave a faint smile. "My mother's marriage to Hugh was the scandal of the year." He handed the book back to her.

She was going to put it in her bag and then hesitated, recalling how he'd come by it. "I asked Lady Ramsay if I could take the book from the library," she said. "But I should have asked you—as your name is in it."

"I am pleased you will get some use from it. I'm sure it hasn't been looked at since the last time I opened it."

His words pulled a laugh out of her. "That's what your mother said, too."

Richard shook his head. "My mother—never one to sugarcoat her words. I daresay she was lurking in the library?"

Celia replaced the book in her bag and he opened the door. "Yes," she said, as she preceded him out. "I didn't even know she was in there until I'd been looking for a good five minutes and she asked if she could help me find something. I'm astounded she can work with the bird noise."

"My mother could work in the middle of a volcanic eruption." Richard led her down the steps and headed in a direction Celia had not yet ventured.

There was plenty of snow on the ground from last night, but it wasn't falling right now. Based on the color of the sky, there would be more tonight.

"You should be flattered she spoke to you—or even noticed your presence," Richard said. "My mother has a habit of ignoring everything around her when she is deep in a book."

"She certainly had a great many of them piled up on her desk. That was why I'd not seen her—she was hidden by a veritable wall of books."

Celia didn't tell him that she'd found the baroness to be utterly charming and unaffected.

Nor did she tell him how she'd hesitated to ask for the book, aware of how it would look—as if she were studying up to snare the baroness's son.

As it turned out, Lady Ramsay hadn't looked surprised or displeased. Indeed, if Celia had been forced to assess her beautiful but rather expressionless face, she would have said the baroness was pleased.

"Hardly anyone comes in here except me, my husband, and Richard," she'd murmured while combing the shelves for the beetle book. "Well, and lately the two parrots, of course."

Celia had laughed at that.

"It's nice to have people putting the room to use," she'd added. And then she'd plucked out a book and handed it to Celia. "Here you are. I daresay this has been here gathering dust for years."

"Thank you, my lady."

"You are quite welcome, Mrs. Pelham." And then she'd turned and gone back to her teetering mountains of books.

"How long have Lord and Lady Ramsay been married?" Celia asked as Richard veered off toward a section of woods.

"Almost eighteen years." He shook a snow-covered branch and lifted it out of the way to expose a trail. "Nobody ever goes this way anymore," he said, pulling back his coat to reveal a long knife strapped in a holder on his thigh. "I'm going to be horribly rude and go first—just because I noticed a good deal of overgrowth when I came out here last week and don't want you to have to hack your way through. Thanks to the thick canopy, there won't be much snow—but there might be a bit of muck."

That was an understatement. It was quite a bit warmer under the dense foliage and meltwater pattered down all around them, running in rivulets along the path.

The trail was barely wide enough for one person and he frequently needed to cut back a branch or bramble.

"My mother married Hugh when Luce and I were ten years old," he said, over his shoulder. "Years ago—long before my mother married my father—Hugh was my father's heir. He got into some sort of trouble so Papa sent him off to the Continent until matters here settled. Unfortunately, his ship was taken by corsairs just the other side of Gibraltar. He didn't return to England for seventeen years."

"Yes," Celia said, "I recall reading something about his adventures—he knew Lady Exley while he was held captive, did he not?"

"He did. It was Hugh who got the marchioness out of Oran after her husband, the sultan, died. Our families have always been close," he added, pausing to step over a log and then turning. "Give me your bag," he said. "You'll need both hands."

Celia could see he was right and handed it over. He slung it over his shoulder and offered his hand. Celia took it and then scrambled rather inelegantly over the soggy, rotting log.

"Thank you." She reached for her bag.

"I'll carry it for you; there are more obstacles ahead." He picked up his basket and continued down the path. "After Hugh returned, he and my mother decided to marry. Because they were nephew and aunt—although there was no blood relation—it was a great scandal."

Much like the one Celia had dragged them through. Although Lord and Lady Ramsay had created a scandal for love. Celia had acted out of nothing but malice.

"My father was over seventy when he married my mother."

Celia stumbled a bit when he offered up this interesting piece of news. "Oh?"

"My mother was seventeen."

"Ah. That's quite an age gap," she said, since it seemed like he was waiting for her to say . . . something.

"Yes," he agreed, trudging. After yet another long pause he said, "Today is my father's birthday."

She was struggling to come up with something—anything—to say.

"It bothers me that my brother didn't remember." He stopped so suddenly she bumped into him. "I'm sorry," he said absently. He was looking down at her, but he seemed to be seeing something other than Celia. "I appear to be the only one who remembers my father."

His gaze sharpened. "I have always been—" He stopped, and his lips curved into a confidently amused expression that was strangely sensual. She suspected the reason she had disliked the expression so much when she'd been eighteen was that it had made her nervous.

Unfortunately, her twenty-eight-year-old self found the expression intriguing and wanted to do foolish, wicked things to and with him.

Richard gave up looking for the right words and shrugged. "Well, let's just say I've always been odd. I'm not sure why I'm so bothered that Luce would forget our father's birthday. After all, he's been dead for almost twice as long as I knew him." He cocked his head and gave her that intense look that made her feel as if she were the only person in the world. "Is it odd for me to be bothered?"

Something about the muted yearning in his gaze caused a wave of sadness to well up in her throat; he was asking if it was wrong for him to still mourn his father. Richard Redvers might appear aloof, but he obviously felt very deeply about some things.

"I don't think it is odd. I think of my own mother every day and she died when I was thirteen." The subject of her mother was another that often drove her to tears. "I—well, I have to admit I have wondered more than once if I would have done the things that I did had she still been alive." She hesitated, and then blurted, "She would have been sickened by the person I became after her death." She gave a bitter snort. "*I'm* sickened."

"You were scared," he said. "You must have known your father was not a man to rely on. If your mother put aside that money for you, she must have known that, too. I have seen people do things when they are afraid that they would never do otherwise."

"I appreciate what you are saying. But don't you believe that it's how you respond under duress that is truly illustrative of what kind of person you are?"

"No. I believe that how you reacted when you were seventeen was just that: the reaction of a seventeen-year-old under tremendous strain. I don't believe human beings are immutable. It is impossible to know whether you would respond the same way now as there are simply too many unique variables." He stopped and shook his head, his expression wry. "Perhaps it is good that I articulated that, because I need to remember it," he said, almost to himself, his gaze once again vague and distant.

"What do you mean?" she asked.

"You must be aware that Dowden and I are not on good terms."

Celia wondered what he'd say if she told him that she knew just how *not* on good terms Sebastian considered them.

Instead, she nodded.

"I'm sure it's no secret to you that I'd prefer he did not marry my sister?"

Again, she nodded.

"Well, it occurs to me that perhaps I've been looking at Dowden and seeing who he was at sixteen. Maybe that is unfair."

"It always seemed there was, er, a history of conflict between you," Celia said carefully, fully cognizant that talking about Sebastian was something she needed to avoid. Not only because of Sebastian's warning, but also because she didn't trust herself not to tell Richard that he *should* be concerned.

But then Antonia Redvers had a loving family to look out for her. Katie only had Celia, three old ladies, and an ancient vicar to rely on. Celia needed to keep her opinions to herself.

Fortunately, Richard did not appear to want to talk about Sebastian, either. Instead, he said, "I think you should talk to Phil."

Celia gave a laugh of disbelief. "What?"

"Yes. You need to talk to her. What happened all those years ago has put Lucien and Phil together, and I believe they—" He cast his eyes skyward. "Lord, I can't believe I'm going to say this, but I believe they are *in love*. You don't need to feel guilty for being the engine of their union. If you want to unburden yourself, it should be over the way you treated Phil."

"And you."

"I already forgave you for writing the note that was meant for me."

"Yes, but what about all the other things I did that Season?"

"You mean things like 'Ode to Odious'?"

Celia groaned, her face heating.

Richard laughed.

"How is what I did to you humorous?" she demanded.

"I don't know—it just *is*. Trust me, Celia, you did not hurt so much as a particle of my feelings. I'm afraid I hardly noticed." He knitted his brows. "Although I confess I always had Dowden pegged as the progenitor of most of that foolishness." He shook his head at whatever he saw on her face—stupefaction, probably. "Dinna fash yersel, as the Scottish say. I'm afraid I'm too thick to have noticed most of what was said about me." He reached up and adjusted his spectacles. "Although I *did* feel terrible about treading on that poor girl's frock." He pulled a face. "And I'm an insensitive clodpole because I don't even recall her name."

"It was Maria Trevallion."

He snapped his fingers, the sound muffled by his gloves. "That's right. Poor thing."

"You were always so kind."

"Hmm?" he said.

"You danced with all the girls that other men ignored."

"Oh, don't put me on a pedestal, Celia. Phil was responsible for that since she was always shoving me at some girl or another."

"I thought that maybe you two . . ."

"What? Phil and me?" He shook his head. "Lord no. It was a wonder she tolerated dancing with me. I told you I was a pupil of her father's?"

Celia nodded.

"Well, he used to fill their house with his students every week for dinner. Poor Phil put up with the lot of us, but it was as brothers, not swains. I don't think she wanted an absentminded, beetle-obsessed husband. She loves her father, but—in a lot of ways—taking care of Sir Gael was probably like having a child." His gaze settled on her and his eyelids lowered slightly. Celia would have sworn the temperature around them went up. "No, it wasn't Phil I fancied. I'm afraid that like every other young man that Season, I only had eyes for one girl."

Celia's mouth opened, but nothing came out.

"Why do you look so surprised? You're not going to tell me some Banbury tale about not being aware of all that masculine admiration?" he asked with no small amount of scorn.

"No, I was a conceited little cat who reveled in that small amount of power," she admitted. "But I never would have thought somebody like you would be susceptible to something so mundane as mere appearance."

"Somebody like me?"

"You always looked so aloof—so impervious to everything around you. I had the impression you held us all in contempt for enjoying such vapid pastimes."

"Oh, Celia, trust me, contempt was the furthest thing I felt for you."

"But—" She needed to swallow as her mouth had inexplicably flooded with saliva at the hungry look on his face.

"But what?" he asked.

"You're a scientist. You've just said you don't believe in love—"

"Ah, but I didn't say that what I felt for you was love. How could it have been? I knew nothing about you; I doubt we exchanged ten words."

"More like five."

"That's true; you were quite adept at managing to ignore me even when I stood right beside Luce."

Lord, but she'd been a nasty little toad! Fortunately he didn't expect a response, because all she had was more apologies.

"What I felt for you was physical attraction. As a scientist, I believe that—just like any other animal—human beings gravitate toward the finest physical examples of the species." He tapped the gold rim of his glasses. "These mean I am not in that group; poor vision would make me both a poor provider, poor hunter, and"—he smirked and lowered his voice—"poor breeding stock."

Celia's pulse pounded in her ears, and it took everything she had not to titter like a widgeon. "But that's absurd—you can correct your vision," she said in a breathy, foolish voice.

"I'm talking about biology—not civilization or society." His nostrils flared slightly. "I'm talking about the overriding urge to mate with the best our species has to offer. It is my belief that *need* or compulsion is something we are all born with; it is built into all humans." His eyes roamed her face, throat, and her rapidly rising and falling breasts before returning to meet her gaze. "I call it a breeding imperative, but we might just as well call it lust."

She had to swallow a few more times. "Er, even beetles feel lust?"

Celia could see by the flicker of glee that passed over his handsome face that her question had delighted him.

"Indeed. They seek out the fittest and most perfect lady beetle of their type. I would imagine they feel a similar physical reaction to what I'm feeling just now," he admitted, not sounding the least bit ashamed.

Celia's breath caught in her throat.

He must have noticed because he shook his head. "But I am not a beetle; I can control my lust. If necessary." He grinned, but then his humor quickly drained away. "And I would never impose myself on a woman who likely spends her life rebuffing unwanted advances."

She opened her mouth and the words tumbled out, like people leaping from a burning building. "What about wanted advances?" As she had in the gallery, she swayed toward him.

But this time, rather than meet her proffered lips, he shook his head, his eyes flickering over her person like a little boy staring greedily through a shop window. "The next time I touch you, I shan't want to stop." His lips curved into a self-mocking smile. "I'm afraid that even my much-vaunted self-control has its limits." He lightly stroked her jaw with gloved knuckles. "You see, I don't want to just kiss you, Celia—I want to be inside you."

She made a mortifying sound that was something between a whimper and a sigh.

He smirked—that maddeningly attractive smug expression that made her want . . . *things*. Things she had not wanted in many years; things that had ruined her life the last time she'd felt anything even remotely similar.

You think Katie ruined your life?

No, she loved her daughter. But there was no denying that her baby's arrival had made Celia's life considerably more difficult.

After those five years in Bath, you should be an expert at avoiding such eventualities.

The accusation should have stung, but it didn't.

This will lead nowhere, Celia, it can't.

I know.

And yet you are ready to take such a foolish leap?

So, it would appear; Celia met his gaze and said, "I want you inside me."

It was clear from his startled reaction that he had counted on her self-control to buttress his faltering restraint.

"It is not my way to deflower servants. I do not wish to marry—and what we are contemplating often creates unwanted . . . results—"

"I'm not a maiden, and I know how to take care of myself. I'm also not seeking a husband." Celia had given up any dreams of marriage a decade ago. As attractive as she found Richard, she knew that a man who loathed Sebastian as much as he did would never look kindly on a woman who'd given birth to his bastard.

Celia was nothing but an afternoon of pleasure for him—a man who could go wherever he wanted and do whatever he wished. For her, an afternoon with him would provide comfort on many lonely nights in the years ahead.

He was regarding her with equal parts desire and curiosity; if she told him that she had changed her mind, he would behave as if this conversation had never happened.

That thought left her feeling empty.

She was sick with loneliness and this was a temporary slice of heaven. She had no virtue to lose—that was long gone—and what else did she have to look forward to?

And so she returned his hungry look. "I want you."

Chapter 31

Richard braced her up against a tree, his action so swift it surprised a laugh out of her. He captured the sound—one of pure joy—in his mouth, greedily hoarding it to himself.

Her hands slid into his hair, knocking his hat off, her fingers clenching hard enough to hurt.

Richard gave an encouraging growl, reveling in her rough handling, his tongue tangling with hers as she stroked into him with a violence that left him breathless and hard.

He met her thrust for thrust, their kisses sloppy, wet, and frantic. They ground against each other's bodies like randy youngsters, her hips pressing and shoving against his in a desperate, yearning way that told him she wanted him every bit as much as he wanted her.

"Mmmm, Celia," he murmured, coming up for air.

She sucked his lower lip into her mouth, pulling so hard he made a noise that was half pained grunt, half aroused laugh.

She released him with a soft, sucking *pop*. "Richard," she whispered, trailing kisses down his chin, nuzzling aside his cravat and lightly biting his Adam's apple.

"Ah, God," he moaned, letting his head fall back. "More, please."

She needed no further invitation and her hot mouth and sharp teeth grazed and nipped and kissed.

Richard shoved his hands beneath her cloak, grabbed her waist and yanked her closer. "Too many clothes," he muttered, bucking against her with slow, deliberate thrusts that could leave her in no doubt of his arousal.

She made a noise that sounded like approval and then bit his ear hard enough to make him yelp.

"Too hard?" she said against his neck, not sounding in the least repentant.

"Never."

She laughed, a wicked earthy sound that made him ache to fill her.

Richard husbanded his rapidly fleeing will and pulled away, amused and aroused by her irritated growl.

"Come, let us go to the cottage."

She stared up at him through lust-hazed eyes.

Richard swallowed and then said what needed to be said. "If you've changed—"

"Lead on."

His mind was a blur as he tore down the path, feet slipping on the slushy mud, ears straining for sounds behind him, half-expecting that he would turn around and find her gone when they reached Weaver's Cottage.

But less than five minutes later, when they broke out of the underbrush, she was breathing heavily beside him, her face taut with anticipation.

The snow here was pristine and unmarked by anything other than bird and small rodent tracks. The sky, he couldn't help noticing, was a darker shade of gray than when they'd started off.

He kicked the mud and slush from his boots and opened the door, holding the basket toward her. "There is a candle on the right side of the door. I'm going to fetch some extra wood before I take off my boots." And he needed to get his rampaging cock under control—or else his afternoon of debauchery would be over embarrassingly fast.

Her arm sagged under the weight of the basket. "What's in here?" she asked.

"It's a surprise. No opening it before I return. The fire is set and there are spills and a flint on the mantel."

He hung up their satchels in the small porch and then went to grab an armload of the wood he'd cut just last week. He'd taken to napping in the little cottage in the middle of the day. The forest on this part of the property was ancient and the fallen old growth was a haven for creatures of all sorts.

He loaded up with wood and went back inside, where Celia was already rubbing her hands before the beginnings of a fire.

After filling the wood box he laid a few more pieces on the grate, stripped off his gloves, and tossed them onto a nearby table.

"Let me warm you," he said, rubbing her cold, far smaller hands between his, his lips curving as he thought about what was in the basket. Once he'd chafed some heat into her fingers, he tilted her chin until she was forced to meet his gaze. "Having second thoughts?"

"No."

He didn't know why he kept asking; she was a widow—an experienced woman and not a maiden.

Instead of interrogating her, Richard slid his hand under her jaw, marveling at the delicacy of her bone structure and the juxtaposition of his sun-darkened skin and her creamy complexion.

He ran his thumb over her lush lower lip, his prick throbbing when she opened, the tip of her tongue darting out to taste him. He groaned. "My God, Celia—you will have me embarrassing myself."

She gave a breathy laugh, her cheeks blossoming with color as she took his thumb into the exquisite softness of her mouth.

Richard couldn't look away from the sight of her plush lips wrapped around him, her cheeks hollowing as she sucked him, the suggestive action almost driving him to his knees.

"Bloody hell," he growled, replacing his thumb with his mouth and plunging into her with his tongue.

She made a muffled sound of need as she absorbed his thrusts, and Richard sank his fingers into the yielding flesh of her hips and pulled her against him, grinding his erection against the gentle swell of her belly.

Celia shoved her hands between the flaps of his coat, her fingers digging beneath the waistband of his breeches, yanking out his shirt-tails. Chilly finger pads stroked against the hot skin of his abdomen and chest.

Richard sucked in a noisy breath.

"Cold?" she asked.

"Mmm, but so goo—*Christ!*" he shouted when she shoved her hands beneath his snug-fitting garments and pinched both nipples *hard* with her freezing fingers.

She laughed.

"You witch," he ground out, backing her against the wall and holding her pinned. "I'm going to have to punish you for that."

Her entire body tensed, telling him what she thought about his threat.

Well, well, well.

Richard grinned as he lowered his lips to her neck, pushing aside her lace tucker and taking a mouthful of tender flesh.

She squirmed against him as he sucked hard enough to bruise. Her questing fingers slid down to his fall and she fumbled with the catches, opening his placket and then tugging on buttons until he heard one hit the floor and bounce off somewhere.

"Ahhh!" he groaned against her throat when her small but strong fist closed around his cock and began to roughly stroke, the angle too clumsy to allow for much finesse. "Celia," he whispered, mapping her contours from waist to rib cage, smoothing his hands over her tight bodice. "You feel so good." He thumbed her stiff nipples through the cheap fabric while thrusting into her hand. He bit out a vulgar word when she grazed the sensitive slit with her work-roughened thumb, slicking his crown and shaft.

While she worked him, Richard pulled up her skirts, questing beneath her petticoats.

It was her turn to hiss in a breath when he parted her slick, swollen folds and thrust a finger up her.

She sucked in a noisy breath and her fist loosened, her stroking faltering and then stopping entirely. "Richard . . . please." She bucked against his hand, tilting her hips to take him deeper.

"I think you need more," he whispered, easing a second finger alongside the first.

She gave a needy whimper, her hands digging into his sides as she ground against his hand, seizing her pleasure.

"Come apart for me, Celia." He rhythmically thumbed her taut bud while penetrating her tight sheath with vigorous thrusts.

Celia began to shake, her head falling back, eyes closing as the first wave of pleasure pulled her under. He slowed his caresses, teasing a second orgasm from her before she finally squirmed, her body too sensitive for more.

Richard released her, kicked her booted feet wide, and then positioned himself at her entrance. "Now?"

"Yes, now—"

He drove into her so hard that he lifted her off her feet.

She made a breathy, surprised sound and clutched at his shoulders, her fingers digging deep, her body contracting around his shaft.

"My God, Celia, you feel divine," he murmured into her fragrant hair.

She clenched her inner muscles around him and he gasped. "Naughty," he hissed in a choked voice. "I approve."

Celia gave a breathy chuckle.

"Up now," he ordered, sliding his hands beneath her lush bottom and straightening his legs, easily lifting her.

She wrapped surprisingly strong legs around his hips and flexed, pulling him deeper.

Richard worked her with deep, thorough strokes, angling himself so that he rubbed against her clitoris each time he pumped into her.

"Richard," she whispered, "so good."

His already tenuous control began to fray; fragile threads snapped with each savage thrust into her silky heat.

She carded her fingers into his hair and then yanked his head down. "Harder," she whispered, and then bit his lower lip, flooding both their mouths with a coppery tang.

He growled, his hips fiercely drumming. Celia grunted with each pounding thrust, tightening around him until it felt as if she would crush him.

His rhythm broke and his thrusts became wild and uncontrolled. "Celia," he gasped, "I can't wait any—"

"Come, Richard."

Her words exploded in his skull, banishing all thought. He closed his jaws around the taut chords of her throat and then hilted himself, emptying in violent spasms deep inside her body.

Chapter 32

Celia came back to herself when Richard carried her across the room, lowering her onto the sheepskin-covered settee.

Once he'd deposited her, he stared down at her.

He was still fully clothed, although his buckskins were halfway down his thighs, baring that most masculine part of his body.

Celia knew her legs were splayed wantonly, but she didn't care. "Undress," she ordered.

He grinned, his hands moving to his mangled cravat, which he pulled off with a dramatic flourish and tossed carelessly over his shoulder.

She laughed.

He cocked an eyebrow. "More?"

"All of it."

"As my lady commands." He shrugged out of his coat, which met the same fate as his neckcloth.

His waistcoat—in contravention of current fashion he wore only one, because Richard Redvers needed no help padding his already broad chest—sailed onto the pile.

And then he reached over his shoulder and pulled his shirt over his head.

Celia reveled in the vision of male perfection. She had enough experience of men to know that his body was rare.

His torso was as sun-browned as his hands and face, the ridged musculature of his chest and abdomen slightly sheened from his recent exertion and flexing enticingly with every move.

He dropped into the chair across from her and brutally toed off first one boot and then the other.

Once again he stood, shoving breeches, drawers, and stockings down with a single push and then kicking them aside.

His half-erect cock lay heavy against one thigh, his jewels pendulous between taut, muscular thighs.

Celia enjoyed a leisurely perusal.

His lips were curved into that maddening smile when she finally reached his face. "Turn around. Let me look at your bottom." Celia knew she was behaving badly, but she'd never get such an opportunity again.

Besides, it was nice to order him about; in her experience she had always been the one on display.

He obeyed her order immediately, turning slowly. His buttocks were firm, compact globes of stark white flesh. A broad, sculpted back flared out from his tightly corded waist, and his well-formed legs were the sort that begged to be displayed in stockings and satin breeches. It was unfortunate those garments were so rarely worn these days.

He raised his arms in mock presentation when he once again faced her, the powerful muscles of his biceps bulging even from such a careless gesture.

She gestured to the marked difference in skin tone. "Do you go about half-naked on your beetle-collecting journeys?" she asked, mainly because she knew that he would enjoy such a question.

His boyish smile told her that she had guessed correctly. "One is often compelled to bathe in the great-out-of-doors when away from the conveniences of town living."

He planted his hands on his narrow hips. "Your turn."

Celia frowned. "But—"

"No buts. Come." He held out his hands; Celia barely hesitated before taking them. She was no longer shy about her body—how could she be?—although it had been four years since she'd shown herself to a man.

"I want to help you undress," he murmured against her hair as he untied her cloak and threw it down to join the rest of the clothing.

Celia gave a protesting laugh. "None of it will be fit to wear if you pile it all on the floor."

"Shhh," he said. "We are living only in the now." His elegant but work-roughened fingers went to the row of buttons that ran down the front of her serviceable brown gown.

"Is that what we're doing—living in the now?" she asked, the slightest of quavers in her voice when a fingertip grazed her breastbone.

"Mmm-hmm." He looked up from his work and smiled, the skin around his eyes crinkling in a charming fashion.

Celia squinted at his mouth.

"What is it?" he said, his fingers not pausing.

"There is blood on your lip." She sucked her own lower lip into her mouth, as if in sympathy. "Did *I* do that?"

He looked amused. "You don't remember?"

"I'm sorry."

"Don't be." He raised heavy-lidded eyes. "I'm not."

Although it wasn't the first time, Celia was horrified by her violent carnality.

His fingers paused and he took her chin in his big, warm hand, forcing her to look at him. He shook his head. "Don't."

"Don't what?"

"Don't start flagellating yourself over your sensual nature." His lips twitched. "If you need flagellation, I shall provide it."

Her body stiffened at his mild threat and she laughed softly, the sound hungry to her own ears—and his—if his dark, heavy-lidded stare was anything to go by.

"How intriguing," he murmured.

Although he had just brought her to climax more than once, her body was ready for more at his knowing, hungry look.

Oh, Celia.

Oh, indeed. How very unfortunate that they were turning out to be so well suited—in so many ways.

"There." He unfastened the last of her buttons and then slid his hand beneath her gown and pushed it off her shoulders.

"Mmmmm." He held her at arm's length, his eyes roving her clean but threadbare chemise and corset. At least she wore her nicest petticoat and newest pair of stockings today, although they were plain and cheap, especially when compared to the simple but exquisite tailoring and materials of his clothing.

Rather than turn her around, he reached behind her to untie the petticoat and push it to the floor before loosening her laces, the action bringing her chest against his.

"You have been cruel to me, Mrs. Pelham."

She swallowed. "Oh?"

"I do not like it when you avoid me."

She gave a noncommittal grunt.

"Indeed," he said in a musing voice, "I rather think you might need to be punished for your willful behavior."

"Uh," was all she could manage.

He chuckled evilly at her pitiful answer. "I should very much like to take a willow—or perhaps my crop—and stripe your delicious bottom." His breath was hot on her head, the words rumbling from his hard chest to her sensitive, taut breasts.

Celia's eyelids fluttered shut and she pressed against him, her blood rushing in her ears.

"Hmmm. I think you would like that," he said in the cool, authoritative tone that somehow made his wicked words all the more arousing.

She *would* like it; it had been far too long since she'd had a lover who understood her needs.

Thoughts of engaging in such erotic debauchery—thoughts which would have shamed her younger self—now made her ache with desire. Especially when she imagined the hand wielding the whip belonging to the masterful man currently obliterating her self-possession with mere words.

Richard pushed the loosened corset to the floor and then pulled her chemise over her head and sent it fluttering.

He held her at arm's length, his hot eyes roaming her no-longer-young, overly lush body. "Celia," he whispered, and then made a hungry, desperate noise that turned her legs to water.

He abruptly caught her up in his arms and crushed her to his chest for a long moment, as if she were . . . precious.

When he laid her out on the settee, Celia noticed that she still wore her ankle boots and stockings.

He sank to his knees in an oddly submissive gesture, gently removing each embarrassingly worn boot. He took his time, his gaze roaming her body, ransacking her with all the subtlety of a Vandal horde, while his touch was so very, very tender.

Something about being the focus of such an intelligent man made his actions all the more erotic. What, aside from the obvious, was he thinking about her?

Don't ask for the moon, Celia, her inner voice warned her, kindly this time.

She swallowed her longing and enjoyed his worshipful ministrations.

When she was down to only her stockings, he lifted her foot to his mouth and trailed kisses all the way up the inside of her leg, stopping where her plain garter tied above her knees. His hot breath on her naked thigh wreaked havoc on her breathing.

He untied the garter and rolled the stocking down, performing a similar ritual on her other leg.

When he was done, rather than ravage her—which she'd half expected—he stood, draped a beautifully woven throw rug over her shoulders, kissed her cheek, and then whispered in her ear. "I've brought a little surprise."

* * *

Richard was not a romantic man.

He was, however, a man capable of learning new things.

After Celia had agreed to accompany him today, he'd immediately hurried down to the kitchen, where he'd cornered Cook and told her what it was he wanted.

Next, he'd gone to Watson and had him unlock the cellar.

After that he'd all-but sprinted back up to his room and picked out two of the items he'd had delivered to the house. Fortunately, the shopkeepers had wrapped his purchases for him.

And now he was ready to execute his first-ever romantic operation.

When he returned to the thick sheepskin rug, he knelt and set the basket in front of Celia, who sat bundled up on the settee, eyeing the hamper with open curiosity.

He unstrapped the leather belt that held the basket closed and opened first one side, and then the other, making the most of his presentation.

Her eyes sparkled as she looked from the glasses and napkins and bottle strapped to one side to the apples, wax paper–wrapped sandwiches, and pastries on the other side.

"You've brought a picnic."

"Why do you sound so surprised? It is a picnic basket, after all." He laid out the small square tablecloth Cook had thoughtfully provided.

"I thought it was full of beetles," she admitted, sliding down to the rug and eagerly eyeing the contents of the basket like a young girl on Christmas morning.

"Let's see what we have," he said, unwrapping packages and setting them out. "Some local cheese, ham sandwiches, plum jam tarts, bread, a knob of butter, and some of Cook's famous apple-and-currant jelly."

He looked up and saw her gaze fall on the two packages he'd left inside the basket.

"Hmmm." He scrutinized her with mock seriousness. "Have you been a good girl this year, Mrs. Pelham?" His handsome face became stern. "Or have you been *bad*?"

She gave a delighted laugh. "I think I know which answer you would prefer."

"As long as you're bad only with me, that's all that matters." He handed her the smaller of the two gifts first.

She stared at it, not reaching out to take it. "What is it?"

"You have to open it to find out."

"Is this something you bought for me?" she asked, giving him a look that was half suspicion, half . . . well, he didn't know what.

"No, actually. This is something Watson bought for you. For your sake I hope that Mrs. Watson never finds out."

She gave a soft snort of laughter. "Your brother's butler terrifies me."

"He terrifies us all. Take it," he urged. "It would please me," he added when she still hesitated.

She could not have looked more cautious and concerned if she'd been sticking her hand into a badger's lair.

"I wanted to get you something for helping me do my Christmas shopping. I would have given it to you on Christmas, but . . ." He shrugged. "I'd much rather give it to you now—just the two of us. Think of it as a practice Christmas."

She laughed at that.

"Open it," he ordered, reaching for the bottle of wine and opener, but keeping his eyes on her.

Celia gave him a put-upon look and shook her head. "You shouldn't have bought me a gift."

"I have a long history of doing things I shouldn't."

"Hmmph. Well, thank you."

"Why are you thanking me? You've not seen it yet. Perhaps I gave you a Goliath beetle."

Her hands froze in mid-tear and Richard laughed. "I promise, there are no beetles within."

Once the paper was off, she opened the slim box, peeled back the tissue, and then shook her head. "I suppose I should have known." She looked up, her chin slightly wobbly, her eyes glassy. "Thank you."

"It's just a pair of gloves." Richard turned to the bottle, embarrassed by the quiet gratitude in her eyes.

"It's a thoughtful and useful and lovely gift," she said softly, tossing the box to the floor and pulling on first one fur-lined red leather glove and then the other. "Mmm."

His jaw sagged as she stroked first her arm, and then her thigh with her delicate gloved hands.

"So soft and smooth," she crooned, her eyes narrowing to sensual slits.

Richard swallowed. "If you keep that up, you'll go hungry."

She chuckled. "I love them. And they will be put to good use."

"I should say *so*," he muttered, his palms sweating as he tugged out the cork, his gaze fastened to her gloves as she carefully removed them, finger by finger. A Parisian courtesan could not have made the action appear more carnal.

Richard jerked his eyes away, his cock once again as stiff as a poker and pointing north. When he poured out a glass and handed it to her, he saw that she was smirking, her gaze on his arousal.

"*Tsk, tsk,* more naughty behavior, Mrs. Pelham. The punishments are just piling up." He raised his glass. "To lazy afternoons."

"To rather *energetic* lazy afternoons," she amended.

They clinked glasses and took a sip.

"This is delicious," she said, swirling the pale liquid in the glass. "What is it?"

"I can't claim credit—it was Watson who recommended it." He cocked his head at her, squinting speculatively. "I'm not sure I should give you your other gift since you behaved so wickedly with the first."

"What if I promised to be even more wicked?"

Richard snatched up the other package with mock urgency, making her laugh.

"I shouldn't be taking gifts from you," she said, holding the red paper–wrapped gift in two hands. "It's a sign of my lax character that I will accept them."

"Or maybe it's a sign that you haven't received nearly enough gifts?"

Her eyes softened as he stared at her. "You are very kind."

Richard's face heated and he was grateful when she turned to the package.

"Hmm, I wonder what this could be," she teased, her voice not entirely steady. When she pulled off the paper, she just stared.

"Celia?" he said, as the moment stretched. "Is something wrong?"

Her throat worked and she made a gulping sound.

Please, God—no tears.

But when a big fat bead of water slid down her cheek, he knew that God had forsaken him.

As she looked up from the ankle boots, several more tears followed the path of the first.

Richard grimaced. "Lord. I didn't mean to make you cry. It's just that I could see your stocking through the—"

"Thank you."

It was his turn to make a gulping sound. "You are welcome."

She turned back to the boots, as if drawn to them by an invisible force. "How did you know my size?"

"I estimated based on a footprint in the snow. I hope they fit."

For a moment he thought she might actually try one on, but she must have recalled that she was naked and all the physical contortions such an action would require.

Richard silently cursed his luck.

"We didn't go into any shops that sold boots."

"No, I just sent a message to the village cobbler and they had these delivered." The boots were a plain, serviceable brown, apparently the only style the bootmaker had in that size. Richard had privately hoped for something red to match her gloves.

"Well," she said, setting them close enough beside her that they touched her leg, as if she couldn't bear to be parted from them. "Thank you."

He busied himself making up two plates. "Some of everything?" he asked, unwrapping a sandwich.

"Yes, please. Although I can't believe I'm hungry again."

"I've got plans to make you even hungrier," he said, making her chuckle.

Once they were both settled with food and drink, Richard shifted so that he could sit beside her, leaning back against the settee.

They munched for a moment in silence.

"Tell me about the most exciting expedition you've taken thus far," she said.

Richard was accustomed to this question. "That would be my trip to North America."

"Why?"

"I found the Florida Territory to have the most remarkable collection of stinging, biting, and urticating insects I've ever seen."

She laughed, her rosy cheeks pushing her eyes into amused crescents.

Richard reflected that there was nothing quite so wonderful as bringing pleasure to another—especially a woman who'd been occupying rather too much of one's mind.

"And that is an endorsement, in your opinion."

He finished chewing and washed down a mouthful of sandwich, nodding vigorously. "It certainly keeps one on one's toes."

"What sort of insects, er, urtic-urt—"

"Urticating—to sting or prickle. Well, let's see, there was the *dasymutilla klugii,* what the locals called the velvet ant. It is not an ant but a female wasp—a *mutillid*. Members of the *mutillidae* family exhibit sexual dimorphism—"

She choked and raised her hand to cover her mouth.

Richard patted her back, waiting until she'd stopped coughing. "All good?" he asked when she reached for her wineglass.

"Yes," she said hoarsely.

"That's what you get for laughing at a *mutillid*."

"What does s-sexually di—what was it?"

"Sexual dimorphism is when the two sexes of the same species exhibit different characteristics beyond just their sexual organs."

"Ahh," she said, nodding vigorously. "I'm finished asking questions now."

Richard laughed. "The red velvet ant's body is covered with a brilliant scarlet coat that is remarkably similar to velvet. I can personally attest that the creature only *appears* cuddly and sweet. It has a sting that is one of the most painful I've ever felt."

"I can see why you enjoyed that particular trip so much."

Richard wagged a chastising finger at her. "Cheeky. You know what that will get you."

Her pupils flared and her lips parted slightly.

Richard lost all interest in his food. "My God you're beautiful, Celia."

She looked away at his words, apparently uncomfortable with compliments while completely comfortable with sexual innuendo.

Richard finished his sandwich and then topped up both their glasses. "Tell me about your life after the Stanford ball," he asked quietly.

She stared at her plate, doggedly chewing her sandwich for so long he thought she might ignore him altogether.

"It was much what you would expect," she said, reaching for her glass and taking a sip before putting aside her unfinished plate. "I didn't leave the house for a week, waiting and waiting for one of my many *friends* to call on me. But nobody came." She paused, her expression bitter, but her eyes distant. "Eventually, my blinders fell away, so to speak. I had already managed to secure my first position as g-governess." She paused, her gaze vague.

Richard would have given a great deal to know what she was thinking.

But her expression shifted in a heartbeat and she continued her story. "It was only a temporary position, until the family moved to the country. After that, I went from position to position. Twice people found out my real identity and discharged me. Sometimes they found out my identity and—" She stopped, picking absently at her half-eaten sandwich.

"Your employer—or their sons, husbands, or male relatives decided you were a woman of easy virtue?" he guessed.

"Yes. Things were far better after I moved away from London."

"And how did you meet your husband?"

She dropped her gaze to the dissected sandwich. "He visited a house I worked in." She paused and then looked up at him. "We were only married a short time before he died of a heart ailment. He was not wealthy, so I needed to find work again." She shrugged, but he could see she was not as untouched as she wished to appear.

"Poor Celia," he said softly. "You really have had rotten luck, haven't you?"

She snorted. "I made a great deal of my *luck* myself."

An uncomfortable silence hung between them for a moment before Richard asked, "And you've been working for Lady Yancy for a year?"

"A year in January. It is not a terrible position, for all that she seems a bit brusque and dictatorial." Her full, sensual lips curved into an impish smile. "I like taking care of the animals. Especially Percy since it means I get to be outdoors often."

It sounded like a lonely, uncertain existence, but he kept that observation to himself.

"Your brother tells me you have your own ship to take you on your voyages?"

"I do own a ship, but I don't always use it for my trips. In order to pay for it, I must transport goods, which often conflicts with my schedule. But Hugh has put one of his ships at my disposal, as well, so usually one of the vessels is available. I tell his captain where and when I wish to go and he secures a cargo so that the journey is not wasted."

"And you are going to the Italian states next?"

"Your eyes light up when you say those words."

"It is a romantic part of the world."

Richard didn't disabuse her; she would know there was poverty and iniquity everywhere without his telling her. "I will go for six months."

"You spend most of your time in the country, I take it?"

"I do, but I will stay with friends in Venice, Milan, and Rome—so I will get *some* culture."

"Whether you want it or not?"

"Exactly." He gestured to her plate. "Have you had enough?"

"Yes, thank you."

Richard put the food and crockery into the basket, poured the remainder of the wine into their glasses, pushed the basket out of the way, and then turned to her and cocked an eyebrow.

She cocked one right back.

Richard grinned. "Lifting one eyebrow is the only skill I possess that Lucien cannot master."

"Somehow I doubt that," she murmured, her eyelids heavy as she shrugged the protective cape from her shoulders and rose to her knees to meet him.

"Oh?" he teased, cupping her firm, heavy breasts in his hands and lowering his head to suck an irresistibly pebbled nipple.

She purred beneath his suckling, threading her fingers into his hair before pulling up his head and claiming his mouth.

Richard adored her confident aggression; he had always been putty in the hands of an experienced woman who knew what she wanted and then took it.

He reveled in the sensation of silken breasts and erect nipples pressed against the hot skin of his chest. Celia held his head hostage while she pushed into his mouth and explored him at her leisure.

Unlike their other kisses, this was deep and languorous—*adagio* rather than *féroce*—a thorough exploration using lips, tongues, and teeth.

Richard slid his hands around her slender waist and pulled her against his erection, pushing against her belly, his thrusts slow and rhythmic.

"Mmmm," she hummed against him, sucking his tongue into her mouth, her intentions blatant.

Just when he was about to flip her onto her back and take her, she shoved his chest. "Lie down," she said in a gruff voice. She stalked him on her hands and knees after he stretched out on the soft but lumpy bed of rugs, blankets, and clothing.

She straddled his hips, staring down at him with an imperious smirk as she positioned his shaft at her entrance, never taking her eyes from his.

She took him into her tight heat with a fierce, greedy savagery that made him gasp.

"Good Lord," he muttered, as she kept him fully sheathed.

Her eyelids flickered and then her body moved in a sinuous ripple that grew with each subtle buck of her hips. She lowered her hands to the middle of his chest, finding the right position to swivel and thrust, grinding against him for her pleasure.

It didn't take long before she contracted so hard around his aching shaft that it hurt.

When her movements became jerky, he grabbed her hips and held her in place, lifting them both off the floor with the power of each driving thrust, losing track of himself.

He came in an embarrassingly short time, his entire body shaking with the power of his orgasm. "Celia," he whispered hoarsely, his cock jerking with diminishing spasms, until he lowered his hips to the floor, his arms dropping limply to his sides.

"Richard." There was a smile in her voice as she stretched out on top of him, her ragged breathing gradually evening out, but not becoming regular enough to suggest sleep.

He was still inside her and decided he would need very little time or encouragement to take her again.

She shifted on him, turning until she was looking down at him, her sweaty, passion-stained face slack, her eyelids low over the lucent blue of her eyes.

Her bruised, puffy lips pulled into a sensual half smile. "You make a comfortable bed, Mr. Redvers."

"It is always good to be of use." He rubbed her body from her hips to her chest, stroking the tender sides of her breasts before moving down her ribs to the nip of her small waist, and then out again to the generous flare of hip.

She stretched like a cat—all sinuous languor—wiggling her body as if settling into him deeper, her inner muscles gripping tightly enough to keep him tumescent. She laid her arms over his chest and rested her cheek on her crossed wrists. "Mmmmm."

And then she fell asleep.

Richard smiled up at the low, cross-beamed ceiling as he listened to her settle into a deep, regular rhythm of breathing, luxuriating in the sensation of a sleep-heavy, satisfied female body covering his.

Part of the reason he preferred widows was their comfort in their own bodies and understanding of their desires.

Another part was that he adored their more mature curves.

Celia epitomized everything he loved about women, and then some. Never before had he been with a lover who'd been as physically demanding—and as rough—as Celia. He would have bites, bruises, and scratches all over his body, and he would treasure them for as long as they lasted. He wondered if she'd feel the same about the marks he'd left on her.

Richard knew that he'd pleased her at least twice—it was a matter of honor for him to make physical joining good for his partner. All too often the women he slept with had unsatisfactory marriages or underwhelming experiences in the bedchamber and he delighted in demonstrating how fulfilling the human sexual act could be if only a person took a little time and effort.

He could stay the way he was forever, sated, relaxed, and still buried in her tight heat.

Richard yawned, his hands moving ever more slowly.

* * *

Celia woke with a start.

The first thing she noticed was the naked body beneath her.

The second thing was the hard, pulsing shaft filling her pleasantly sore passage.

And the last thing she noticed was the pair of warm, brown, unmagnified eyes staring up at her.

"Hello," he said, his beautiful mouth smiling.

Celia flushed at his piercing look—a ridiculous reaction given what they'd done only a short time before.

"Hello," she said.

"Are you warm enough?"

She nodded.

"Do you—" His hips pushed up and they both hissed in a breath as he penetrated her more deeply.

Celia tightened her inner muscles in response, and he groaned, his powerful arms coming around her body and holding her as he rolled them gently onto their sides, their bodies still joined.

He stretched out an arm and she laid her cheek on his biceps, staring into his eyes, his hips thrusting in slow, deep undulations while his free hand rested on her hip.

They made love without speaking or kissing, eyes locked as their measured thrusts became sharper, less controlled, until Richard slid a hand between them and brought her to climax, his hips pumping in increasingly powerful thrusts, until he hilted himself deep inside her and released a flood of warmth.

The next time Richard woke he saw they must have slept for some time as the fire had burned down to embers.

A quick glance at Celia showed she was still deeply asleep. He reluctantly and carefully withdrew his half-erect cock from her body and then fumbled around in the dim room for his watch before taking his glasses off the side table where he'd laid them.

Richard grimaced when he saw the time; it was almost five o'clock.

He'd drawn the heavy curtains when they'd entered, so there'd been no way to tell the time. He went to the windows that faced east and pulled back the drapes just enough to take a quick look outside.

Richard could only gape. When they'd come into the cottage—it couldn't have been later than noon—the sky had been gunmetal gray.

It was now almost dark, only a sliver of daylight on the horizon illuminating the thick, fluffy white world beyond the window.

The heavens had opened their vaults sometime in the past few hours—probably closer to three given the drifts that had built beside the woodshed.

He felt movement beside him and turned to find Celia, wrapped in one of the blankets.

"I had no idea it was so late," she said, her warm breath tickling his arm and causing goosepimples all over his body. "We should get going—it will be dark soon." She turned and hurried back to the tangle of clothing, quickly finding her chemise, dropping the blanket she'd been covering herself with, and slipping the garment over her head.

When Richard didn't move, she looked at him, her hands smoothing down the worn garment. He doubted she knew that pressing the fine fabric against her body made her look more nude than nude. Richard was not going to tell her.

He couldn't recall her ever looking more beautiful: flushed, tousled, her stiff pink nipples pressed against the fine muslin chemise, the alluring triangle between her thighs a shadowy promise.

She was perfect, from her messy dark hair to her pretty pink toes.

"Why aren't you getting dressed?" she asked.

"We can't go out in that."

"*What?* But we have to."

"It's a thirty-minute walk in good weather, Celia. Right now—with upwards of a foot and a half of snow—it'll take twice as long.

You'll catch your death in that thin cloak." He'd been tempted to buy her a new cloak, as well. Now he was glad he hadn't since it gave him a good excuse to keep her here.

"Surely you cannot mean to *stay*?"

"Why not? My valet will know where we are—I always tell Buckle exactly where I am headed when I go out."

"But—but—"

"Yes?"

"I shall be disgraced—I'll lose my position with Lady Yancy."

"Do you think she'd rather you go out in a blizzard and become ill?"

"Yes, actually."

Richard laughed. And then saw she was not speaking in jest. He went to her and took her bunched-up gown from her hands, tossing it to the side.

She stared up at him, the notch between her glorious eyes telling him how anxious she was.

He smoothed the furrow with his thumb, pushing back her heavy mass of hair with his other hand. "If the woman cares more for your reputation than your life, you don't need her." He was hard again and he pressed his engorged cock against her belly. "I want you again," he murmured, stroking himself against her.

She sucked in a breath and her pupils flared; for a moment he thought desire could overcome her other concerns, but then she shook herself and took a step back.

"It's not just a position, Richard—it's a job that pays very well. You don't understand what it's like to—" She broke off and shook her head. "Never mind." She reached for the dress he'd just tossed to the side.

"I don't know what it's like to . . . what, Celia?"

She whipped around. "What it's like to make your own way in the world. If I don't get paid for this quarter, I won't have any money for the next."

"Why don't you let me take care of you?"

Celia couldn't have looked more surprised than Richard felt.

"What?"

Now that the idea was out there, he realized it had been floating around in his mind since she'd kissed him in the portrait gallery. He'd become aroused every time he'd thought about a mere kiss—when was the last time a woman had had such an effect on him? Never.

"Let me take care of you."

She stared at him, arrested. "You mean you'd pay for a place for me in London?"

"Yes, if that is where you'd like to live—I'll get you a house wherever you want."

She nodded, her expression considering. "And I would have pin money—perhaps a maid, a cook, that sort of thing?"

Richard smiled, relieved this was so much easier than he'd imagined; he had never engaged a mistress before. He took a step toward her, until he could place his hands around her waist, his body aching at the thought of having her waiting for him when he came back from his journeys.

"I would be generous, Celia. I'm not as rich as Lucien, but you were right when you said I would never be in want. Neither would you."

"You would come to visit me—when, exactly?"

"Whenever I was in the city, I would stay with you."

"And I would be there waiting for those visits?"

Richard's forehead furrowed at the strange question. "Well . . . yes."

"Waiting for you to return and mount me."

He frowned, dropping his hands from her body and taking a step back.

This time it was Celia who came toward him and he recoiled at the fury—the *rage*—on her face. "Do you think that you are the first man to offer me the honor of being your *whore*, Richard?"

He opened his mouth.

She gave a bitter laugh, her eyes suddenly wild. "If I had a shilling for every *gentleman* who offered me the privilege of spreading my legs for him, I wouldn't be working for Lady Yancy."

He raised his hands in a placating gesture. "Celia—"

"Go straight to hell, *Mister* Redvers." She spun on her heel, snatched up her garments, shoes, cloak, and everything else that belonged to her and stormed toward the bedroom, slamming the door hard enough to rattle all the windows.

"Well . . . bugger," Richard muttered, shoving a hand through his hair and staring at the door.

What in the world had just happened?

Chapter 33

Lucien pulled the servant cord and glanced at Phil, who was looking as anxious as Lucien felt.

"Do you think he is still out with Mrs. Pelham?" Phil asked, speaking the same words that were rattling around in his head.

"I don't know. But Buckle will be able to tell us." The door opened and a footman stood in the doorway.

"Yes, my lord?"

"Go fetch Mr. Buckle for me, Charles."

Once the door shut, Lucien asked Phil, "Have you spoken to Toni?"

"She said that everyone else is here."

"Except Richard and Mrs. Pelham."

Phil nodded. "That is what Lady Yancy said—that Mrs. Pelham wasn't in her room. But she had no idea where she went."

"If we are fortunate, *we* are the only ones who know Rich and Mrs. Pelham are together."

The door swung open and Buckle came bustling into the room, his curly red hair uncharacteristically disarranged. He bowed. "My lord, my lady. I encountered Charles as he was coming to fetch me. I'm afraid Master Richard hasn't returned from his day trip."

"Did he tell you where he was going?"

"Weaver's Cottage, my lord."

"Yes, that's where I thought he might be." Lucien glanced at his watch. It was ten after six. He looked at Buckle. "You may go—don't tell anyone else that Richard hasn't returned."

"Of course not, my lord." Buckle looked hurt, but Lucien didn't have time to soothe his ruffled feathers.

The valet reached for the door but it opened before he touched the handle.

Richard stood in the doorway, snow covering his hat and coat, his face rosy from the cold.

"Thank God," Lucien said as Richard entered the room, leaving a trail of snow behind him. "We've been looking for you."

Richard pulled off his gloves and handed them to his hovering manservant. "I came in the sunroom door so as not to attract any notice," he said while Buckle fluttered about brushing away snow, unmindful of the mess he was making on the library floor.

"Did you see—" Lucien began.

"Yes." Richard cut a sharp look at his valet. "I'll be there in a few moments, Buckle—have a bath waiting for me."

"Of course, sir." Buckle hustled out.

When the door shut, Richard said, "I thought it wise that I enter by a different door than Celia. I daresay Lady Yancy is looking for her?"

Alarm thrilled through him at his brother's use of the woman's first name. "Yes, she is. Care for a brandy?" he offered when Rich shivered.

"Lord yes, I could murder one."

"Phil?" he asked.

"I'd take a sherry," she said. The request surprised him; his wife rarely drank. "Go stand in front of the fire, Rich."

Once they were all in possession of glasses, Lucien said, "What happened?"

"We kept waiting and waiting for it to slow, but when it didn't—well, it was a bugger going down that trail in the dark in two feet of snow." He took a big sip. "I take it you are the only ones who've noticed that I am late?"

"And Buckle," Phil said.

"Good. That means Mrs. Pelham might be able to keep her job."

"God, Rich—it was mad to drag her through this weather. You should have stayed put," Phil said.

Rich opened his mouth, cut a look at Phil, but then merely said, "She didn't want to cause the old lady worry."

Lucien snorted. "You mean the old cat would have given her the sack."

"Likely."

"I hope she is going to have time to rest and get warm," Phil said, showing her characteristic mothering instinct, even for a woman she loathed. She stood, put down her largely untouched glass, and headed for the door. "I'm going to go make sure she gets what she needs." She frowned at whatever she saw on their faces. "What? It wouldn't look good if somebody died at our house party, would it?"

Lucien made it to the door in several long strides and opened it for her. "You're a good egg. Has anyone ever told you that?"

"Ha!" she said, marching into the hall without another word.

Lucien loved her more than ever, prickliness and all. He regretfully closed the door on his wife and then leaned his shoulders against it, crossing his arms and staring at his brother.

"What?"

"Tell me what happened."

"Why should I? You're not my confessor," Richard said, throwing back the remains of his drink and heading for the door, himself.

Lucien stayed where he was, waiting until Rich was right in front of him before saying, "I hope you didn't compromise a servant under my roof, Richard."

"Leave off playing the lord of the manor with me, Luce." He reached for the handle, but Lucien wouldn't move.

"I'm not *playing* at anything. This is my house and I'm head of this family. What you do here reflects on me."

"Well, you needn't worry about anything getting back to you."

Lucien narrowed his eyes. "Did you take her to that cottage to bed her?"

Richard sneered, an expression Lucien had not seen since they were very young boys. "What is it, Luce? Jealous that I might have had something you wanted?"

Lucien's fist flew, hitting his brother just below the ear and knocking him back a few feet.

"Bloody hell!" Richard shouted, holding a hand over his jaw. "What the devil is wrong with you?" He experimentally moved his jaw from side to side. "Christ! That damn well *hurts*."

Lucien closed the distance between them. "When you utter such insulting words, you dishonor yourself as well as me and my wife."

Richard dropped his hand and heaved a sigh. "Fine. You are right. I apologize for saying such a rude, foolish thing. But that doesn't mean you'll be privy to my personal business. Stay out of matters that don't concern you, Luce."

This time, Lucien didn't try to stop him when he shoved past.

Phil didn't think she'd ever be able to get Lady Yancy out of the quarters she shared with Mrs. Pelham.

Finally, after assuring the old lady that a footman—Daniel, who'd already tended to Lady Yancy's animals on occasion—would take care of the dog for the next *three* walks that evening and two in the middle of the night, the old woman had agreed to be escorted down to the Yellow Salon.

Phil had instructed a servant that Mrs. Pelham's belongings be moved to a room just where the family wing met the guest wing. It used to belong to Hugh before he and Lady Ramsay moved into a new suite of rooms that was closer to their children. The room had an oversized tub rather than the hipbath that was in most of the guest rooms.

Lady Yancy could go one night without Celia as she had a lady's maid to do for her, even though Phil suspected that the sour old servant was accustomed to delegating the least appealing tasks to her mistress's dogsbody.

As Phil made her way to Celia's room, she told herself she was doing what she was doing for the other woman's health.

But that—while not completely a lie—was not exactly the truth, either. What she really wanted was a few minutes in private with Celia—something she would never find in the normal course of the day given Celia's propensity for hiding and Phil's family's efforts to protect her from any contact with the other woman.

She knocked and waited, not wishing to catch Celia still soaking.

But the door opened a few seconds later and Mrs. Pelham stood swathed in a heavy flannel robe that Phil had sent over, a fluffy towel wrapped around her hair. Other than some windburn on her cheeks and the tip of her nose, she looked her usual beautiful self.

"Oh, my lady." She dipped a hasty but graceful curtsey and stepped back, gesturing for Phil to come in. "I'm sorry. Had I known it was you, I would have—"

Phil waved the apology aside. "How do you feel?"

"A bit tired, but otherwise I'm fine." She hesitated and then said, "Thank you so much for moving me to this room—and also for seeing that Lady Yancy is taken care of."

Phil didn't want the woman's thanks. What she wanted was to ask her some very personal questions. Unfortunately, she didn't know exactly how to go about getting what she *did* want.

It turned out that she didn't have to broach the subject, after all.

"You're worried I have designs on Mr. Redvers."

It wasn't a question, but Phil nodded.

Rather than look offended, Celia gave her a weary smile. "I'm seeking neither a husband nor a protector." Her smile grew wry at whatever she saw on Phil's face. "I give you my word."

"Does Richard know that?"

"Oh yes, we neither of us have expectations beyond a mild flirtation." Her cheeks flushed and Phil wondered what the term *mild flirtation* meant to the other woman.

And then decided she didn't want to know.

"There is one thing I feel I should tell you."

"Oh?" Phil said, fear closing like a fist around her heart.

"I want to apologize—for all of it. I've already apologized to your husband and he said—" She bit her lip, as if debating whether or not to tell Phil something.

Phil wanted to grab the woman and shake the words out of her.

"He thanked me for what happened that night at the Stanford ball."

Phil couldn't have heard her correctly. "What?"

"He said if not for my mean-spirited behavior, he never would have met you, and that—in his words—would have been a tragedy."

Phil could only stare.

Celia smiled, and it was a sort of smile Phil had never seen on the beautiful woman's face: a kind smile. "I have to admit that his words lifted a great weight off my heart, my lady. I know I don't deserve it, but I can at least forgive myself for what happened to the two of you. As for all the times before that Season—well, it seems the Redvers brothers are destined to impart critical pieces of information without realizing it. Richard told me the truth about your mother."

"My mother?"

"Yes. You see, it doesn't excuse me, but maybe it will explain my behavior. Or perhaps you don't care any longer?"

Phil was tempted to lie and tell her she didn't even recall that long-ago pain, but the woman had been honest and she'd also told her the most joyous piece of information that Phil had ever received in her life—other than hearing both her children were born healthy and hearty.

Phil owed her a bit of honesty. "I'd like to know why you disliked me so. I admit it was—" She broke off and shrugged.

"Horrid?"

Phil nodded.

"I am so sorry, my lady—and I was sorry even before Richard

told me how you'd taken care of your mother, who suffered for years. You see, from my adolescent perspective, you had everything."

"*Me?* I thought *you* had everything."

"Then I did an excellent job of pretending. Every day from the moment my mother died until the night of the Stanford ball was a day lived, if not in terror, then at least worry. At school I daily feared being ejected for lack of payment." She paused and then said, "Did Mrs. Bennington not tell you that?"

"She would never discuss such private matters with another student."

"No, I should have known that. In any case, our lives were worse than hand to mouth. My father was a gambler, and I never knew whether there would be a home to go home *to* if I were told to leave school. I thought that you had everything—a loving family, friends who cared for you, even the owner of the school respected you and held you up to other students as a role model. I . . . well, I envied you and so I made your life hell. And I am deeply sorry."

Phil stared at the other woman, amazed by how tangled both their lives had been by misperceptions.

At Phil's hesitation Celia said, "I know that isn't enough to make up for—"

"I wasn't hesitating to make you feel bad. I was hesitating because I couldn't help marveling at how very wrong we both were."

"Yes, but you didn't torment me."

"True—but not because I didn't want to."

Celia laughed, and Phil laughed with her. "How sad is that? I *wanted* to persecute you but did not know how."

"I think that speaks of a sterling character, my lady."

Phil felt an amazing lightness and knew it was due to Celia's words about Lucien. Her husband had thanked this woman for bringing them together. He didn't love or want Celia; he'd only wanted to thank her.

Phil was suddenly in love with the entire world. She saw that

Celia was looking at her oddly and stifled her delirious grin. "I'll have supper sent up—unless you wish to come down."

"No, please, that would be lovely, if it's not too much trouble."

"Not at all." Phil hesitated. "You don't have to hide in your room, Mrs. Pelham. I think it is time to put the past behind us. It is Christmas—a time of forgiveness."

"You are far kinder than I deserve. Thank you, my lady."

"I hope you will feel free to join the festivities during the few days that remain of the house party—and that includes tomorrow night's ball."

"I'm afraid that balls and dancing are things that exist only in my past."

Phil didn't argue with her; she'd done her part by extending the invitation. She'd been magnanimous to the woman who'd deviled her existence for over fifteen years.

And Lucien was grateful that he'd married her.

Celia closed the door behind the mistress of Lessing Hall and then slumped against the cool wood.

Well. So that hadn't been as horrible as she'd feared.

It appeared Richard had been right.

Richard.

Celia groaned, closed her eyes, and let her head fall back with a *thunk.* She'd been a beast to him after he'd offered her a carte blanche. It wasn't as if anything he'd said had been unusual—nor should it have offended her. What was he supposed to think after she had just thrown herself at him and voluntarily warmed his bed? Why wouldn't he have made such an offer?

And she had turned on him like a shrew.

Most of her anger had been directed toward herself—for wanting to accept him so badly.

Did she never learn? She could not head down that road again. Especially not with a man she actually cared about.

Hopefully her behavior would be enough to keep him at bay

these next few days, and she wouldn't have to worry about throwing herself at him a third time.

Given all the activities Miss Antonia had packed into tomorrow and Saturday, there would be little time to wander off alone with him and make a fool of herself.

Or do something that would get you discharged or attract Sebastian's attention.

For the next few days she would avoid everyone except Lady Yancy. She did not have the leisure to nurse a broken heart or indulge her foolish fancies. She needed to keep this position until the end of the year, collect her bonus, and then find another job that had no connections whatsoever to the Redvers family.

Chapter 34

Phil stared at her reflection, wondering at the stranger in the glass.

She'd been smiling like an infatuated schoolroom chit for the last two days, even before Celia told her what Lucien had said.

The last two days had been magical. Her husband of almost a decade had behaved as if he were . . . courting . . . her.

Lucien had schemed and connived to get her alone—to keep her to himself, he'd said—and he'd been delightfully successful, even though their house was crawling with guests.

It had been everything Phil had always dreamed of.

Well, *almost* everything.

Phil knew that Lucien had been serious about not coming to her bed. Honestly, when she thought of their experiences in her bedchamber, she could not blame him.

So, this next step was Phil's to take, and take it she would, no matter how terrifying.

Barnes finished the one hundredth stroke and put down the ivory-handled brush, a gift from Lucien on their second anniversary.

Phil's husband never neglected a birthday, anniversary, or Christmas. Not only that, but his gifts were always thoughtful. She sometimes wondered if William selected and purchased the gifts, but—as comfortable as she and Will were—she couldn't bring herself to ask him.

"No, Barnes," she said as her maid prepared to divide her heavy hair into three sections and plait it.

The older woman frowned. "If you sleep on it loose, it will be like a thicket in the morning, my lady."

Phil stared at her servant—who'd once been her mother's maid—without speaking.

Barnes's eyes widened and her pale cheeks flushed.

No doubt Phil's face looked similar, based on how hot it felt. Phil knew that servants were always watching; she was positive that the last few days had sparked speculation down in the servant hall.

Barnes swallowed and nodded—the gesture careful, as if she didn't want to startle a shy forest creature. She glanced at Phil's nightgown, opened her mouth, and then closed it.

"What is it?"

"That is one of your older nightgowns, my lady."

Phil waited.

"I thought perhaps—" She broke off at whatever she saw on Phil's face. "You've the lace nightgown in your bride chest." Barnes blurted the words out so fast that Phil's brain took a moment to translate what she'd said.

She recalled the gown. It was something she'd made when her mother was still alive. She'd sat beside her sickbed and they had giggled like girls over the delicate, feminine garment.

It was thanks to all those hundreds of hours she'd sat with her mother that Phil was skilled at tatting. The nightgown in question was perhaps the most beautiful lace she'd ever made. It was a cobweb-thin lawn with inset lace panels that had taken her over a year to finish. The pattern was so complex she could only work on it while sitting in blazing sunlight.

And she had never worn it.

She met Barnes's gaze in the glass. "Go and fetch it."

The woman grinned—as if *she* were the one who would be wearing it.

As if *she* would be the one knocking on her husband's door and presenting herself like a sacrificial lamb for the slaughter.

Terror shot like lightning down her spine and Phil opened her mouth to call her servant back.

Tarry too long and you will lose him forever.

She shut her mouth with a snap and stared at her reflection. And then looked away because the last thing her reflection did was give her confidence.

Especially not since the last person she had seen before coming upstairs for the night was Celia Pelham.

Although the woman had not come to dinner, Lady Yancy had summoned her down to the drawing room when Toni had decided to have a bit of dancing.

"Oh, we have no shortage of pianists—you needn't disturb her," Toni said after the old lady offered Mrs. Pelham's services.

Toni's eyes had darted around the room and Phil had known she was looking for her mother, whom Phil had watched slink off after they'd left the men to their port and cigars.

Lady Ramsay was notorious for hiding in the library when the house was full of guests. Only when the men returned—and Hugh went and rooted his wife out of her hiding spot—would Daphne return.

Phil couldn't play because she had ten thumbs, Toni would want to dance herself, and so would the other young ladies.

Lady Ramsay was an accomplished pianist and Phil was about to offer to go and find her when Lady Morton—who had a voice like a saw cutting tin—spoke.

"Nonsense, the gel needs to earn her keep, and all the young ladies will want to dance." She waved at one of the footmen positioned on either side of the door. "You there, go fetch Mrs. Pelham. Tell her she is wanted immediately."

Phil met Toni's aggravated look and gave a slight shrug. The girl was marrying into Dowden's family and had better learn to rub along with her abrasive aunt-to-be.

The men had returned not long afterward and helped the servants shove aside furniture and roll up carpets to make a smallish dance floor. Although Lessing Hall had a lovely ballroom—which would be used for the grand ball—it was far too large for tonight's entertainment.

Phil had been surprised at how quickly Mrs. Pelham had arrived, gowned in a hideous brown dress and wearing an ugly mobcap. But she supposed the woman knew her employer well enough to expect such a summons.

Celia had immediately sat down at the piano and commenced to provide two solid hours of entertainment before Hugh brought Lady Ramsay to relieve her.

Celia must have slipped out of the room because Phil had not seen her again until she'd met her on the stairs, three-quarters of an hour ago, with the blind dog in her snow-covered arms. Celia—once the *ton*'s darling, had clearly accepted her unpleasant lot in life. Even though she was destined to a future filled with drudgery, she had still smiled cheerfully at Phil when she'd bade her good night. For the first time ever, Phil had felt sorry for the other woman.

"Here it is, my lady," Barnes said, breaking into her thoughts, holding up the nightgown that Phil hadn't seen in over ten years. "Shall I give it a quick pressing?" she offered, showing Phil several creases.

"Yes, do," Phil said, less interested in the wrinkled gown than buying herself another quarter of an hour before she had to do what she had promised herself she'd do.

She didn't want to think about that just now.

Instead she thought back to earlier in the evening, to when Celia arrived in the drawing room—rather breathless—in response to the summons.

It just so happed that Phil was looking at Dowden when Celia entered the room. If she hadn't been, she would have missed the look of fury that flickered across His Grace's handsome features. Phil had to give the duke credit—he managed to mask the look in less than a second, but she'd seen it.

Phil had looked from Dowden to the woman, whose face was

pale, her eyes suddenly downcast—as if she were afraid of something. Or someone.

Despite her humble status, at least one thing about Celia Pelham had not changed over the years, and that was her ability to draw the eyes of every man in her vicinity.

Even Jonathan and his young mates had cast yearning glances at Celia as she'd hovered near the door, clearly trying not to be seen.

Phil had almost laughed. Truly, Celia could as well try to hide a fireworks display as her beauty.

The emotions that realization released had surprised Phil, because among envy, jealousy, dislike, and a half dozen of the less elevated feelings battering her was one she never would have expected: pity.

Because it was clear to even a woman who disliked her that Celia would have rather been almost anywhere else than in that drawing room.

Men from all parts of the large room seemed to be pulled toward her like iron filings to a magnet. Only Dowden and Hugh appeared immune, although Dowden was staring at her.

Hugh was staring at his prospective son-in-law, the handsome lines of his face hard and intent, more suited to a duel-to-the-death than an evening of dancing and party games.

Surprisingly, it was young Jonathan who got to Celia first.

Celia's smile had been glorious and genuine. For a moment. And just as quickly it was gone, and her eyes darted elsewhere without hesitation.

Phil didn't want to look—didn't want to see which of the men she was looking at, but her body turned without permission. Although Lucien, she saw, was watching the events with as much interest as any of the other older adults in the room, it was Richard whom Celia was staring at.

Richard looked amused, rather than irritated, to see that his young brother had captured the prize.

"Here we are," Barnes said, shaking Phil from her wool gathering. The older woman was holding up the smooth, creaseless gown.

"Goodness, that was fast," Phil said, standing on strangely weak legs.

All too soon she was dressed in the new garment.

Phil stared in fascination at the virginal yet sensual gown her own two hands had made. *What* could she and her mother have been thinking? Why, she looked almost—

"My lady?"

Phil pivoted away from her provocative image and frowned. "Oh, Barnes. Surely that is, er, too much?"

Barnes marched toward her, holding the magnificent peacock blue silk robe before her. "It is perfect, madam—and this color suits you more than any other. Her ladyship knew what she was doing when she brought this back for you."

Phil smiled at that, perfectly aware it had been Hugh—and not her mother-in-law, who could barely dress herself—who had chosen all the gifts they'd brought back for the family.

It was the most beautiful and exotic piece of clothing Phil owned, the wide lapels made from a heavy cream satin that flattered the embroidered peacock whose body was on one flap with the enormous fanned tail covering the back, the tips of the feathers wrapping around to the other flap.

Phil chewed her lip. She would look like a fool in this magnificent gown. Mutton dressed as lamb.

You'll look like a fool no matter what, the dry voice in her head offered. *You might as well look like an attractive, well-dressed fool.*

Phil held out her arms and allowed her maid to swathe her in peacock blue silk.

Chapter 35

Lucien had just dismissed his valet when there was a knock on the door.

The connecting door.

He frowned and looked at the clock; it was almost one.

He put aside the book he'd just picked up—a primer on fertilizer use in lowland farms—took off his reading glasses, and got to his feet.

Only Phyllida would knock on that door.

His steps faltered slightly as the thought struck him.

Could it be . . .

He opened the door and his jaw dropped: It was his wife, but it was not his wife.

For the first time ever, he saw her hair down. Rather than the straight fawn-colored locks he'd expected, she was surrounded by a wavy, glossy froth that hung almost to her waist.

The robe she wore must have come from China—his parents would have brought it back.

Lord. Whoever had chosen it—Hugh, he suspected—could not have picked better. The vibrant blues, violets, and greens brought out the striking gold ring around her sea-colored irises.

"May I come in?" she asked, her voice brittle.

Lucien stepped back immediately. "Of course—please do," he

added rather stupidly. She walked into his room, looking around as if she'd never seen it before.

"Here, sit by the fire," he said, amused when she stopped in front of his bed and pivoted on one heel, walking quickly away from the big four-poster as if it were some sort of dangerous animal.

"Would you like something to drink?" he offered, gesturing toward the tray that held glasses and two decanters. "Or I could ring for tea?"

She looked at his glass. "I'll have whatever you're having."

"It is brandy."

She gave a jerky nod, her bottom barely perched on the edge of the chair. Lucien turned to pour her a drink, his mind racing; he had never seen her so nervous.

His cock knew what her nervousness meant before his brain acknowledged what was happening: his wife had come to his chambers. For sex.

The decanter rattled noisily against the lip of the glass.

For God's sake, Lucien—take hold of yourself. You're not seventeen—you're almost thirty.

But he felt far younger—the way he had that night all those years ago with his mates at that brothel.

He scowled at the thought, schooled his features, and turned to give her the glass, pleased to see that his hand was steady.

"Thank you."

He sat across from her and picked up his drink, more for something to do than because he needed liquor. Indeed, he was feeling bizarrely intoxicated for all that he'd had only one small glass of port and half a brandy.

She sipped, pulled a face, and then glanced around the room again. "This is nice."

"You've not seen it before?"

"When would I have seen it?"

"Yes, I suppose that is true." *True and very, very sad.* "I assumed you saw it when it was refurnished a few years ago."

"I chose the color palette," she said.

"But you never saw the results."

Why are you talking about draperies and wall hangings? The voice in his head was frantic. *Take her to bed. It has been ages*—years—*and you need to strip off that nightgown and mount her. You need—*

Shut up, Lucien snarled silently.

Phyllida's hand shook as she lifted the glass to her mouth, and she made a slight gulping sound, wincing yet again.

His heart went out to her, and part of him knew he could take charge of matters—have her stripped and bedded in mere moments.

It would be easier and quicker, but that wasn't what he wanted.

"Tell me what you want, Phil. I am yours to command." His face heated at the pet name, as if he were taking liberties. But he could see, by the way her muscles relaxed, that it had been the right thing to say.

"I—I have no experience with—" She squeezed her eyes shut and shook her head, her expression one of supreme mortification.

Lucien leaned toward her. "Open your eyes—look at me."

She opened her eyes, her expression dogged.

"Do you find me repellent?" he asked.

She gave a startled laugh. "Of course not."

"I find you extremely desirable." He knew they both heard the harsh rasp of desire in his voice, and her cheeks flushed.

But then she just sat there, her eyes flickering over him, her confusion clear. His wife didn't lack the courage to act; she simply did not have the knowledge. For all that he'd been inside her body more than a dozen times, she was as good as a virgin when it came to making love.

And whose fault is that?

He pushed aside his shame at the thought; this wasn't about him or his shame. This was about his wife and what she wanted.

"Do you want to talk about—"

"No talking."

Lucien nodded. "All right."

Phil grimaced. "I don't mean that. Of course I want to talk—but not now."

"Good. Me either."

Her head whipped up and he grinned; why bother to hide the joy he felt inside? "I'm so very, very glad you are here."

Her lips parted, as if she were surprised. Oh, he had been a foolish, stupid, bumbling husband to his wife. He wanted to drop to his knees and beg for her forgiveness.

Nothing like whining and groveling to put a woman in the mood . . .

The voice was right; he needed to take charge—at least to begin with. "Would you like to undress me? Or for me to undress myself?"

She swallowed several times. "Is that usually how it is done?"

He opened his mouth to tell her it could be *done* any way she liked, but she didn't need more confusion. "It is what pleases me," he admitted.

She nodded, jerkily rather than authoritatively. "Then yes—but you do it," she said in a whisper.

Lucien smiled and stood. "It would be my pleasure." He ran a hand over his jaw and frowned at the sound of bristles against skin. "I'm afraid I didn't have Peel shave me—should I—"

"No, don't stop," she blurted. "Er, I don't care—about the shaving, that is." Her gaze was fixed somewhere at the level of his chest.

Lucien bit his lip to hold back a laugh. He had undressed before a good many women in his life, but never had one looked at him as if she were facing a problem—as if he were a tricky piece of legislation on Catholic Emancipation or a field full of crops that refused to drain properly.

He glanced around at the candles. "Would you like to have fewer candles?"

"No." She gave another shake of her head, this one emphatic.

Lucien toed off his slippers first, wishing he had more clothing. Not that he was modest or ashamed of his body, but he didn't want to startle or shock her. And his current state of arousal was rather shocking—even to him. He wanted her with a fierce hunger; he'd never been so hard for a woman.

But fear tinged his arousal—fear that he might frighten her away. Still, he could hardly stand here taking off his slippers all night.

He was glad that he'd put on a nightshirt this evening. Generally he slept without one, but the weather was frigid.

Lucien pulled the sash on his robe and then shrugged out of it, tossing it over the chair behind him.

Her chest was moving in shallow jerks. He was torn between being grateful that she was breathing and worried that she might faint from overstimulation. He was feeling a bit overstimulated himself as her eyes—huge and dark—skittered over his person, becoming stuck around the level of his waist.

His cock, ever the opportunist, jumped at even the slightest sign of interest and her lips parted, giving him more ideas than he needed just now.

And so he reached behind his neck, grabbed his nightshirt, and pulled it over his head.

Chapter 36

Phil knew she was staring and the cold air on her tongue told her that she likely looked like some witless yokel.

But really, how could she *not* stare?

He was . . . well, magnificent, obviously. But he was also shocking. She'd had *that* inside her. No wonder it had hurt.

She'd grown up in a scientist's household, she knew what a penis was, why it became engorged, and what its function was. Phil hadn't needed to sneak books to educate herself; her father had given her an anatomy text when she'd turned sixteen, his face blushing wildly. "It's good for everyone to know such things," he'd muttered, handing her a book full of wonders.

Her aunt had, of course, told her what to expect on her wedding night.

What had happened when she and Lucien had eventually coupled had matched her aunt's description almost perfectly: he'd pushed himself into her, stroked her, spent, withdrawn, thanked her, and gone back to his room.

And then Phil had cried. Each and every time.

She had loved the feel of his body against hers—the weight of him when he'd relaxed on top of her for that agonizingly brief moment before leaving her alone, her head spinning, her body strangely . . . wanting.

The worst part had been that she'd known his businesslike approach had been her fault.

Lucien had offered, the first time he came to her, to prepare her—to give her pleasure. But she'd lied and told him she preferred it to be quick. The thought of him making love to her body, rather than just mounting her, had been far more terrifying than the idea of losing her virginity.

It had hurt—that first time. And again three years later, after such a long abstinence. But, by then, she'd begun to experience certain . . . sensations, for lack of another word.

Right now, looking at him—especially the hard, ruddy, jutting part of him—was giving her that tingling feeling between her thighs.

"Phil?"

She looked up, momentarily startled to find the head of her sophisticated, urbane husband attached to this *warrior's* body. He was breathtaking—his fair skin as pale as hers, the light blond hair dusting his chest—around his small nipples—almost invisible. It became darker and darker as it led down toward—

She jerked her head up again. Less surprised to find him looking at her this time.

"Would you like me to undress you?"

"No!"

The sharp word startled them both, but Lucien only nodded. "You needn't do anything you don't want, love."

She flinched at the endearment, but he didn't seem to have noticed, his expression patient and kind and wanting.

The notion that this gorgeous creature wanted *her*—after all, that was what his engorged organ signified—caused her own sex to throb in a most distracting fashion.

Phil squeezed her thighs together and then had to bite her lip.

"Do you want to touch me?" he asked, making her realize that he'd been standing before her—like a rather spectacular statue on display—for some moments. He cleared his throat. "Would you like me to touch you?" he asked, his voice husky.

Phil seemed to have lost the power of speech as his offers ricocheted around in her skull like two trapped bullets.

Touch him.

Yes. That was what she wanted. How many times had she touched him without multiple barriers between them—layer after layer of clothing? Not often.

Phil met his gaze and he smiled at whatever he saw, taking a few steps toward her, not needing to ask what she wanted. No doubt her desire—her lust—for him was shining from her eyes.

How many lovers has he had?

She gritted her teeth at the unwanted thought.

"Phil?"

She looked up.

"What were you just thinking?"

Her face heated. "It was nothing," she lied.

He stared for a long moment, and then sat down beside her on the settee. "Think about *us*, Phil. Because that is what I'm thinking about. I'm thinking about how badly I want your hands on my body. *Your* hands. My wife's hands. Please," he said, his chest rising and falling with labored breaths, "I've waited a long, long time for you to touch me. Please—" His eyelids fluttered and his head tipped back as she lowered a hand to his thigh—high up, where his skin was soft, hairless, and so thin she could see the faint blue-green of the veins beneath.

"Yesss," he hissed, his muscular body shuddering beneath her hand. "More. Please."

Hearing this strong, powerful man beg for her hand almost doubled her over with desire. This was her husband, her lord.

"Lucien," she whispered, too soft for even herself to hear. Her left hand slid up the other thigh, stroking from the unspeakably tender skin toward the ridge that separated thigh from groin, the V of muscle like those she'd seen on the classical sculptures in the Lessing sculpture garden, which her in-laws didn't drape, allowing all who explored the gardens to look at the perfect musculature of gods like Aries, Hermes, and more.

And here was her own personal god.

As she stroked her fingers over the ridges of his abdomen, his muscles tensed and he groaned, his breeding organ hard, slick, and jutting straight up between his sculpted thighs.

"God, Phyllida."

She looked up to find him staring, his eyes heavy with need, his pale skin passion mottled.

"I'm—I—" He gave a breathless laugh. "Clearly I'm having difficulty forming complete sentences." His almost black eyes moved from her face to the part of him that was pointing toward her. "I'm also afraid I'll embarrass myself—and probably you." His hand slid around the base of his organ and Phil stared, enthralled as his broad palm and long fingers tightened around the thick shaft, the veins and muscles of his forearm flexing as he squeezed, his teeth gritted, his expression one of near pain. The action caused several more diamonds to leak from the tiny slit.

Phil couldn't pull her eyes away from this obvious sign of arousal; her own thighs were sticky, their bodies both preparing for each other.

Suddenly, she could not wait to have him inside her. She pushed to her feet, her legs wobbly, and he stood with her, facing her.

Phil leaned against his broad chest, pressing herself against him while her hands pushed between their bodies to yank and pull at her sash.

"Shhhh," he whispered, his breath hot in her hair, his hands covering hers, his nimble, sure fingers untying the knot. "Look at me," he said as he pulled open the sash and pushed the dressing gown over her shoulders.

His mouth covered hers the instant she turned to face him, his lips hot and soft as his hands closed around her waist, pulling her tight to his body, his hot length pressing against her while his hips subtly pulsed.

"Phyllida," he murmured, leaving a trail of kisses over her mouth, his tongue tracing the seam of her lips, pushing between them and entering her, the intimacy of his actions more erotic and shocking than anything she'd ever experienced. Not even when he'd penetrated her body had she felt so joined with another person.

"Mmmm," he hummed against her. "I want you. I want to be inside you."

She didn't trust her voice, so she nodded.

She felt his lips curve against the thin skin of her temple, and then he bent slightly and slid one arm behind her back and another beneath her knees, lifting her to his chest and pausing a moment to look down at her. "I'm so pleased that you came to me. I've been thinking about this for a long time."

He laid her out on the bed and hesitated. "May I take off your nightgown?" His darkened eyes flickered over the garment. "It's lovely and gives me delicious peeks of your body but I want to see you. All of you. I want to feel your skin against me when I come into you."

Phil's head swam at his words, his look—hungry and demanding. "Yes."

His fingers worked the tiny buttons with a skill that tried to pull her mind in other directions, toward other nightgowns . . . other women.

She slid a hand over his chest, willing the destructive thought away.

"Yes," he praised, his eyes flickering to hers while his fingers worked. "I love feeling your hands on me. Touch me anywhere, everywhere. Up," he urged, raising the hem of the gown over her calves, thighs, and the dark triangle of hair.

He made a low, needy noise and muttered something she couldn't hear as he lifted the gown over her chest.

Her chest.

If there was one part of her body she could change, it would be her almost nonexistent breasts. But it was too late to hide herself when he pulled the gown over her head, carefully scooping up her hair and freeing it from the fabric.

Phil hastily caught her hair, pulling half of the thick, heavy waves over each shoulder, hoping perhaps—

"So beautiful."

She almost didn't hear him, he spoke so softly.

When she looked at his face, she saw his eyes were on her breasts.

Her nipples, mortifyingly hard and peaked, thrust between the strands of hair, leaving her looking more naked than if nothing covered her.

She opened her mouth to say something—to apologize for their unwomanly size, nothing like the high, white mounds that Celia tried unsuccessfully to hide with ugly gowns.

But he wasn't paying her any mind, and when his mouth lowered over one breast, every other thought fled.

She was so tiny—slender and perfect, her breasts small, high, and firm, the tips dark and puckered. He suckled and kissed and tugged, alternating from one to the other as he carefully caged her with his arms, kneeling between her thighs and nudging her wider.

His quiet, severe wife was transformed by his lips, mouth, and tongue, her body twitching, bucking, thrusting as he teased and nibbled her nipples until they were tightly budded.

Her hands slid into his hair and pulled him closer, her actions asking—no, demanding more. Lucien sucked the tender skin beneath her breast, hungry to mark her.

He pushed her legs open, never pausing his licking and kissing, one hand sliding over her taut belly, his fingers delving into her curls.

It was his turn to groan and shudder. "So wet, darling." He parted her folds and stroked from her slick, swollen entrance to her taut nub, caressing her until she whimpered, her hips pushing and jerking, thighs spreading wantonly as she lifted her bottom off the bed.

Lucien chuckled softly against the plum-colored bruise he'd left on her white flesh, and then he pushed a finger inside her.

Phil made a soft, keening sound as he worked her, glorying in her tight heat.

"Mmmm," he hummed against her, sliding a second finger in beside the first and pumping her deeply, his thumb circling her sensitive bud. Her hips began to meet his hand, thrust for thrust, every muscle in her body tightening as she dug her heels into the bed, gaining better leverage to grind against his hand.

"That's right, sweetheart," he encouraged when she began to move jerkily. "Take your pleasure, Phyllida."

She cried out something unintelligible, her inner muscles contracting around his fingers. Lucien gentled his stroking, careful not to touch her too-sensitive core while she bucked and convulsed around him.

Once she'd stopped trembling, he positioned himself at her entrance. "Will you take me, love?"

She met his gaze with heavy-lidded eyes and wrapped her legs around his hips, pulling him down into her.

Lucien penetrated her with one long, smooth thrust, pinning her slender body to the bed and holding her still and full. "You're so tight and hot, darling."

She jolted at his crude words, flexing and squeezing his length.

Lucien gritted his teeth against the sharp stab of pleasure; he wanted this to last and last and last.

"Is it good?" he whispered, covering her body completely with his, reveling in the feel, scent, and sound of her.

"So good," she murmured, a dazed smile on her slack lips.

He lifted onto his forearms and began to work her with slow, thorough strokes.

She held his gaze and Lucien lost himself in her eyes, his world reduced to sensation, to pleasure, to need. As he pumped harder, faster, and deeper, she tilted her hips, taking even more of him.

And then she clenched around him.

"Good Lord! Do it again, darling," he begged, driving into her with savage thrusts.

She squeezed her eyes shut, her expression one of intense concentration, and he knew she was trying to repeat what she'd done. He grinned, loving her more for the effort she put into pleasing him.

He laughed, the sound breathless and joyous. When she opened her eyes he said, "You're so beautiful."

Her body tightened reflexively and he reached between them, before he lost himself, finding the source of her pleasure and caressing her as he buried himself deeply with each thrust.

He worked her until her breathing roughened and her body began to tense.

"Come with me, Phil," he murmured, his hips pounding harder as she tightened around him.

With a hoarse shout he hilted himself and froze, his body clenching as he emptied deep inside her, his hips jerking, each successive spasm less intense than the last.

"Ah," he mumbled, unable to hold himself up any longer, lowering onto her in a boneless slump. "My Phyllida."

Chapter 37

Celia stared at the canopy over her bed, unable to sleep. The clock said it was just past three in the morning: the witching hour.

She'd been lying there for hours, with nothing to read because she'd left her book in her satchel in Lady Yancy's room.

She chewed her lower lip and considered her options. Staring at the ceiling until dawn, braving the house to go fetch another book from the library, and then braving the massive library to *find* a book, or going to Lady Yancy's room and fetching her book.

The last option was best. The older woman slept like the dead, her snores often audible a floor away in the Harrogate house.

Celia put on her nightcap and tied it under her chin and then slipped on her ugly—but warm—old gray cloak and rammed her feet into her threadbare slippers. She opened the door a crack, checked to make sure the coast was clear, and then darted toward the servant stairs rather than the main staircase; the last thing she wanted was to encounter any guests who might be sneaking back to their own rooms after an evening of trysting.

Lady Yancy slept like a corpse and neither Alexander nor Percy was in the room to notice and alert their mistress to an invader. She knew the two animals were in a spare room so that a footman could come and walk the elderly dog three times without disturbing Lady

Yancy. That only left Mr. Fusskins, who briefly glared at her from his place near the hearth before falling back to sleep; he had no interest in Celia unless she had a deviled kidney in her possession.

She snatched up her novel and took the book on beetles for good measure.

She made it back to her floor and was just congratulating herself on her stealth when a door five or six doors down from hers opened and a woman—a maid—came staggering out.

Celia stepped back into the stairwell, her heart pounding in her chest, and then peered carefully around the corner.

The young woman was oddly hunched over and had turned to listen to somebody still in the room.

A hand, with the index finger pointed, stuck out of the open doorway and a very familiar profile followed it.

It was Sebastian's room.

He actually *poked* the girl in the chest and said something Celia couldn't hear.

The door shut and the girl slumped against the wall, her shoulders shaking with silent sobs.

Celia watched for a moment that seemed to stretch forever, one foot poised to move forward, the other rooted to the wooden floorboards.

Mind your own business, Celia. This will be nothing but trouble for you.

Yes, but since when did that matter to her?

She tucked her books under her arm and rushed toward the maid, who must have heard her feet because she looked up, her expression shifting from mute agony to horror.

Celia held a finger over her lips and shook her head, and then beckoned toward her room. She opened the door, waved the girl in, and then soundlessly shut the door behind her, locking it for good measure.

"What happened?"

The girl was already shaking her head, "Oh, no, ma'am—I couldn't—"

"I'm no ma'am, I'm a servant just like you," Celia said. "Did he interfere with you?"

The girl hesitated, and then nodded, her expression miserable.

"Is this the first time?"

She shook her head, tears silently coursing down her cheeks.

Celia said a very vulgar word and the girl flinched.

"What's your name?"

"Amy, Miss."

"Amy, you need to cleanse your body. If we do it soon enough it will—"

"Aye, I know, Miss—it might help prevent a baby. It's just—"

"Just what, Amy?"

"I don't know how." She dissolved into tears once more and Celia wanted to join her.

Instead, she slipped her arms around the girl and led her toward the overlarge bathing chamber. "I know how, Amy. I'll help you. Afterward, I want you to tell me exactly what happened."

Chapter 38

Phil woke slowly, feeling almost drugged as she gazed around at the strange surroundings.

She was in Lucien's room.

She blinked rapidly, staring at the flickering candles.

"Mmmm."

Something big and warm and solid moved beside her.

"Are you awake?" Lucien rumbled, his voice coming from around her collarbone.

That's what was tickling her nose—his hair.

She swallowed and carefully pulled away, realizing that she'd thrown her leg over his hip at some point.

But a big arm snaked around her body and stopped her. "Where are you going?"

"Er, it is late. I thought I'd return to my bed."

He pulled back just enough to look up at her. "Why?"

Her mouth opened, but she couldn't think of anything to say.

His arm tightened, pulling her closer. "Stay," he growled, something hard and hot jamming against her hip.

Her heart thrilled at the physical evidence of his lust for her, but . . .

Once again he pulled back, this time his arm moved and he released her. "I'm sorry," he said, "I shan't keep you if—"

"I don't want to go," she said as he disengaged and moved until no part of their bodies was touching. "I just need—" How could she do this without ruining what they had between them?

But there were things she *had* to know.

His hand closed around hers, which she'd unknowingly clenched.

"You want to talk?" he asked.

She nodded.

"Come, let's sit up a bit. Or would you rather get dressed?"

"No. Let's stay in bed." Her face heated at her forward words, but he didn't notice as he was shoving pillows against the headboard and pushing himself up, his chest bare and muscular and gorgeous in the candlelight.

Phil wasn't quite ready for that level of intimacy, so she pulled the sheet up over her breasts as she sat.

"Shall I fetch your robe?" he offered, his smile gentle and understanding.

"No, this is fine." She considered asking him to fetch his own robe; his body was a powerful distraction, but decided she would rather look at him, even if the sight did scatter her wits.

He sat patiently and she realized he was waiting for her to speak.

Phil swallowed. How did she put it? Where did she—

"You are wondering whether I keep a mistress."

Her eyes darted up to his face. She nodded.

"There is nobody." He took a deep breath and then let it out slowly, the flexing muscles in his jaw telling her this was not easy. "I won't lie to you, Phil. When you—er—"

"Said you were not welcome in my bed and told you to take a mistress?" she suggested.

He snorted, the sound one of surprise and amusement. "I was angry and hurt," he said, his fair skin flushing at the confession. He glanced at her, as if wondering just how honest he should be.

"I know you took lovers because I overheard women talking once."

He briefly closed his eyes. "Lord. I'm sorry you—"

Phil shook her head. "No, don't apologize. You did what I told you to do—what I forced you to do."

"This must have been some time ago," he said.

"Yes, it was years ago. They mentioned your m-mistress." Her heart pounded in her ears as that long-ago fury and jealousy raged inside her. "A woman named Louisa."

"She was the last."

Phil gaped. "But, that was—"

"A long time ago," he agreed. "I was miserable, Phil—absolutely miserable. I took those lovers in anger. I wanted to prove to myself that I didn't care that you didn't want me. But the truth is, well, I grew up seeing real love—a *real* marriage. Two of them, actually, and that is what I had always wanted and expected. I was ashamed by the way I was behaving. And then—hell," he swore, shaking his head.

"You don't have to go on," Phil said, his obvious agony making her feel some shame of her own.

"Yes, I want to tell you. I need to."

She nodded.

"Well, Hugh found out what I was doing." His face flamed in the candlelight. "He never said anything to me, but the look on his face was like a mirror. And so I quit behaving like a thwarted angry child." He shrugged. "I was lonely, but loneliness was better than disgust."

Phil was stunned. All these years she'd believed he was happily slaking his needs.

He took her hand in his and gave her fingers a gentle squeeze. It was a small gesture, but it made her feel closer to him than the physical joining they'd just engaged in. It was such a casual but precious intimacy.

"Here then, what's this?" He reached out and wiped a tear from her cheek.

"Oh," she said, mortified. "I didn't even—"

"I'm sorry, Phil—so very—"

"Shhh." She placed a finger over his lips. "I'm not crying because of what you told me." She gave a watery chuckle. "I have to admit that I'm jealous about that—and furious, but at myself. These are happy tears, Luce. I'm so happy. But there is sadness, too—that we wasted so much time."

He pulled her closer, sliding an arm around her shoulders and leaning down for a long, lingering kiss.

Phil had never guessed just how sensual and intimate a kiss could be, and her husband was a master of the art. By the time he broke away, she was boneless with desire and passion drunk.

"You are the love of my life, Phil."

Phil's head spun, the lump in her throat making it impossible for her to respond.

Lucien was undaunted by her silence and dropped a light kiss on the tip of her nose. "It might have taken us longer than it should have to discover this part of our marriage, but you are worth waiting for, my love." His beautiful lips curled into a smile that caused a throbbing between her thighs. "We'll just have to work extra hard to make up for all that wasted time."

And then he pulled her close and turned words into deeds.

Chapter 39

Richard woke with the sniffles.

After all his worrying and chiding of Celia, it was he who'd somehow managed to get a stuffy head.

He could only hope that she'd not been stricken with anything worse. He resolved to find her first thing and make sure she was fine.

Despite what Lucien had said to him last night.

"Stay. Away. From. Her."

His brother had grabbed him on their way from the after-dinner port to the drawing room—where Richard hoped there might be a game of charades, rather than the dancing that Toni had threatened—and dragged him into the nearby linen closet.

"I hope this won't take long, Luce." Richard loved charades and was quite good at them. He didn't want to miss any of the fun while being chastised by his brother.

"Listen to me, for once," Lucien began. "You need—"

"This is none of your concern. I know what—"

His brother dug his fingers into Richard's shoulder. Hard.

"Shut up. If you make a mull of Toni's wedding, she will kill you. And then I will kill you. And if there is anything left of you, Hugh will kill you."

"Duly noted, Brother. I will get killed. Now, was that all?"

It turned out that *hadn't* been all and Richard had needed to endure a five-minute raking before he could break free.

"I need to walk Newton. He'll be crossing his hind legs right about now."

Luce had turned him loose with a warning. "If I see you with her one more time—"

Richard had walked away before he heard the rest of the threat, but he could well imagine it.

The night had gone downhill from there. Instead of charades, there'd been the dreaded dancing. Dowden's fool aunt had insisted on rousting Celia—as if she were a performing bear—and dragging her out of bed to play the piano.

Richard had been furious that Phil hadn't put a stop to such foolishness. But, at least it had been Jonathan who'd turned pages for her and kept her company. Although Richard hadn't danced, he'd hung about to make sure that neither Dowden nor either of his repellent cronies bothered her.

He'd left when his mother arrived to spell poor Celia, hoping to catch her before she escaped back to her room.

But the woman was as slippery as an eel.

Richard would not allow her to evade him again today.

He shoved back the covers and plucked his glasses off the nightstand, squinting at the clock: it was just past five thirty.

He shaved and bathed himself with cold water rather than ring for Buckle, who would be forever in his fussing.

Once he was dressed, he took Newton out for his morning constitutional. The old boy was not amused to be confronted by snow drifts three times his height. So, Richard shoveled a path for the basset, who walked only far enough to relieve himself before turning around and marching back to his warm bed. Newton was no fool.

By the time Richard entered the breakfast room, it was seven and there was no sign of Celia or anyone else.

He poured himself coffee, ransacked the buffet, and settled down with the paper he needed to edit before the beginning of the New Year.

Richard was making excellent progress with his editing and on his third pot of coffee when the door opened two hours later. He looked over hopefully, only to have his hopes smashed to flinders.

"Good morning, my brother-in-law-to-be," Dowden bellowed, wearing a shockingly bright blue frockcoat. Even Richard knew that sort of toggery had gone out of fashion years ago.

"Hallo, Your Grace," he muttered, turning back to his work and hoping the other man would take the hint.

Naturally, he hoped in vain.

Richard was still listening to Dowden bore on endlessly about some curricle race when the door opened. He couldn't help noticing the duke's head whipped around as quickly as his own.

But it was just Phil.

And she was *smiling*.

Richard pushed his glasses up his nose and squinted. No. She was *glowing*.

"Good morning, Rich. Good morning, Your Grace." She floated over to the buffet.

Richard met Dowden's questioning gaze and shrugged. The fact that even the self-centered duke noticed Phil's strange expression told him something was amiss.

He'd never seen his assertive sister-in-law look so . . . well, *dreamy*.

When Phil turned to the table he couldn't help staring; she'd piled her plate a good three inches high.

Heedless of his surprise, she sat down beside him and commenced to polish off her mountain of food, replying to both his and the duke's questions in monosyllables.

Shortly after her arrival the guests began to drift in fast and thick.

Fortunately, Dowden buggered off with some vague twaddle about decorating sleighs or some such, and Richard was spared any more of the man's incessant chatter.

He leaned toward Phil after yet another giggling trio of girls drifted in. "Why is everyone so early?"

"Hmm?"

"Early. Guests. Breakfast. Good God, Phil—did you hit your head on something?"

Her cheeks flushed a fetching shade of pink. "Oh, it's the sled races."

He frowned. "Races?"

"Mmm-hmm."

"Is that what it sounds like?" he asked. "People getting on sleds and racing down the one hill in the vicinity? Competing against each other?"

She gave him an odd look. "What else would it be?"

"Does Toni make *everything* into a competition?"

But Phil had gone back to whatever it was that was distracting her.

By eleven o'clock Richard had finished the minor corrections on his paper, his eye-teeth were floating, and his arse was sound asleep from sitting. Phil had left ages ago and the room was filled with a fresh crop of gigglers.

There was still no sign of Celia.

He rose, tucked his papers under his arm, and stalked toward the main staircase.

"Richard!"

He just about jumped out of his skin. "Lord, Toni," he said as his sister charged toward him, her hair flying wildly and her cheeks flushed, looking dashed pretty. Far too pretty and lively for that pillock Dowden.

"You *are* coming to the races?"

"Er . . ."

"You missed the shopping, you missed the decorating, the skating, and now you're thinking about missing the sled races?" Her voice was gaining in volume; Richard was sure that ships out in the Channel would hear her soon. She must have inherited the skill from her father.

"No. I'll be right behind you. I just need—"

She grabbed his coat in her remarkably strong fist "No. You'll shab off—you always do." She yanked on him, almost pulling him off his feet before dragging him toward the foyer.

His sister was *strong*.

"But I came to the garland thing and the snowman thing," he protested.

"And then you left and never came back—you weren't even there when the winners were announced."

Well, she had a point, there. "I have to walk Newton."

"I just passed Buckle on the back terrace when I was looking for you. *He* was walking Newton. Or did you mean some other Newton?"

"No," he admitted mildly, "that was the Newton I meant."

There was the sound of booted feet moving quickly down the stairs and they both turned.

Richard stopped, grinned, and said, "Ah, Mrs. Pelham. I was just looking for you."

"You were?"

"You were?"

The two women spoke at the same moment, their voices almost sounding like one. They looked at each other, Toni frowning suspiciously and Celia faintly amused.

"I wanted to see if you'd suffered any ill effects after yesterday?" He glanced at Toni, but she was staring fixedly at Celia. "I heard you were caught out in the weather," he added.

"I was, but only briefly. I am well, thank you." She paused and then said, "You sound as if you might have something of a head cold?"

Richard appreciated her slightly smirky look; he deserved it. He opened his mouth to say something taunting in return, but Toni wasn't about to allow this conversation to proceed without her.

"Are you not well, Rich?" Toni glanced speculatively at Celia. "Perhaps you shouldn't go sledding, after all."

"Are you going to miss that?" Celia inquired with an innocent look he knew was entirely false. He watched, rapt, as she pulled on her gloves. The gloves he'd given her yesterday. Hmm. Perhaps she wasn't as angry with him as he'd thought. She cocked her head. "You should probably go back to bed. I can have Lady Yancy's maid send over a posset. She makes a most effective brew using ewe's milk and aspic."

Toni shuddered. "That sounds awful."

"It is," Celia agreed. "But most effective."

"As what? An emetic?" Richard asked.

Toni laughed.

"I feel fine," Richard said. "I believe I shall go along to the sledding festivities—even if it is only for a little while."

Toni gave him a look of approval. "There, I knew you were a good 'un. Now, I've got to go and find Mama. She promised she'd be there, but she's gone to ground."

"Try the library," he suggested, but she'd already bolted off in that direction.

"Is your sister always so . . . energetic?" Celia asked.

"Always. I'm surprised you're going sledding."

"Why?"

"Just because you've been so reclusive these past few days."

"That is over," she said with a grim smile.

"What happened to change things?" Richard fell into step with her, smiling when he saw she was wearing the boots he'd given her, as well.

"Are you going dressed like that?"

"Hmmm?" Richard asked.

She stopped and gestured to his person.

Richard realized that he was in his morning suit with a sheaf of papers in his hand. "Oh. I suppose I had better change."

"I suppose so," she agreed.

"Wait for me?" he asked. "I shall only take five minutes."

"I can't. I must attend to something for Lady Yancy, first. But I will meet you over at the sled track. Or grounds. Or whatever one calls it." She turned before he could answer, striding off with as much sense of purpose as Toni.

"His Grace? No, he's not here. He had something important to do in town," Lord Davenport said, his gaze flickering toward the next group of contestants. He frowned at his son. "No, Marcus, do *not* hold onto your uncle by the face, please."

The earl turned to Celia and shook his head as his son commenced to tackle his smaller uncle. "He really is a little savage. I shouldn't be allowing him to participate, but the curate dangled the race as a reward for good behavior, so I can hardly go back on his word. I just hope the two young monsters don't break their legs—or necks," he muttered, more to himself.

"And they're *off*!" Baron Ramsay shouted, his voice so loud it shook snow from the nearby trees.

"He's worse than the boys," Lucien said, following her line of vision.

Celia laughed.

"What did you need Dowden for? Perhaps I can tell him when I see him."

Celia could just imagine *that* conversation. "It is not urgent," she lied. "I shall talk to him later." In fact, that would probably be better. Why give him any time to ponder what she was about to tell him?

She could surprise the bastard with what she knew when she arrived at the ball. Why shouldn't she go, just because her dress was a decade old and more suited to a girl of eighteen than a widow? She would go. And perhaps she might even dance with Richard.

The moment Sebastian raised so much as an eyebrow at her, she would take him aside and tell him what she would do if he didn't break off his engagement.

Celia wanted to leap and cheer and—

"Are you going to give it a go?" Lucien asked.

"Hmm?" She looked away from the sledders, three of whom seemed to have collided with one another near the bottom. None of them were the two young boys. "I'm sorry, what was that?" she asked.

"The sled race? Will you try it?"

"What is the object?"

"Toni has several different competitions, farthest, fastest, and something else I can't recall."

"I'd better not." Celia said, wincing as two young men sledded right into each other.

"Why not?"

She was racking her brains for a suitable response when Lord Davenport's eyes flickered over her shoulder. A hint of a frown creased his brow. "Ah, Rich. Come to race? Mrs. Pelham says she won't be doing it."

"Oh?" Richard said as he came up and then stood beside his brother. The image of the two of them right next to each other was startling. And then Richard took off his spectacles and handed them to Lord Davenport. "Hold these for me, will you, Luce?"

Now, there was no way to tell them apart other than their clothing and Richard's tan and slightly shorter hair.

His lips curled into that sensual smirk that made her want to kiss him breathless. "Remarkable, isn't it? We used to enjoy fooling adults when we were younger."

"But never Papa," Lucien said.

Richard turned slowly to his brother, arrested. "You remember?"

"Of course, I do. He always knew who was who right away."

"He did."

Celia watched Richard stare at his brother for a long moment and knew that he was grateful his brother hadn't forgotten their father, even if only in little things.

Lucien didn't seem to be aware of what had happened and

merely turned to smile at Celia. "Sure you won't change your mind?"

"No. I'd better just—"

"Buwooock, bwock bwock."

Celia stared at Richard. "Did you just call me a chicken?" she demanded.

Richard shrugged. "If the shoe fits . . ."

Lucien laughed. "Quite good at that, isn't he? You should hear him do a cricket sometime."

Richard, meanwhile, continued to make astoundingly realistic clucking noises.

"Childish," Celia said. But then she slipped her satchel off her shoulder and thrust it at Lucien. "I'll do it. But I'm not sharing my sled with anyone."

Richard smirked triumphantly and said to his brother, "Still works as well as it did on you when we were ten, Luce."

Richard propped his soaking wet feet closer to the roaring fire.

"How's the ankle?"

He looked up to find his persecutrix smiling down at him. "The foot will probably need to be amputated."

She chuckled. "I brought you this."

This was a steaming cup of what smelled like wassail. "A peace offering, is it?" He held the cup up to his nose and inhaled. "Ah, nectar of the winter gods," he said, and then took a big swallow.

She sat down on the bench beside him. "I'm sorry about your ankle. I didn't mean to run over you."

He cocked a brow at her. "So you've said."

"I *am* sorry. But you shouldn't have been in the way."

"Anything to win, that's your motto—is it?"

She laughed—more of a choked gurgle, actually. And Richard realized, with a foolish chuckle of his own, that he'd do just about anything to make her laugh.

Good God. When did this happen to you, old boy?

Richard didn't have to ask his superior mental companion what *this* meant.

"So, was the prize worth mangling my foot?"

She took a small inlaid wooden box from her satchel and opened it. A magnificent magnifying glass lay in a bed of black silk.

"Ooh, that's quite nice." He reached for it. "What strength is—Ow!" he said when she snapped the box shut on his fingers.

"No touching. And I know that didn't hurt so quit looking so pitiful."

"I think you broke my finger."

"No, I didn't. Here, let me look at it." She grabbed his hand and held it up closer to her face. "I don't see anything wrong."

"It's internal damage." That earned him another laugh. "Perhaps you should kiss it better," he said in a lower voice.

Instead she squeezed it. Hard.

"Ow," he squawked, again, snatching his hand away. "What a vicious shrew you are."

She looked pleased by the accusation, put her prize into her satchel, and stood.

"What are you doing?"

"Everyone is leaving." She waved a hand around them.

He saw it was true. The races had dragged on for hours. There had been more than a few re-matches. But the wind had picked up around four and Lucien had dragged the children home, both boys clearly unhappy.

"I'll go with you," he said, getting to his feet and forgetting he was supposed to wince.

"Your ankle isn't hurt at all, is it?"

"It is," he insisted, holding out his arm. "I'll need to lean on you if I'm to make it."

She gave an inelegant snort and strode in the direction of the other sledders.

"You should at least share your prize with me," he complained, having to trot to catch up with her. For a small woman she had a brisk stride.

"How can we share a magnifying glass?"

"You could keep it one week; I could keep it the next," he said.

"It would cost a fortune to mail it back and forth."

"Not if we lived close to each other."

He saw her smile fade and he realized what meaning she put on his words. Before he could correct her misapprehension, a voice called out behind them.

"Yoohoo! Oh Celia, Rich! Do wait up."

Richard groaned. "Good God."

"Be civil," Celia chastised.

"Why? It's not *your* bedroom door she knocks on at least once a night."

Celia goggled. "No, she doesn't?"

"Does, too."

Steff was panting by the time she caught up with them.

"Where were you all afternoon?" Celia asked. "I didn't see you by the sleds or by the fire."

Just then one of the younger men—Jeremy something or other, a mate of Jonathan's—came jogging from the same direction as the countess had come.

Stephanie saw their shocked expressions and laughed. "Don't be so prudish."

Jeremy trotted past with only a smug smirk and a quick "Hallo," and ran up to join a group of young men.

"Come," Steff said, linking arms with each of them. "I need to get back. I'm already terribly late to get myself ready for tonight."

"Late?" Richard said. "Why, it's not even five o'clock. Dinner isn't until eight; the ball doesn't start until—"

"You silly man." Steff gave a grating giggle and Richard couldn't help wondering why he found Celia's laugh so addictive and the other woman's only annoying. "Do you remember how long it used to take us to get ready, Ceelie? All day, sometimes." She sounded wistful.

Who the devil would want to spend all day getting ready to go to a bloody dinner and ball?

"Those were the days," Celia said, cutting Richard a sly look, as if she knew exactly what he was thinking.

"Well, it's a shame you won't be attending this evening. Toni says people are coming from as far as Tunbridge Wells and staying at that charming little inn."

The Pig and Whistle would be doing a good business tonight.

"Actually," Celia said, her tone almost *too* nonchalant, "I will be going."

"Oh, how lovely. I could have sworn Seb said you'd decided against it. Well, in any case, do let me know if you need a gown. I daresay my Higgins could alter something of mine quickly enough to fit you."

"That's kind, but I shan't need it. I have the gown I wear in Harrogate. It's not a ball gown, of course, but it shall suffice."

Richard smiled to himself, wishing he could be in Celia's room when she discovered what was waiting for her.

Celia kept looking at the dress and then at the card, as if one or the other would suddenly disappear.

But, no, they were still there. The ridiculous celestial blue gown from the little shop in town, complete with a divinely soft pair of opera gloves in a shade of white that glowed like pearls.

And the note: *Just shut up and wear the dress. R.*

She looked up and caught sight of her reflection in the mirror: she was grinning like an idiot.

You can't wear this.

She watched as her smile fell.

Of course, she couldn't wear it; Lady Yancy would be horrified if she appeared at the ball kitted out as if she were—

The door to her bedroom swung open and Lady Yancy marched in, staring at a gaudy diamond bracelet on her wrist. "I think the catch is broken, Pelham. And I just sent—" She looked up, her eyes caught by the brilliant blue silk. "My goodness, Pelham. I thought you said you'd only brought your dark green."

Celia quickly hid the note in a fold of her skirt. "Oh, well I decided to throw this in at the last minute."

"Well. It certainly is something." She turned and eyed Celia with a critical look. "You were considering *wearing* it, I gather?"

No, I was considering eating it, but found that I've misplaced my knife and fork.

She smiled tightly at her employer. "Not if you think it . . . inappropriate."

Lady Yancy inhaled deeply and then gave a long sigh. "Well, yes, it is, rather."

A surprising pain stabbed her at the other woman's words. Surely, she should be used to such disappointment after all these years? When would she ever—

"But then it *is* a ball and you were invited. By Lady Davenport herself—twice."

Celia blinked. "Twice?"

"Yes, she mentioned it again last night, just as I was coming up to bed. She said it would be a favor to her as there were so many more men than women." Lady Yancy frowned at this improbable piece of information. "Shabby planning, that's what. It never would have happened in my day." She shrugged. "So, I don't see anything wrong in wearing it under those circumstances." She looked away from the gown, losing interest. "I need you to look at the catch. You are always so clever with these things. And when you're done, I'd like you to run down to the kitchen and request they send up some raw liver for Mr. Fusskins. All this cooked meat is playing havoc with his system. I'd say to ring for it, but I just know they'll mess it up somehow."

Celia was so giddy at the prospect of the ball that she didn't point out that the kitchen was all the way at the other end of the house. Nor did she mention that raw liver was, pretty much, raw liver and difficult to confuse with any other substance. And she certainly didn't point out that it was only three-quarters of an hour to dinner. Instead she smiled and said, "It would be my pleasure, Lady Yancy."

And she even meant it.

Chapter 40

Richard had just taken a mouthful of his stepfather's prized brandy when Celia entered the drawing room on the arm of Lady Yancy.

Inhaling brandy down his windpipe had both Hugh and Lucien thumping his back and asking, repeatedly, if he was all right.

Why did people insist on asking a choking person questions?

By the time he could breathe again and answer their questions, Celia and her employer had settled with a group of ladies who were lingering near the blazing fire. Heating Lessing Hall in winter was an uphill battle and he imagined it was more than a little chilly for women in their gauzy finery.

He wasn't at all surprised when Lady Yancy decided to send Celia for another shawl, or a different shawl, or some other necessity less than five minutes after she'd entered the room.

"Steady on, old man," Hugh muttered, his single eye discerning plenty. "She'll be back."

He looked up at his stepfather, his head getting hot at the look of amusement on Hugh's face.

"Finally got you, did it?" Hugh chuckled.

Richard didn't need to ask what *it* meant. Neither did he argue. The truth was, if Steff hadn't come barging along and clung to them both like a barnacle all the way back to the house he would have amended his offer of yesterday. Indeed, he'd done damned little sleeping last night as he spent most of the hours before dawn marveling at what an utter cod's head he'd been to offer her a carte blanche.

"With the right woman it's the best thing that can happen to a man," Hugh said softly.

Richard had to ask. "How do you know when it's the right one?"

"Is thinking about her keeping you awake?"

"Yes."

"Are you inventing new and creative reasons to be around her?"

Richard thought about his willingness to go shopping, an activity he despised. "Yes."

"Will you make a fool of yourself just to hear her laugh?"

Richard's mouth opened, and then he shut it, and then he stared in amazement.

Hugh nodded and took a sip from his glass.

"So you're saying that I'm in *love*?" he asked in a low voice.

Hugh gave one of his bellowing laughs, drawing the eye of every person in the large drawing room. "You say it as if you've contracted a case of crab lice."

"No," Richard said through clenched teeth, irked by the other man's superior amusement, "because I actually believe in the existence of lice. Love, on the other hand—"

"Yes, yes, yes, I've heard your theories about love. Hell, I've *read* your theories." He shrugged and smirked down at Richard. "This just goes to prove you are wrong. Or, wrongity-wrong-wrong, as David would say."

"You *do* realize that you just quoted a five-year-old?" Richard asked, not bothering to wait for an answer. "How do I know this isn't simply an especially virulent case of another four-letter L-word?"

"If you can't tell the difference between lust and love you've got my pity, lad." For once, Hugh didn't sound as if he were making mock of him. "I've lived almost six decades and have only encountered the feeling once." He looked around the room for the woman in question.

Richard followed Hugh's gaze to where his mother's dear friend,

Squire Dibbley—an ancient political philosopher who was invited to Lessing Hall so often Richard sometimes wondered if the man lived there—stood alone, staring vacantly into space.

Hugh took out his watch. "Where the devil *is* your mother?" he muttered. "I daresay I shall have to drink up and chase her down."

"You see?" Richard said. "There is an excellent example."

"I'm sorry, but an excellent example of what?"

"You and Mama and the fact you have nothing in common. You're actually looking forward to this wretched party tonight while Mama is likely burrowed under a pile of books somewhere. Even when she *does* manage to make an appearance, she'll only talk to old Dibbley. Or maybe you or one of her children. I don't understand it. You are social and know more people than anyone I've ever met. My mother would be happy if she knew nobody other than Dibbley and her family."

"What's your point?"

"My point?" Richard sputtered. "I should think that is obvious: how can you be in love with someone when you have positively nothing in common?"

Hugh chuckled. "Ah, you poor, poor lad. Love is not commonalities or lack thereof."

"Then what *is* love comprised of?" Richard demanded, getting a bit annoyed with the older man's smirking condescension.

"Love is one of life's mysteries, Rich."

Richard wanted to howl at the frustrating vagueness of such a statement. "That is utter balderdash. Twaddle," he added for good measure.

Before Hugh could respond one of the footmen approached and leaned close to say something in his ear.

"What? *Now?*" he asked the servant.

"Yes, my lord."

Hugh heaved a sigh and turned to Richard. "Excuse me, old man. I've been summoned by your mama."

Richard nodded absently and glanced at his watch. "You've only got twenty minutes until dinner," he reminded him. Something suddenly occurred to him. "Lord, do you think Mama remembered that it's the ball tonight?"

Hugh, who was tossing back the last of his drink, choked. "Good God! I'd not thought of that." He handed his empty glass to the hovering footman and hastily strode toward the door.

Richard stared at his stepfather's departing back, his mind still stuck on the subject of their conversation: love.

He also wondered just where the hell Celia was.

Celia had just found the *new* handkerchief Lady Yancy so desperately needed when there was a knock on the door. Well, that was odd. Everyone should know the guests—all except for dogsbodies—were down in the drawing room.

She opened the door and smiled. "Good evening, Daniel. I'm afraid Lady Yancy is down in the Yellow Salon."

"It's you I'm looking for, ma'am. Lord and Lady Ramsay would like a moment of your time in his lordship's study."

"Right *now*? But it is only twenty minutes until dinner."

"Right now, ma'am."

"I'm afraid I don't know where his study is."

"If you'll follow me, I'll take you there now."

What the devil was this about? Had Sebastian somehow found out what Celia knew? Her chest froze in fear—what if he'd found Amy and threatened her?

Why did she suddenly feel ill?

No matter what Sebastian has done, you have nothing to worry about this time, Celia. It's not at all like when you were summoned to the Duke of Stanford's study.

She tried to keep telling herself that, but, even so, her feet seemed to get heavier and heavier with each step.

Several moments later the servant stopped in front of a room she'd never entered and scratched on the door.

"Come in," a loud male voice called.

When the footman opened the door, Celia wasn't sure where to look first.

It wasn't just Lord and Lady Ramsay, but Lord and Lady Davenport, Miss Antonia Redvers, Sebastian, and . . . *Amy*.

Turn around and run, Celia, the usually cool voice in her mind advised.

"Please, come in, Mrs. Pelham," Lord Ramsay said, coming toward her. His face, which was almost always creased in a smile, was now stern and rather terrifying. He stopped far too close to her, towering over her. "Why don't you have a seat," he said coolly, gesturing to a chair that was slightly away from all the others.

Celia walked on legs that seemed to have become boneless.

"We have some rather upsetting information, ma'am," the huge man said.

Celia turned and looked at Sebastian. She recognized the barely suppressed glee in his hydrangea blue gaze and knew that she had—yet again—made a terrible misstep.

"His Grace tells us—"

The door to the study opened, and the only people who'd been missing to complete her misery stood in the doorway.

Lord Ramsay frowned. "Lady Yancy, Rich—I'm afraid I don't—"

"I sent for them, my lord," Sebastian said, taking control of the play that he had no doubt scripted. "I thought Lady Yancy should know the character of her employee and—" He bit his lip, as if in chagrin, but she knew he was secretly overjoyed. "And I'm afraid that Mrs. Pelham may have been insinuating herself with Mr. Redvers, so it only seems fair—"

Richard strode into the room. "I beg your pardon, Dowden, but you should watch what you're saying when you speak of Mrs. Pelham."

Sebastian gave the rest of the occupants of the room a look that said, *You see what I mean?*

"Richard," Lady Ramsay said, her voice soft, but stern. When her son turned to her, she said, "If you're going to stay, take a seat."

Lady Ramsay looked at her husband and then Sebastian. "It was ill-done bringing these two into this, Your Grace, but it is too late now to send them away."

"I beg your pardon, my lady," Sebastian said, bowing his head, but not before Celia saw the spark in his eyes: His Grace did not care to be chided, not even when the person doing the chiding would soon be his mother-in-law.

"What is this about, Pelham?" Lady Yancy demanded when Celia stood and helped her into a chair.

Celia just returned to her seat.

When everyone turned to Ramsay to continue, Celia couldn't help noticing the infamous privateer looked displeased. Unlike earlier, that displeasure was aimed at the duke, rather than her.

"You came to us with this, Dowden. Perhaps you should handle it," Ramsay said, his expression one of distaste.

"Of course, my lord," Sebastian said smoothly. He then stood and went to stand beside Amy. When she cringed, he gave her shoulder an avuncular pat. "It's quite all right, Amy. You shan't be punished for telling the truth. Tell them what you told me."

Amy's eyes jumped to Celia and then dropped back to the floor. "I, er, Mrs. Pelham told me that she wanted to play a prank on His Grace. That I was to say he'd, er—" She broke off and looked up at Sebastian with pleading eyes that were leaking tears. "Oh, please, I don't want to cause no trouble. I never—"

"Shhh, Amy, don't cry. It's better to just get it all out and let your master and mistress decide what to do about it," he said. "Go on, Amy."

Amy gulped convulsively and then blurted, as if spitting out a rotten piece of food, "Mrs. Pelham wanted me to tell youse that His Grace had, er, interfered with me against my will."

Lady Yancy gasped and her head whipped around. "My goodness! Tell me this isn't true, Pelham."

Every eye in the room was on Celia, so nobody saw the look that Sebastian gave Amy's cringing form. She knew him well enough to decipher his expression: the game was up and all she could achieve now by trying to fight him was to make more misery for the girl.

And herself.

Celia met Richard's stunned—but flatteringly disbelieving gaze—and nodded. "Yes, it's true."

Other than Lady Yancy's horrified squawk, the room was utterly silent. Celia didn't bother to look at anyone else but Richard. She knew what everyone would be thinking because she could see it on Richard's face when she confessed: disbelief, hurt, and—yes—disgust.

Well, then. It seemed she'd not need to worry about another offer—of any kind—from him.

"If you'll all excuse me." She stood and strode to the door quickly enough to beat even Lord Ramsay.

Behind her, the room erupted as everyone came back to life.

Celia was halfway down the hall, not sure if she was heading in the right direction, her eyes blurred with tears, when she heard Richard's voice.

"Mrs. Pelham."

Celia ignored him.

"Celia."

When a hand closed around her arm, she jerked away and whirled on him. "Leave me alone, *Mr. Redvers*," she hissed through clenched teeth, unable to see him through the veil of tears.

"What happened in there, Celia? I've known Amy all her life. She grew up on the estate with Toni and my other young siblings. Why would she lie about something like this?"

Celia's jaw dropped. "You think she's *lying*?"

"Well, isn't she?" he asked, his honest, penetrating gaze burning into her.

"Richard?"

They both turned to find Lucien striding toward them. The rest of the group from the study—all except Hugh and Richard's mother—were already walking in the opposite direction.

"For God's sake, Rich. What the hell are you doing?" Lucien demanded.

"Something isn't right, here," Richard said. "It just isn't logical."

"I don't give a bloody goddamn about logic. I'm telling you that you need to go and support our sister tonight."

Richard stared mulishly.

"Dinner began five minutes ago—without our entire family," Lucien said. "We need to go now or this will all become public knowledge."

Richard stared at Celia, his eyes pleading with her to deny everything.

"Just go," she ordered.

But he would not budge.

Lord Davenport gave a disbelieving snort. "If we do not salvage this situation, the entire world will learn that Lady Infamous is back to her old tricks."

Richard turned on him. "You will mind your tongue, Brother," he said, coldly menacing.

Lucien raised his hands and took a step back. "I apologize," he said to Celia. "That was uncalled for."

Based on what Sebastian had just said, Celia thought Lucien's comment was remarkably mild.

Richard turned back to Celia. "He's right—I have to appear at dinner. But we will talk about this immediately after the ball." Whatever he saw on her face made him say, "Don't go *anywhere*."

Celia glanced at Lucien; his face was unreadable, but she knew well enough what he was thinking.

"I won't go tonight," she promised. "But his lordship is correct: your sister deserves to have her family around her this evening."

Richard ground this teeth, visibly displeased, but finally said, "Fine. In the morning, then."

Celia nodded.

"I want your word, Celia."

She looked up into his beautiful brown eyes; eyes that were raw with worry. And then opened her mouth and lied to him. "I give you my word, Mr. Redvers."

Richard honestly felt as if his blood were boiling.

"What the hell is wrong with you?" Lucien demanded, striding beside him. "Do you realize the entire family is going to be late for your sister's wedding ball dinner and you were prepared to make everyone even later by pandering to a—"

Richard had never once laid a hand on any of his siblings. His calm and cool nature was legendary. But when he slammed Lucien up against the wall, he felt nothing but righteous fury coursing through him. "Whatever you are thinking about saying, don't."

Hugh's huge, four-fingered hand landed on Richard's shoulder. "Rich. Not now."

"Richard! Lucien! That is enough."

It had been a good fifteen years since he'd heard their mother use that tone.

Richard yanked his arm from Hugh's grasp and marched toward the dining room.

A footman scrambled to open the door and Richard forced his lips into a—likely grim—imitation of a smile.

They were only ten minutes late, but he knew it would be obvious to everyone else in the room that something unpleasant had happened.

All a person had to do was look at any of their faces.

Old Lady Yancy appeared to be in a fugue state, her smile fixed and her eyes blank.

Toni looked . . . well, Richard didn't know what her expression meant. He'd never seen his confident sister look anything other than poised.

Lucien continued to glare at Richard—as if expecting him to run from the room at any moment—and ignored the young ladies on his left and right.

Phil and Hugh, the most socially adept and gregarious members of the family, chatted with their dinner partners, but were uncharacteristically stiff and subdued.

Only Dowden looked perfectly at ease.

The duke took his chair like a king settling onto his throne, apologized to his dinner companions for his tardiness, and immediately went to work charming them.

Richard reached for his watch, not caring how rude the gesture appeared; it was approximately six minutes since he'd last spoken to Celia.

Tonight was going to be the longest night of his entire life.

Chapter 41

It was no accident that all Celia's possessions fit into just one bag.

Even with all the gifts from Richard, her single piece of luggage was not overfull. Celia had learned her lesson the hard way—long ago, when she'd first become a servant—after she'd been tossed out of two houses without warning and little time to gather her things.

If she only kept enough to fit in one bag, then she only had one bag to carry if she found herself out on the street.

Garbed in one of her two grim gowns, Celia carefully wrapped the blue silk in the paper it had come in. It would get wrinkled in her small portmanteau, but it was hers and she would not leave it behind. It was the most beautiful garment she'd ever owned. More importantly, it was bought by a man she suspected did not often purchase clothing for women. Richard had selected the gown after she'd paused beside it while they shopped for gifts for his family. She'd not lingered near the dress longer than a few seconds—it was too painful to want things she had no use for and could never have—but he had noticed. Because he was the sort of man who'd devoted his life to observation and paying attention to tiny details. For a while, at least, he had found Celia worthy of his notice.

It was foolish of her, but her one great regret this evening was that she hadn't been able to dance with Richard.

Celia left her old boots beside the bed with a note asking the maid to give them to someone in need.

Once her bag was packed, she rang for a servant and then sat at the small desk and wrote a brief letter to Lady Yancy while she waited. She didn't tell the old woman where she was going. She did let her know that she would write Lord Yancy about her remaining wages. There would be no bonus, of course, but she was still owed for the last quarter.

She had just put the letter on the desk in Lady Yancy's room when the door opened.

Celia smiled. "Ah, Daniel, I was hoping it was you."

The handsome young footman blushed, his gaze wandering to her bag and cloak, which she'd set next to the door. He did not look surprised. Celia had spent enough time in servant halls over the past decade to know that nothing that happened upstairs went unremarked.

"Do you know when the mail coach stops in Eastbourne?"

"The Brighton mail, or the London, ma'am?"

"Either." She could not be choosy at this point.

He scratched his head and glanced at the clock on the mantel; it was already after eleven thirty. "The London one will be gone soon—even in this weather. But the Brighton doesn't come until three." He hesitated, and then said. "You're not thinkin' to walk, ma'am?"

It was only three miles and she'd done it the day she'd gone sailing on Jonathan's boat. "I was."

"It's too cold, ma'am, and there is word of more snow. My brother works in the stables—John is his name—he can run you over and nobody will be the wiser."

Celia hesitated. She didn't want to ask Daniel or his brother to lie, and Richard would surely ask the servants where she went when he discovered her absence the next morning.

"There is another way," he said, when he saw her hesitation. "John and I have permission to spend tomorrow with our family, as we'll be working on Christmas. His lordship is kind enough to let us use the dogcart to go home. We could drop you at the inn in Pevensey. There's no mail that stops there, but the coach runs to Tunbridge Wells at eight in the morning."

That would serve just as well. "I shall need to leave early." *Preferably right now, but . . .*

His gaze was knowing. "Aye, we'd planned to go at five, ma'am, but John'll have sent the last guest carriages off around three. Would four be early enough? You'd have to sit about the inn and wait for the coach for a few hours," he warned.

"Thank you, Daniel. Four will work nicely. I believe I shall wait in the library, rather than here." The last thing she wanted was to be in Lady Yancy's room when the older woman returned from the ball, which she was likely to do any minute.

Daniel bent to pick up her valise.

"That's quite all right. I shall keep it with me."

"No, ma'am," he said, suddenly quite mulish. "I shall carry it for you."

They walked in silence down the servants' stairs. This side of the house was as empty as a graveyard, every servant and guest engaged in the revelry of the ballroom.

As usual, a fire flickered in the huge hearth in the library.

Alexander and the Great Sou'wester were both sleeping on their perches near the fireplace, their giant heads tucked beneath their wings.

Celia turned to thank the footman and found him staring at her, his expression one of misery.

"I know somethin' bad happened with Amy tonight, ma'am. She was called to the baron's study—like you were. She wouldn't talk to me, after." He hesitated and then added in a choked voice, "We'd planned to marry next summer, when a cottage comes free, but yesterday Amy told me she'd changed her mind."

Another pair of lives that Sebastian had ruined.

Celia felt for the boy. "I can't tell you what happened, Daniel, because it's not my secret to share. But I *can* tell you that Amy is probably in need of a friend right now. Don't give up on her."

Daniel nodded, his eyes glassy as he set down her bag. "Thank you, ma'am. I'll come fetch you at four."

Celia laid her cloak over the nearby settee and made her way toward the big desk that was obscured behind towers of books. A quick peek over one of the shorter stacks satisfied her that Lady Ramsay hadn't sneaked away from the evening's entertainment.

She heard the door open behind her and turned. "Did you forget—"

Sebastian closed the door and leaned against it. "Did I forget what, darling?"

"How did you find me and what do you want?"

"I went to your room to speak to you and saw you with the servant. I'd hoped you would have the sense to leave the house entirely, but—lo and behold—I followed you here. As to what I want?" He smirked and sauntered toward her, magnificent and intimidating in his evening blacks. "I came to tell you not to be a sore loser, Celia. I won, you lost—again."

"Do you think this is some sort of game, Sebastian? These are people's lives you are ruining—Amy's, her family, the young man who hoped to marry her."

"Listen to you, Celia! A champion of the servant class." He chortled.

"Why?"

"Why what?"

"Why did you do all this?"

"You mean why did I ruin your reputation?" He laughed. "Not that there was much to ruin."

"No, that is the only thing I *do* understand; you did what you did tonight because I was about to ruin your plans. No, I mean why do you have such plans to begin with? Why are you marrying this poor girl? I know you don't love her, and you don't need her money."

"Love?" He laughed to show her what he thought about that.

"As to her money? Well, times are difficult for men of my station, Celia. The vast estates we hold have become a burden, the merchant class encroaches daily on our power, and we are under siege by the same riffraff who owe their very lives to us. So, yes, as a matter of fact, Celia, I do need a wealthy bride."

She enjoyed a surge of satisfaction at the thought of Sebastian worrying about money. But her satisfaction was short-lived when she recalled the poor young woman he was using to solve his problem.

"Surely there are plenty of women who are wealthier than Miss Redvers?"

"I don't think you understand the riches her father accumulated during his years as a privateer. The only other marital prospects as well-dowered as Antonia are the daughters of wealthy cits. While that type of woman might be well enough to plow when my blood is hot, they are hardly the sort of female in which I wish to plant my seed."

Celia could only stare.

He chuckled, visibly amused by her loathing. "You ask me why I want to marry her? I counter with the question: Why shouldn't I? She is passably handsome, young and nubile, and eager to be molded into the perfect duchess. Her father's blood is ancient—nothing to mine, of course, but acceptable."

His lips curled into a sensual smile that made her gorge rise. "If Lady Ramsay's fecundity is anything to go by, then her daughter shall make excellent bloodstock." He paused, his eyes glinting unpleasantly "For all that Toni aspires to become a great political hostess—like her sister-in-law—that is not the future awaiting her. She will discover that she is actually more content living at my country estate, where she can stay out of my way and anticipate being bred with pleasing regularity."

"You are a lying, revolting—"

He flicked one elegant hand dismissively. "Yes, yes, yes. I already know what you think of me, my dear." He sighed. "But if you believe that Toni is a schoolroom chit and ignorant of my ways, think again. My wife-to-be is surprisingly worldly for all her tender years. She knows I keep a mistress in town and is quite sanguine about it."

"I doubt she'll be so *sanguine* when she discovers your true plans for her."

His smirk grew. "I shall enjoy working any kick from her gallop. Not that I believe much exertion on my part will be necessary; Antonia has been raised to know a woman's place and be satisfied with her role. She will make a most obedient and accepting wife."

Celia could not believe the man was so stupid—had he not *seen* the high-spirited and strong-willed young woman this past week? As for being raised to know a woman's role, her mother was hardly a pattern card of tractability. No, Antonia Redvers would not have the *kick worked from her gallop* so easily. Sebastian would eventually break her to bridle, but he would crush her spirit in the process.

"Your mistresses are one thing; do you think she will be as accepting when she learns that you rape your servants?"

Sebastian propped a hip on the back of the settee that separated them, crossed his arms over his chest, and smiled. "I think she'll accept whatever I tell her to accept. Once we are married and she is mine under the law, I shall make sure of her compliance."

Celia shivered at what she saw in his pitiless eyes.

He cocked his head. "But, tell me: why do you care about her so much? You don't even know the chit. You barely know her fam—"

His eyes widened and a slimy grin spread across his face. "Oh, Lord!" He slapped his thigh. "But this is *delicious*. You have fallen in love with Odious." He threw his head back and laughed. Celia wondered if she had time to grab the fireplace poker before he turned his attention to her.

He shook his head as he brought his gaze back to her. "Priceless, my dear. Positively priceless." He chuckled. "Oh, I can see you are still filled with feminine rage toward me, Celia. If you are considering doing anything foolish—although I can't imagine what—I want you to remember that I know where to put my hands on our daughter."

"And I want you to know that I am not a defenseless seventeen-year-old girl anymore, Sebastian."

His brows arched, his expression one of tolerant amusement. "Oh, I can see you are all grown up, my dear."

"After you threatened me that first morning, I wrote a letter to the family my daughter lives with. They are not wealthy or powerful, but they also are not ignorant or frightened. They are now on notice and prepared should you—or one of your thugs—come calling and threaten *my* daughter." She narrowed her eyes. "The name of my daughter's father—as far as the law is concerned—is Thomas Pelham. I have several witnesses who will testify to that. The only reason I have submitted to your threats these past few days is because I did not want to cause trouble here and lose my position." She gave him an unpleasant smile. "My worries on that score are now over. I warn you: If I get so much as a whiff of your stench in Katie's vicinity, I shall write a letter to every newspaper in Britain exposing you for the conscienceless rapist you are."

"You would never do that," he scoffed, although Celia could see a hint of doubt in his eyes. "If you did, all of Britain would know about your bastard. You might expose yourself to more ridicule, but never her."

"You're right that my fears for Katie have kept me mute all these years. But your threats have changed that." She cocked her head, giving him a confident smirk that she was far from feeling. "You've forgotten that I don't have to live in England, Sebastian. I can find dogsbody work anywhere in the world. But it will be a bit more difficult for *you* to outrun a reputation as a rapist. Your august position might protect you from ever going to gaol for your sins. But not all prisons have bars, Sebastian—as I well know. Your status will also become your curse because wherever you go, people will whisper. And *everyone* will know the truth about you. It will haunt your steps for the rest of your life."

His mouth tightened. "Are you threatening me?"

"Call it whatever you like, Your Grace. Just stay away from my daughter."

For a moment, she thought he might strike her.

But then, as quickly as it had slipped, his mask was back in place.

He flashed her a condescending smile. "It amuses me that you'd think anyone would ever take your word over mine, Celia. You might think the accusations of an infamous whore will matter. But the truth is, nobody will believe you." He stood. "Now, as much as I'd love to stay here and chat, my dance card for the evening is rather full."

When he reached the door, he paused and turned. "If you know what is good for you, Celia, you will be gone well before breakfast."

Celia waited until the door shut behind him before dropping into her chair, shaking with impotent rage, frustration, and terror.

He was right: nobody would ever believe her.

When have you ever tried to tell the truth, Celia?

Celia blinked at the question.

Never. Never had she tried to expose Sebastian for what he was. She'd always been too terrified of what he would do. These past few days had shown just how willing he was to use Katie as a club to beat and subdue and bring her to heel.

She was terrified of him—a person would be a fool not to fear the power of a duke—but if she left here tonight without sharing the truth, she would be condemning another woman to a lifetime of abuse and degradation.

Speaking out—even if it meant exposing her own shame in the process—was not about exacting revenge on Sebastian, although that would certainly be a benefit; it was about doing the decent and moral thing.

Celia picked up a taper from the glass on the mantelpiece and lit it before making her way through the gloom to the book-covered desk.

She lighted the candles in the candelabrum, lowered herself into the massive chair, and assembled a quill and paper.

And then she began to write.

Chapter 42

The door to Lucien's bedchamber flew open so hard that it slammed against the wall.

"She's *gone*!" Richard yelled at him.

Lucien was profoundly grateful that he'd gone to Phil's chamber last night so that his wife wasn't lying naked and ravaged in his bed.

Instead, she was lying naked and ravaged in *her* bedchamber, where he'd left her sleeping a mere hour earlier.

He allowed himself to enjoy that image for only a moment before engaging in what he *knew* would be a most challenging discussion.

"You may go," he said to Peel, waiting until the valet was gone before turning to his brother. "Perhaps you could keep your voice down as it is still not quite seven in the morning and most of the household did not retire until four."

Richard stalked toward him. "She. Is. Gone."

Lucien finished putting in his cufflinks before taking up his coat. "Help me on with this, since you drove away poor Peel."

Richard snatched the coat from Lucien's hands and looked ready to tear it in half.

"Help me finish dressing and then I shall help you," Lucien said coolly.

"Was it you who sent her away?"

"No." Although it had certainly occurred to him to have her taken to the Pig and Whistle last night. But Phil, his mother, Hugh, and even Toni had protested that such an action would be inhumane. When he found himself backed only by Dowden, Lucien gave in.

Richard grunted and then held out the coat.

For the next minute they both struggled while Lucien shoehorned himself into it.

"Bloody hell," Richard snapped once the coat was finally on. "Why in the name of God would you wear such a ridiculous garment?"

Lucien cut a speaking look at the coat his brother was wearing. The pockets sagged from being stuffed full of . . . well, whatever. The cuffs were frayed from hard use and you could easily put a fist between his chest and the front of the coat. Quite frankly, his twin looked like a traveling tinker.

"Where the hell could she have gone?" Richard demanded, clearly uninterested in bickering about clothing. "It didn't snow again last night, but it was bloody cold."

"What does Lady Yancy say?" Lucien asked as he tweaked his cravat, which Rich had smashed with his utter lack of valeting skills.

"She didn't even know she was gone until I went looking for her."

Lucien spun on his brother. "Christ, Richard! I thought Lady Yancy came to *you*. You mean you went knocking on the old lady's door at seven in the morning?"

Richard shoved a hand through his already disheveled hair. "It was actually closer to five," he admitted without any visible sign of shame. "After learning nothing from the old woman I took a ride to the Pig and Whistle, but they said Celia didn't buy a ticket on either the London or Brighton mail. I've spent the last hour talking to servants."

"And none of them have any idea where she's gone?"

"They claim they don't, but I know they are hiding something."

Lucien frowned. "Please do not accuse my servants of dishonesty without evidence."

Richard didn't seem to hear him. "It is as though she simply disappeared."

Lucien heard the anguish in Richard's voice and felt his brother's pain sharply for a moment. Richard had finally fallen in love. The fact that he'd chosen the most inappropriate and infamous woman they knew was pure Richard. If there was a way to do something sideways or awkwardly, his brother would find it.

"You must see that this is for the best, Rich."

Lucien wouldn't have been surprised to find himself slammed up against a wall again, like last night.

But Richard's anger seemed to have dissipated. In its place was something even more concerning: despair.

"Where would she go?" Richard asked, speaking more to himself than Lucien.

"Perhaps Lady Yancy—"

"She knows nothing." He fixed Lucien with a penetrating look. "I learned from Watson that you sent Amy home to her family last night?"

"Yes," Lucien admitted. "The poor girl was—"

"I want to talk to her."

"I won't have you badgering one of my servants, Rich."

"That's unfair, Lucien," Richard said, his voice suddenly quiet. "I would never frighten Amy."

Lucien sighed. "You are correct. I apologize. Hugh and I already spoke to her—without anyone else there to coerce her—if that's what you're thinking."

"I want to talk to her."

"Fine." Lucien recognized his twin's expression; Richard wouldn't stop until he got what he wanted. "But wait until you are calmer, Rich. Right now you look wild around the eyes."

"That's because the bloody ball didn't end until three-thirty and I did nothing but pace until it was a respectable hour," he muttered.

Lucien found it amusing that his brother thought five o'clock a respectable hour to knock on anyone's door.

Richard looked him up and down and then frowned. "Why do you look as fresh as a daisy?"

"Because I'm used to a far faster pace in London. While you, I know, go to bed with the hens, er, beetles. Now, have you had breakfast?" he asked, already guessing the answer.

"No. I'm not hungry."

"Now I *know* you aren't well." Lucien gripped his brother's shoulder and was startled by how brawny he had become. "Lord, no wonder I look scrawny compared to you," he said. "You're as solid as a cart horse. You'll need to eat to keep your strength up," he added quickly before Richard could come up with any resistance. "Come on, we can discuss how to find her while we're eating. You know there won't be anyone else down for hours yet."

Richard's body was stiff for a moment, but then he sighed heavily and nodded.

Unfortunately, there *was* somebody down there: Dowden.

The duke had the nerve to grin at them. "I thought I'd be the only one up and about after last night." He chuckled heartily. "I ordered Toni to stay abed until at least noon. I want her to get plenty of rest before tomorrow."

Lucien could feel Richard radiating hostility beside him.

"Do you know where Celia went?" Richard demanded, his tone extremely uncivil.

The duke's eyebrows knitted. "No, as a matter of fact, I do not."

"I think you're a bloody liar."

Lucien stared at his brother. Richard didn't even sound like Richard—at least not the Richard he knew. Instead, he sounded like something predatory and dangerous, like one of the man-eating creatures he was always encountering on his far-flung expeditions.

Dowden's mouth tightened at the insulting tone. "I'm going to give you the benefit of the doubt, Redvers, because I know Celia is capable of casting quite a net around a man and—"

"Oh?" Richard sneered. "And just how do you know that, *Your Grace*?"

"Because I recall her tricks from a decade ago, when she almost snared your brother."

Lucien had heard the saying *his hackles rose*, but never had he seen it happen.

Richard took a long stride toward the other man, until only the breakfast table was between them.

"Gentlemen," Lucien said, putting a hand on Rich's shoulder. "Let's not—"

"You wanted her gone because she knows something—something about you and how rotten you really are."

The duke tossed aside his napkin. "You are dangerously close to crossing a line, Redvers."

"Consider me having one foot over it, *Dowden*." Richard seemed to double in size, his thighs pressed against the table and his fisted hands resting on its surface while he leaned toward the duke.

Dowden showed his teeth, but you couldn't call it a smile. "Right now it is only your future status as my brother-in-law that is keeping me from—"

"Keeping you from *what*? You vile, poxy, pusillanimous—"

The duke shoved back his chair with an earsplitting screech.

What happened next was a blur.

One second Richard was beside Lucien; the next he was scrambling over the table, sending Dowden's unfinished kippers, steaming coffee, and a half-full rack of toast flying.

Before Dowden could get away from the table Richard launched himself across the polished wooden expanse right into the duke's lap. The impact slammed Dowden's chair onto its back and flung both men to the floor.

"Stop them!" Lucien roared at the gawking footman as he ran around the length of the table toward the grappling men.

Richard was straddling Dowden, who heaved and bucked below him, trying to roll aside and protect his face from Richard's flying fists.

"Good God! Richard, stop." Lucien grabbed his brother's right biceps and pulled back, the footman doing the same on his left arm. When they began to lift him, the duke got his right arm free and delivered a punishing blow to Richard's temple, sending his spectacles skittering across the polished wooden floor.

"Hey there!" Lucien shouted at the duke. "Stop or I'll—"

Dowden took another swing just as Richard wrenched his arms free.

Rich threw himself forward, punching the duke in the jaw even as he absorbed a hit to the chest.

"Goddammit!" Lucien yelled as one of Dowden's fists hit his open hand and bent his finger back.

"We need some help in here!" Lucien yelled over his shoulder, shaking out his right hand and grabbing Richard's shoulder with his left as the footman pinned the duke.

They'd just managed to pry the brawling men apart when the breakfast room door flew open and hit the wall.

"Just what the devil is going on in here?" his stepfather roared.

Richard was only vaguely aware of giant hands clamping onto his shoulder.

"Richard, come, let go of him," a deep voice urged.

At some point he'd lost his spectacles. The duke's face was a blur, but he was pleased to see smears of blood on his pale brow.

Or perhaps that was blood from the cut in Richard's eyebrow, which was trickling into his eye and making his already bad vision worse.

When he tried to bring his fist around, he realized he was immobilized.

"*Richard!* Stop it right now." The cold female voice startled him, cutting through his rage even as several pairs of hands pulled him off the duke.

He quit resisting and allowed himself to be led a few feet away from Dowden, who was currently struggling with his own team of handlers.

"Can I release you?" Hugh asked him a moment later.

Richard jerked out a nod, his pulse so loud in his ears that everything was muffled.

"Here." Something pressed into his hand and he looked down to see his spectacles.

"I think the frame is damaged," Lucien said, his voice breathless.

Richard slid the glasses onto his face, having to bend them to stay on his nose.

Across from him, Dowden jerked his arm away from one of the footmen and began to straighten his clothing.

Richard's fists clenched and he took a step toward the other man; Hugh's hand landed on his shoulder. "Don't even think about it."

"What happened here?" Toni demanded.

Richard turned to find his sister standing on Dowden's side of the table.

He opened his mouth to speak, but then realized she was staring at the duke.

Dowden snorted, his face distorted by an ugly sneer that, for once, showed his true character. "Your lunatic brother attacked me—without provocation, I might add." His voice was cool, but his hands shook as he tried—and failed—to straighten his ludicrous cravat.

Toni strode toward the duke and Richard noticed that she was clad in her dressing gown—a gorgeous scarlet and gold garment. Her hair, which she always wore unbound, appeared to be unbrushed and stood out in a wild golden-red corona. She didn't look like his little sister; she looked like a stern, angry goddess from a Greco-Roman painting.

She looked bloody magnificent.

She stopped a few feet from Dowden. "I want to talk to you."

The duke took in his betrothed's dishevelment, a flicker of distaste on his handsome face. "Now is hardly the time, Antonia; you are not even decent."

Toni gave a sharp bark of laughter that made the duke flinch. "*I'm* not decent. That is rather rich coming from you, Sebastian."

Dowden's eyes narrowed. "I'm not sure I care for your tone, my dear. If you wish to speak to me, let us go somewhere more—" His gaze flickered around the room, which now held at least a dozen servants and several curious early morning guests as well as the original occupants. "—appropriate. After you have dressed yourself."

"No. I think right here, and right now, is extremely appropriate." She raised her left hand, which held a crumpled sheet of parchment. "This is a letter from Mrs. Pelham."

Richard saw the lightning-fast flash of fear in the other man's eyes before Dowden could smother it with a condescending smirk. "Please tell me you aren't going to believe anything that slattern says."

Both Hugh and Lucien grabbed Richard as he lunged forward.

Dowden looked over at him and laughed, then winced when the action opened the split on his lip.

Toni didn't allow his amusement to distract her from her purpose. "My mother brought this letter to me as soon as she found it, just before dawn this morning. Once I read it, I sent a servant to fetch Amy back. We had a brief, but enlightening, conversation just ten minutes ago."

Dowden's mouth tightened, but he merely shrugged. "The words of *another* slattern."

"For such an upstanding, respectable man, you seem to be surrounded by slatterns, Sebastian."

The duke's mask slipped, and this time he let it fall. "Have a care, Toni," he warned. "You are treading in dangerous waters. You don't want to say something you will regret."

"You are right, *Your Grace*. I don't want to *say* anything I might regret."

He nodded smugly, as if the planets had come back into alignment, just the way he'd known they would.

"But there is something I want to *do*. If I don't, I shall regret it for the rest of my days."

Richard saw her tall, slender body tense and he dropped his gaze to her right hand.

She was almost as tall as the duke and her roundhouse punch hit its target—his jaw—squarely. Just as he and Luce had both taught her, Toni put her weight behind the punch and followed through.

Dowden's body spun in an oddly graceful pirouette before he slammed back into the breakfront and slid down to the breakfast room floor.

"Well done, Toni!"

"Excellent follow-through!"

Richard's and Lucien's voices blended together.

Their sister didn't seem to hear them as she stood over Dowden's vanquished body. "Just in case I wasn't clear enough, Your Grace, our engagement is over."

Chapter 43

Celia stared around at the tiny, but clean, ground-floor room and sighed. It was the last room the inn had, and one that was usually occupied by an employee, but it was better than being snowbound on some country lane, freezing on top of a mail coach.

As Celia sat on her narrow cot and stared at the blank wall across from her, she wondered if she'd done the right thing by leaving last night.

She'd considered staying—especially after she'd written that letter to Toni, confessing almost everything. For the first time ever, she had told somebody outside her small circle of intimates about Katie.

By doing so, she had done the one thing she'd feared more than anything else these past ten years: she had admitted on paper that Sebastian had a blood claim on her daughter.

If Toni believed her, then Celia might have saved her from a miserable fate.

But if she didn't . . . Was Antonia Redvers the sort of person to misuse the information Celia had given her? Knowing what she did about Richard, and his honorable nature, Celia did not think so.

But she was terrified of what Sebastian might do if he learned about the letter.

Celia needed to get back to Katie, even though she knew that Molly and her sisters would be protecting the girl with their lives.

Besides, what was the point of staying? Even if Richard had believed what she had to say about Amy, Celia would no longer be able to keep the truth from him. And when he learned about her and Sebastian . . . ?

You looked into his eyes and lied to him, Celia.

She groaned, infuriated by the remarkably persistent thought. All night and all day—until the coach had gone off the road into a ditch, at which point other concerns had occupied her mind—she'd thought of nothing but Richard and how he'd looked when she'd told him that she would wait.

Celia squeezed her eyes shut, as if that would banish the image.

It didn't.

Thanks to the shocking amount of snow that continued to fall it was likely she'd get to keep thinking about Richard tonight and all day tomorrow, rather than spending Christmas with Katie and Henson and the rest of her friends—something she'd not done in years.

The sound of heavy boots clumping up the narrow wooden stairs pulled her from her thoughts and brought her to her feet.

Hopefully this would be her bag, which the ostler had sent a pair of lads to fetch from the stranded mail coach and—

Her door swung open and she had to step back to keep from getting clipped.

Celia gawked at the figure who loomed in the small doorway. *"Richard?"*

Richard strode toward Celia. "Why do you sound so surprised?" he demanded. He knew he sounded rough and angry, but that was because his heart wouldn't stop hammering at his ribs.

"What are you doing here? How did you find me?" Her gaze flickered to his snow-crusted overcoat. "Did you *ride* all the way here?"

"I'm here to have the conversation you promised me. And I found you by using my brain—even if it took me far too many hours. To answer your last question, look." He pointed to the room's single window, which faced the stables. The only activity in the courtyard was a monstrous black horse that was pawing the ground, gouts of steam shooting from its flared nostrils while a groom stood at a safe distance. "To my shame, I rode poor Sunshine shamelessly hard."

Celia gave an unladylike snort of laughter that warmed him to his core. "That beast is called Sunshine?"

Richard took both her hands and clutched them hard, even when she tried to pull free. "You are not getting away from me again."

Celia opened her mouth.

"You *lied* to me, Celia. You gave me your word." Richard didn't care if he sounded hurt; he *was* hurt, by God.

Celia closed her mouth, sighed, and then said, "I did it for your own good."

"Bollocks."

Celia jolted.

"I beg your pardon," he muttered. "But that's one thing you should know about me before we marry: I can be rather vulgar at times."

"Marry?"

"Yes, marry. There are other things you'll need to know, of course, but nothing too terribly surprising, darling."

"Darling?"

Richard leaned down and brushed his cold lips over hers. "You've been spending too much time with parrots, sweetheart."

She kissed him back—but only for a heartbeat, and then she turned away, making a sound of distress. "Why would you undertake such a ride? The roads are icy, there is very little—"

"Shhh," he murmured, leaning in and stealing another quick kiss before rapping on the window and nodding to the groom, who gingerly approached Sunshine.

He turned and unbuttoned his frozen overcoat, drinking her in with his eyes, as if it had been a year since he'd last seen her.

"Come stand by the fire," she said, sounding beyond grim to his ears.

"You're upset with me," Richard said. "You didn't want me to come here."

Her lips twisted, her expression one of regret and yearning. "It's not that, Richard. It's just—"

"Just what?" he prodded when she stalled.

"What about the wedding? It's in the morning—aren't you going to miss it?"

"Oh, that. It's been called off."

"What?"

"Did I forget to mention that?" He grinned. "That's the effect you have on me, darling. You'll need to learn to distract me less when you're in the field with me." He got a speculative, thoughtful look. "Perhaps if I train you as my assistant and—"

"Richard."

"What?"

"Tell me what happened."

"What happened to what?"

She heaved a sigh. "What happened to end the betrothal."

"Well, first I hit Dowden—"

"You hit Sebastian? But why?"

It was his turn to snort. "Please, his face begs to be punched."

She gave a helpless laugh, "But—"

"And then Toni hit Dowden—"

"What?"

"Yes, she did. Followed through quite properly and knocked him to the ground." He clucked his tongue. "I don't know what you put in that letter to her, darling, but my entire family would like to thank you for bringing her to her senses."

"Oh. You . . . you didn't read the letter?"

"No, only Toni read it—she wouldn't let anyone else see it. And then she burned it. She said if you wanted me to know the contents, you could tell me yourself."

"And Sebastian?"

"He didn't look too well when the footmen carried him up to

his chambers. I was all for tossing him out immediately, but Phil is far kinder. Besides, there are no rooms available at the Pig, so my brother is stuck with Dowden until he can travel. But I don't want to talk about him. I want to talk about us."

"Oh, Richard, there is no us."

"I want you to be my wife."

Rather than look pleased, she only looked pained. "That's not possible."

"Why? Are you already married?" A horrid thought stabbed at him. "Lord, is Pelham still alive?"

"There never was a Mr. Pelham."

Richard frowned. "You're *not* married?"

"No. And I never was."

"Why did you take the name Pelham? Ah," he said, before she could answer, "you did it so people wouldn't recognize you."

Celia inhaled deeply, and then said the words she'd been dreading. "No, Richard. I did it so that my daughter would not have to face the world as a bastard."

Chapter 44

Rather than regard her with disgust, his passionate gaze gentled.

"I'm sorry," Celia said, "that was . . . obnoxious. And if anyone else called Katie a bastard, I would be enraged."

"Here, sit," Richard said, pulling one of the chairs closer to the small hearth, and then sitting in the other one. "Perhaps you might start at the beginning, Celia."

"It all goes back to that night. After what happened at the Duke of Stanford's house, I was . . ."

"Alone? Vulnerable? Frightened?" he guessed.

"Yes to all three. I kept expecting somebody—at least one of the people I'd thought were my friends—to come visit me. But for days on end, there was nothing. And then, finally, a caller came."

"Let me guess—Dowden?"

Celia nodded.

Richard's nostrils flared and his pupils shrank to pinpricks. "Did that bastard force you?"

"No, he did not. After so many days alone, I was easy prey to Sebastian's not inconsiderable charm."

"So, it was not rape, but it was not all that far off—taking advantage of a young girl who had no other choices in her life. And then he left you when he discovered you were pregnant?"

"No, of that, at least, he is not guilty. I did not tell him." She didn't want to confess everything, but if there was to be a chance for them—no matter how slender—Richard needed to know the truth. "Sebastian tired of me before I even found out I was pregnant." If that wasn't the most mortifying admission to make to the man you loved, Celia could not imagine what was. She forced herself to look at him.

Richard's expression was grim. "What did you do?"

"He found me a position—with *Monty*."

A low, menacing growl rumbled deep in his chest. "Did he—"

"Again, no, I was not forced." There was no point telling him that she'd not been forced, but neither had she had any other choice without money. "I became his mistress." She continued to stare at Richard, no matter how much she wanted to look away.

The muscles in his jaw flexed and he was pale beneath his tan. "Go on."

"I left his employ before my condition began to show and went to a small village where one of my old servants lived. Molly Henson had once been my mother's dresser." Celia's lips twisted. "I'd been a dreadful ogre to her for years, but she was still kind to me. Henson inherited the house with her sisters and invited me to live there. My daughter was born in their home and they were delighted to keep and raise her—they had no children of their own. While I agreed to leave Katie with them, I knew I could not live off their charity."

He took her hands in both of his. "My poor Celia."

His simple, heartfelt sympathy was almost enough to undo her; she wanted to crawl into his arms and never let him go.

But she was not yet finished with her dreadful story.

"Henson and her sisters wanted me to stay, but I knew I had to find work if I wanted to send Katie to a decent school. It would be the only way to equip her for a life that would certainly include working. To afford that, I would need to earn a great deal more money than I could make as a teacher or companion."

"You became a man's mistress," he said when she could not

make her mouth form the words. His voice was quiet, calm, and sympathetic, which was almost worse than angry shouting.

Celia nodded. "I couldn't work in London—not without being recognized—so I went to Bath. I decided that I would need to work for at least four years. I kept each protector a year—it was easier to end things before they became—" Celia chewed her lip; she hadn't realized how bad—how coldly calculating—it sounded until she'd spoken the words out loud.

"Too attached to you?" Richard guessed.

She dropped her gaze. "Yes. Over the course of four years I whored with—"

He released her hands and grabbed her shoulders, his fingers digging deep as he shook her. "Look at me," he ordered, waiting until she lifted her head.

His expression was angry—furious, even. "Don't you dare, Celia. Don't *ever* disparage yourself for doing what you needed to do to survive. I have had dozens of lovers in my life and nobody calls me a whore or shames me. You did it to make a better life for your daughter after some—some—" He made a noise of disgust. "After Dowden took what he wanted, walked away, and left you with the consequences. Don't you *dare* blame yourself for any of it. You should be proud not only of surviving, but of ensuring a better life for your daughter."

Celia wiped at the tears that were streaming down her face.

"Oh, Lord," he said, reaching into his coat and pulling out a handkerchief. "I didn't mean to—"

"You didn't make me sad, Richard."

"Then why are you crying, sweetheart?"

Celia gave a half sob, half laugh, dabbing at her cheeks. "It doesn't matter. Let me finish my story. I am known as Mrs. Pelham in the small community where my daughter lives. I took that name so I would not bring shame on my friends or Katie. They put about a vague story that I was married to a distant cousin of theirs. They saved my life. In the early days, after my father left and when I learned I was to have a child—" She didn't want to confess the thoughts she'd had.

"So Dowden never knew?"

"I didn't think he did, but when I saw him at Lessing Hall, he threatened me if I told anyone about Katie. He said he'd take her away from me."

Richard muttered an extremely vulgar word. "I beg your pardon, Celia, but what a vile, loathsome devil."

They were certainly in agreement about that.

"He told me to stay away from all of you." Celia gave a watery chuckle, her hand squeezing his. "Of course you made that impossible, Richard."

Richard guessed that the feeling currently raging through his body was jealousy, an emotion he had little experience of.

He knew that people expected him to envy his twin the earldom and all the money and power that came with it, but the truth was that Richard would have hated such a life.

If he were the earl he'd never get to travel and his days would be taken up with hundreds of tedious responsibilities. Lucien had five estates; God only knew how many people depended on him.

Richard had the perfect life; he went wherever he wanted, whenever he wanted.

He'd always had everything he wanted. He'd never yearned for a woman he couldn't have, nor had he ever experienced unrequited love.

But now, for the first time, at almost thirty, his emotions were consuming him.

"I can see by your face that you are disgusted," Celia said. "Maybe now you will understand why I left. And why you should never have come after me." The words came out in a furious rush, her chest rising and falling rapidly. "I think you need to leave."

"You do me a great disservice, Celia."

Her eyes sparked with anger. "Are you telling me you aren't seething right now?"

"No."

She blinked at his admission.

"Of course I'm angry about what Dowden did to you. I should think that's a perfectly normal response. It's what I do with my resentment and jealousy that determines my character, isn't it? Surely I am allowed some time—a few minutes, at least—to digest such momentous news?"

"Will it really make any difference? I have an illegitimate child by a man you hate, and I was a whore for four years. Do you think that is the sort of wife you should bring home to your family?"

"The next time you refer to yourself as a whore, I will turn you over my knee. And it won't be a pleasurable sort of spanking," he added when her cheeks reddened. "My family loves me, Celia. All they want for me is my happiness. You just spent a week with them; did they strike you as the sort of people who are concerned by what society thinks?"

"You are right, Richard—they are kind people who want the best for their children. But am I really the best for you? You'll never be able to take me out in public. It's possible your knighthood might even be jeopardized if your name were associated with mine."

"I daresay I could survive the disappointment of losing such an honor. Don't you understand? I *love* you, Celia."

Her jaw dropped in a way that made him chuckle. "Can you really be so surprised? I've followed you about like a lovelorn boy since the day you arrived at Lessing Hall. The night of the ball I wanted to ask you to marry me. I was furious with myself for asking you to be my mistress. I wanted to talk to you immediately after I'd bungled matters, but one thing after another seemed to happen." His lips twitched. "It was my plan to ambush you during our very first waltz together. Can you believe I was actually looking forward to dancing, Celia? I stunned myself," he answered. "I'd decided that if you said no to me—or if I accidentally stepped on your hem and tore off your ball gown"—she snorted inelegantly—"then I was going to pursue the topic again during the supper dance and all through the meal."

"Provided I wasn't naked after having my gown torn off."

His nostrils flared. "I'm not sure it's a good idea for you to say words like *naked* around me, just now." Richard took his raging emotions in hand. "There will be time for that later," he promised. "Now, I know you don't love me, but I do think we could rub along well together." Richard leaned closer and nuzzled her neck, as if to demonstrate.

She yelped. "Richard! Your nose is freezing."

"I might have permanent damage from that long, freezing ride. What if my nose needs to be amputated?" He could feel her body shaking with silent laughter. "Cruel woman! See how I suffer for you, without complaint? What more could you want in a husband?"

"It's not just a matter of wanting, Richard. It's what I need." Her magnificent blue eyes were brilliant even in the dim light of the room. "And I need a man I can love, look up to, and respect."

He stared down at her, his heart doing that *thing* again—leaping up into his throat and then getting stuck there. He searched her serious face for any hint that he might one day be such a man.

She smiled, her eyes softening. "It's a good thing that I already love you, Richard."

He made a mortifying gulping sound and then cleared his throat. "So," he said gruffly. "There's one thing checked off your list—what were the others? Oh yes. Well, you already look up to me." He gestured with one hand to indicate their differing heights.

Her eyelids grew heavy as she gazed up at him. "That's true, I do look up to you."

"I guess that only leaves respect." He stared at her, waiting.

And waiting.

"I'm sure it will come. In time," she said solemnly. And then gave one of those choked little snorts that he adored so much.

"You witch. I'll show you some respect," he muttered, catching her up in an unbreakable embrace and claiming her mouth.

Their teeth and tongues clashed as they consumed each other, as if they'd been apart for years.

It was Richard who finally pulled away. "Will you marry me, Celia?"

She groaned. "I know it is wrong of me to accept you, but . . . I will," she said, her eyes glinting with unshed tears.

They kissed until it felt as warm in the chilly little room as if it were the middle of summer rather than Christmas Eve. As if—

Christmas.

Damn, he'd almost forgotten . . .

Once again, it was Richard who—reluctantly—broke away.

Celia groaned. "You keep doing that. I thought you were teaching me some respect. I'm not yet feeling nearly respectful enough," she said, squirming against him in a way that made it difficult to remember what it was he was supposed to be doing.

Oh, yes—Christmas, box, pocket, gift . . .

"Reach into my pocket, darling. I brought you something."

"Not another present. I didn't get you anything."

"Oh, you will," he promised her smugly.

She pulled a large velvet box out of his pocket and gave him a shy look. "What is it?"

"It's a box, darling—haven't you ever seen one?"

She laughed.

"Hurry and open it so we can go back to your respect lesson. I sense you are a willful student who will require a great deal of discipline."

"Richard."

He grinned. "Open it."

She removed the lid and then gasped when she saw what was inside. When she looked up at him, her expression was one of wonder. "How did you know I wanted this?" she asked, stroking the Goliath beetle's slick carapace with one delicate finger.

"Your husband-to-be is a very wise man, darling."

"It's so big, Richard," she murmured.

"So I've been told, my dear." He lifted his wicked eyebrow and leered.

"You are shameless. Are you sure you can bear to give this up?"

"Well," he admitted, "I wouldn't have given it to you if you hadn't agreed to marry me."

She chuckled. "I don't know why I'm laughing, because I *know* that you're serious about that."

"I never joke about beetles, sweetheart."

Celia cut him a sly look that did interesting things to his already overexcited body. "What if I decide to keep it for myself in a drawer under lock and key?"

"I'm hoping you won't be greedy—perhaps you'll allow me to look at it, on occasion. Or perhaps you might even want to merge your collection with mine? We could keep them together—in our house."

Her lips parted as she gazed up at him with love, longing, and hope in her beautiful blue eyes. "Oh, Richard," she said softly, no longer laughing. "Are you *quite* sure about this? I will always be Lady Infamous—I will never be welcome in society, no matter how influential your connections."

"I don't give a toss for such things. And when you marry me, you shall become Mrs. Richard Redvers, and you'll have to lose that honorific. I'm going to be a mere knight and I can't have a wife outrank me."

"Are you *sure*? If you want me to—"

"Shhhh." He placed a finger over her lips. "I want you, and I want to get to know Katie. I want us all to live together and even travel together, if you wish it." He dropped a lingering kiss on her mouth. "I love you, Celia. Only you. Now," he said, forcing himself to sound brisk, "answer my pretty proposal properly. Say, *Why, thank you, Mr. Redvers, I'd love to marry you.*"

"Why, thank you, Mr. Redvers, I'd love to marry you."

He raised both brows. "Good girl," he praised. "Now tell me you love me."

"You love me," she said, smirking.

Richard threw his head back and laughed. There couldn't possibly be a more perfect woman for him in all the world.

She wrapped her arms around him. "I love you, Richard Redvers. Merry Christmas—the best one I've ever had."

Richard caught her up in an unbreakable embrace. "Merry Christmas, my love—the best so far, but the first of many."

Epilogue

One Month Later
Lessing Hall

"I now pronounce you husband and wife."

The vicar smiled beneficently on Richard and his new wife. "You may kiss the bride."

Richard grinned down at Celia as he pulled her close.

"Behave," she said, able to speak through her smile.

"Where is the fun in that, Mrs. Redvers?" And then he leaned down and claimed her mouth with the sort of crushing kiss he couldn't resist.

He moaned against her soft lips, his mind already on tonight.

One very long month he'd had to wait since their last evening together at that little roadside inn, where they'd spent a delicious, far too brief, night of lovemaking. Richard had wanted to keep her there for a week, but even more he'd wanted to get her to Katie on Christmas Day.

She'd only returned to Lessing Hall two weeks ago. He had hoped that they would take up where they'd left off, but the entire house had been in a state of around-the-clock wedding pandemonium.

Richard wasn't sure he could wait until tonight. He might have to sneak her off somewhere—perhaps Weaver's Cottage—and—

Somebody cleared their throat.

Richard opened his eyes and saw that he was in front of dozens of people.

Well, damn.

The next half hour passed in a blur as everyone gathered in the large sitting room before going into the dining hall for their wedding breakfast.

Even though the house had been far more crowded before Toni's canceled wedding, Richard had not known most of the guests so he'd been allowed to go his own way. *This* wedding was a great deal more intimate.

Thoughts of his sister made Richard seek her out in the mingling throng.

Toni was standing beside Jonathan. Based on her vehement gesticulations, she was delivering a scold to their younger sibling. For his part, Jonathan wore the forbearing expression of a man long accustomed to weathering such storms.

Although his sister had appeared more disgusted than brokenhearted by the discovery of her betrothed's soiled character and many transgressions, Richard knew the event had left Toni deeply shaken.

"She is already the better for the experience," his mother had said—speaking with her characteristic, if rather brutal, bluntness—when Richard mentioned the matter to her. "Your sister has always been altogether too sure of knowing what is best, regardless of the evidence. We can only hope that she will not be so headstrong in her next foray into romance. Which, if we are fortunate, will not be for a very long time."

"What are you doing hiding over here, Richard?"

He turned to find Hugh grinning down at him.

"Er . . ."

"Can't lurk in a corner at your own wedding," Hugh teased.

"No," Richard agreed, even though he'd been trying to—at least for a few minutes.

But he was quickly discovering that one's own wedding was far different from attending somebody else's. He knew every person currently packed into the drawing room, and they all seemed to want to talk to him.

He was grateful that the wedding was small—at least by Redvers standards—and only family and very close friends were present.

"Well, Sir Richard, who would have believed this day would ever come?"

Richard turned away from Hugh to find the Duchess of Tyne smirking up at him.

"I'm going to take that as congratulations, Your Grace."

Eva laughed and hiked the squirming infant in her arms higher on her hip. "It *is* congratulations."

If anyone thought it odd behavior for a duchess to cart around her own offspring—especially at a wedding breakfast—nobody in the room was brave enough to say anything.

Eva's astonishing violet eyes slid to Hugh and she scowled up at the towering man, who had to be a good foot and a half taller than she. "And *you*."

Hugh grinned. "Me?"

"Being an indulgent papa is well and good, but if you do not put somebody other than your infant children in charge of naming your horses, I shall have to take steps."

"Ooh, that sounds . . . intriguing," Hugh taunted.

Eva opened her mouth, but her husband, Godric, came up beside his wife and scooped up their child—a little girl, Richard thought, although it was difficult to tell from the child's grubby face.

"Are you threatening our host with bodily harm, darling?" the duke asked his diminutive wife.

Eva ignored her husband and said to Richard, "Rolly-Polly. That's what your stepfather named a seventeen-hand hunter whose sire is Victorious and dam is Dancing Fire—some of the finest bloodstock in the world." She turned to stare up at Hugh again. "Rolly. Polly."

Hugh laughed.

The duke squinted at his daughter. "Good Lord," he muttered. "What the devil is this?" He pried the little girl's mouth open and then dug something brown and soggy out of her mouth.

Richard was intrigued. "What is it?"

Godric shook his head in amazement. "It's part of a pinecone. Eva," he said, turning to his wife. "How did Dorothy get a pinecone in her mouth?"

Eva was fuming and glaring at Hugh, who, predictably, was pulling faces.

She shrugged. "Don't fly into a pucker, Godric. It's just a pinecone—it won't hurt her."

The duke turned to Richard, shaking his head in wonder. "You'd think that I'd be used to it by now," he said, bouncing the fat, extremely healthy-looking child on his hip. "I still recall the time she put Philip, our eldest, down for a nap in the kennels with a bitch and her litter."

Still locked in visual combat with Hugh, Eva said over her shoulder, "It's an excellent way to bond with one's hounds."

Godric rolled his eyes.

"How many children do you have?" Richard asked.

"Dotty makes six—four boys and two girls." The duke sounded more than a little proud, as if he, rather than his tiny wife, had given birth to a half-dozen children.

"Oh, she's so very lovely," Celia said as she came up beside Richard. "May I hold her?" she asked the duke. "It's been an age since I've held a little one."

"She's, er, a bit sticky—pine sap, I think." Godric grimaced. "Are you sure you want her?"

Celia laughed. "I'm sure." She took the beautiful dark-haired child into her arms. "Just look at your magnificent eyes," she said to the infant, using that voice people always seemed to adopt around young animals and babies.

Lady Exley, who was Eva's stepmamma, cooed beside Celia, the two women speaking gibberish to the little girl, whom Richard would swear gave him a long-suffering look that was remarkably like the one her mother was giving Hugh.

Something bumped against his arm and Richard looked down to find his stepdaughter beside him, bouncing up and down in her pink satin slippers, her hands cupped together.

Katie jerked her chin for Richard to follow and led him away from the chattering adults, over to one of the many settees, this one vacant.

The two weeks he'd spent getting to know his new stepdaughter had convinced him that the child was a genius.

They sat and Richard nodded. "Let's see what you've got."

She slowly lifted her upper hand.

"She's lovely," Richard murmured, holding out his far larger hand.

Katie gently nudged the spider's abdomen and it leapt into Richard's palm.

"What kind is she, Richard?"

"Where is your loupe?" he asked.

She scowled. "There are no pockets in this dress."

They exchanged looks of mutual disgust.

Richard fished around in the pocket of his trousers until he found the tiny loupe he always kept on him, and handed it to her. "Take a look," he said. "She is a *marpissa muscosa*, commonly known as a fencepost jumping spider. Look at her eyes," he suggested.

Katie leaned close and the little spider reared up, it's distinctive cephalothorax giving the small arachnid a very human aspect.

"Why, they are *blue*," she said, glancing up at Richard with her own beautiful blue orbs.

"The male of the species has black eyes," Richard said. "Do you remember what that is called?"

Her smooth forehead furrowed. "Dimorphism?"

Richard nodded. "Exactly."

Katie leaned closer to the little spider, which had turned around, as if to examine the girl.

"Where did you find her?" Richard asked.

"She was on the tapestry behind the piano. If she hadn't moved, I never would have found her." Katie closed the loupe and handed it back to him. "Is she a house spider?"

"Not in general. She must have wandered inside at some point. But she's lucky to be indoors in winter."

"Should I return her to the tapestry?"

"I think the best place for her might be the orangery."

Katie nodded and held out her hand.

"Do you want me to take her?" Richard offered.

"No, I want to do it." The eagerness on the girl's face made Richard grin: she was hooked—he recognized that expression because he'd felt that way a thousand times over the years as he'd studied one creature or another.

Richard sat back on the sofa as she hurried off, a perfect child, in his opinion.

Celia lowered herself beside him with a chuckle. "I can guess what you're smiling about."

"The girl is a natural entomologist. Or perhaps arachnologist." Richard looked down at his wife's beautiful face and his heart did that foolish thing it did only for her. "You sound tired, my love."

"This has been a very hectic two weeks—even though Toni and Phil did most of the work."

Richard slid a hand around her waist, pulled her closer and murmured, "Tonight you can just lie back and let me do all the work, darling."

She snorted. "Poor Richard, it has been a long month, has it not?"

"It has been an eternity." He nuzzled her neck.

"Richard, people are looking."

"Don't let that concern you," he said, "My mother and Hugh behave far—"

"I hope I'm not interrupting anything?"

Richard looked up at the sound of Martin Bouchard's distinctive French drawl. "Uncle Martin, what perfect timing," he said.

Martin laughed, his unusual yellow gaze flickering over Celia's form in a way that made Richard bristle. No wonder so many men had challenged the handsome Frenchman to duels over the years. Interesting that Richard had never noticed until now.

Martin smirked as if he knew exactly what Richard was thinking. "I understand you will be accompanying my nephew on his next, uh, *bibitte, eh*—what's the English word?" he asked.

Richard snorted. "Insect, although *bibitte* is quite charming."

Martin snapped his fingers. "Ah, yes, insect. So, you will be going insect hunting?" he asked Celia.

She smiled up at the far too attractive man. "Well, I won't be, er, *bibitte* hunting, myself, but my daughter Katie is looking forward to it."

Martin's eyebrows jumped. "*Non*? A girl who likes insects?"

Martin's wife, Sarah, arrived just in time to hear his words. "You'll have to excuse my husband's surprise. You see, I'm the one who has to rescue him whenever he finds a, er, *bibitte* in our house."

Celia and Richard laughed.

"Pfft!" Martin scoffed, but Richard couldn't help noticing that his cheeks darkened slightly. "That was only the one time," he explained.

Sarah winked at Richard and Celia. "You must pay us a visit when you pass through Tuscany on your upcoming journey," she said. "I'd love to entertain you while Richard and Katie explore the local flora and fauna."

"That would be lovely," Celia said, her eyes shining at the prospect of their impending wedding trip.

"It is an excellent time to visit our vineyards," Martin added.

"Did somebody say vineyard?" Luce asked, coming to join them along with Phil.

Richard couldn't help noticing that his brother and sister-in-law stood close enough to touch, brushing against each other, from time to time.

Luce had confided in him only yesterday that Phil was pregnant. "We're waiting until after your wedding to make the announcement," he'd said, happier than Richard had seen him in years.

Richard had been tempted to share his own news with his brother, but he and Celia had decided they would keep their announcement a secret until at least a month after the wedding. Although his family was not conventional, there was no need to shock them more than necessary.

Besides, he was in no hurry to endure Hugh and Luce's endless ribbing. Already they'd teased him mercilessly about falling in love after disputing its existence for so long.

Not that being married to Celia wasn't worth some teasing. He glanced down at his wife of less than an hour, marveling at his remarkable good fortune.

Her eyes were sparkling with happiness as she conversed with the guests who'd clustered around them, discussing what to see and where to go when they visited the Continent.

Luce and Phil, his mother and stepfather, and the rest of his family and friends had all welcomed Celia warmly, regardless of what had occurred a decade ago.

As Richard looked at his brother and wife, he had to admit that what had happened *That Night* at the Stanford ball had yielded far more joy than misery.

While their journey—not just his and Celia's, but Luce and Phil's, too—toward each other might have been long and rocky, Richard couldn't help thinking that their happiness was all the more precious for being so hard earned.

Celia leaned close, her warm breath sending goose bumps over his body. "What are you thinking of so deeply and with such a serious look on your face, Richard?"

Richard looked from his gathered friends and family down into his lover's warm blue gaze and smiled. "I'm thinking I must be the luckiest man in the world, darling."

Don't miss the book that started it all, *Dangerous* by Minerva Spencer, available now!

"A delight from start to finish."
—*New York Times* bestselling author Elizabeth Hoyt

Lady Euphemia Marlington hasn't been free in seventeen years—since she was captured by Corsairs and sold into a harem. Now the sultan is dead and Mia is back in London facing relentless newspapermen, an insatiably curious public, and her first Season. Worst of all is her ashamed father's ultimatum: marry a man of his choosing or live out her life in seclusion. No doubt her potential groom is a demented octogenarian. Fortunately, Mia is no longer a girl, but a clever woman with a secret—and a plan of her own . . .

Adam de Courtney's first two wives died under mysterious circumstances. Now there isn't a peer in England willing to let his daughter marry the dangerously handsome man the *ton* calls The Murderous Marquess. Nobody except Mia's father, the desperate Duke of Carlisle. Clearly Mia must resemble an aging matron, or worse. However, in need of an heir, Adam will use the arrangement to his advantage . . .

But when the two outcasts finally meet, assumptions will be replaced by surprises, deceit by desire—and a meeting of minds between two schemers may lead to a meeting of hearts—if the secrets of their pasts don't tear them apart . . .

"Readers will love this lusty and unusual marriage of convenience story."
—*New York Times* bestselling author Madeline Hunter

"Georgette Heyer, BUT WITH SEX!"
—RITA-award winning author Jeffe Kennedy

For David and Amelia

M.W.

For Charlie

B.F.

For information address: Candlewick Press, 2067 Massachusetts Avenue, Cambridge, Massachusetts 02140.

This edition published by The Trumpet Club, Inc., a subsidiary of Bantam Doubleday Dell Publishing Group, Inc., 1540 Broadway, New York, New York 10036, by arrangement with Candlewick Press.

First published in the United States in 1993
by Candlewick Press.
First published in Great Britain in 1991
by Walker Books Ltd., London.

ISBN 0-440-83510-0

Printed in Hong Kong
January 1995

1 3 5 7 9 10 8 6 4 2

The artwork for this book was done in watercolor.

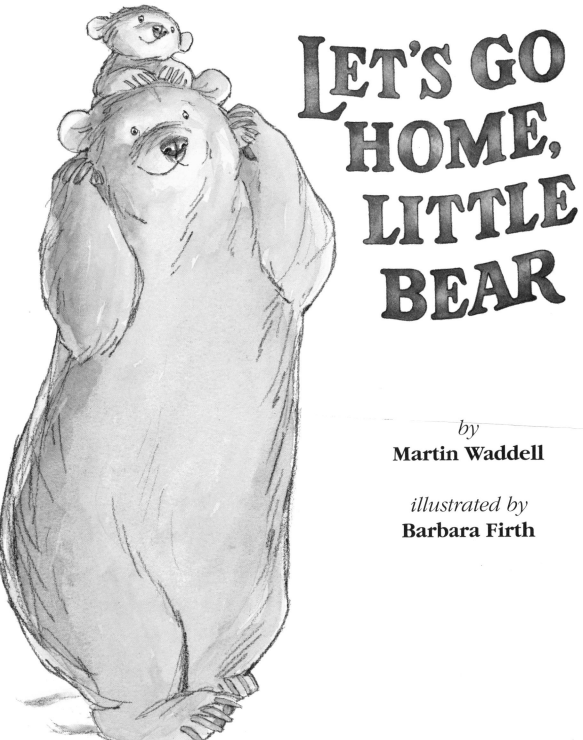

LET'S GO HOME, LITTLE BEAR

by

Martin Waddell

illustrated by

Barbara Firth

A TRUMPET CLUB SPECIAL EDITION

Once there were two bears.

Big Bear and Little Bear.

Big Bear is the big bear

and Little Bear is the little bear.

They went for a walk in the woods.

They walked and they walked and they walked until Big Bear said, "Let's go home, Little Bear."

So they started back home on the path through the woods.

P L O D   P L O D   P L O D

went Big Bear, plodding along.

Little Bear ran on in front,

jumping and sliding

and having great fun.

And then . . .

Little Bear stopped

and he listened

and then he turned around

and he looked.

"Come on, Little Bear," said Big Bear,
but Little Bear didn't stir.
"I thought I heard something!" Little Bear said.
"What did you hear?" said Big Bear.
"Plod, plod, plod," said Little Bear.
"I think it's a Plodder!"
Big Bear turned around and
he listened and looked.
No Plodder was there.
"Let's go home, Little Bear," said Big Bear.
"The plod was my feet in the snow."

They set off again on the path
through the woods.
PLOD PLOD PLOD
went Big Bear with Little Bear
walking beside him,
just glancing a bit, now and again.

And then . . .
Little Bear stopped
and he listened
and then he turned around
and he looked.

"Come on, Little Bear," said Big Bear,

but Little Bear didn't stir.

"I thought I heard something!"

Little Bear said.

"What did you hear?" said Big Bear.

"Drip, drip, drip," said Little Bear.

"I think it's a Dripper!"

Big Bear turned around, and he listened and looked. No Dripper was there. "Let's go home, Little Bear," said Big Bear. "That was the ice as it dripped in the stream."

They set off again on the

path through the woods.

PLOD PLOD PLOD

went Big Bear with Little Bear

closer beside him.

And then . . .

Little Bear stopped

and he listened

and then he turned around

and he looked.

"Come on, Little Bear," said Big Bear,
but Little Bear didn't stir.
"I know I heard something this time!"
Little Bear said.
"What did you hear?" said Big Bear.
"Plop, plop, plop," said Little Bear.
"I think it's a Plopper."

Big Bear turned around,
and he listened and looked.
No Plopper was there.
"Let's go home, Little Bear,"
said Big Bear.
"That was the snow plopping
down from a branch."

P L O D   P L O D   P L O D

went Big Bear along the path

through the woods.

But Little Bear walked

slower and slower

and at last he sat

down in the snow.

"Come on, Little Bear," said Big Bear.

"It is time we were both back home."

But Little Bear sat and said nothing.

"Come on and be carried,"

said Big Bear.

Big Bear put Little Bear
high up on his back
and set off down the path
through the woods.

W O O   W O O   W O O

"It is only the wind, Little Bear,"
said Big Bear and he walked
on down the path.

C R E A K   C R E A K   C R E A K

"It is only the trees, Little Bear,"
said Big Bear and he walked
on down the path.

P L O D P L O D P L O D

"It is only the sound of my feet again," said Big Bear, and he plodded on and on and on until they came back home to their cave.

Big Bear and Little Bear
went down into the dark,
the dark of their own
Bear Cave.

"Just stay there, Little Bear,"
said Big Bear, putting Little Bear
in the Bear Chair with a blanket
to keep him warm.
Big Bear stirred up the fire
from the embers
and lighted the lamps
and made the Bear Cave
all cozy again.
"Now tell me a story,"
Little Bear said.

love Gran

And Big Bear sat down in the Bear Chair
with Little Bear curled up on his lap.
And he told a story of Plodders
and Drippers and Ploppers
and the sounds of the snow
in the woods,
and this Little Bear
and this Big Bear
plodding all the way . . .

HOME